In the town
are men w...
and

Montana Passions

Three thrilling and satisfying romances from
three beloved Mills & Boon authors!

Montana Passions

CHRISTINE RIMMER
ALLISON LEIGH
PAMELA TOTH

All the characters in this book have no existence outside the imagination of the author, and have no relation whatsoever to anyone bearing the same name or names. They are not even distantly inspired by any individual known or unknown to the author, and all the incidents are pure invention.

First published in Great Britain 2010
Harlequin Mills & Boon Limited,
Eton House, 18-24 Paradise Road, Richmond, Surrey TW9 1SR

MONTANA PASSIONS © by Harlequin Enterprises II B.V./S.à.r.l 2010

Stranded With the Groom, All He Ever Wanted and *Prescription: Love* were first published in Great Britain by Harlequin Mills & Boon Limited in separate, single volumes.

Stranded With the Groom © Harlequin Books S.A 2005
All He Ever Wanted © Harlequin Books S.A 2005
Prescription: Love © Harlequin Books S.A 2005

Special thanks and acknowledgement are given to Christine Rimmer, Allison Leigh and Pamela Toth for their contribution to the MONTANA series.

ISBN: 978 0 263 88047 2

05-1010

Printed and bound in Spain
by Litografia Rosés S.A., Barcelona

STRANDED WITH
THE GROOM

BY
CHRISTINE RIMMER

Christine Rimmer came to her profession the long way around. Before settling down to write about the magic of romance, she'd been an actress, a sales clerk, a janitor, a model, a phone sales representative, a teacher, a waitress, a playwright and an office manager. Now that she's finally found work that suits her perfectly, she insists she never had a problem keeping a job—she was merely gaining "life experience" for her future as a novelist. Those who know her best withhold comment when she makes such claims; they are grateful that she's at last found steady work. Christine is grateful, too—not only for the joy she finds in writing, but for what waits when the day's work is through: a man she loves who loves her right back and the privilege of watching their children grow and change day to day. She lives with her family in Oklahoma.

For Montana readers everywhere.
Welcome to Thunder Canyon, Montana.

Chapter One

"A mail-order bride," Katie Fenton muttered under her breath. "What were they *thinking*?"

In Thunder Canyon, Montana, it was the first Saturday after New Year's—and that meant it was Heritage Day.

The annual celebration, held in the big reception room of Thunder Canyon's sturdy stone-and-brick town hall, included rows of brightly decorated booths, some serving food and others displaying endless examples of local arts and crafts. There was always a pie auction and a quilt raffle and, as evening drew on, a potluck supper and dancing late into the night.

Also, this year, the Thunder Canyon Historical Society had decided to put on a series of historical reenactments. In the morning, they'd presented the local legend of the great Thunder Bird, a mythical figure who took the form of a man every spring and met his mortal mate on sacred ground. According to Native American lore, their joyous reunion caused the spring rains to fall, the leaves and flowers to emerge and the grass to grow lush and green.

At two in the afternoon, there was the discovery of gold in 1862 at Grasshopper Creek—complete with rocks the size of baseballs, sprayed gold to look like huge nuggets.

And now, at four-thirty, it was time for the mail-order bride—played by Katie—arriving by train to meet and marry a man she'd never seen before.

Katie stood huddled on the narrow stage at the west end of the hall. Perched on a makeshift step behind a rickety cardboard mock-up of a steam engine and a red caboose, she kept her shoulders hunched and her head down so she couldn't be seen over the top of the fake train.

Utterly miserable—Katie hated, above all, to make a spectacle of herself—she stared at the door hole cut in the caboose. On cue, she was supposed to push it open and emerge to meet her "groom."

Outside, the wind howled. A storm was blowing in. Though the local weatherman had promised nothing much worse than a few flurries, most of the Heritage Day crowd had departed the hall during the past half hour or so and headed for the safety of their homes.

Katie herself was more than ready to call it a day.

But unfortunately, this year for the Heritage Day revels, a local merchant had come up with the bright idea of providing free beer on tap. The beer booth was a big hit. Certain of the citizenry had been knocking it back since eleven or so. They couldn't have cared less that the predicted flurries seemed to be shaping up into a full-blown blizzard. They were too busy having a grand old time.

Out on the main floor, someone let out a whistle. Katie heard the impatient stomping of heavy feet on the old, well-polished hardwood floorboards.

"C'mon, where's the bride?"

"Get on with it. We want the bride!"

"The bride!"

"The bride! Give us the bride!"

Katie cast a desperate glance to the tiny wing area at the edge of the stage where sweet old Emelda Ross, one of the few members of the Historical Society who'd yet to go home, hovered over an ancient reel-to-reel tape recorder.

"The bride, the bride!"

"Wahoo, let's see her!"

Katie gave Emelda a shaky nod. Emelda turned on the tape and two loud train whistles erupted: her cue.

Sucking in a big breath and letting it out slowly, Katie tugged on her 1880s-style merino wool frock, adjusted her bonnet and pushed open the cardboard door.

The beer drinkers erupted into a chorus of catcalls and stomping.

"The librarian!" one of them shouted. "Hey, the librarian is the mail-order bride!"

Another let out a whoop. "Hey, Katie! Welcome to Thunder Canyon!"

"We love you, Katie!"

"If your groom stands you up, I'll take you, Katie!"

Lovely.

With care, so as not to knock over the train, Katie emerged to face the crowd. She smoothed her dress again, her nervous hands shaking. How, she wondered miserably, had she let herself get roped into this one?

With great effort, she forced a wobbly smile and waved at the beer drinkers, who obligingly clapped and stomped all the louder. She stared out over the seventy or so grinning faces—many of them looking downright woozy by then—and longed to be anywhere but there.

It was all dear old Ben Saunders's fault. The high school history teacher had been the one to propose the mail-order bride reenactment. The Historical Society went wild for the idea—all except for Katie, who was lukewarm on the concept at best.

Since most of Katie's fellow society members were well into their forties at least and the other two younger ones were already slated to play the legendary Thunder Bird and his mortal love, it was decided that Katie should play the bride.

She had tried to say no, but who listened? *No one,* that's who. And now, here she was, alone in front of the cardboard train, a ludicrous spectacle for the Heritage Day beer drinkers to whistle and holler at.

Ben himself was supposed to be her groom. Unfortunately, the history teacher had awakened that morning with terrible stomach cramps. He'd been rushed to Thunder Canyon General for an emergency appendectomy. And then, when the sky darkened and the wind came up and the first snowflakes began to fall, pretty much everyone from the society except Emelda had decided to go home. *They* made the plans and now Katie stood on the stage alone, shaking with nerves and stuck with the follow-through.

Since her "groom" was in the hospital, she'd almost succeeded in canceling this ridiculous display. But then, a half hour ago, an out-of-towner named Justin Caldwell had agreed to step in and take Ben's part. Caldwell was a business associate of Caleb Douglas—Caleb being a local mover and shaker who owned half the property for miles around and also happened to be a second father to Katie. Caleb had ribbed the stranger into playing the groom. The poor guy resisted at first, but when Caleb kept after him, he couldn't refuse.

And speaking of Justin Caldwell...

Where was he?

Frantically, Katie scanned the noisy crowd for her impromptu pretend groom. Good gravy. In a moment, one of the drunken men down on the floor would be staggering up to take his place.

But no—there he was.

He stood off to the left, at the edge of the crowd, wearing the ill-fitting old-time garb—complete with silly red suspenders and clunky nineteenth-century-style boots—intended for the potbellied Ben Saunders. Katie met the stranger's piercing blue eyes and a crazy little thrill shivered through her. Even in the ridiculous outfit, the guy still somehow managed to look absolutely gorgeous. She felt the grateful smile as it quivered across her mouth. If she had to make a fool of herself, at least it would be with the best-looking man in the hall. And beyond being handsome, there was the added attraction that he appeared to be sober.

"The groom!" someone shouted. "Where's the damn groom?"

"Right here," Justin Caldwell answered easily in a deep, firm voice. He took off his floppy felt hat and waved it high for all of them to see.

"Get up there and claim your bride!"

"Yeah, man. Don't keep her waiting!"

Justin Caldwell obliged. He mounted the steps at the side of the stage and came toward Katie, his long strides purposeful and confident. When he reached her, he gallantly swept off the floppy hat a second time. Her overtaxed heart raced faster still.

And then, of all things, he reached for her hand. Before she could jerk it away, he brought it to his full-lipped mouth.

Katie stood stunned, staring into those gleaming blue eyes of his, every nerve in her body cracking and popping, as he placed a tender kiss on the back of her hand.

The crowd went wild.

"That's the way you do it!"

"Oh, yeah!"

"Way to go!"

His lips were so warm—and his hand firm and dry. Her hand, she knew, was clammy and shaking. Gulping, Katie carefully pulled her fingers free.

Caleb's business partner nodded and put his absurd hat back on. He looked so calm. As if he did this sort of thing every day. He leaned in closer, bringing with him the subtle scent of expensive aftershave. "Now, what?" he whispered in that velvety voice of his.

"Uh, well, I..." Katie gulped again. She just knew her face was flaming red.

"Kiss 'er!" someone shouted. "Lay a big, smackin' one right on 'er!"

Everyone applauded the idea, causing Katie to silently vow that next year, under no circumstances, would there be free beer.

"Yeah," someone else hollered. "A kiss!"

"A big, wet, juicy one! Grab 'er and give it to 'er!"

Justin Caldwell, bless him, did no such thing. He did lift a straight raven-black eyebrow. "The natives are becoming restless," he said low. "We'd better do *something...*"

Do something. His soft words echoed in her frazzled mind. "The, uh, ceremony..."

He smiled then, as if mildly amused. "Of course." He suggested, "And for that we would need..." He let his voice trail off, giving her an opportunity to fill in the blank.

She did. "The preacher." Her throat locked up. She coughed to clear it. "Uh. Right."

"Get on with it!" someone yelled.

"Yeah! Get a move on. Let's see the rest of the show!"

Outside, a particularly hard gust of wind struck the high-up windows and made them rattle. Nobody seemed to notice. They kept laughing and clapping.

"So where is this preacher?" her "groom" inquired.

"Um, well…" Katie wildly scanned the crowd again. Where was Andy Rickenbautum? The balding, gray-haired retired accountant was supposed to step up and declare himself a circuit preacher and "marry" them, but Katie couldn't see him among the crowd. Evidently, like most of the Historical Society members, he'd headed home.

Maybe Caleb, who'd gotten such a kick out of the whole thing, could help out and play Andy's part.…

But no. Caleb appeared to be gone, too. And Adele, his wife, who had taken in a teenaged Katie and raised her as her own, was nowhere to be seen, either. Now what?

At the Heritage Museum several blocks away, the society had set up a wedding "reception," complete with finger food and beverages and an opportunity for folks to see up-close the artifacts of the life the mail-order bride and her groom would have lived. The idea was to lure everyone over there behind the "bride" and "groom," in the museum's prized refurbished buckboard carriage. They'd all enjoy the snacks, look around—hopefully make a donation—and then head on back to the hall for the potluck supper and dancing that would follow.

But without the fake wedding first, how could they hold a pretend reception?

A couple of the beer drinkers had figured that out. One of them yelled, "Hey! Where's the preacher?"

"Yeah! We need the dang preacher to get this thing moving!"

What a disaster, Katie thought. It was definitely time to give up and call the whole thing off.

Katie forced herself to face the crowd. "Ahem. Excuse me. I'm afraid there's no one to play the preacher and we're just going to have to—"

A resonant voice from the back of the crowd cut her off. "Allow me to do the honors." Every head in the room swiveled toward the sound. The source, an austere-looking bearded fellow, announced, "I'd be proud to unite such a handsome couple in the sacred bonds of matrimony."

Someone snickered. "And just who the hell are you?"

The tall fellow, all dressed in black, made his way to the front of the crowd. He mounted the steps and came to stand with Katie and her "groom." "The Reverend Josiah Green, at your service, miss," he intoned. He dipped his head at Katie, then turned to Justin. "Sir."

Someone broke into a laugh. "Oh, yeah. *Reverend.* That's a good one...."

"He's perfect," someone else declared. "He even looks like a real preacher."

Looking appropriately grave, the "reverend" bowed to the crowd. The usual whistles and catcalls followed. "Reverend" Green turned his gaze to the spindle-legged antique table a few feet from the cardboard train. "I see you have everything ready." On the table, courtesy of the Historical Society, waited a Bible, a valuable circa-1880 dip pen and matching inkwell and a copy of an authentic late-nineteenth-century marriage license.

Emelda, smiling sweetly, emerged from the wings. A smattering of applause greeted her as she got the Bible and handed it to the "reverend."

"Ahem," said the "reverend." "If you'll stand here. And you here..." Katie, Justin and Emelda moved into the positions Mr. Green indicated.

The man in black opened the old Bible. A hush fell over the crowd as he instructed, "Will the bride and groom join hands?" Caldwell removed his hat. He dropped it to the stage floor, took Katie's hand and gave her an encouraging smile. She made herself smile back and didn't jerk away, in spite of the way his touch caused a tingling all through her, a sensation both embarrassing and scarily exciting.

The fake preacher began, "We are gathered here together..."

It was so strange, standing there on the narrow wooden stage with the cardboard train behind them and the wind howling beyond the stone walls as the pretend reverend recited the well-known words of the marriage ceremony.

The rowdy crowd stayed quiet. And the words themselves were so beautiful. Green asked if there was anyone present who saw any reason that Justin and Katie should not be joined. No one made a sound. If not for the wind, you could have heard a feather whispering its way to the floor. Green said, "Then we shall proceed...."

And Katie and the stranger beside her exchanged their pretend vows. When the "reverend" said, "I now pronounce you husband and wife," Katie had to gulp back tears.

Really, this whole weird situation was making her way too emotional.

"You may kiss the bride."

Oh, God. The kiss...

It hadn't seemed so bad when it was only good old Ben. But Justin Caldwell was another story. He was just so good-looking, so exactly like the kind of man any woman would want to kiss.

Truth was, Katie wouldn't mind kissing him. Not at all. Under different circumstances.

Maybe. If they ever came to really know each other...

Oh, why was she obsessing over this? The final vow-sealing kiss was part of the program. It wouldn't be much of a pretend wedding without it.

Almost over, Katie silently promised herself as Caldwell turned to face her. With a small, tight sigh, she lifted her chin. Pressing her eyes shut and pursing up her mouth, she waited for her "groom" to lean down and give her a quick, polite peck.

The peck didn't happen. Warily, she opened her right eye to a slit. Caldwell was looking down at her, apparently waiting for her to look at him. When he saw she was peeking, one corner of that full mouth of his quirked up and he winked at her.

A ridiculous giggle forced its way up in her throat and almost got away from her. She gulped it back, straightened her head and opened both eyes. At the same time as she was controlling her silly urge to laugh, the man before her reached out his hand. He did it so slowly and carefully, she didn't even flinch.

He took the end of the bow that tied her bonnet under her chin. One little tug and the bow fell away.

Gently, he guided the bonnet from her head. Her brown curls, which she'd hastily shoved in beneath the hat, fell loose to her shoulders. Justin—all of a sudden, she found she was mentally calling him by his first name—tossed the hat to Emelda and then, with tender, careful fingers, he smoothed her hair.

Oh, God. Her throat had gone tight. She felt as if she would cry again. This pretending to get married was darned hard on her nerves—or maybe she had a little natural-born performer in her, after all. Maybe she was simply "getting into" her part.

Their formerly boisterous audience remained pin-drop quiet. How did people in the theater put it? The phrase came to her. She and Justin had the crowd *in the palms of their hands....*

Justin braced a finger under her chin and she took his cue, lifting her mouth for him.

His dark head descended and his lips—so gently—covered hers.

That did it. The Heritage Day revelers burst into wild applause, sharp whistles, heavy stomping and raucous catcalls.

Katie hardly even heard them. She was too wrapped up in Justin's kiss. It was a kiss that started out questioning and moved on to tender and from there to downright passionate.

Oh, my goodness! Did he know how to kiss or what? She grabbed onto his broad, hard shoulders and kissed him back for all she was worth.

When he finally pulled away, she stared up at him,

dazed. He had those blue, blue eyes. Mesmerizing eyes. She could drown in those eyes and never regret being lost....

"Ahem," said the "reverend," good and loud, gazing out over the audience with a look of stern disapproval until they quieted again. "There remains the documentation to attend to."

Katie blinked and collected herself, bringing a hand up and smoothing her hair. Justin turned to face Josiah Green, who had crossed to the spindle-legged table. He picked up the old pen and dipped it in the ink and expertly began filling out the fake marriage license. "That's Katie...?"

"Fenton."

"Speak up, young lady."

"Katherine Adele Fenton." She said her whole name that time, nice and clear, and then she spelled it for him.

"And Justin...?"

"Caldwell." He spelled his name, too.

They acted it all out as if it were the real thing, filling in all the blanks, signing their names. When the "reverend" called for another witness besides Emelda, one of the guys from down on the floor jumped right up onto the stage and signed where Josiah Green pointed.

When the last blank line had been filled in, Green expertly applied the sterling silver rocker blotter. Then he held up the license for all to see. "And so it is that yet another young and hopeful couple are happily joined in holy wedlock."

As the clapping and stomping started up again,

Emelda stepped forward. She waited, looking prim and yet indulgent, her wrinkled hands folded in front of her, until the noise died down. Then she announced that, weather permitting, there was to be a reception at the Heritage Museum over on Elk Avenue. "Everyone is welcome to attend. Help yourself to the goodies—and don't forget that donation box. We count on all of you to make the museum a success. Just follow the bride and groom in their authentic buckboard carriage."

Evidently, the crowd found that suggestion too exciting to take standing still. They surged up onto the stage and surrounded the small wedding party, jostling and jumping around, knocking over the cardboard train and almost upsetting the antique table with its precious load of vintage writing supplies. Laughing and shouting, they tugged and coaxed and herded Katie and Justin down the stage steps, across the main floor and out into the foyer.

Katie laughed and let herself be dragged along. By then, the crazy situation had somehow captured her. The day's events had begun to seem like some weird and yet magical dream. Her lips still tingled from the feel of Justin's mouth on hers. And she was pleased, she truly was, that her little reenactment, skirting so close to disaster, had ended up a great success.

In the foyer, the crowd surged straight for the double doors that opened directly onto the covered wooden sidewalk of Old Town's Main Street. They pushed the doors wide and a blinding gust of freezing wind and snow blew in, making everyone laugh all the louder.

"Brrrr. It's a cold one."

"Yep. She's really movin' in."

"Gonna be one wild night, and that's for certain."

The snow swirled so thick, the other side of Main Street was nothing more than a vague shadow through the whiteness. The horse, a palomino mare, and the buckboard were there, waiting, the reins thrown and wrapped around one of the nineteenth-century-style hitching posts that ran at intervals along Main at the edge of the sidewalk, bringing to mind an earlier time.

Katie herself had requested the horse, whose name was Buttercup. The mare belonged to Caleb. He kept a fine stable of horses out at the family ranch, the Lazy D. A sweet-natured, gentle animal, Buttercup was getting along in years—and, boy, did she look cold. Icicles hung from her mouth. She glanced toward the crowd and snorted good and loud, as if to say, *Get me out of this. Now…*

Really, maybe they ought to slow down here. The snow did look pretty bad.

"Um, I think that we ought to…" She let the sentence die. She'd always had a too-soft voice. And no one was listening, anyway.

The revelers herded her and Justin into the old open, two-seater carriage. It creaked and shifted as it took their weight.

"Use the outerwear and the blankets under the seat!" Emelda shouted from back in the doorway to the hall foyer. A frown had deepened the creases in her brow. Maybe she was having her doubts about this, too.

But then Emelda put on a brave smile and waved

and the wind died for a moment. Really, it was only two blocks west and then three more northeast to the museum. And, according to the weather reports, the storm *was* supposed to blow itself out quickly.

It should be okay.

Justin brushed the snow from a heavy ankle-length woolen coat—a tightly fitted one with jet buttons down the front and a curly woolen ruff at the neck. He helped her into it, then put on the rough gray man's coat himself. There was a Cossack-style hat for her that matched the ruff at her neck. No hat for Justin, and he'd left the silly, floppy one back in the hall. But he didn't seem to mind. There were heavy gloves for both of them.

They shook out the pile of wool blankets and wrapped up in them. Justin pulled on his gloves and Josiah Green handed him the reins.

"Bless you, my children," Green intoned, as if the marriage vows he'd just led them through had been for real.

"Thanks," Justin muttered dryly. "Looks like we'll need it." He glanced at Katie. "Okay…" He had a you-got-us-into-this kind of look on his handsome face. "Where to?"

"If you want, I'll be glad to take the reins."

"I can handle it. Where to?"

Even if he didn't know what he was doing, it should be all right, she thought. Buttercup was patient and docile as they come. "Straight ahead. Then you'll turn right on Elk, about three blocks down."

"What? I can't hear you."

She forced herself to raise her voice and repeated the instructions.

Justin shook the reins and clicked his tongue and Buttercup started walking. Her bridle, strung with bells, tinkled merrily as they set off, the beer-sodden townsfolk cheering them on.

The wind rose again, howling, and the snow came down harder.

A half block later, the thick, swirling flakes obscured the hall and the knot of cheering rowdies behind them. A minute or two after that, Katie couldn't hear their voices. All at once, she and this stranger she'd just pretended to marry were alone in a whirling vortex of white.

Katie glanced over her shoulder. She saw nothing but swirling snow and the shadows of the buildings and cars on either side of Main.

The snow fell all the harder. It beat at them, borne by the hard-blowing wind. Katie huddled into the blankets, her cheekbones aching with the cold.

Buttercup plodded on, the snow so thick that when Katie squinted into it, she could barely see the horse's sleek golden rump. She turned to the man beside her. He seemed to sense her gaze on him. He gave her a quick, forced kind of smile—his nose was Rudolph-red, along with his cheeks and chin and ears—and then swiftly put his focus back on the wall of white in front of them.

For a split second, she spied a spot of red to the side—the fire hydrant at the corner of Elk and Main. Wasn't it? ''Turn right! Here!'' Katie shouted it out good and loud that time. Justin tugged the reins and the horse turned the corner.

They passed close to the fire hydrant. Good. This was the right way. And as long as they were on Elk Avenue now, they'd literally run into the museum—a sprawling red clapboard building that had started out its existence as the Thunder Canyon School. It sat on a curve in the street, where Elk Avenue made a sharp turn due east.

The palomino mare slogged on into the white. By then, Katie couldn't see a thing beyond the side rails of the buckboard and Buttercup's behind.

Good Lord. Were they lost? It was beginning to look that way.

Hungry for reassurance, Katie shouted over the howling wind, "We *are* still on Elk Avenue, aren't we?"

Justin shouted back, "I'm from out of town, remember? Hate to tell you, but I haven't got a clue."

Chapter Two

Just as Katie began to fear they'd somehow veered off into the open field on the west side of Elk Avenue, the rambling red clapboard building with its wide front porch loomed up to the left.

"We're here!" she yelled, thrilled at the sight.

Justin tugged the reins and the horse turned into the parking lot. Ten or twelve feet from the front porch, the buckboard creaked to a stop—at which point it occurred to Katie that they couldn't leave poor Buttercup out in this. "Go around the side! There's a big shed out back."

He frowned at her.

She shouted, "The horse. We need to put her around back—to the left."

His frown deepened. She could see in those blue eyes that he thought Buttercup's comfort was the leas of their problems right then. But he didn't argue. Shoulders hunched into his ugly old-fashioned coat, he flicked the reins and Buttercup started moving again.

When they got to the rear of the building, Katie signaled him on past a long, narrow breezeway and around to the far side of the tall, barnlike shed. "I'll open up," she yelled and pushed back the blankets to swing her legs over the side. She opened the gate that enclosed a small paddock northwest of the shed. Justin drove the buckboard through and she managed to shut the gate.

The snow was six or eight inches deep already. It dragged at her heavy skirts and instantly began soaking her delicate ankle-high lace-up shoes as she headed for the shed doors around back. How did women do it, way back when? She couldn't help but wonder. There were some situations—this one, for instance—when a woman really needed to be wearing a sturdy pair of trousers and waterproof boots.

There was a deep porchlike extension running the length of the shed at the rear, sheltering the doors. She ducked under the cover, stomping her shoes on the frozen ground and shaking the snow off her hem. Even with gloves on, her hands were so stiff with cold, it took forever to get the combination padlock to snap open. But eventually, about the time she started thinking her nose would freeze and fall off, the shackle popped from the case. She locked it onto the hasp.

And then, though the wind fought her every step of the way, she pulled back one door and then the other, latching them both to hooks on the outside wall, so they wouldn't blow shut again. She gestured Justin inside and he urged the old mare onward.

Katie followed the buckboard inside as Justin hooked the reins over the back of the seat and jumped to the hard-packed dirt floor. "Cold in here." He rubbed his arms and stomped his feet, looking around, puzzled, as Buttercup shook her head and the bells tinkled merrily. "What is this?"

"Kind of a combination garage and barn. The Historical Society is planning on setting it up as a model of a blacksmith's shop." She indicated the heavy, rusting iron equipment against the walls and on the plank floor. "For right now, it'll do to stable Buttercup 'til this mess blows over." There were several oblong bales of hay stacked under the window, waiting to be used for props in some of the museum displays. Buttercup whickered at them hopefully.

"Go on through there." Katie indicated the door straight across from the ones she'd left open. It led to the breezeway and the museum. "It's warm inside. And a couple of ladies from the Historical Society should be in there waiting, with the food and drinks."

He looked at her sideways. "What about you?"

She was already trudging over to unhook Buttercup from the buckboard. "I learned to ride on this horse, I'll have you know. I'm going to get her free of this rig and make her comfortable until someone from the ranch can come for her."

"The ranch?"

"She's Caleb's, from out at the Lazy D."

He stomped his feet some more, making a big show

of rubbing his arms. "Can't someone inside take care of the horse?"

"Anna Jacks and Tildy Matheson were supposed to set out the refreshments for the 'wedding reception.' They're both at least eighty."

"Maybe someone else has shown up by now."

Doubtful, she thought. And even if they had, they'd most likely be drunk. "I'd rather just do it myself before I go in."

He gave her an appraising kind of look and muttered, heavy on the irony, "And you seemed so shy, back there at the hall."

She stiffened. Yes, okay. As a rule, she *was* a reserved sort of person. But when something needed doing, Katie Fenton didn't shirk. She hitched up her chin and spoke in a carefully pleasant tone. "You can go on inside. I'll be there as soon as I'm through here."

He insisted on helping her. So she set him the task of searching for a box cutter in the drawers full of rusting tools on the west wall. When he found one, she had him cut the wire on a couple of the bales and spread the hay. Meanwhile, she unhitched Buttercup from the rig, cleaned off the icicles from around her muzzle and wiped her down with one of the blankets from the buckboard.

"Okay," she said when the job was done. "Let's go in."

He headed for the still-open doors to the pasture. "I'll just shut these."

"No. Leave them open. The walls cut most of the wind, so it won't be too cold in here. And Buttercup can move around a little, and have access to the snow when she gets thirsty.''

He shrugged and turned to follow her out—which was a problem as the door to the breezeway was locked from the outside. They ended up having to go out the big doors. Hunched into the wind, with the snow stinging their faces, they slogged through the deepening snow around the side of the shed and back through the gate that enclosed the paddock.

Once under the partial shelter of the breezeway, they raced for the back door, the wind biting at them, tearing at Katie's heavy skirts.

It was locked. Katie knocked good and hard. No one came.

Justin wore a bleak look. ''What now?''

''No problem.'' Katie took off her right glove and felt along the top of the door frame, producing the key from the niche there. She held it up for him to see before sticking it in the lock and pushing the door inward onto an enclosed back porch. He signaled her ahead of him and followed right after, pulling the door closed to seal out the wind and snow.

By then, it had to be after six. It was pretty dark. Katie flipped on the porch light and gestured at the hooks lining the wall next to the door that led inside. ''Hang up your coat,'' she suggested, as she set her gloves on a small table and began undoing the jet buttons down her front. The porch wasn't heated and she shivered as the coat fell open. ''Whew. Cold...''

''I hope it's warm in there.''

''It is,'' she promised as she shrugged out of the long gray coat and hung it on a hook. He hung his beside it. She swiped off her hat, shook out her hair and tossed the hat on a porch chair.

"This way." Katie unlocked the door and pushed it open into the museum's small, minimally equipped kitchen area. Lovely warm air flowed out and surrounded them.

"Much better," Justin said from behind her.

She led him in, hanging the key on the waiting hook by the door and turning on the light.

The long counter was spotless, and so was the table over by the side windows. A few cups dried on a mat at the sink. No sign of Tildy or Anna.

They moved on into the big central room, which a hundred years before had been the only schoolroom. The room was now the museum's main display area—and pitch-dark. Years ago, when rooms were added on around it, the windows had been closed up. Katie felt for the dimmer switch near the door, turning it up just enough that they could see where they were going.

The light revealed roped-off spaces containing nineteenth-century furniture arranged into living areas: a bedroom, a weaving room, a parlor, a one-room "house" with all the living areas combined, the furniture in that section rough-hewn, made by pioneer hands.

"No sign of your friends," Justin said.

"They probably got worried about the storm and went home."

A quick check of the two other display rooms confirmed their suspicions. They were alone.

"No cars out there," Justin said once they'd

reached the front reception area, where trays of sand-wiches, cookies and coffee, tea and grape drink waited for the crowd that wasn't coming. "Remem-ber? The parking lot in front of the building. It was empty." She did remember, now that he mentioned it. He asked, "What now?"

It was a good question; too bad she had no answer to it. "I guess we wait."

"For?"

She wished she knew. "For the storm to die down a little so we can leave?"

He gave her a humorless half smile. "Was that an answer—or just another question?"

Katie put up both hands, palms up. "Oh, really. I just don't know."

Justin studied her for a moment, wearing an ex-pression she couldn't read. Then, out of nowhere, he plunked himself down into one of the reception chairs and started pulling off his boots.

The sight struck her as funny, for some crazy rea-son. She laughed—and then felt stupid for doing it when he glanced up from under the dark shelf of his brow, his full-lipped mouth a grim line. "These damn boots are at least a size too small."

Katie winced. "Sorry."

With a grunt, he tugged off a boot. "For what?"

She sank to a chair herself. "Oh, you know. Caleb shouldn't have roped you into this. And I should have spoken up and called the whole thing off."

He dropped the boot to the floor, pulled off the other one and set it down, too. "Are you capable of that?"

"Excuse me?"

That dry smile had gone devilish. "Speaking up."

She sat straighter and brushed a bit of lint off her skirt. "Now and then, absolutely."

His smile got wider. "Like with the horse."

She nodded. "That's right." Blowing out a weary breath, she let her shoulders slump again. "But back in the hall—oh, I just hate getting up in front of a lot of people. Especially a lot of people who've had too much beer."

"I hear you on that one." He looked down at his heavy wool socks—and wiggled his toes. "Now, that's more like it."

Her own feet were kind of pinched in the narrow lace-up shoes. What the heck? She hiked up her soggy skirts—which gave off the musty scent of wet wool— and set to work on the laces. When she had both shoes off, she set them neatly beside her chair, smoothed her skirt down and straightened to find him watching her. There was humor in his eyes and something else, something much too watchful. She found herself thinking, *What's he up to?* And then instantly chided herself for being suspicious.

What *could* he be up to? Except wishing he hadn't let Caleb talk him into this.

The watchful look had faded from his face as if it had never been. He asked softly, "Now, isn't that better?"

"What?"

"Without your shoes…"

She felt a smile tug at her mouth. Oh, really, he was much too good-looking for her peace of mind.

She answered briskly, "Yes, it is." And she picked up a tray of sandwich triangles from the reception desk. "Help yourself. It's probably the closest thing to dinner we're going to get."

He took one and bit into it. "Ham and American. With mayo. The best."

"Oh, I'll bet." She took one for herself and gestured at the big stainless steel coffee urn, the hot water for tea and the glass pitcher of grape drink. "And coffee. Or a cold drink..."

He got up. "You?"

"Coffee sounds good. With a little cream."

He poured them each a cup, splashed cream from a little stoneware pitcher into hers and handed it over with a courtly, "Mrs. Caldwell."

She played along. "*Mr.* Caldwell." Really, she was grateful he was taking this so calmly.

He sank into his chair again and sipped the hot brew. "Now we're married, I think you're going to have to call me Justin."

She had that silly, nervous urge to laugh again. She quelled it. "By all means. And please. Call me Katie. I firmly believe married people should be on a first-name basis with each other."

"I agree. Katie." He finished off the rest of his sandwich. She held out the tray and he took another. She took one, too. He asked, "So how was that train ride?"

She rolled her eyes. "I should have taken a club car."

About then, the false cheer they were both trying to keep up deserted them. They sat silent, like the strangers they really were, eating their sandwiches, listening to the wind whistling in the eaves outside.

Eventually, he turned to her, his expression grave. ''Will anyone else show up?''

''In this?'' She gestured at the six-over-six front windows. Beyond the golden glow of the porch light, there was only darkness and hard-blowing snow. ''I don't think so.''

He turned and looked at the round institutional-style clock on the wall above the desk. It was six thirty-five. ''How long will we be stuck here?''

He *would* have to ask that. She cleared her throat. ''Maybe, if we're lucky, the snow will stop soon.''

''And if it doesn't?''

Katie sighed. ''Good question. We'll just have to wait and see how bad it gets.''

''Should we call someone, let them know we arrived here and we're safe?'' He felt in his pockets. ''Damn…''

''What?''

''I left my cell in my own clothes, back at the hall.'' He produced a handsome calfskin wallet and waved at her. ''The good news is I've got plenty of cash.''

Katie forced a grin. ''Whew. I was worried. What if we wanted to do a little shopping?'' He made a sound halfway between a grunt and a chuckle, and she added, on a more somber note, ''And cell phones don't work all that well around these parts, anyway. Lots of mountains. Not many cell towers.''

''I knew that,'' he said, his mouth twisting wryly.

She set her coffee cup on the edge of the reception

desk, reached for the phone and put it to her ear. "Dead." Carefully, she set it back in its cradle.

"Terrific."

"Count your blessings," she advised, trying to keep things positive. "At least we still have heat and electricity. And plenty of water, as long as the pipes don't freeze."

He didn't look too reassured, but he got the message. "Right. Might as well look on the bright side."

"Exactly."

Rising, he went to the trays of food and chose another sandwich.

The museum had propane heat throughout, but there was also the remains of a fire in the potbellied stove in the corner. Katie got up and put in another log. She jabbed it with the poker until it was well nestled in the bright coals. The red flames licked up.

She shut the stove door and turned—to find him watching her again. "Is something the matter?"

He frowned. "No. Of course not—well, except for the situation we're in here."

"You keep looking at me strangely."

His gaze remained far too watchful—for a moment. And then he shrugged. "Forgive me. I'm just... curious about you, I guess. Caleb Douglas told me you're the 'little girl he never had.' He raised you, I take it?"

She had no idea why she felt reluctant to answer him. What was there to hide? She said, "My mother and Adele were both from Philadelphia, best friends at Bryn Mawr—you did meet Addy, didn't you?"

''I did.'' He looked like he was waiting to hear more.

So she elaborated. ''They had an instant connection, my mother and Addy, from the way Addy tells it. And their families were friends. When my parents died, I was fourteen. There was really no one left in my immediate family to take me. Addy came and got me.'' Katie smiled at the memory—Adele, with her suitcases at her feet in the foyer of the Center City brownstone near Rittenhouse Square that had belonged to Katie's grandparents and their parents before them. When Katie came down the stairs to meet her, Adele held out her arms, her blue eyes shining with tears....

Katie swallowed down the emotion the memory brought with it and Justin asked, ''Adele brought you here, then—to Thunder Canyon?''

''That's right, to live with her and Caleb.''

''And you loved it.''

''Yes, I did. From the first.''

''Because?''

She hesitated. Could he really want to hear all this? But he was looking at her expectantly. So she told him, ''It was...just what I'd needed. A close-knit community, where people looked out for each other. I lived at the Lazy D through my teenage years, went to Thunder Canyon High and then on to college in Colorado. As Caleb told you, he and Addy never had a daughter, so it worked out beautifully. For all of us.''

''All?''

''Caleb. Addy. And Riley. Have you met Riley?''

He nodded. "Their son. Caleb introduced me to him a few days ago—and I suppose he's like a big brother to you?"

She picked up her soggy skirt so it wouldn't drag on the floor and padded to one of the front windows, where she looked out at the porch, the darkness and the driving snow beyond. "Yes. I think of Riley like a brother...." She turned back to him. "They're fine people." Did she sound defensive? A little. She wasn't really sure why. Something hostile in the way he'd spoken of Riley, maybe.

But why in the world would Justin Caldwell be hostile toward Riley, whom he'd only just met? Clearly, the stress of their situation was getting to her, making her read things into his tone that weren't there.

She tried for a lighter note. "Caleb is so pleased that you've invested in his ski resort." Caleb had always been a wheeler-dealer. The resort was a long-time dream of his and it was finally coming true. He'd opened an office on Main Street for the project—complete with a model of the future resort in the waiting room—and hired a secretary. Thunder Canyon Ski Resort would be built on a ridge about twenty miles out of town on land the Douglases had owned for generations. Caleb had worked for months, hunting down investors. Everything had finally fallen into place in the past few weeks. Caleb had told her proudly that Justin's company, Red Rock Developers, was the main reason it was all working out.

"I think it's a solid investment," Justin said.

"Good for everyone, then."

"Yes. Absolutely."

Another silence descended. Oh, this was all so awkward. If she had to get herself stranded in a blizzard, you'd think it might have been with someone she knew. Or at least, maybe someone less...attractive.

He was almost too good-looking, really. And she felt a certain fluttery sensation in her midsection every time she glanced his way. Her excited response to him made her wary.

She wondered if he knew about her money. There *was* a lot of it. Katie mostly ignored it and let the estate managers handle everything. Her interests were in her family—and to her, that meant the Douglases—and in her town and in the Thunder Canyon Public Library, which she had generously endowed and where she was privileged to work at a job she truly loved.

But she could never completely forget that she was the sole heir to large fortunes on both her mother's and her father's side. Everybody in town knew it, of course. She'd even had a couple of boyfriends who'd turned out to be nothing more than fortune hunters in the end. From them she'd learned the hard truth: when it came to men, she had to be careful. If a man seemed interested, there was always a chance that his interest was more in her money than in Katie herself.

Sometimes she wished she could be like other women, and just go for it, when it came to guys. But she had a shy streak and she had too much money, and both made her more guarded than she would have liked to be.

She kept thinking of that kiss, back in the hall, kept remembering the feel of his mouth against hers....

But really, other than that kiss, which had only been for show, he'd made no moves on her. He wasn't even blaming her for the fact that they were stuck here for Lord knew how long.

She could have been stranded with worse, and she told herself firmly to remember that.

"Deep thoughts?" Justin asked softly.

"Not at all." She gestured at the trays of food. "If you've had all you want, I think we should go ahead and put this stuff away...."

He gave her a level look. She knew what he was thinking. They could very well end up enjoying those sandwiches for breakfast. "Let's do it." He rose and picked up a tray and the pitcher of grape drink.

She grabbed another tray and followed him through the main display room, to the kitchen at the back.

Twenty minutes later, they had everything put away. They returned to the reception room and sat down again. They made halting conversation. He told her a little about his company, said he'd started from nothing and had "come a long way."

"You're based in...?"

"Bozeman."

"Did you grow up in Montana?"

"No. I was born in California. We moved a lot. To Oregon for a while and later to Colorado, Nevada, Idaho..."

"Brothers and sisters?"

"Single mom—and she only had me. She died two years ago."

"It must have been tough for her...."

"Yeah. It was." He'd rested his dark head back against the knotty pine wall. He glanced her way. "We could use a television. Or at least a radio."

Boy, could they. "We can look around for one."

So they returned to the kitchen and went through the cabinets. Nothing but pots and pans and dishes and such. In the storage room off one of the side display rooms, where the society kept the donations they were collecting for their next rummage sale, they did find a battered old boom box.

Justin scanned the small room. "Any plugs in here?"

"Just the one in the light." They both looked up at the bare bulb above. The cord wouldn't stretch that far. "Why don't we take it with us out front?"

"Fine," he said, glancing around. "Lots of clothes in these bags..." They shared another look and she knew they were thinking along the same lines. If they didn't get out of here soon, they could always go through the bags, maybe find something more comfortable to wear.

The idea depressed her—that they might be stuck here long enough to need a change of clothes.

"Look at it this way," he advised gently. "We're safe and warm. And we've got plenty of sandwiches."

They took the radio out through the silent display rooms to the front. Justin plugged it in and turned the dial. Nothing but static.

Thoroughly discouraged, Katie went to the window

again. She wrapped her arms around herself and stared out for a while at the steadily falling snow.

Justin spoke from behind her. "Those old beds in the center display room…"

She faced him. They shared a grim look.

He asked, "Are you thinking what I'm thinking?"

Her nod was resigned. "It does begin to look as if they're going to get some use tonight."

Past midnight, Justin Caldwell lay wide-awake staring at the shadowed rafters in the museum's central room. He'd taken the narrow, hard little cot in the one-room pioneer cabin display and stretched out, fully clothed but for those damn too-small boots, under the star-patterned quilt. He'd had to pull out the sheet at the bottom of the bed. It was too short by a foot and his stocking feet hung out over the edge.

But at least the bedding was clean. Katie had told him it was all antique stuff donated by local families. The Historical Society took pains to keep it laundered and in good repair.

Katie…

He could hear her soft breathing from the "bedroom" on the opposite wall, where she lay in a wide four-poster with pineapple finials that some pioneer family had probably dragged across the plains in a covered wagon. He smiled to himself.

She was…a surprise. A quiet woman; self-contained. With those wide honey-brown eyes, that tender mouth and the shy way she had about her, she seemed, in some ways, so young—younger than her age, which he knew was twenty-four.

Yes. Very young. And yet, at the same time, she had that self-possessed quality that made her, somehow, seem older.

He knew much more than she'd told him so far. He'd paid and paid well to learn all about her—and about Caleb, Adele and Riley Douglas, as well.

Katherine Adele Fenton was the only child of the jet-setting Paris and Darrin Fenton. She'd been born in Venice, Italy—and immediately turned over to a nanny. Into her teens, Katie hardly saw her parents. She was fourteen and living a sheltered life with a governess in London when both Paris and Darrin died tragically; their private plane crashed on the way to a society wedding.

That was where the Douglases came in. As Katie's godmother, Adele had gone back east to claim the orphaned child of her dear college friend.

From what Justin had been able to learn, the Douglases considered Katie one of their own. She was, though not by blood, a full-fledged member of their family. She was the daughter Adele Douglas never had. Though he'd taken her into his home and treated her as family, Caleb had never made any effort to lay claim to a red cent of Katie's considerable inheritance. And from what Justin knew of Caleb Douglas—who loved nothing so much as making big deals involving large sums of money—that was saying something.

Justin pushed back the quilt. When he returned to the hard pallet laughingly called a bed, he'd leave off the blankets. The old building's heating system seemed to have one temperature: high. He sat and swung his legs soundlessly to the floor.

Rising, he ducked under the rope that was supposed to keep visitors away from the displays, and went to the door that led out to the reception area. It opened soundlessly and he shut it without letting the latch click.

In the men's room off the reception area, he flicked on the light and used the urinal. At the sink, he splashed cold water on his face and avoided meeting his own eyes in the mirror.

Back in the reception area, he stood by the window. The snow was still coming down. It lay, thick and white and sparkling, covering the steps up to porch level.

If it kept up like this, they could be stuck here for a day or two. Maybe longer. Who the hell knew?

Lots of time alone, just him and Katie…

Though he generally preferred a more outgoing, sophisticated type of woman, he *was* drawn to her. In the end, he supposed, there was no predicting sexual chemistry.

She felt attracted to him, too. He'd seen it in those big brown eyes of hers, known it in the way her body softened and melted into him during that kiss that had sealed their fake vows back there at the town hall.

Maybe he had something here. Maybe he ought to consider taking advantage of the way this sudden winter storm had thrown them together.

But he would have to watch himself. He couldn't let things get *too* hot and heavy. He had nothing with him to protect her from pregnancy and he'd have wagered half his assets that Katie Fenton wasn't on the pill.

No. He couldn't take the chance that she might become pregnant. He'd grown up without a father and he knew what that could do to a kid.

But he could certainly draw her out a little. No doubt she knew things about the Douglases—things that even his expert, high-priced sources couldn't have dug up. Knowledge *was* power and the more he had of it, the better his position would be in this special game he was playing.

And in spite of her wariness, Katie should be approachable if he took the right tact with her—if he were frank and friendly; helpful and easygoing…

It wouldn't have to go too far. Just enough for her to trust him, to tell him her secrets—and those of the Douglases. Just enough that she would *believe* in him as a man. Just enough that she'd come to…care for him.

In the end, if he worked it right, she'd be brokenhearted. He regretted that. But when it came time for payback, a man had to accept some degree of collateral damage. She would be hurt—and the people who cared most about her would hurt *for* her. It would add a certain…turn of the knife, you might say.

Justin flicked off the porch light. No need for it at this late hour. The window became a dark mirror. He saw his own reflection faintly, a lurking shadow in the glass.

Hell.

Maybe not.

He'd always been a man who did what needed doing. Still, he was having a little trouble getting around the fact that Katie Fenton was a good woman. An innocent in all this.

He should leave her out of it.

But then, if it worked out according to plan, he wouldn't be hurting her *that* bad. Just a little. Just enough to get to Caleb. She'd get over it in time.

And there was no saying that he could even fool her. She might be innocent, but she was also smart. It was just possible she'd see him coming and refuse to let him get close enough to make her care. They'd be locked in here for a day or two and she would merely tolerate him until their time of forced proximity had passed. She'd escape unscathed.

Maybe.

But then again, there *was* the real attraction between them. If he let himself go with that, he wouldn't be faking it. And he would tell her the truth—just not all of it.

Taking it forward from that angle…

Say it was all the same, except for the fact that she'd been raised by the Douglases. Say she was only the town librarian playing the mail-order bride and he'd been a stranger talked into taking the part of her groom. Say they ended up here, alone, snowed in at the museum, just as they had.

Take away her connection to the Douglases and he would still be intrigued with her, would still want to pursue her, to hear her secrets, to hold her in his arms and steal a kiss or two.

So in the end, he would only be doing what he

would have done, anyway: getting to know a woman who interested him.

Yes. He could look at it that way. He could take it from there and go with it. Be friendly and open and willing to talk about himself—to hear about her and her life and the people she cared for.

Maybe nothing would come of it.

Or maybe, in the end, he'd have found a second, more personal way to make Caleb Douglas pay for his sins.

Chapter Three

Katie woke to the smell of coffee brewing.

That was the good news.

Everything else? Not nearly so pleasant. Her mouth tasted like the bottom of someone's old shoe. Her wrinkled wool dress gave off a distinctly musty odor. And she had a crick in her neck from sleeping on a too-fat pillow.

She let out a loud, grumpy groan—and then snapped her mouth shut. After all, there was a virtual stranger in the bed across the way—or wait. Probably not. He must be the one who'd made the coffee.

Katie sat up. She'd left the dimmer set to low, so the light was minimal, but she could see that Justin Caldwell's narrow cot lay empty, the covers pulled up and neatly tucked in.

Anxious, suddenly, to know what time it was, to

find out if the storm had ended, if it might be possible that she could go home to her own comfy house on Cedar Street, Katie threw back the covers and jumped from the old bed. Ducking under the rope that marked off her "room," she pulled open the door to the reception area—and blinked at what she saw.

Beyond the windows, a wall of snow gleamed at her in the gray light of a cloud-thick Sunday morning. It was piled above the porch floor now. Though the wild winds of last night had died in the darkness, the snow itself continued to fall, a filmy white curtain, whispering its way down.

The clock on the wall read seven-fifteen. She picked up the phone. Silence. With a heavy sigh, she set it down again and headed for the ladies' room, where she used the facilities, rinsed her face and made a brave effort to comb her tangled hair with her fingers.

Snowed-in without even a hairbrush. Definitely not her idea of a good time.

In the kitchen, Katie found Justin sitting at the table by the window, wearing jeans and a cable-knit red and green sweater with reindeer leaping in a line across his broad chest. On his feet were a battered pair of black-and-white lace-up canvas All-Stars.

"It's true," he announced at her look. "I have raided the rummage sale bags and I feel no shame."

"Love the sweater," she muttered glumly. "Phone's still dead." Beyond him, out the window, the snow kept coming down. "They won't even be able to get the plow out in this."

"Relax," he advised with an easy shrug. "Have some coffee." He toasted her with his stoneware mug. "I even found a smaller pot, so we don't have to brew it up for a hundred every time we want a cup." He gestured at the plateful of sandwiches on the table. "And did I mention there are plenty of sandwiches?"

"Wonderful." She padded to the counter, poured herself some coffee, added cream from the carton in the fridge and plunked herself down in the chair opposite him.

"Better?" he asked after she'd taken a sip.

"A little. Though I'd give a good number of stale sandwiches for a toothbrush. And a comb." She put a hand to her tangled hair. "If we're stuck here much longer, I may consider raiding the museum displays for some long-gone pioneer lady's sterling silver dresser set."

He looked very pleased with himself—and, now she thought about it, he looked as if he'd shaved. And his hair was wet—was that shampoo she smelled?

She set down her cup. "You found a razor in the rummage sale bags—and you washed your hair."

He laughed. It was a low, velvety kind of sound and it played along her skin like a physical caress. "Was that an accusation?"

She sat back in her chair and regarded him with suspicion. "You're much too cheerful."

"And you are very cranky." He took another bite of his sandwich, chewed and swallowed. "If you don't be nice, I won't let you have what's in that bag over by the sink."

She glanced where he'd indicated. The bag sat near the edge: a plain brown paper bag. "What's in it?"

He pushed the plate of sandwiches toward her. "Eat first."

She reached for a sandwich, raised it to her lips—and lowered it without taking a bite. "Just tell me. Is there a hairbrush in there?"

He nodded. "More than one. And combs. And a few toothbrushes—still wrapped in cellophane. And travel-size toothpaste. And sample bottles of shampoo and lotion, boxed-up shower caps and miniature bars of soap—oh, and did I mention razors and travel-size shaving cream cans? Looks like someone held up a drugstore, raided a motel supply closet and gave what they stole to the Historical Society rummage sale."

"Shower caps," Katie repeated wistfully.

Justin grunted. "Yeah. No need for those."

"Since we don't have a shower."

"But remember. It could be worse. The heat could be out and there could be no wood for the stove. The ladies from the Historical Society could have failed to leave us these delicious sandwiches." He waved one at her.

"You have a surprisingly vivid imagination."

"Thank you. And what I meant is, we're doing okay here. And after you eat, you even get to brush your teeth."

She supposed he had a point. "You're right. I should take my own advice from yesterday and keep a more positive outlook on our situation."

He faked a stern expression. "See that you do."

Katie ate her sandwich and took a second, as well.

Her spirits had lifted. If she wasn't getting out of here today, at least she'd have clean teeth and combed hair.

Once she'd spent twenty minutes in the ladies' room using various items from the brown paper bag, Katie went to the storage area and chose a bulky sweater and a pair of worn corduroy pants. She even found thick gray socks and jogging shoes that were only a half size too big.

"Lookin' good," Justin remarked with a wink when she returned to the kitchen where he sat reading yesterday's newspaper.

"The fit leaves something to be desired—but I have to admit, I'm a lot more comfortable."

"And less cranky."

"Yes. That, too." She gave him a smile, thinking how even-tempered and helpful he'd been since she got them into this mess. Really, she could have been stranded with worse. She added, in an effort to show him her friendlier side, "While I was choosing my outfit, I found some old board games. Maybe we can haul them out later. I play a mean game of checkers."

"Sounds good." The paper rustled as he turned the page.

"Justin…"

He lowered the paper and gave her an easy smile.

"I just want you to know I appreciate how well you're taking all this."

He gestured toward the snow beyond the window. "This is nothing, believe me."

Really, this positive-attitude approach could be carried too far. "Oh. So you're telling me this kind of thing happens to you all the time?"

"Only once before."

"Oh. Well. Only once. That's nothing—and you're joking, aren't you?"

"No. I'm not. When I was thirteen, we lived in this vacation-home development in northern Nevada. I got snowed-in there alone for a week."

She couldn't have heard right. "Alone for a week—at thirteen?" He nodded. "But what about your mom?"

"She was supposed to be home, but she didn't make it. The situation was similar to yesterday's—a sudden storm that turned out much worse than predicted. It got bad fast and she couldn't get to me."

"But...where was she?"

His expression turned doubtful. "You sure you want to hear this? It's not that exciting. And as you can see by looking at me today, I got through it just fine."

She'd been planning to go check on Buttercup. But that could wait a minute or two. She pulled out a chair and slid into it. "I do want to hear. Honestly."

He studied her for a long moment, as if gauging the sincerity of her request. Finally, he folded the paper and set it aside. "At the time, we were living in this one-room cabin not far from Lake Tahoe."

"You and your mom?"

"That's right. The cabin was one of those ski chalet designs. On a two-acre lot. Intended as a vacation home. It had a single big, open room with lots of windows, the roof pitched high, a sleeping loft above?''

''Yes. I can picture it.''

''My mother was in real estate at that point. She went off to show someone another cabin identical to ours. A bad storm blew in. She couldn't get back to me, so I was stuck on my own. It was…a learning experience, let me tell you.''

''Yikes. I can't even imagine.''

''Yeah. It *was* pretty grim, looking back on it. The phone line went dead the first day. Then, the next day, the power went out. But I had plenty of candles and a woodstove for heat. I kept the fire going and tucked into the canned goods when I got hungry.''

''But what did you *do,* alone for all that time?''

One corner of his full mouth quirked up. ''I got pretty damn bored, now you mention it. Bored enough that I taught myself solitaire with a dog-eared deck of cards I found in a kitchen drawer. When that got old, I started working my way through all my school-books. For a thirteen-year-old boy to do every prob-lem in his math book for recreation, *that's* despera-tion.''

''But there was plenty of canned food, you said?''

He made a low sound in his throat. ''For some reason, my mom had a case each of canned peaches and cream of mushroom soup. To this day, I can't stand the sight or smell of either.''

''I'll bet—but what I can't imagine is how you made it through something like that.'' She scanned his face. ''Thirteen,'' she said softly. ''It's too hor-rible. You must have been scared to death.''

He shrugged. "The wood lasted 'til the end of the sixth day. I got out the axe and chopped up my mother's oak-veneer kitchen table and chairs. Once I'd burned them, I kind of lost heart. The fire died and I piled every blanket in the place on my bed and burrowed in there for the duration. I have to admit, by that time I was getting pretty damn terrified."

"But then you were rescued."

"That's right. The snowplow arrived at noon the next day with my mother, in her Blazer, right behind it. She was seriously freaked, I can tell you."

Katie almost wished his mother could have been there, with them, right then. She'd have had a thing or two to say to her. "Your *mother* was freaked. What about you? *You* were the child, for heaven's sake. How could she leave you alone like that?"

He let out a low chuckle. "Katie. Settle down."

Easier said than done. His story had seriously hit home for her. She shifted in her chair, crossing her legs and then uncrossing them, feeling antsy and angry and definitely not *settled down.* "I'm sorry, but it just, well, it fries me, you know? Children are so vulnerable. Parents have to look out for them, take *care* of them, pay them some attention now and then...."

He sat back in his chair. "Why do I get the feeling you're talking about more than what happened to me when I was thirteen?"

She wrapped her arms around her middle and looked out the window at the falling snow, blinking against the glare of all that shimmery white.

"Katie?"

She faced him. "You're right," she confessed. "I was thinking about how things were for me, before Addy came and got me, when my parents were still alive."

"Rough?" Those blue eyes had a softness in them, as if he understood—and from what he'd just told her, she had a feeling he did.

She hugged herself harder. "I rarely saw them. They enjoyed traveling. They had a flat in London, the family brownstone in Philadelphia, villas in France and Italy. And where they didn't have a flat or a villa, they had *friends* who had one. You know the words. 'Globe-trotting.' 'Jet-setting.' My parents *were* the beautiful people. They came from fine families and the money was always there. They never had to work. So they didn't. They didn't even have to take care of their child. There were nannies and governesses, plenty of hired help for that."

"So you weren't left alone," Justin said, his eyes direct. Knowing.

"No, I wasn't."

"But you *were* lonely."

"Exactly." She looked down. Her arms were wrapped so tightly around her middle, they made her rib cage ache. With a slow, deep breath, she let go of herself and folded her hands on the tabletop. "I never knew a real family—'til Addy and Caleb." She smiled to herself. "And Riley. He was all grown up by the time I came to them, twenty-three, when I moved to the ranch. How many young guys in their twenties have time for a gawky fourteen-year-old girl? Not many. But Riley did. He was so good to me, you know?'' Justin made a sound of understanding low in his throat. ''What the Douglases gave me was something so important. The two big things I'd never had. Their time. Their attention. Riley taught me to ride—''

''On Buttercup.'' He grinned.

''That's right.'' She glanced toward the door to the back porch, thinking she should get out there and check on the old mare. Soon.

But it was so…comfortable. Sitting here with Justin, talking about the things that had made them who they were. ''So you don't blame your mother for leaving you alone in that cabin?''

He shook his head. ''It's tough for a woman on her own, with a kid. She'd been left high and dry, pregnant with me by the no-good bastard who used her and then walked away from her when she told him she was having his baby. She was…a good mother and she took damn good care of me. But there was no getting around that she had to make a living and that meant when the storm blew in, I was at the cabin, and she wasn't. It's the kind of thing that can happen to anyone.''

''It's the kind of thing that could scar a child for life, that's what it is.''

He pressed a fist to his chest right over the row of reindeer prancing across the front of his sweater. ''That's me. Deeply damaged.''

She tipped her head to the side, considering. ''Well. I guess it's good that you can joke about it.''

He was quiet for a moment. Then he said, ''It happened. I survived. And I've done just fine for myself, though I never had a father, never had much formal education and started, literally, from scratch.''

"In…development?'' She laughed. "What does that mean, exactly, to be a 'developer.'''

"Well, a developer 'develops.'''

"Sheesh. It's all clear to me now.''

He grinned. "Property, in my case. We start with several viable acres and we develop a project to build tract homes. Or say I got hold of just the right business-district lot. I'd start putting the people and financing together to build an office complex. A developer is someone who gets the money and the people and the plans—and most important, the right property—and puts it all together.''

He hadn't told her anything she couldn't have figured out herself, but she was discovering she enjoyed listening to him talk. She liked the way he looked at her. As if he never wanted to look away.

She said, "Like Caleb's ski resort? He's got the property and you'll work with him to 'develop' it.''

"That's right. But don't misunderstand. It's his project, his baby. He'll be in charge, though I'll be involved every step of the way.''

She looked down at her folded hands. She was just about to tell him how much the project meant to Caleb. Caleb *was* getting older and Katie knew that sometimes he worried he was losing his edge—but no.

Katie kept her mouth shut. Yes, she was finding she liked Justin. A lot. However, the last thing Caleb would want was for her to go blabbing his secret doubts to a business associate.

She glanced up and found Justin studying her again, his dark head tipped to the side. "Question."

"Ask."

"Yesterday. Didn't you mention that you went to college in Colorado?"

"That's right. CU."

"I'll bet you had straight A's in high school."

She gave him a pert little nod. "You would win that bet."

"High scores on the SAT?"

"Very."

"Then why not Bryn Mawr, like your mother, and Adele Douglas? You'd have been a legacy, right—pretty much guaranteed to get in—even if your grades and test scores hadn't been outstanding?"

"I liked CU. They have a fine curriculum. Plus, it was closer to home."

"Home being here, in Thunder Canyon."

"That's right—and you? Where did you go to college?"

"I told you. No real formal education. I went to real estate school and then got my broker's license a couple of years later."

"You started in real estate because of your mother's connections?"

He chuckled at that, though there wasn't a lot of humor in the sound. "My mother had no connections. She'd been out of the real estate business for years when I started. It didn't work out for her. Like a lot of things…"

She might have asked, *What things?* But he wore a closed-in, private kind of look at that moment and she didn't want to pry. She coaxed, "So you started in real estate…"

He blinked and the brooding shadows left his eyes. "Yeah. By the time I was twenty-five, I'd branched into property development."

"A self-made man."

"Smile when you say that."

She *was* smiling. But to make sure he noticed, she smiled even wider. And then her conscience reminded her that she had Buttercup to think of. She stood.

He put on a hurt look. "Just like that. You're leaving. Was it something I said?"

"What you said was fascinating. Honestly. And I'll be back soon."

"The question is, where do you think you're going?" He tipped his head toward the window and the still-falling snow outside. "I hate to break it to you, but I doubt you could get beyond the front porch."

"I want to check on Buttercup."

He rose. "I'll come with you."

She started to argue—that it was cold out there and she could take care of the job herself and he didn't really need to go. But then again, it wasn't as if he had a full schedule or anything.

He ushered her out to the back porch, where they put on their antique outerwear. Then they pushed open the door to the breezeway.

The snow had piled four feet or so on either side, sloping to the icy ground, leaving a path maybe a foot wide. "After you," Justin said. "Watch your step. It looks pretty slick."

In the shed, Buttercup snorted in greeting and came

right to Katie. She stroked the old mare's forehead and blew in her nostrils. "How're you doing, sweetie? Kind of lonely out here?" The horse whickered in response. "And I'll bet you wish I had some oats. Sorry. That hay'll have to do you for a while." She patted Buttercup's smooth golden neck and pulled out one of the brushes she'd brought from inside. It was hardly a grooming brush, but nothing else was available.

She brushed the old mare's knotted mane and spoke to her in low whispers for a while. Then she and Justin broke open another bale of hay.

"Watch out," he warned when they were spreading it around a little. "It's damned amazing how much manure one horse can produce in a sixteen-hour period."

"It is at that."

"Just don't step backward without looking behind you first."

She found a shovel in the corner and took it to him. "Get to work."

"Shoveling horse manure?"

"That's right."

"But where am I going to put it?" The gleam in his eyes said he already had a pretty good idea.

"Just shovel it up, carry it out those open main doors there and toss it as far as you can into the snow."

"That snow's piling up pretty high out there. This could be dangerous."

"So pay attention when you throw it. Wouldn't want it to come flying right back at you."

He pretended to grumble, but he started right in. She looked around and found another shovel. With both of them scooping and tossing, they had the mess cleared away in no time at all.

As they went to put the shovels up, Justin remarked that if the snow got much higher, swamping out the shed was going to be a real challenge.

"We'll manage," she told him. "Somehow…" She set her shovel against the wall and turned so fast, she almost ran into him.

"Watch it." He laughed down low in his throat, the sound emerging on a cloud of mist.

She laughed, too.

And then, all at once, she wasn't laughing and neither was he. They were just looking at each other— staring, really. And the cold air seemed to shimmer between them.

Oh, my goodness. Those lips of his…

Too full, for a man's lips. Really. Too full and yet…

Exactly perfect.

If only she didn't already know how delicious those lips felt pressed against her own. Maybe, if she didn't know what a great kisser he was, she wouldn't be standing here, sighing out a big breath of misty air and lifting her mouth to him.

He said her name, on a fog of breath. "Katie…"

She was so busy imagining what it was going to feel like when his lips met hers, that she didn't register how close Buttercup was behind him—not until the mare let out a low whinny and head-butted Justin a good one.

"Hey!" He surged forward, right into Katie. She went over backward and down they went into the newly spread hay. He ended up on top of her.

Katie blinked up at him and he looked down at her and there was a lovely, strange, breath-held kind of moment. He was so...warm and solid, pressed all along the length of her—and heavy, too, but in a good way. He looked deep in her eyes and he said her name again and she held up her lips to welcome his kiss.

But Buttercup wasn't finished. She bent her head and started nipping the back of Justin's baggy old coat.

He rolled away from Katie to glare up at the mare. "Knock it off."

Buttercup whinnied again and clopped off toward the double doors. A moment later, she was outside beneath the overhang, lipping up snow.

Justin canted up on an elbow and looked down at Katie. "That animal has it in for me."

Katie was thinking that she really ought to sit up. Her hat had come off when Justin landed on top of her. She knew she had hay in her hair. But she felt kind of...lax. Lax and lazy and oh-so-comfortable, lying there in the hay on the frozen dirt floor.

"Hmm," she said, and the sound was every bit as low and lazy as she was feeling. "Maybe Buttercup thinks you're up to no good."

He leaned in closer. She gazed up at his thick black lashes and his red nose and that wonderful, soft, oh-so-kissable mouth. "I'm perfectly harmless."

"Perfect?" she heard herself answer, her tone as

husky and intimate as his. "Maybe. Harmless? Oh, I don't think so...."

There was a silence, a quiet so intense she could hear the soft sound of the snow falling outside and the faint rustling noises Buttercup made beyond the shed doors. Slowly, his mouth curved into a smile. And his eyes...

Oh, it was just like right before he kissed her, in front of everyone, back in the hall. His eyes kind of sucked on her. They drew her down.

"I don't think that mare wants me to kiss you."

And she probably *shouldn't* kiss him. "Well, Justin. Okay, then. Let me up and we'll—"

He cut her off by placing a gloved finger against her lips. "Not yet." She probably should have protested, told him firmly to let her up.

But she didn't. She watched, entranced, as he lifted his hand, took the tip of the glove's finger between his white teeth and pulled it off. He dropped the glove beside her and then he touched her lips again—skin to skin this time. That brush of a caress made her mouth tingle, made her whole body yearn.

He let his hand drift over until it lay against the side of her face. "Soft," he whispered. "So pretty and soft..." He lowered his mouth.

She expected a hot, soul-shattering kiss. But he only brushed his lips sweetly, one time, across hers— and then he lifted away again and she was looking in those haunting eyes once more. "What's another kiss? Between a man and his wife."

Now she felt truly torn. She longed to kiss him— yet she knew it was probably a bad idea. "We shouldn't…get anything started, you know? We hardly know each other and—''

''But that's just it. I *want* to know you better. What about you, Katie? Do you want to know me?''

She did! And that seemed…dangerous, somehow. That seemed foolish and scary and simply not right. ''I—I don't really want to start anything *casual,* you know?'' She found her throat had gone desert-dry. She paused to swallow and then rushed to continue before he could do anything that would make her thoughts scatter and fly away. ''I know it's probably every guy's fantasy to get stranded with a woman who, uh, knows what she wants and knows how to get it—not that I don't know what I want. It's just, well, I don't want…*that.*''

He only smiled. ''*That,* huh?''

''Yes.''

''That…what?''

Oh, this wasn't going well. ''Look. I just don't want to start anything I know I'm not going to finish. Okay?''

''Katie?''

She glared at him. ''What?''

''It's only a kiss.''

''Oh, I just don't—''

''Katie. Do you *want* to kiss me?''

''We've just about talked this to death, don't you think?''

''But do you want to kiss me?''

''Oh, all right, damn it.'' Katie rarely swore. But right then, *damn it* seemed the only thing to say.

''But do you?''

"Yes." The word came out breathless-sounding. "I do."

"Good." He lowered his mouth to hers.

Katie sighed once and she sighed again.

Her hands slipped up to encircle his neck and she held on for dear life as he played with her mouth. With that clever tongue of his, he traced the seam where her lips met, teasingly at first and then with a more insistent pressure. She couldn't resist him— didn't *want* to resist him. Shyly, she let her lips relax and he swept that tongue of his inside.

It was a shocking, thrilling thing, the way Justin Caldwell could use that mouth of his. And it was a truly wonderful thing, the way his body felt, so warm and close, pressed against her side, the way he smelled of soap and shaving cream.

His cold nose touched hers and his hot breath burned her icy cheek. As he kissed her, he stroked her with his hands. That was wonderful, too. Each separate caress left a burning trail of longing in its wake. He wrapped his arms around her and rolled a little, so they were both on their sides, and his hand moved lower, to the small of her back. He rubbed there, a sweet, firm pressure, soothing muscles cramped from sleeping on that lumpy ancient mattress last night.

She moaned and pressed herself all the tighter against him. His hand swept lower. He cupped her bottom and tucked her up into him.

That was when she felt the hard ridge in his jeans.

Oh, my.

Time to stop.

Time to stop right *now*.

She braced her hands on his shoulders and tore her mouth away from his. "That's enough." She looked at his face and she feared...

What?

She realized she didn't know. Her fear was formless, and yet she did feel it.

Remember the others, she reminded herself. *They were after your money. They hurt you. He could so easily do the same....*

But even as she thought of that, she didn't believe it. Oh, he might hurt her, yes. But in her heart, she simply didn't believe it would be for her money.

Which probably made her the biggest fool in Montana.

He loosened his hold on her. With a deep sigh, he pressed his forehead to hers. "You're right," he said. "Enough."

She slid her hands down to his hard chest. Beneath her palms, she could feel his heat, and his heart racing. His breath came out in ragged puffs—just like hers.

She whispered, "We'd better go in."

He touched her hair. She thought that she'd never felt anything quite so lovely in her whole life as that—the tender caress of his hand on her hair. He threaded his chilled bare fingers up under the tangled strands and cupped the back of her neck. She took his cue and tipped her head up to look at him.

"Yeah," he said. His mouth was swollen from what he'd been doing to her, his eyes twin blue flames. "We'll go in. Now." He pressed one more quick, hard kiss on her lips—as if he realized he shouldn't, but couldn't resist. Her mouth burned at the contact.

Then he reached across her to grab his discarded glove. Rolling away from her, he rose. She scuttled to a sitting position.

"Here," he said.

She stared at his outstretched hand. It seemed...too dangerous to take it.

Her gaze tracked upward, to his face. She knew by the heated look in his eyes that if she reached out, he would only pull her close and start kissing her again—and the thrumming of her blood through her body left her no doubt that she would end up kissing him right back.

No. Not going to happen. She'd known this man less than twenty-four hours. And she refused to end up rolling around naked with him on a bed of hay in a freezing old shed.

"I can manage, thanks." She pulled off a glove and felt in her hair. It was just as she'd suspected: threaded through with bits of hay. "Oh, just look at me...."

Justin let his hand drop to his side. "I am." His voice was husky and low. And in his eyes she saw desire—*real* desire. For her.

And not only desire, but also something dark and lonely, something that might have been regret.

Katie's mouth went dust-dry. *This* was danger—a danger far beyond any threat a mere fortune hunter might pose. Peril to her tender heart, to her very soul.

No doubt about it. She wanted him—with a kind

of bone-melting yearning, with a merciless desire the like of which she'd never known before.

It was…a physical aching. A hunger in the blood.

Oh, she would have to watch herself with him. She would have to exercise a little caution, or she'd be in way over her head.

Somewhere far back in her mind, a taunting voice whispered, *Katie. Come on. You're already over your head. Over your head and falling fast.…*

Chapter Four

He shouldn't have kissed her.

It had been a major error in judgment and Justin damn well knew that it had.

He shouldn't have kissed her. Not so soon, anyway—and certainly not in a prickly bed of hay on the frozen dirt floor of the shed out back, with that irritating old mare looking on.

Getting hot and heavy so fast had spooked her. She had her guard up and now he couldn't get past it.

They spent the rest of the endless day playing checkers, watching the snow fall, stoking the fire in the stove out front and reading books and magazines they found stacked in the storage room. Whenever they spoke, she made sure it was in polite generalities.

The snow kept falling. The radio played only static. And the phone stayed dead.

Justin could have kicked himself with his rummage sale Converse All-Star. The big loss of ground with her was his own damn fault. He'd sucked her in beautifully, had her right in the palm of his hand once he'd told her the story of that lonely week in the cabin when he was thirteen. He'd hit the perfect common nerve: a lonely childhood; parents who weren't all they should have been.

It was going so well.

Until the kiss.

And even that could have been okay—could have been tender and sweet and worked beautifully to lure her closer.

But he'd gotten his arms around her and her mouth under his and that sweet body pressed close against him...

He'd lost it. Lost every last shred of control.

The bald truth was that he'd seriously underestimated the power of his own lust for the shy brown-eyed librarian with too much money and an adopted family he despised.

It was funny, really—though he wasn't laughing. A royal backfire of his basic intention: *he* was supposed to seduce *her*.

Not the other way around.

At six that evening, they sat at the kitchen table, reading—or at least, Katie was reading. He knew it because he kept sneaking glances at her and losing his place in the thriller that should have been holding him spellbound—or so it said in the cover notes. As "taut" and "edge-of-your-seat" as the book was supposed to be, he kept having to go back and read the same paragraph over and over again.

Katie, though...

She seemed to have no trouble at all with her concentration. She'd laid the heavy volume she'd chosen open on the table, rested her forearms on the tabletop and bent her brown head to the page. She'd barely budged from that position for over an hour. He knew. He'd timed her. Occasionally, she'd catch her soft bottom lip between her teeth, worry it lightly and let it go. Sometimes she smiled—just the faintest hint of a smile. As if what she read amused her.

Justin scowled every time she smiled like that. He wanted her to look up and smile at *him*, damn it. But she didn't.

And he ought to be glad she didn't look up. If she caught him scowling at her, he'd only lose more ground than he already had.

And what the hell was his problem here, anyway? He was getting way too invested in this thing with her. She had nothing to do with the main plan and if she never let him get near her again it wouldn't matter in the least.

So why should he care if she smiled at him or not?

He decided he'd be better off not thinking too deeply on that one.

Luckily for him, he'd just looked down at his book again when she glanced up and announced, ''You know, when we went through the cupboards in here yesterday, I noticed some cans way in the back.''

There was something in her tone—something easier, a little more friendly.

His pulse ratcheted up a notch and he quelled a satisfied smile. *Better,* he thought. *Now, don't blow it....*

He shut the battered paperback without marking the page. Next time he picked it up, he'd have to start over, anyway. ''Yeah,'' he said, sounding a hell of a lot more offhand than he felt. He gestured toward the cabinets on the far wall. ''In the bottom, on the left.'' He started to rise.

''No. I'll look.''

He sank back to his seat and she got up and went over there, leaving him debating whether to follow her. He decided against it. She *was* loosening up a little. Better let her get looser before he got too close.

She went to her knees, pulled open the cupboard and stuck her head in there. He looked at her back-side. Great view. Even with the ugly baggy sweater and too-loose frayed corduroy pants.

''Yes,'' she said, her voice muffled by the cabinet. ''Here they are.'' She pulled her head out and craned around to grin at him. ''Lots of soup, but I see some canned fruit, too.''

He got up, after all, and went to stand over her— just to be helpful. She passed him the dusty cans and he set them on the counter above the cabinet.

''That's it.'' She shut the cabinet doors and stood to read the labels. ''Vegetable beef, chicken noodle, cream of asparagus, pears, applesauce...'' She gave him a pert look. ''Justin. Not a single can of cream of mushroom soup. And no peaches.''

Absurdly pleased that she'd remembered the details of his childhood ordeal, he allowed himself to chuckle. "That's a relief. I admit I was getting worried."

"No need to." She brushed his arm—the lightest breath of a touch. Beneath the green sleeve of his sweater, his skin burned as if she'd set a match to it.

Their eyes met. *Zap.* His heart raced faster and the air seemed to shimmer around them. Damned amazing, her effect on him.

Katie smiled wider, a nervous kind of smile. Yes. She *was* trying. She wasn't cutting him out anymore. "So...soup with your sandwiches?"

He nodded. "Vegetable beef—unless that's your favorite?"

She admitted, "I have this thing for cream of asparagus."

"Well, then. Looks like we both get what we want."

Katie went to get ready for bed at ten. Justin said he wanted to read a little longer and then he'd be in.

She knew it was only a pretense. In the hours they'd sat reading, he'd hardly made it through the first few chapters in that book of his. No. He was being thoughtful, giving her a chance to get ready and go to bed in private.

In the ladies' room, she rinsed out her underwear and hung it over the stall door. She washed up and dressed for bed in a wrinkled old pair of red flannel pajamas—thanks, again, to the bags of clothing in the storage room.

She looked at herself in the mirror over the sink and scrunched up her nose at what she saw. Tomorrow, if they were still stuck here, she would have to wash her hair. Maybe she could find some bath towels in the rummage sale stuff—or if not, well, she'd work it out somehow. And really, Justin didn't need to be sitting in the kitchen pretending to read, respecting her need to keep her distance from him after the kiss that had gone too far out in the shed.

"Stupid," she muttered to her own reflection. "I'm being stupid about this and I need to stop." There was nothing alluring or lust-inspiring about the sight of her in flannel pajamas. They buttoned up to here and bagged around her ankles. If Justin saw her getting into bed in them he would not be the least tempted to make mad, passionate love to her.

Truly. In pajamas like these, she was safe from the potential to have sex of any kind.

She peered closer at herself, craned her head forward so her nose met the glass. The question was, why did that depress her?

Oh, come on. She knew why.

Because there had not been nearly enough sex—of any kind—in her life.

"I, Katherine Adele Fenton," she whispered, her breath fogging the glass, "am a cliché. I'm right out of *The Music Man.* I'm Marian the librarian—hiding in the stacks, waiting for some cocky con man to show up and let down my hair for me."

Really, it had to stop. She owed it to librarians everywhere, who, she knew, were a much more outgoing, ready-for-anything bunch than most people gave them credit for.

She pulled back from the mirror and then used her

flannel sleeve to wipe the steamed-up place her breath had left. She stood straight and proud. "I *wanted* him to kiss me and I'm *glad* he kissed me," she announced to the sink and the toilet stall and her soggy underwear hanging from the stall door. "I'm not afraid of my own feelings. I'm an adult and I run my own life and I do it very well, thank you." She *liked* Justin and he clearly liked her and she wasn't running away from that. Not anymore.

Yes, there was always danger—when you really liked someone, when you put your heart on the line. Things that mattered inevitably involved a certain amount of risk.

Her shoulders back and her head high, Katie marched to the ladies' room door and pulled it wide.

Justin looked up from his book when she entered the kitchen. The bewildered expression on his handsome face made her want to grab him and hug him and tell him it would be all right. She didn't, of course. There were a few things that needed saying before they got around to any hugging.

"Katie? Everything okay?"

She marched over, yanked out the chair opposite him and dropped into it. "It was very sweet of you, to sit in here with that book you're not really interested in and wait until I had time to put on these ugly old pajamas and get into bed. But it's not as if we had to share a bathroom or anything." She raised her arms and looked down at her baggy bedroom attire. "And as you can see, this outfit reveals absolutely nothing of my, er, feminine charms. We're both perfectly safe from any, um, dangerous temptation, don't you think?'' She lifted her head and met his eyes.

They were gleaming. ''Well, Katie. I don't know. You look pretty damn tempting to me.''

''Liar,'' she muttered, flattered in spite of herself.

He put up a hand, palm out, as if testifying in court. ''Sexiest woman I ever saw.''

''Oh, yeah, right.''

''Must be the color. You know what they say about red. The color of power. And sex.''

She sat up straighter. ''Power, huh? I kind of like that.''

In his eyes she could see what he almost said: *But what about sex?* He didn't, though.

Probably afraid she'd get spooked and shut him out again.

''Justin?'' Her heart pounded painfully inside her rib cage. She had things to say and she was going to say them, but that didn't make it easy.

''Yeah?''

''Justin, are you after my money?''

With zero hesitation, he replied, ''No.''

She peered at him through narrowed eyes. ''Are you *sure*?''

''Yeah. Money's not an issue for me. I have plenty of my own. Now, anyway. And I earned every damn penny of it.''

Her face felt as if it had turned as red as her pajamas and her heart beat even faster. She did believe him. If that made her a total fool, well, so be it.

He added, ''But don't take me wrong. I don't mind

that you're rich. Hey, I'm glad you are. It's always better, don't you think, to have money than not to?''

Katie thought about that. ''Sometimes I'm not so sure. Money can...isolate a person. It can make it so it's hard to believe that someone might like you, just for yourself.''

''Katie.''

She put her hand against her heart. Really, did it need to keep pounding so awfully fast? ''Yeah?''

''I do like you. For yourself.''

She realized she believed that, too, and her galloping heart slowed a little. But she wasn't finished yet. ''There's more.''

''Shoot.''

''Did you know that I was...?'' Oh, this was so awkward.

He helped her out. ''Rich?''

She gulped. ''Yes. Did you know I was a wealthy woman before you got up on that stage at the town hall and 'married' me?''

''I did.''

She blinked. ''Who told you?''

He chuckled. ''Some of those spectators were pretty damn drunk. When they heard I'd be playing your groom, I got a lot of ribbing. You know the kind. How you were not only a cute little thing, you were loaded, too. How, if I played my cards right, I might catch myself an heiress.''

Katie scrunched up her nose. ''A cute little thing?''

He shrugged. ''Drunk talk. You know how it goes. And you might like to know, I got more than one warning that I'd better be good to you. They were joking—but the look in every eye said I'd pay if I messed with their favorite librarian.''

That brought a smile. ''They did? They told you to be good to me?''

He nodded. ''So you've got backup, in case you were worried.''

She looked him directly in the eye. ''I guess I *was* worried. And scared. The truth is, in the past couple of years, I've had a tendency to let fear run my life. But I've had a little talk with myself. Fear is not going to rule me. Not anymore. I…well, I like you. And I think you like me.''

''I do. Very much.''

A sweet warmth spread through her. ''So then. I'd like to get to know you better.''

His gaze didn't waver. ''And I want to know you.''

Chapter Five

They talked for hours, lying in their separate beds in the central display room.

Katie told him about Ted Anders. She'd met Ted at CU. He was tall and tan and blond, a prelaw student. Interesting to talk to, with a good sense of humor—and charming, too. Extremely so. Ted had lavished attention on Katie. She'd started to believe she'd found the right guy for her—until she went to a party up on "the hill," where a lot of the students shared apartments. The place was packed, a real crowd scene. She got separated from Ted and when she found him again, he had his arm around a cute redhead.

"He was so busy putting a move on her, he didn't even see that I was watching," Katie said. "I heard him tell her how he'd like to, uh, 'jump her bones,' but he couldn't afford to. He had a 'rich one' on a string and he wasn't blowing that 'til he'd clipped at least a couple of her millions.''

''I hope you reamed him a new one right there and then.'' Justin sounded as if he wouldn't have minded doing that for her.

She laughed—and it felt so good. To think about something that had hurt so much at the time and realize it was just a memory now, one with no power to cause her pain. ''In case you didn't notice, I'm not big on public displays.''

He chuckled. ''Well, yeah. As a matter of fact, I did notice. So, what *did* you do?''

''I went home to my apartment. Eventually, Ted must have realized I'd left. He came knocking on my door. I confronted him then. He started laying on the sweet talk. But I wasn't buying. Once he saw he couldn't talk his way back into a relationship with me, he said a few rotten things, trying to hurt me a little worse than he already had. But he knew it was over.''

''And that made you sure every man you met would be after your money?''

''Well, there was another, er, incident.''

''At CU?''

''No. Right here in town, not long after I came home to stay and took the job as librarian. He was a local guy, Jackson Tully. He'd grown up here and gone to Thunder Canyon High ten years before I did. After high school, he'd moved away—and then moved back and opened a souvenir shop on Main. He asked me out and he seemed nice enough. We had several dates and…oh, he was funny and sweet and I started to think—''

''That he was *the one*.''

She made a face at the shadowed rafters above. ''Oh, I don't know. I thought that we had something good, I guess. That it might really go somewhere.''

''As in wedding bells and happily ever after?''

''That's right.''

''So then…?''

''Well, he proposed.''

''Marriage?''

''What else?''

He made a low sound. ''I can think of a few other things, but I won't go into them. So the money-grubbing shop owner proposed and you said yes.''

She pushed the blankets down a little and rested her arms on top of them. ''Well, no. I didn't say yes. I did…care for him, but I wasn't sure. I said I wanted to think about it. And while I was thinking, his mom came to see me. She's a nice woman, Lucille Tully is. A member of the Historical Society, as a matter of fact.''

''Isn't everyone?''

''In Thunder Canyon?'' She considered. ''Well, just about everyone over forty or so is.''

''And Lucille Tully said…''

''That she loved her son, but I was a 'sweet girl' and she couldn't let me say yes to him without my knowing the truth.''

''Which was?''

''Jackson had had two bankruptcies. His souvenir shop—which Lucille had given him the money to open—wasn't doing well and he'd told his mother more than once that as soon as he married the librarian, she could have her money back. He'd close the store. Why slave all day long, catering to pushy tourists in some stupid shop when he'd be set for life and he could focus on enjoying himself.''

"Spending your money, I take it?"

Katie sighed. "Lucille cried when she told me. I felt terrible for her. It just broke her heart, the whole thing.''

"So you said no to the gold-digging Jackson Tully."

"I did."

"And where is he now?"

"Couldn't say. His shop went under and he left town. So far as I know, he hasn't been back."

"And what about the mother?"

"What do you mean?"

"Come on, Katie. I've known you for two whole days and I can already guarantee that you took care of her."

"Well, if you must know, I had Caleb buy the shop."

"With *your* money."

"That's right. Caleb made sure Jackson paid Lucille back. Then Caleb sold the shop for me. At a profit. Everybody came out all right—financially, at least. And by then, Jackson had moved on. Lucille doesn't talk about him much, not to me, anyway— and you know, now I look back on both Jackson and Ted Anders, I realize I was pretty darn lucky. At least I didn't marry them. At least I found out what kind of men they really were before I took any kind of irrevocable step.''

There was silence from the narrow cot on the other side of the room.

She grinned into the darkness. ''Justin? Have I put you to sleep?''

''I'm wide-awake.''

''You sound so serious…''

A pause, and then, ''Those two were a couple of prime-grade SOBs—and you're right, at least you didn't marry either of them.''

''No, I didn't. And Justin…''

''What?''

''I did have a *nice* boyfriend or two. Nothing that serious, but they were good guys. I actually enjoyed high school. How many people can say that?''

''Good point.'' The way he said that made her sure he was one of the ones who couldn't.

''And I went to both proms—junior and senior. For my senior prom I wore a—''

He made a loud snoring sound.

She sat up and the bed creaked in protest. ''I might have to unscrew one of these pineapple finials and throw it at you.''

He sat up, too. ''Please don't hurt me.''

They looked at each other through the darkness. For pajamas, he'd found a pair of cheap black sweats in the storage room. In the minimal light, he was hardly more than a broad-shouldered shadow. But then his white teeth flashed with his smile.

She flopped back down. ''I promise to let you go to sleep. Soon.''

His blankets rustled. "No hurry. As it happens, I don't have any early appointments tomorrow."

"Okay, then. But remember. I offered to shut up...."

"And I turned you down."

She raised her arms and slid her hands under her hair, lacing them on the too-fat pillow, cupping her head. "Sheesh. I'm starting to feel as if I know you so well. But I don't even know where you live—in Bozeman, right?" He made a noise in the affirmative. "Your house...what's it like?"

"Four thousand square feet. Vaulted ceilings. Lots of windows. Good views."

"And redwood decking, on a number of levels— with a huge hot tub, right?"

"How did you know that?"

"Oh, Justin. How else could it be? And come on. Fair's fair. Women?"

He let out a big, fake sigh. "Okay. What do you need to know?"

She thought of the way he'd kissed her out in the shed—and when they got "married." And she realized it had never occurred to her that there might be someone special in his life. A live-in girlfriend, or even...

A wife.

No. No, that couldn't be. He could never have kissed her like that if there already was a special woman in his life—not the way he had when they'd pretended to get married.

And certainly not the way he'd kissed her out in the shed.

And if he *could*...

Oh, God. Here she'd made such a big deal about asking him if he was after her money. And she hadn't bothered to find out if he had a wife.

"It's too damn quiet over there." His voice was deep and rough—and teasing.

"Justin, are you married?"

There was dead silence, and then, "What the hell made you think that?"

"Nothing. It's just that I never asked—and you never said."

He swore under his breath. "I've done one or two things I'm not...thrilled I had to do, I'll admit." She wondered what, exactly. But before she had time to ask, he said, "But I never will do that—play one woman when I'm married to another." He sounded totally disgusted with the very idea.

Which pleased her greatly. "Er...that would be a no?"

"Yeah. A no. A *definite* no—and let me guess your next question. Do I have a steady woman in my life?"

She was grinning again. "Yep. That would be it."

"That's a no, too."

"Well." She put her arms down on the blankets again. "Okay, then. Were you *ever* married?"

"Never. Too busy making something from nothing. Serious relationships just didn't fit into the equation."

"You're career-driven?"

"I guess one of these days I'll have to slow down and get a life. But I like what I do."

"What about...a high school sweetheart?"

A brief silence, then, "High school. Now, that was a long time ago."

She realized she didn't know his age. "You're how old?"

"Thirty-two. And as I think I told you, when I was growing up, we moved around a lot—no chance to fit in. I dated now and then. It never went anywhere."

"You make yourself sound like a lonely guy."

He grunted. "No need for a pity party. There have been women, just not anything too deep or especially meaningful."

There have been women...

Well, of course there had. He had those compelling good looks. That kind of dangerous, mysterious air about him. A lot of women really went for the dangerous type. And yet, he could be so charming, so open, about himself and his life. And then there was the way he could kiss....

Katie slipped her hand up, to touch her lips, remembering.

Oh, yes. A guy who could kiss like that would have had some practice.

But there was no special woman. No secret wife.

In spite of that aura of danger he could give off, Justin Caldwell was an honest guy—and Katie really did like that in a man.

The next day was Monday. They woke to find the snow still coming down, though not as thickly as the day before. On the ground, it reached halfway to the porch roof. After they'd dressed and had their fresh coffee and two-day-old sandwiches, they both went out to the front porch, though the door could barely clear the spill of snow that sloped onto the boards of the porch floor.

"Shoveling our way out of here will be a hell of a challenge," Justin said.

She nodded. "If it would only stop coming down. Give us a chance to take a crack at it, give the snowplow a break. It's piling up faster than anyone could hope to clear it."

Back inside, the phone was still out. And the boom box picked up the usual crackling static.

They made their way along the narrow covered path to the shed, where they spent a couple of hours cleaning up after Buttercup and keeping her company. Twice, the horse got feisty with Justin. She tried again to head-butt him into the hay. And once, in a deft move, she actually got the collar of his jacket between her teeth. She yanked it off him.

When he swore at her, she instantly dropped it. White tail swishing grandly, she turned for the doors that led out to a wall of snow.

"See?" he demanded. "That horse hates me."

"Could be affection," Katie suggested.

"Yeah, right." He picked up the old coat and brushed it off.

"Hey, at least it didn't land in a pile of manure."

He made a low sound, something halfway between a chuckle and a grunt, and slipped his arms into the sleeves. "Are we done here?"

She agreed that they were.

Back in the museum, Katie decided to get busy on the day's main project: clean hair.

Over her baggy tan pants, she put on a wrinkled white T-shirt with a boarded-up mine shaft and Stay Out, Stay Alive! emblazoned across the front. The rummage sale bags didn't come through with a bath towel. But hey. She had plenty of personal-size bottles of shampoo—in herbal scent and "no tears." And there was a stack of dish towels in the kitchen cupboard. She'd make do with a few of them.

Then came the big internal debate—to use the bathroom sink: more private. Or the one in the kitchen: bigger.

Bigger won. Justin had seen her in her ugly sweater and saggy pants wearing zero makeup; he'd seen her in the distinctly unflattering flannel pajamas. He could certainly stand to get a look at her bending over a sink with her hair soaking wet.

Glamour just wasn't something a girl could maintain in a situation like this.

Justin sat at the table playing solitaire with a deck he'd found in the desk out front and tried not to sneak glances at Katie while she washed her hair.

The faint perfume from the shampoo filled the air, a moist, flowery scent. And the curve of her body as she bent over the sink, the shining coils of her wet hair, the creamy smoothness of her neck, bared with her hair tumbling into the sink, even the rushing sound of the water, the way it spilled over the vulnerable shape of her skull, turning her hair to a silken stream and dribbling over her satiny cheek and into her eyes....

He couldn't stop looking.

He had a problem. And he knew it.

There was something about her. Something soft and giving. Something tender and gentle and smart and funny...and sexy, too. All at the same time.

Something purely feminine.

Something that really got to him.

Every hour he spent with her, he wanted her more. It was starting to get damn tough—keeping it friendly. Not pushing too fast.

Too fast? He restrained a snort of heavy irony liberally laced with his own sexual frustration.

Too fast implied there would be satisfaction.

There wouldn't be. And he damn well had to keep that in mind.

Even if she said yes to him, there was no way he was taking her to bed while they were locked in here.

He couldn't afford that. Not without protection. And though the bags in the storage room seemed to have no end of useful items in them, what they didn't have were condoms.

He knew because he'd actually checked to see if they did.

And since he'd checked, he'd found himself thinking constantly of all the ways a man and a woman could enjoy each other sexually short of actual consummation.

He grabbed up a card to move it—and then couldn't resist stealing another look.

She'd rinsed away most of the flowery-scented shampoo, but there was a tiny froth of it left on her earlobe. She rinsed all around it, but somehow the water never quite reached it.

He gritted his teeth to keep from telling her to get that bit of lather on her ear. He ordered his body to stay in that chair. Every nerve seemed to sizzle.

Damned if he wasn't getting hard.

Ridiculous, he thought. *This has to stop....*

He looked down at the card in his hand—the jack of spades—and couldn't even remember what he'd meant to do with it.

This was bad. Real bad.

Some kind of dark justice?

Hell. Probably.

He meant to use her as another way to get to Caleb. Too bad he hadn't realized how powerfully—and swiftly—*she* would end up getting to *him.*

At last, she tipped her head enough that the water flowed over that spot on her ear. The little dab of lather rinsed away and down the drain.

Late that afternoon, Justin went out to the front of the museum to stoke the fire in the stove. Katie busied herself in the kitchen, putting away the few dishes that stood drying on the drain mat, wiping the table and the counters. The tasks were simple ones, easily accomplished.

After she rinsed the sponge and set it in the little tray by the sink, she found herself drawn to the window. She wandered over and stood there watching the snow falling through the graying light, wondering how long it would be until they could dig out, until the old mare in the shed got a little room to stretch her legs and a nice, big bucket of oats.

Justin returned from the front room. She glanced

over and gave him a smile and went back to gazing out at the white world beyond the glass.

He went to the sink. She heard the water running, was aware of his movements as he washed his hands and then reached for the towel. A moment later, she heard his approach, though she didn't turn to watch him come toward her.

It was so still out there. Snowy and silent. The museum sat at the corner, where Elk Avenue turned east. There was a full acre to either side, free of structures—what had, years ago, been part of the schoolyard. Katie could see the shadowy outline of the first house beyond the museum property. The Lockwoods lived there—a young couple with two children, a boy and a girl, eight and nine: Jeff and Kaylin, both nice kids. Kaylin loved to read. She and Jeff always attended the library's weekly children's story hour, run by Emelda Ross.

There was a light on in the Lockwood house, the gleam of it just visible, through the veil of falling snow. Katie hoped the Lockwoods were safe in there, with a cozy fire and plenty to eat.

"Katie…" Justin brushed a hand against her shoulder. The warm thrill his touch brought lightened her spirits—at least a little. "Watching it won't make it stop coming down."

She thought of the noisy beer drinkers back at the hall, of dear old Emelda, who'd stuck it out when all the other members of the Historical Society had left. "I was just thinking of everyone back at the hall. I hope they're all safe."

"They had food, didn't they?"

She looked from all that blinding white to the man beside her. "Yes. The potluck, remember? People brought all those casseroles."

"So they'll get by." He gave her a steady look, a look meant to reassure. "They have food. And restrooms. Water—and the sidewalks on Main are all covered. That's going to make it a lot easier for them to get out than it will be for us."

He was right. She added, "And the first place the snowplow will be working is up and down Main."

"See? They'll be okay."

But there were others—the ones who'd left the hall before Katie and Justin. "What about the people who left for home? We don't even know if they all made it."

He took her by the shoulders—firmly, but gently. His touch caused the usual reactions: butterflies in her stomach, a certain warmth lower down....

"Katie, you can't do anything about it. We just have to make the best of a tough situation. And so will everyone else."

In her mind's eye, she saw Addy's dear long, aristocratic face, her sparkling blue eyes and her prim little smile—and then she pictured Caleb, in that white Stetson he liked to wear, a corner of his mouth quirked up in his rascal's grin. "I don't even know where Addy and Caleb went. One minute they were there, in the hall, and then, when we were up there on the stage, just before the 'Reverend' Green stepped up, I looked out over the crowd and I didn't see either of them."

"They probably went home. Or maybe you just

didn't spot them and they're both still there. Either way, there's not a damn thing you can do about it. Just let yourself believe they're safe—which, most likely, they are.''

''But if—''

He didn't let her finish. ''Worrying about them won't help them. All it'll do is make *you* miserable.''

''But I only—''

''It'll be okay.'' He shook her, lightly. ''Got it?''

She made herself give him a nod.

He studied her for a long moment. Then he demanded, ''Why the hell do you still look so worried, then?''

She only shrugged. What was there to say? He was right. There was no point in worrying. But when she thought of Addy and Caleb—when she looked at the Lockwood's faint light across the snow-covered museum yard—she simply couldn't help it.

''Hey,'' Justin murmured. ''Hey, come on…'' He pulled her to him.

She didn't even consider resisting—why should she? Maybe she'd had her doubts about him at first. But gently and tenderly, he'd dispelled her reservations. She knew she could trust him now.

He wrapped those long, hard arms around her and she pressed herself close to him, tucking her head under his chin, laying her ear against the leaping reindeers on the front of his sweater, right over his heart, which beat steady and strong, if a little too fast. She smiled to herself—a woman's smile. His embrace brought more comfort than words could. And the sound of his heartbeat, racing in time to hers?

That wasn't comforting, not in the least. That sound thrilled her. It stole her breath.

She hoped—she *prayed*—that everyone else trapped by the storm was at least safe and warm with plenty to eat.

For herself, though, there was no place she would rather be than right here in the Thunder Canyon Historical Museum held close and safe in Justin's arms.

For herself, she was beginning to believe that getting snowed-in with Caleb's business associate was the best thing that had ever happened to her.

She felt his lips against her hair and snuggled closer. "Justin?"

"Hmm?"

She tipped her head up to find those blue eyes waiting.

And his lips...

It just seemed the most natural thing. To lift her mouth, to let her eyes drift shut.

His mouth touched hers—so lightly. Heat flared and flowed through her. Her lips burned. Her pulse raced.

Then he lifted away.

She didn't want that.

Oh, no. She wanted more. Much more.

"Justin?" She opened her eyes to look up at him again.

"Hmm?"

"Justin, do you like kissing me?"

He muttered something very low, probably a swear word. "I do. I like it too damn much."

"I like kissing you, too," she confessed. "I like it a lot."

His gaze scanned her face. "So…?"

She slid her hands up to encircle his neck. "Please. Kiss me some more."

"Katie," he whispered, and that was all. Then his mouth swooped down and covered hers.

Chapter Six

They kissed, standing there at the window, with the white hush of the snow drifting down outside, for the longest, sweetest time. When Justin finally lifted his head, he asked, husky and low, "Convinced?"

She blinked up at him. "Of what?"

"That I like kissing you?"

She pretended to consider that question—which, truthfully, required no consideration at all—and then at last, she said, "I think you should kiss me again— just to make sure."

"Ah. To make sure…"

"That's right."

He cupped her face—cradled it, really. His hands were warm and cherishing against her cheeks. And then he lowered his head again and his mouth touched hers and…

Oh, there was nothing like it. Kissing Justin.

Kissing Justin was everything kissing ought to be. His mouth played on hers and his arms slid around her to hold her close and she felt his heart beating, hard and steady, against her breasts, keeping pace with hers.

That time, when he lifted his head, she said in a voice gone husky with pleasure, "I'm getting it now. You like kissing me."

"Yeah. I do."

And to prove it, he kissed her again—a hard, deep, long one that melted her midsection and turned her knees to rubber.

She clutched his shoulders and sagged against him, feeling very aroused, totally shameless. She liked this feeling. She liked it a lot. There was so much she'd been missing. Not anymore, though. "I don't know. If you're going to *keep* kissing me, I might just have to sit down."

"Let me help you with that." He grabbed the nearest chair, spun it around and dropped into it—pulling her with him, onto his lap.

Her breath hitched as she landed.

"Better?" he asked.

"Oh, I think…"

He nuzzled her neck, pressed a burning kiss at the place where her pulse beat close to the skin. A lovely shiver went through her and she sighed.

"You think what?" He breathed the words against her throat—and then he caught her earlobe between his teeth. He worried it, lightly, as she clutched his shoulders and sighed some more.

"Oh, Justin…"

His tongue touched the place where his teeth had been, a velvety moist caress. He licked the tender hollow behind her earlobe. Briefly, with the very tip of that bold tongue, he dipped into her ear.

She let out a low moan. She was supposed to be telling him…something. The question was what. "I…well…"

He threaded his fingers up into her hair and he brushed a line of butterfly-light kisses along her jaw. "What you think…"

"Think?" The word sounded alien. Not surprising. At that moment, thinking was the last thing on her mind.

He cradled the back of her head, holding her still, bringing his mouth a breath's distance from hers. "You were telling me…what you think…"

"I…well…"

One corner of his mouth lifted in a knowing smile. "Well, what?"

"I forgot." And she had.

She'd forgotten everything. Nothing mattered, at that moment, but this man and the drugging pleasure of his hands on her body, his mouth so close to hers. "Kiss me. Again."

He obeyed. His mouth covered hers and she wrapped her arms around his neck and kissed him back with boundless enthusiasm.

This time when they came up for air, he took her by the waist and held her away from him. "We'd better stop." His voice was rough—almost curt.

She started to argue. She didn't want to stop. But

maybe he was right. Where could they go from here, except to the bed with the pineapple finials?

Was she ready for that yet?

As much as she liked kissing him and feeling his hands on her body…as much as she liked *him*…as much as she couldn't help but start to think that there was something very special going on here, between them…

That was a big, fat…maybe. Even given what she'd decided that morning—about the lack of sex of any kind in her life, about how she was going to stop being a cliché. Even given all that, well, they didn't need to rush this, did they? There was nothing that said they couldn't take their time. Though she was determined to get herself a sex life one of these days very soon—and with Justin—she *was* old-fashioned in some ways. She believed making love should be special. And it *shouldn't* be rushed.

He smoothed a wild curl of hair off her cheek. "Listen." His eyes teased—and burned, too. "I want you to get up. And I want you to do it very carefully."

She frowned, and then she understood. Oh, my. Yes. She could *feel* him and it was just like out in the shed the day before. He was very happy to be near her.

"Oh. Oh, well. You're, uh—"

"Katie."

"Uh. Yeah?"

"We don't need a lot of discussion here."

"Oh. Well, no. Of course, we don't." She put her feet on the floor and stood, backing off a little. Her gaze dropped to—oops. Blinking, she yanked her chin up and gave him a nervous smile. "Is that better?"

"Not really." The chair legs scraped the floor as he turned to face the table—a deft movement, in spite of the pained grunt that accompanied it. Now his lap, and the obvious bulge there, was hidden by the tabletop. "In a few minutes, I'll be fine."

"Well. Good."

He folded his hands on the tabletop. "It would help if you wouldn't stand there looking so damn... thoroughly kissed."

Her wobbly smile widened. "But Justin. I *am* thoroughly kissed."

He commanded sternly, "Think of an activity. One that doesn't involve kissing."

She pretended to give his request great thought. "Well, now...we could go out and visit Buttercup again."

He scowled. "Let me qualify. Something that doesn't involve kissing *or* that mean old mare."

"Hmm. It's a tough one."

He shifted in his chair, wincing. "Work with it."

An idea came to her. "I know. We could tour the museum."

"Why? I've seen it."

"Now, wait a minute. I'll admit, you've seen about all there is to see in the central room. But the two side rooms...why, Justin, you've hardly had a look. And you know, on second thought, you've only *slept* in the central room. That's not the same as a tour."

He let out a dry chuckle. "I've been up close and

personal with that dinky narrow cot of mine. Isn't that enough?''

''Oh, no. You have to see it all. I insist. The rich and varied history of Thunder Canyon is right here, only a few steps away. You owe it to yourself to explore it.''

''I can't wait.''

''Don't get so excited,'' she instructed, deadpan.

He tipped his head toward his lap. ''I'm trying.''

She couldn't help it, she burst into a laugh—and then she frowned. ''You know, now I think about it, it's not really fair that I always get the big bed.''

''Katie. I'm fine with the cot.''

''But still, it's only right that we—''

''Stop. I *love* that cot of mine and you can't have it. Now, I want you to go on ahead of me, reconnoiter the display rooms, get your tour guide rap down pat. Let me, er, relax a little here.''

She decided not to remark on what might need relaxing. ''Hey, we could even take some rags in there, dust the display cases...''

He sent her a pained look. ''The fun never ends.''

She was dusting a case full of old gold-panning equipment in the south room when he joined her. She handed him a rag and one of the two bottles of spray cleaner she'd found in the storage room.

''I thought this was a tour,'' he groused. But he was grinning as he took the rag and bottle.

''The museum is a community effort,'' she told him tartly. ''We all have to pitch in.''

"Hey. I'm all for that." He saluted her with the spray bottle.

They set to work dusting the cases. As they sprayed and polished, she explained about the Montana gold rush that had begun in Idaho, with the Salmon River strike. "Gold fever came to Montana in 1862. John White and company, en route to the Salmon River mines, found gold on the way—at Grasshopper Creek." She paused to point out the exact location on the big laminated territorial map on the wall. "Bannack—" She pointed again. "—Montana's first boomtown, sprang up during that rush."

"Just like in the reenactment Saturday."

"That's right." She beamed at him. "For a man who didn't have the benefit of a Montana education, you're a very good student."

"Thank you. I try."

"Shall I continue?"

"By all means."

So she explained that the gold rush had lasted into the early 1890s, starting with placer mining and then, as the streams petered out, panning and sluicing gave way to hardrock mining. "There were a number of mines right here in the Thunder Canyon area. Caleb still owns one, as a matter of fact. It's called the Queen of Hearts."

"So I heard."

"From Caleb?"

"More or less." At her questioning look, he explained, "I'm in business with Caleb. My people have gone over his books, with Caleb's full knowledge and consent, of course. As a result, I know a lot about what his assets are, as well as which pies he's got his fingers in. I understand the gold mine's been shut down for years. 'Played out,' isn't that what they say in the trade?''

"That's exactly what they say—and I'll bet you didn't know that Caleb's great-grandfather, Amos Douglas, won the Queen in a card game." She sprayed and rubbed with her cloth. "Or so the legend goes.''

"Fascinating."

She glanced his way, and found he was watching her. Her body went warm all over. "Less staring, more cleaning,'' she advised.

Once they'd finished in the mining display, she took him to the central room, where they dusted the tables and she told him the origins of the most interesting pieces.

She gestured grandly with her dusting rag in the direction of the big bed with the pineapple finials and the heavy, dark bureaus, vanity set, bed tables and chairs that surrounded it. "This bedroom suite was used at the Lazy D during Amos Douglas's time. It's of the finest mahogany.''

"Only the best for the Douglases." There was something in his tone—something way too ironic, even cynical. She sent him a puzzled look, but he only shrugged and bent to dust a bedside table.

And she had to agree with him. "It's true. Only the best. For generations, the Douglases have been the wealthiest, most influential family in the area.''

"Don't forget to dust those pineapples."

"That's right. If you don't watch it, I may still have

to throw one at you. I want it dust-free if I do.'' She reached up—but the intricately carved end-piece was too high. She couldn't get her rag around it.

Justin stepped closer. "Allow me."

Her pulse kicked up a notch, just to have him standing so near, eyes gleaming at her with humor and heat. "Oh, by all means." She bowed and moved back and he did the honors.

Once every surface in the central room had been wiped clean of dust, they proceeded to the north addition, where the personal artifacts of life in Territorial and early-statehood Montana waited to be admired—and the cases that protected them, dusted.

Justin went straight to the tall case containing a mannequin in a faded red satin dress. Cinched tight at the wasp-thin waste, the dress had a deep neckline and lots of black lace trim. The mannequin wore several ropes of fake pearls around her neck, a thick bracelet of glittering jet stones and an ostrich feather in her pinned-up hair. In one hand, she carried a black fan edged with lace. The other hand held the red skirt high, revealing a froth of red and black petticoats— and a fancy black silk garter.

Justin wolf-whistled. "Love that red dress."

Katie grinned. "That dress belonged to one of Thunder Canyon's most memorable early citizens. The Shady Lady, Lily Divine."

"Is this the part where I say, 'Ooh-la-la'?"

"That would be appropriate, yes. Back in, oh, 1890 or so, Lily owned the Shady Lady Sporting House and Saloon. The building still stands at the corner of Main and Thunder Canyon Road, though the place is now a restaurant and bar called the Hitching Post. The original bar from the Shady Lady is still there, in the building. And a very risqué painting of Lily hangs above it.''

''Risqué, how?''

''In it she wears nothing but a few wisps of strategically draped semitransparent cloth.''

''I have to see that.''

''And if it ever stops snowing, you just might.''

He tipped his head toward the low case beside the mannequin in the red dress. ''A few of Lily Divine's things, I take it?''

''That's right.'' Katie moved in beside him. They looked down at the tortoise shell dresser set in a gold floral design studded with rhinestones, at the black lace gloves and the faded filmy undergarments. There was even a corset—a black one, dripping with red silk ribbons.

''It looks to me like the Shady Lady was a very fun gal.''

Katie shrugged. ''So they say. And not only fun, but a suffragist, as well. Or so some accounts claim.'' He looked up from the case and when their eyes met, she realized she never wanted to look away.

Back to the Shady Lady, some wiser voice in the distant recesses of her mind instructed.

She tuned out that wiser voice. ''Oh, Justin...'' The two words escaped her lips, full of hope and longing, and having nothing at all to do with either the notorious Lily Divine, or with getting the dusting done.

He whispered her name.

Her heart seemed to expand in the prison of her chest.

And at that moment, *not* to kiss him...

Well, that was impossible. It just wouldn't do.

She set down her rag and her spray bottle on the glass case beside her. He did the same.

"Justin," she whispered, thinking she should really try a little harder to resist the overwhelming urge to feel his lips on hers.

"Katie..."

A long moment elapsed. She looked at him and he looked back at her and—

"Oh, Justin, I think we're in trouble here."

He only nodded. His eyes said he knew exactly what kind of trouble she meant.

"We shouldn't," she whispered. "We told ourselves we wouldn't."

"That's right," he agreed, his voice rough and low. "No more kissing."

"It's not a good idea."

"Things could...get out of control."

"Easily."

"It's crazy."

"Wild..."

"Dangerous..."

"Oh, I know," she said.

And then he reached for her.

With a glad cry, she reached back. His arms went around her and all doubt fled.

Eager and oh-so-willing, she lifted her mouth to receive his kiss.

Chapter Seven

"We...have to...be careful..." He whispered the words between quick, hungry kisses.

She nodded. "Oh. Yes. Careful. You're so right."

His mouth closed on hers again, drugging. Magical. She slid her hands up his broad chest to wrap them around his neck, and he caught her wrists. He guided them down, so her arms were straight at her sides.

His fingers slipped over the backs of her hands and he wove them between hers, lightly rubbing—in and out and in again, never quite clasping, flesh brushing flesh, little tingles of excitement zipping through her with every featherlight caress. All the while, as his fingers teased hers, he kissed her, his tongue sweeping her mouth, his lips hot and soft and oh-so-tender.

She moaned as he finally twined his fingers with hers, tightening, curling his hands to fists, so her hands were cradled in his palms, her fingers captured between his. A thoroughly willing captive, she smiled against his lips as he guided her hands around behind her.

Their joined fists resting at the small of her back, he kissed her some more. She sighed at the wonder of it, and gave her mouth up to his.

After forever of the two of them kissing and kissing as if they would never stop, he began walking her backward.

She stumbled at first, surprised. A giddy laugh escaped her; he chuckled in response.

Quickly, she regained her balance, and, as he guided her, she backed up toward the open door to the central room. It was like a dance, a beautiful, slow, erotic dance.

He waltzed her through the open doorway, his mouth locked to hers. On they went, slow, delicious step by slow step, to the turn in the roped-off walkway, and then down toward the wide, high bed that had once graced a guest room at the Lazy D.

There, with only a stretch of rope keeping them from the waiting bed, he paused. She swayed in his hold, her mouth fused to his.

A small cry of loss escaped her when he lifted his head. He eased his strong fingers free of hers and stepped back.

"We should stop now."

For a suspended moment, she gazed up into his gleaming eyes. And then, with a sigh, she rested her head on his shoulder. "You know, you keep saying that."

His arms closed around her, tight and warm. She felt the sweet brush of his lips in her hair as she breathed in the scent of him: of the motel-issue shampoo they'd both used, of his clean skin and a faint hint of the inexpensive aftershave he'd found in the brown bag. "I know I keep saying it," he muttered against her hair. "I just don't seem to be *listening* to myself when I say it."

She lifted her head and captured his blue, blue gaze again. Boldly, she suggested, "We could just go ahead and slip under the rope. We could kick off our shoes, stretch out on the bed...."

His arms dropped away. "And then what?"

She swallowed. "Well, and then, we could...take it from there."

"Take it from there," he repeated, gruffly. "I'd like that. Way too much. But we can't lose our heads here. We've got to be sensible."

Now she was the one repeating after *him*. "Sensible."

"That's what I said."

"I have to admit, I don't feel all that sensible recently. Not since I met you."

That brought a smile to his beautiful mouth. "All my fault, then."

She tipped her chin higher. "No. This thing between us, it's fifty-fifty. You're not leading me anywhere I don't want to go."

He studied her face for a long moment—long enough that she felt a blush begin to burn her cheeks. And then he said flatly, "I've got no condoms. I don't suppose you do?"

"Uh. No. Sorry." She looked down, not embarrassed, exactly, but definitely feeling in over her head.

He put a finger under her chin and made her look at him again. "It's something that has to be considered."

"Oh, I know. You're right. I just…well, we could be careful, couldn't we?"

He swore under his breath. "I keep telling myself the same thing. But I don't feel all that damn careful, and that's the hard truth. Once I get my arms around you, caution flies right out the door."

"I could…be cautious for us." Even as she suggested it, she knew that wouldn't work. When he kissed her, words like *careful* and *caution* vanished from her vocabulary.

He gave her a rueful smile. "No doubt about it. Time to go out and check on that mean mare."

The snow stopped around seven. They were sitting at the table eating applesauce and more of the never-ending sandwiches, when Katie looked across at the light in the Lockwood's window and realized there was no curtain of white obscuring it.

Justin noticed, too. "Tomorrow we can probably start digging out."

"Hey, the phone may even be working soon." She'd checked it just a half an hour before. "And if the snow doesn't start in heavy again, the plow should get to us by tomorrow sometime."

"And we'll be free."

They stared at each other across the expanse of the

tabletop. "Free..." She repeated the word softly. And somehow, she couldn't keep from sounding forlorn.

She looked out the window again, at that golden light from the house across the museum yard.

No question that stale sandwiches, wearing other people's ill-fitting cast-off clothes, and sponge baths at the sink in the ladies' room got old very fast. She'd be grateful for a shower, something different to eat, her own clothes to wear. And more than any of those minor inconveniences, it would be a huge relief to know that everyone she cared about had come through the unexpected blizzard safe and sound.

But still. They *had* made themselves a private little world here, in the center of the storm. She would miss it—miss just the two of them, all alone. Talking through the night. Kissing. Laughing together. And kissing some more....

She would miss it a lot.

Would she see Justin again, once they were out of here?

She frowned. Well, of course she would. Really, she didn't need to even ask herself the question.

They had a...connection, something special going on between them. She felt it in her bones. This was different from anything she'd known before. Even after what had happened with Ted Anders and Jackson Tully, she had no doubts about Justin.

None at all.

He spoke then. "For someone who's probably going to be out of this place tomorrow, you're looking pretty glum."

She turned from the golden light across the way to

meet his waiting eyes. "I want to see you again, when this is over. Do you want to see me?" She was proud, of the steadiness of her voice, that she'd put her own intention right out there, hadn't waited for him to make the first move, handing him all the power and then hoping he'd give her a call.

Oh, yes. Katie Fenton, a cliché no more.

"I do want to see you again. I want that very much."

Her heart leaped—and then something in his eyes spoke to her. Something...not right. "But?"

He blinked. "No buts. I want to see you when we get out of here."

And I will. She thought the words he didn't say.

The silence stretched out. Painful. Empty. She wanted to demand, *And will you?* But somehow, that seemed one step too far. He should say it of his own accord, or not at all.

She wanted him. She *cared* for him. She had no doubt that he wanted and cared for her.

Would it go any further than that?

That secret something behind his eyes was telling her no. "Justin?"

"Yeah?"

"Is there...something else you want to say to me?"

Justin looked at the incredible woman across from him and never wanted to look away.

His chest felt tight—as if something strong and relentless was squeezing it. His gut twisted.

The urge was there, in his clenched gut and his tight chest—an urge almost too powerful to deny.

To tell her everything. To throw over his carefully constructed plans.

To lay it all out for her: what Caleb really was to him and how he meant to make the older man pay for the cruel things he'd done.

To hit her with the whole truth: how from the first night fate threw them together, he'd felt the heat between them and decided to make use of it, to toss her into the mix. How he'd purposely set out to take advantage of the situation, and of her.

It was crazy, even to think he might open his mouth and...

No.

He wasn't going to blow it. He'd waited too long to get to the man who'd ruined his mother's hope and happiness. He had to remember....

All of it. The times she didn't come home until he was sick with fear and worry. The nights she *was* home, when he'd wake and have that strange, lost feeling and come out of his room to find her at the kitchen table or curled up on the couch, her eyes swollen and red from crying, the end of her cigarette glowing like a burning eye in the dark.

He had to remember....

The suicide attempts. The never-ending new starts that always went wrong. Caleb's name on her lips like an unanswered prayer the day that she died....

Of lung cancer. She never would give up those damn cigarettes until the last few months of her life. And by then it was too late. Lung cancer got her—

but Caleb Douglas killed her as sure as if he'd put a gun to her head and pulled the trigger.

Caleb Douglas broke her heart and she never did find a way to mend it again. Justin, just a kid, had been powerless to help her.

He wasn't powerless anymore.

And damned if he was giving up now.

He was set on a course and it was a just course. What he would do was perfectly legal; he had the power now—power Caleb himself had put in his hands—and he would use it.

In the end, if all went according to plan, there would be big profits for everyone. Including Caleb.

That was the beauty of it. Everybody would win.

At least in terms of the bottom line.

He only wished...

Wished.

It was a word for fools, for helpless little boys who spent too much time alone, for boys with no fathers, whose mothers too seldom came home....

He wasn't a little boy anymore.

And he wasn't going to spew his guts to anyone—not even to sweet Katie Fenton who was turning out to be a hell of a lot more woman than he'd ever bargained for.

Those amber eyes were still waiting.

He couldn't stand the disappointment he saw in them. "I *want* to see you when we get out of here, Katie. I want to see you and I *will*."

And I will.

Now, where the hell had that come from?

He'd been so careful. He'd never actually lied to her.

Not until now.

But then again, he *did* want to see her again.

Though he knew damn well he shouldn't, he wanted to keep on seeing her. He wanted...

A whole hell of a lot more with her than he was ever going to get.

He shouldn't have lied. But the words were out now. No calling them back. In future, he'd just have to keep a closer watch on his tongue.

He silently vowed he would do just that as she watched him with worried eyes.

Chapter Eight

Katie opened her eyes to the sight of the shadowed rafters overhead.

For a second or two, with the soft mist of sleep still fogging her mind, she wondered where she was.

And then she placed herself: the four-poster bed in the Historical Museum. With no windows to let in the light from outside, she couldn't begin to guess what time it was. There *was* one clock. An intricate gold leaf ormolu piece with Cupid strumming a lyre perched on top. It sat on the mantel in the "parlor" area.

She couldn't see the face of it from the bed. Plus, it wasn't wound and always read ten-fifteen.

And what did it matter, anyway, what time it was? She and Justin weren't going anywhere until the snowplow finally showed up. They could sleep all day and stay up all night. There was no schedule, just whatever suited them.

Justin...

What was going on with him?

There had been a certain...reserve—a new distance between them, since dinnertime, when she told him she wanted to see him after they got out of here and asked him if *he* wanted to see her.

He'd definitely withdrawn from her after that. From then on, when she spoke, he gave her single-sentence replies. When she looked at him, his gaze would slide away. Also, it had seemed to her that he was careful to avoid touching her. He kept his distance emotionally—and physically, too.

All evening she'd told herself to let it be. The guy didn't have to be hanging on her every word every minute of the day. Maybe he just wanted a little time to himself. In such close quarters, there was no easy way for him to claim some private space.

But in her heart, she knew it wasn't about lack of privacy. It was about them seeing each other after they got out of here.

It hurt a lot, to admit it to herself, but she was beginning to think she'd gotten things all wrong. She'd read more into this thing between them than was actually there.

Oh, not in terms of herself. She knew how she felt. It was real and strong and...maybe it was love.

Or something very close to it—something that *could* be love, given the time and space to grow.

But just because she was feeling something didn't automatically mean he had to feel it in return.

She'd gone to bed, however long ago that had been, ahead of him. And she'd lain here waiting for him.

He'd yet to come in when she finally fell asleep.

Was he even here now?

She sat up.

Across the room, the too-short, too-narrow cot lay empty, the star quilt smooth and undisturbed, the flat little pillow without a wrinkle.

He hadn't even come to bed.

Quietly, carefully—as if there was someone in the empty room she might disturb should she make a sound—she lay back down.

And popped right back up again.

No. This was wrong. If he didn't want to get anything going with her, well, that was his prerogative and she would learn to accept it.

But she wasn't going to just lie here, worrying. And what about tomorrow? What about whatever time they had left here until the plow came? If she spent that time tiptoeing around him, keeping her head down and her mouth shut, well, wouldn't that be just like the woman she'd told herself she wasn't going to be anymore? Wouldn't that be like Katie, the cliché?

She needed to clear the air between them.

How, exactly, to do that, she wasn't quite sure. But it certainly wouldn't get done with her lying here in bed agonizing over what had gone wrong and him off somewhere in another room doing whatever the heck he was doing.

She shoved the covers back and slid her stocking feet to the floor.

* * *

"Justin."

He turned from his own dark reflection in the window to find Katie standing in the doorway to the central room, wearing her wrinkled red pajamas and a pair of fat wool socks, blinking against the bright overhead kitchen light.

A slow warmth spread through him, just to see her standing there. It was that feeling of well-being and contented relief a man gets when he comes in from the cold and finds a cheery fire waiting—that feeling multiplied about a thousand times.

Damn, she looked good, all squinty-eyed with a sleep mark on her soft cheek and her dark hair a tangled halo all around her sweet face. Had there ever been a woman so outright adorable? Not in his experience, and that had been varied, if not especially meaningful.

She stuck out a hand in the direction of the book that lay open on the table in front of him. "Still on chapter three, I'll bet."

He glanced down at the book in question, then back up at her, an ironic smile twisting his lips. "Page sixty-seven, to be exact."

She wrapped her arms around herself. Her soft mouth was pursed tight. "Look. Mind if I sit down?"

The set of her mouth, the determined look in her eyes, her defensive posture—they all told him more than he wanted to know.

No doubt about it. Katie had questions.

Which meant he would have to try to answer them honestly, but without ever telling her the whole truth.

Things got ugly when a man had too much to hide. He probably should have known that when he started this whole charade. Hell. He *had* known it. And he'd been willing to live with the ugliness.

Then.

He gave her an elaborately casual shrug and closed the book. "Sure. Take a seat."

She marched over, yanked out the chair opposite him, and plunked herself down into it, unwrapping her arms from around herself and folding her hands in her lap.

"Okay..." He drew the word out, eyeing her sideways. "What's up?"

She craned around to get a look at the kitchen clock. When she faced him again, she replied, "Well, *you* are. It's three-fifteen in the morning and you're just sitting here, staring out the window."

He lounged back in his chair, displaying an ease he didn't feel. "And this is a problem for you?"

"No. No, of course not." She huffed out a frustrated-sounding breath. "You can sit here all night if you want. What's bothering me is..." She ran out of steam, sucked in another big breath, and started again. "Look. I spent most of last night staying out of your way, and *you* spent most of it avoiding looking, talking or getting too close to me. I just, well, I'd like that to stop and I came out here to ask you what I could do to make that happen."

Her distress was palpable. He hated to see her so miserable, and he hated worst of all that he was the cause of her unhappiness.

But what the hell did he have to tell her?

Half-truths.

And when half-truths failed him, outright lies.

He wanted out of this—out of this damned museum, away from the reality that he was using her.

He didn't want to use her anymore. It had been a bad idea from the first and he wanted to walk away from it.

But there was no walking away now. The damage was done. She cared for him. When it all went down, she would be hurt, and hurt bad. There was no getting away from that now.

Even if he gave up his original plan to see that Caleb Douglas paid—which he wasn't about to do—he would still end up hurting her. It was simply too late to walk away and leave her untouched.

Untouched.

An interesting word choice given the plain fact that all he wanted to do was reach out.

And touch...

"Justin," she prompted, when he went too long without answering her. "Did you hear one thing I said to you?" A deep frown creased her brow.

He resisted the powerful urge to rise, to go to her, to smooth that frown away. "I heard you. Every word. Go on."

"Ahem. Well. The truth is I know very well why I stayed out of your way—because it seemed to me that you were avoiding me. *Were* you?"

"Yeah." What else was there to say? "I was."

"Why?"

Why? He should have known that one was coming. What to say now? How to weasel out of this one...

And then, out of nowhere, the exact right words seemed to well up of their own accord. "Because I want you. Because I want to *be* with you. And because it scares the hell out of me, that I do—and how much I do."

The words took form and he let them out and…

Damned if they weren't the absolute truth. More truth than he wanted to face himself, let alone share with her.

But he *had* shared them.

What did that mean?

Where was he headed with this?

Hell if he even knew.

Her soft face had gone softer still, all the worried tension melting out of it. Her eyes shone and her pursed-up mouth had relaxed to its usual sweet fullness. "Oh, Justin…" She lifted a hand from her lap and stretched it across the table to him. "Come on. Take a chance. Take a chance on me."

And before he could think twice, he was leaning toward her, reaching right back. Their hands met and heat shot up his arm, broke into a million swift, burning arrows that splintered off in all directions, hitting every nerve in his body at once.

All he could say was one word: her name. "Katie."

And then, as one, they stood. They stepped around the barrier of the table and there was a moment— painful and electric—when he almost managed to make himself let go, almost stepped back, almost told her, *Katie, I can't. Can't touch you, can't hold you…*

But the pull was too strong. It wouldn't be denied.

He gathered her in and she landed against him, soft

and warm and so willing, smelling of shampoo and sweetness, naked beneath the fuzzy red flannel.

"Katie." He buried his face in her fragrant hair. "Katie."

She nuzzled his chest, pressed her lips there, sent a warm, thrilling breath through the wool of the old sweater. The warmth spread, borne on that breath, a caress of hope and life itself. He held her tighter.

And she turned her head, pressing her mouth to his neck, a velvety pressure. Her lips opened slightly. He felt the wet brush of her tongue.

He groaned deep in his throat and an answering sound came from her, a soft, heated, purring sound. It vibrated through him, that sound, right down to the core of him.

He felt himself harden in an instant, and he did what he had to do, what he longed to do, sliding his hands down, over the tempting swell of her hips and under, tucking her into him, making her feel him, feel his need and his hunger.

She gasped, the sound purely female, speaking better than any words could of her eagerness, of her complete surrender.

Mine. The word exploded in his brain, bright as a shooting star in a dark winter world. *Mine.*

She gasped again and she tipped her head back, offering her mouth.

He took it, his blood roaring in his ears, his body burning, on fire.

All his lies, all his scheming, his lifelong quest for justice—all that was nothing. There was only Katie, the promise of Katie, the *truth* of Katie, held close in his hungry arms.

As he plunged his tongue into her eager mouth and cupped her bottom in his hands, pressing her harder into him, as his blood pounded through his veins and his heart beat so hard it was like thunder in his ears, he knew....

This...*this* was what mattered. This woman's tender heart, her lips, her breath, her yearning, willing body.

This was his truth. His real justice.

The truth that could save him.

The truth he could never claim.

He knew he had to stop this, that he owed it to her. Somehow, from some deep hidden resource of rightness within him, he managed to break the never-ending kiss.

He tore his mouth from hers, groaning at the effort. "Katie."

But she only reached up, touched his mouth and whispered, "Shh, it's okay."

He bit the soft pad of her finger. She cried out—not in pain; it had been a gentle bite—but in hunger, with a fire that answered his own.

Her cry of need broke him. His last resistance shattered into a thousand tiny shards. He surrendered to the pounding of his own blood, the yearning like fire spreading through his veins.

She pulled her hand from his mouth and he cupped her head and claimed her lips again.

He kissed her and she kissed him back and he took a step and she moved with him.

No stumbling, not this time. Backward she went, knowing where he guided her, through the open door to the central room, down the roped-off walkway to...

The big, old bed with the pineapple finials, the bed that had once stood in a Douglas bedroom over a hundred years ago.

Was that irony?

Probably.

Did it matter? Did he care?

Not right then. Right then, there was nothing and no one but Katie in the world.

Nothing mattered, nothing even existed, but her tender lips and the wetness beyond, her soft, willing body, her eager sighs, the light and heat that seemed to radiate from her, warming him down to a place that, until she had found him, had lain forever cold, forever shadowed.

A place unknown even to him.

He held her close, his willing prisoner, with one arm. With the other he reached back, found the hook that held the thick rope to the pole and released it.

He let it drop. With a heavy, final thumping sound, it hit the hardwood floor.

She clasped his shoulders.

And then *she* was the one waltzing *him* backward, around the carved trunk at the end of the bed, to the knotted rag rug that waited beside it.

She pushed him onto the tangled blankets. The bed was high; he had to lift himself up to it, and he did, with little effort, bringing her with him, so she rested on top of him, a tempting pressure all along the length of him.

Until he rolled and captured her beneath him.

"Oh!" Her lids fluttered open and he looked for the briefest, sweetest moment into those honey-brown eyes. "Oh…" And her lashes settled, feather-soft, against her cheeks.

He shut his own eyes and lost himself in the sensation.

Of kissing her. Of touching her.

He slid to the side a little and put his weight on one arm, bringing the other up, laying his hand between her small, soft breasts, feeling the heat of her and beneath that, the strong, hungry beating of her heart.

The buttonholes on the old pajamas were worn and loose. The red plastic buttons slipped free with no difficulty at all. He undid them, one by one, only pausing when he once again got so lost in her kiss he could do nothing but press his mouth tighter to hers.

When all the buttons were undone, he eased the sides of the top open to reveal her beautiful white breasts. He took one in his hand.

"Oh," she cried, and "Oh!" again, as he positioned the hard, pink little nipple for his mouth.

He took it, closing his lips around it, and she moaned as he caught it lightly in his teeth and flicked his tongue across it, felt the puckered nub of flesh tighten all the more. She arched her back and clutched his head, her fingers threaded in his hair. He drew on her sweetness and more cries escaped her. The pleading, hungry sounds enflamed him, driving him on.

To know her.

In spite of everything, in spite of the lies he'd told

and the harm he would do her. To know her, anyway, in the deepest, most complete way.

To find the truth in spite of himself, here, in this moment, in the dark windowless quiet, with the artifacts of other, long-lost lives all around them.

Here among the ghosts of the past.

His body on fire with her, her scent all around him, her yielding flesh under his hands, his heart pounding out her name, it seemed to him he could sense them, those long-lost souls, that he could *feel* them.

The pioneers who came before. The hopeful families seeking a brighter future, the miners struck hard by gold fever, scouring streams, digging into mountainsides, after a fortune destined to elude all but a fortunate few. The merchants, the cattle barons, the Shady Lady in her red dress, lounging provocatively against the bar in her sporting house saloon.

They came to Thunder Canyon with desperate ambition, a grasping, undaunted will to match his own. How many found the dreams they sought?

It was too long ago. He would never know.

He only knew that, for this night, in this moment, he held the happiness he'd never understood he was seeking. *She* was his happiness.

He couldn't hold her past this night. Cold, hard reality *would* intrude. He knew that, too.

But for now, for this brief time in this old bed with Katie in his arms, he was someone else.

He was…

Her groom. And she was his sweet mail-order bride, come in on the train intending to marry a stranger—himself—and start a new life with him out here in the raw, untamed West.

They had said their vows before a drunken crowd of well-wishers and the buckboard pulled by the mean old palomino mare had brought them here.

A sudden blizzard had snowed them in, forcing them, with astonishing swiftness, to know each other.

To want each other.

And now, it was finally time. To seal their vows in the age-old way.

Yes, in some cynical corner of his mind, Justin was more than aware that such wild flights of imagination, such absurd leaps of logic, were ridiculous in the extreme.

But right then, with Katie soft and willing in his arms, he believed them, anyway.

And that was the greatest miracle of all: that right then, Justin Caldwell *believed.*

He captured her other breast in his mouth and she groaned low in her throat, her body arching, offering him more. He moaned in answer, his fingers skimming the creamy flesh of her belly, dipping lower...

"Oh! Oh, yes..."

He murmured soothing, ardent sounds against her breast and he continued to explore the warm, soft curves and hollows of her body.

The pajamas tied at the waist.

Easily dispensed with. He pulled on the tail of the little bow she'd made and the bow gave way. It was a simple matter then to slip his hand beneath the worn flannel...

She gasped and clutched his head tighter against

her breast. He drew on her nipple more strongly and her hips began to rock against the lumpy mattress. She moaned, her fingers loosening in his hair. He lifted his head enough to glance up at her sweet face as she tossed her head on the blankets, her dark hair, alive with static, clinging where it rubbed.

He stroked the inward curve of her smooth belly, dipping a finger into her navel.

Her breath caught. She made small, hungry mewing sounds. He wanted to kiss those sounds from her lips.

And he did, letting go of her breast and taking her mouth once more, as his hand slid upward, to caress the sleek flesh high on her stomach, to clasp the side of her slim waist, to trace the lower curve of her ribs where they arched above her midsection.

By then, the sounds from her throat were pleading ones.

He dared to ease his fingers beneath the flannel again, to stroke the silky curls at the place where her soft thighs joined. She stiffened, but only for a moment.

Soon enough, her hips began rocking again.

He dipped farther down, parting the soft curls, easing a finger into her moist cleft. She bucked hard against his hand and he cupped her, steadying her as he kissed her deeply, his own body aching with the need to be buried within her.

No.

Not yet. This part was for her—and, yes, for him, too.

He wanted to feel her give herself over; he wanted to give her satisfaction first, before he took his own.

Right then, as he stroked her, as her body moved in rhythm to his intimate touch, it came to him. Like a blinding, painful light switching on in velvet darkness, he realized...

It wasn't going to happen.

Ridiculous fantasies of past lives aside, crazy dreams of a mail-order marriage come true to the contrary, he wasn't going to have her fully.

Even tonight she couldn't be really his.

He had no condoms and she didn't, either.

This. Right now. Her body moving in hungry yearning under his hand, her mouth eager and soft against his own, this was all he could have.

All he would ever have.

He groaned in agony at the thought and pressed himself, hard and aching, against the side of her thigh.

She clung to him, whimpering, as he slipped that finger inside again, even daring to ease in another, stretching her a little. She was tight and very wet.

So good, so right.

He realized he was whispering the words against her parted lips. "So good, so right..."

"Yes," she answered, soft and sweet and oh-so-willing. "Oh, Justin, yes...."

Her hips moved faster. He followed the cues her body gave him, finding the nub of her greatest pleasure, rubbing it, stroking it....

She said his name again against his mouth, on a low breath of yearning and building excitement.

And then he felt it. The soft pulsing beneath his stroking finger, the silky spurt of wetness as she came...

She cried out and he caught that cry, kissing her deeply, as below the tiny, hot, wet pulsing continued.

In the end, her body went loose and boneless. She gave a final, gentle sigh.

His body *hurt*. He ached for more, and yet...

It was good. Better than good, just to be here, in this old bed with her, to know she'd hit the peak and loved every minute of it, that he had done that for her.

She lifted a lazy hand to stroke the side of his face and he raised his head to look down into her shining eyes.

"Oh, Justin..." Her sweet mouth trembled on a smile.

He kissed the tip of her nose. And then, slowly, reluctantly, he took his hand from that wet, hot secret place between her sleek thighs and smoothed her pajama bottoms to cover her to the waist. He took the sides of her top, one and then the other, bringing them together, proceeding to slip the buttons back into their too-loose holes.

She caught his hand. "Oh, don't..."

He gave her a dark look. "Katie. We've got to be careful. You have to know. That was as far as we can go."

She only looked at him, eyes dazed, mouth swollen from his kisses, cheeks flushed: a woman more than willing to go on from here.

Willing? Hell. Eager.

Ready.

For him.

With a low groan, he fell back on the bed, throwing his arm across his eyes, ordering the bulge in his jeans to subside.

Now.

It didn't happen—which hardly surprised him.

The bed shifted as she sat up. He dared to steal a peek at her from under the shadow of his arm.

She was taking off her pajama top.

"What the hell are you doing?"

Her high, cute breasts bounced as she tossed that top aside. "Getting undressed." It flew over and hooked on the vanity mirror. "And so should you. Now."

He shouldn't be peeking. He should cover his eyes again.

But somehow, he couldn't. The bulge in his pants only got bigger as she slithered out of the pajama bottoms and tossed them over to land with the top.

Now, all she had left were those thick, gray socks of hers. Her skin seemed to glow in the dimness, rich as vanilla ice cream, but with a pearly kind of luster, too. The sable hair between her soft thighs was shiny with moisture.

And the scent of her...ripe. Purely sexual. The scent of a woman aroused and satisfied. It clung to his hand.

Exercising every last shred of will he possessed, he held back a groan.

This was not going well.

She got rid of the socks, ripping them off, one and then the other, and tossing them to the rag rug beside the bed. "Okay, Justin. I'm naked."

As if he didn't know. As if every inch of him wasn't painfully aware.

He pressed his arm hard against his eyes. He was not going to look. Not again. No matter what.

She spoke again. "Justin. I want to get into bed. But you're on the blankets..."

"Uh. Right. Sorry." He shut his eyes tight and jumped from the bed, letting out another groan as his jeans dug in at the crucial spot.

He stood there, eyes shut, body rigid and burning, facing away from her. Behind him, he heard the covers rustling.

"Safe to look now," she said at last, her tone just slightly teasing. "I'm all covered up."

He yanked his sweater down low over his jeans, to mask the clear evidence that his body refused to be ruled by his mind. And then, with a deep breath and a silent vow that he would not climb onto that bed with her again, he turned to face her.

She sat against the pillows, shining dark hair soft and wild on her satiny shoulders, the blankets pulled up to cover those tempting breasts, looking achingly sweet, and not quite as confident as a moment ago. "I...well, I can't help it. It's crazy, but I almost feel as if we *are* married, you know? As if making love with you is the most natural, *right* thing for us to be doing."

It was exactly what he'd been thinking not long before.

But so what? his cynical side reminded him. *So damn what?* They *weren't* married. They would never be married. In a week she would hate him and know him for the enemy he was and had always been.

And, all sentimental talk of "feeling" married aside, they had no protection. They shouldn't have gone as far as they had.

And they damn well weren't going to go any further. "Katie." His voice was rough. Pained. Pushed out through his clutching throat, threaded with his own frustration. "We can't. You know we can't."

She picked at a thread on the velvet patchwork spread, eyes cast down, lashes wisps of silk against her cheeks. "You're right. I know..." She looked up. Those honey-brown eyes captured him, held him—a prisoner of his own burning need for her. "But couldn't we just..." She paused to swallow, convulsively—and then didn't seem to be able to go on.

"Couldn't we, *what?*" he demanded way too gruffly.

She swallowed again and licked those soft lips with a nervous pink tongue—an unintentionally provocative action that inflicted yet another blow to his barely held self-control.

"Well," she suggested, all wide eyes and innocence, "you could put on those black sweats you sleep in. I'll put my pajamas back on, too. You can...come to bed with me."

"Come to bed with you." There was nothing— *nothing*—he'd rather do. And it was exactly what he was *not* going do. "Katie—"

She cut him off before he could tell her no. "Oh, listen. Please..."

"We can't—"

"No, see. Just listen. We won't do anything more. I promise...to be good."

They shared a look—hot and hungry, crackling with need.

And then, out of nowhere, she laughed, a happy, startled, captivating trill of sound.

That laugh was infectious. He laughed, too—and then he stopped himself and glared at her. "What the hell are we laughing at?"

"Well, Justin, it's only...me, sitting here naked. Promising not to try anymore to seduce *you*. Who would have guessed *that* would happen?"

He only looked at her, making no attempt to smile. He was thinking that she'd been seducing him since the first moment he saw her, when Caleb introduced them and he got his first look into those wide, soft brown eyes.

There was just something about her. She got to him in ways he'd never been gotten to before.

"Please," she said, so sweetly.

"Hell," he replied.

"Please," she said, once more.

And once again, there was no stopping the wrong words from escaping his mouth.

"Put on those damn pajamas," he growled. "I'll be right back."

Chapter Nine

"Spooning," Katie whispered.

They lay on their sides, her slim back tucked into him, her legs cradled on his, his arm across her waist. He nuzzled her hair, cuddled her closer, in spite of the fact that holding her tighter only aroused him more.

"Yes," she said. "Spooning."

"What in hell are you talking about?"

She chuckled. The sweet sound vibrated through him. "What we're doing, tucked in this bed together, fully clothed, with you curved all around me. We're spooning."

He grunted, smoothed a wild coil of fragrant hair away from his mouth, and muttered, "We're driving me crazy, that's what we're doing."

"Hmm," she said, and wiggled her bottom against him.

He took a slow breath. "That was completely uncalled for."

"Sorry."

"Liar."

"But seriously, courting couples used to do this, in the old days...lie down together, with their clothes on, tucked up nice and cozy, like spoons in a drawer. Thus, spooning."

"Spooning." He laid his hand over hers, stroking the back of it, until she opened her fingers and he slid his between. She tucked their joined fists against her soft, flannel-covered breasts. He growled in her ear. "Frankly, I'd rather be shtupping."

She giggled. "I don't believe you said that."

"The truth hurts. Let me tell you, it really, *really* hurts."

She elbowed him lightly. "I'll distract you."

"Don't worry, you already are."

"I mean, from your, er, pain."

"Oh. That. Good luck."

"Back to spooning... Soldiers have done it, far back in history, spooning in the trenches to ward off the cold on a freezing night before a big battle. They'd keep warm using each other's body heat."

"Speaking of which, it's too damn hot in here." He pulled his hand from hers and readjusted the covers, pushing them down on his side.

"Umm." She wiggled in against him again. "Better?"

It was agony, but at the same time... "Yeah."

"Give me your hand back, please." He obliged. She tucked it under her soft chin. "Yes," she said on a gentle sigh. "This is nice…"

Nice wasn't exactly the word for it.

Spooning.

Never in a million and a half years would he have pictured himself, lying here, *spooning* Katie Fenton.

But he *was* lying here, with her sweet-scented softness plastered all along the front of him, holding her tight, both of them covered in clothing from neck to ankle. He *was* lying here, never wanting to let her go.

He knew he'd never get any sleep like this. But he closed his eyes, anyway.

He woke abruptly as Katie threw back the covers and jumped from the bed.

He sat up. She was already past the rope he'd dropped last night, racing for the door to the front reception room.

He raked the hair back from his forehead. "Huh, wha—?"

She sent him a dazzling smile and hauled open the door. "The phone's ringing."

It rang again as she slipped through the doorway.

Katie picked up the phone in midring. "Hello?" No one spoke. She asked again, more urgently, "Hello?"

"Katie, darling? Oh, thank goodness."

She felt the huge smile burst across her face. "Addy."

"You're there…you're safe?"

"Oh, Addy. Yes. I'm fine. Justin and I got stuck here, at the museum. But we're okay. We're safe. Buttercup's even okay—though she's getting pretty cranky, trapped in the shed out back with only hay to eat."

"You're safe." The relief in Addy's dear voice was achingly clear. "We've been so worried...."

"I'm fine. Really. And so is Justin. Don't worry anymore. Everything's great, but what about you? And Caleb? And Riley?"

"Safe. We're all safe." A gentle chuckle followed. "Riley made it home from the hall before the snow got too bad. Caleb and I and Mr. Sy Goodwin got stuck in that office in town."

"The ski resort office?"

"You know Caleb. Sy's visiting from Billings. He expressed interest in the project and Caleb wanted to take him right over there to show him what a good investment he'd be making. I tagged along. By the time we realized we needed to get home, it was too late. But we all three made it back to the hall, and spent Sunday and Monday and three endless, uncomfortable nights there, with the others who didn't make it home. It was an adventure, I'll tell you."

"Where are you now?"

"The snowplows started working last evening. Thunder Canyon Road was cleared by seven this morning."

Katie looked at the clock on the wall—ten thirty-five. "So you're at the Lazy D?"

"That's right. Home safe and sound."

Katie clutched the phone tighter. "Oh, I'm so relieved. I was worried about everyone."

"Nothing to worry about. We're all safe, and Caleb wants to talk to you."

"Okay, I—"

Before she finished her sentence, Caleb's deep voice was blustering in her ear. "Katie. Honey, you're all right?"

Katie smiled all the wider. "I'm fine. Really. Safe and warm, and we had food to eat, sandwiches left by the Historical Society ladies. We're pretty tired of ham and cheese, but it all worked out. Truly."

"Justin Caldwell?"

The sound of his name on Caleb's lips made her blush, for some silly reason—or maybe it was the memory of last night. "He's here, with me. Safe. I promise."

"All right, then. Katie, honey, you'll be out of there in no time. I'm making a few calls to see that plow gets to you right away."

"Caleb, that's really not necessary. We're perfectly safe and we can wait."

Caleb wouldn't hear of that. "I'm getting you out of there, and I'm doing it quick. Just sit tight now and hold on." He spoke to someone—Addy, no doubt—on his end of the line. "Addy wants you to come on out to the ranch for dinner tonight. We'll celebrate how we all got through the worst blizzard of the century—so far, anyway—safe and sound. She says to invite Caldwell, too. Can't have an out-of-towner thinking we don't know how to treat a guest."

He chuckled again. "Especially one who happens to be my business partner."

Nice idea, she thought. *Lovely* idea. "I'll ask him."

"Good. I'm going to let you go now. I want you to call me if that plow doesn't show up in the next hour."

She wouldn't, of course. She and Justin could wait as long as it took. But Caleb always enjoyed pulling strings for the people who mattered to him. "Thanks, Caleb. I love you—Addy, too."

He made the usual, gruff, blustering sounds. "Well, now, who's my girl?"

"*I* am. Always. Bye now."

She hung up and turned to find Justin leaning in the doorway to the central room, one bare foot crossed lazily over the other. Her heart set to pounding and her breath caught at the sight of him—at the memory of last night that seemed to shimmer in the air between them.

"That was Caleb and Addy." She sounded breathless. Probably because she *was.* "They were worried. I told them we were fine. And they said everyone else is safe, too."

"Good." He straightened from his easy slouch and came toward her, the predatory gleam in his eyes causing her knees to go weak and something low in her belly to go soft as melting butter.

She suffered dual urges—to back away from him; and to throw herself against him and lift up her mouth. In the end, she did neither. She held her ground, waiting, as he stalked toward her.

He reached her, his eyes still burning into hers.

A nervous laugh escaped her. "Justin, you look so…" The sentence trailed off. She didn't know quite how to finish it.

He lifted a hand. With a light finger, he guided a stray coil of hair behind her ear. A little shiver went through her. "Cold?"

"No. No, not at all. Justin, are you okay?"

His hand dropped to his side and he stepped back. "So, today we're really getting out of here."

She nodded. "If we're lucky, the plow should be here in the next few hours."

He turned from her, abruptly. "Let's get the coffee going."

She caught his arm. "Justin…"

He swung back, his eyes dark. Turbulent. His bicep was rock-hard with tension beneath her hand. "What?"

She let go, fast. "I…well, you almost seem angry. I just don't get it."

He kept staring at her, giving her that strange, hot, dark *devouring* look, for an endless, tense moment and then…

His eyes changed. Softened. His wonderful, sensual mouth went soft, too. "Hell." And he reached out and pulled her into his strong arms, squeezing the breath right out of her.

"Justin, what—?"

"I don't want to lose you." The rough, whispered words seemed dredged up from the deepest part of him.

"Oh, Justin." She held on, tight as he was holding her. "You won't. Of course, you won't."

A low, pained sound came from him and he crushed her so close, as if he would push himself right into her, meld their separate bodies into one undividable whole.

An image flashed into her mind: of the boy he once was, a boy all alone when he shouldn't have been, standing at a wide window, watching the snow come down, wondering what was going to happen to him.

"You can count on me," she whispered, meaning it with every fiber of her being. "You can hold on to me. I'll always be here."

He held her close for an endless moment more and then, with a shuddering sigh, his arms relaxed. She raised her head to meet his eyes and a rueful half smile lifted a corner of his mouth.

"Damned if I wasn't kind of getting to like it here."

She surged up, pressed a kiss on his beard-shadowed jaw. "Me, too. Oh, Justin...me, too."

Over morning coffee and the inevitable sandwiches, she relayed Addy's dinner invitation.

His eyes shifted away for a split second, and then he shook his head. "Wish I could. But I need to get back to Bozeman, ASAP. In my business, there are a hundred issues to deal with on a daily basis. I've been away since Saturday morning and that's three days too long."

She set down her stale sandwich and resisted the urge to work on him to stay. The guy had a demanding job and if they were going to get anywhere together, she'd have to learn to live with that—and on second thought, there were no *ifs* about it. The way he'd held her, as if he'd never let her go, out in the reception room a while ago, had banished all doubts on that score.

"I'm disappointed," she said, matter-of-factly. "But I do understand."

"Will you thank Adele for the invitation—and express my regrets?"

"You know I will—and it could be tough to get home at this point. You realize that?" Well, okay, she couldn't help hoping that maybe bad road conditions would keep him in town tonight, after all. He could stay at her place.

They could catch up on their spooning.

She might even make a quick trip to the drugstore, take care of the contraception problem. She'd never bought a condom in her life and old Mr. Dodson, the pharmacist, might give her the lifted eyebrow when she plunked the box down at the cash register counter. But it would definitely be worth the slight embarrassment, to make tonight extra special, a night to remember.

Always...

But then Justin said, "It's not even twenty miles. And by later today, at least, I'm sure they'll have the highway cleared."

He was probably right. Darn it.

The plow came within the hour. By then, Caleb had called a second time to tell her not to worry about Buttercup. A couple of hands would be over a little later with the snowblower and other necessary equipment to free the mare from the shed out back. Emelda

Ross had called, as well, just to check and see that Katie was all right.

Katie and Justin, still dressed in their rummage sale clothes, bundled in the coats and gloves they'd arrived in, shovels in hand, waited on the porch as the plow lumbered up the street. It turned into the museum parking lot and kept on coming, right up to the steps. Katie waved at the driver, a local man whose wife and kids paid frequent visits to the library, and shouted, "Thanks!"

The driver gave her a wave in return and then backed to the street again. The plow, which had already made the Elk Avenue curve, headed east at a crawl, toward what was known as New Town, clearing the high white drifts into yet higher piles at the sides of the street as it went.

Justin turned to her. "Well. What next?"

A dragging feeling of sadness engulfed her: for all they had shared in the dim rooms behind them, for the uncertain future—which, she told herself firmly, wasn't uncertain at all.

She and the man beside her had found something special. Nothing could change that. "Where's your car parked?" she asked with a cheery smile.

"In the lot behind the town hall."

"It's not far, and mine's there, too. Let's get the steps cleared off and put the shovels away and then we'll start walking."

All along Main Street, folks were out with their shovels. The roar of snowblowers filled the icy air.

People called out and waved as Katie and Justin walked by.

"Katie, how you doin'?"

"Some storm, eh?"

"Talk about your New Year's surprise!"

"Come on. This is nothin'. Five or six feet. Piece a cake."

"And they say it's turning warm right away. In the fifties by Friday. What do you think of that?"

They waved back and called greetings and when they reached the hall, they found the front steps already cleared and the driveway to the back parking lot passable, as well.

They went in the front to ask after the things they'd left behind the night of the storm. Rhonda Culpepper, well past sixty with a white streak in her improbably black hair, waited at her usual post behind the reception desk.

Rhonda greeted Katie and nodded at Justin and announced with a wink, "I'll bet I know what you two are after." She bent down behind the desk and came up with Katie's purse and Justin's briefcase, phone and keys, along with a big bag for each of them filled with their own clothes and shoes. "Have I got everything?"

"Looks like it. Thanks, Rhonda."

"Always glad to help."

They went down a side hall and out a door at the back. A couple of guys were at work there, clearing the snow between the vehicles so people could get them out. Katie exchanged greetings with the men and then Justin asked which car was hers.

She pointed at the silver-gray Suburban, near where the men were working. "In a few minutes they'll have me dug out."

"Let's get the snow off the roof and the windshield cleared, then," he suggested.

She caught his hand. Even through their heavy gloves, she felt his warmth. Her pulse quickened. "It's okay. Doug and Cam will help me." She gestured at the two busily shoveling men.

"You're sure?"

"Absolutely. Where are you parked?"

His black Escalade was near the edge of the lot, not far from the drive that led around to the front. The snow had already been shoveled away around it.

She helped him knock some of the snow off the roof and the hood and he got inside and turned the vehicle on, ducking back out with a scraper. He set to work. She went on tiptoe and pushed more snow off the Escalade's roof as he cleared the windshield.

It wasn't all that long before he had the wipers going and he was ready to head out.

He cast a glance toward Cam and Doug, still shoveling away between the snow-covered cars and pickups. "Come here." He grabbed her hand and towed her to the back of the Escalade, where they were out of sight of the working men. She went eagerly into the warm circle of his arms.

"Time to get out of here." His breath came out on a cloud.

"Drive safely. I want you back soon. Very, very soon..."

By way of answer, he bent and pressed his lips— cold on the outside, so warm within—to hers.

The icy day, the growls of snowblowers on Main Street, the scraping of shovels on the frozen blacktop a few feet away—all of that faded to nothing. There was only Justin, his arms tight and cherishing around her, his mouth claiming hers in a bone-melting kiss.

With a regretful growl low in his throat, he lifted his head. "I'll call you."

She let out a laugh. "Good luck with that. You don't even have my number."

"Katie, you're the town librarian and you're like a daughter to Caleb Douglas, who happens to be a colleague of mine. I don't think you'll be that hard to track down. Plus, I'd bet the last strip mall I built that you've got a listed number."

"Now, how did you know that?"

"You're the listed-number type."

She gave him a frown. "That's good, right?"

He kissed her nose, her cheeks and even her chin, his lips warm now against her cold skin. Then he pulled away enough to look at her, a deep look, a look she couldn't quite read. "I have to go." His arms fell away and he turned toward the driver's door.

She followed, already missing him, feeling bereft. He climbed up into the seat and shut the door. She went around the front of the vehicle to the other side, getting out of his way.

He saluted her—a gloved hand to his forehead. She mimicked the gesture. And then he was backing out, turning to get the right angle, and rolling forward. She watched as the big, black SUV disappeared around the side of the town hall, her heart pounding hard and heavy as lead beneath her breastbone.

She knew he would call her. Hadn't he just told her he would? Still, she had the strangest, scariest feeling right then that she would never see him again.

Chapter Ten

Dinner at the Lazy D was a festive affair. Adele had the cook prepare a juicy prime rib and Tess Little-hawk, the ranch's longtime housekeeper, set the long table in the formal dining room with the best china and crystal.

Riley, who'd been out earlier checking the stock, came in from his own place a half a mile from the main house to join them, his dark hair slicked back, wet from the shower he must have just taken.

"I was the lucky one," he said, smoothing his linen napkin on his lap and sparing a wink of greeting for Katie. "Safe and sound at my place before things got too rough."

Sy Goodwin, a feed-store owner and family man who'd decided to stay the night before heading back to his wife and four kids in Billings, laughed with

Caleb and Adele over their shared "ordeal" in the hall—especially Sunday morning, when most of the others were suffering from an excess of beer the day before.

"A number of extremely discouraging words were exchanged," Goodwin reported, his expression jokingly solemn, a definite gleam in his eye.

The creases in Caleb's nut-brown face etched all the deeper as he let out his big, boisterous laugh. "I tell you, Katie, a bottle of aspirin that first day was worth its weight in gold."

Sy laughed, too. "And anyone with a box of Alka-Seltzer could have gotten a fortune for it."

Adele and Caleb agreed that Sy wasn't exaggerating.

Caleb asked, a little too meaningfully as far as Katie was concerned, "And what about you and Justin? Stuck there in that musty old museum with nothing but mining equipment and Indian artifacts for company."

Adele was shaking her head. "What *did* you do for all that time?"

We kissed, Katie thought. *Forever. We spooned. All night. And I dropped in at State Street Drugs this afternoon and bought myself a box of condoms.* Mr. Dodson hadn't even batted an eye when she plunked it down on the counter.

She said, offhand as she could make it, "Oh, we found some books and board games in the storage room. We managed to occupy ourselves."

Addy clucked her tongue and sent Katie a sly look. "A handsome guy, that Justin."

Katie put on her sweetest smile. "Yes. He is. Very."

Adele added, "I do wish he'd been able to stay and join us tonight."

"He had to get back," Katie said. "Business, you know."

"Yeah," Caleb agreed. "That man's a real go-getter. Started from nothing and now he's the biggest developer in western Montana—and not even thirty-five yet." Those devilish green eyes of his were twinkling. "And our Katie's gone and married him."

Addy and Riley shared a glance and Sy Goodwin looked confused.

Adele had to explain to him about the mail-order bride reenactment they'd missed when they went down to the ski resort office.

"We heard after we got back to the hall that it was quite an event, that marriage of yours," said Caleb. "Heard some old character named Green stepped up to play the preacher. Got right into the part. Even called himself 'Reverend.'"

"Yep," Katie agreed, keeping it light, but thinking of Justin. Of his low, teasing voice through the darkness that night they'd talked and talked. Of his kiss. Of his hands on her body. She should have gotten his number. But no. He'd said he'd call. And of course he would. "That 'wedding' was...really something."

Maybe tonight, she thought. At least by tomorrow...

The talk moved on to other subjects. After coffee and dessert, Caleb and Addy urged her to stay. They didn't want her driving home on the icy roads in the dark.

She said she really had to get back. The roads to town had been cleared and salted and the snow hadn't started up again. She'd be just fine.

It was after eleven when she let herself into her two-story farmhouse-style Victorian on Cedar Street.

She'd been home earlier, after Justin left her in the town hall parking lot, and she'd turned up the thermostat then, so the house was cozy-warm and welcoming. Switching on lamps as she went, she headed for the phone in the kitchen in back, where she found the message light on her machine glowing a steady red.

No one had called.

He didn't call Wednesday morning, either. Katie went to the library at nine and jumped every time the phone rang, though there was really no reason he'd call her at work when all he had to do was look up her home number in the book.

Still, whenever the phone rang, her heart would race and the clerk would answer.

And it wouldn't be him.

Emelda, who put in a lot of volunteer hours at the library, arrived at two. "It's going to be fifty degrees today, can you believe it?" she marveled as she peeled off her muffler and hung up her heavy coat. "Snow's already melting. It'll be gone in no time if this keeps up." She clucked her tongue and got to work shelving some new novels Katie had waiting.

At three, Emelda took over the check-out desk so

the clerk, Lindy Peters, could have a break. The phone rang just as Lindy left the desk. Katie raced over and grabbed it on the second ring, though Emelda was moving down the counter toward it.

"Thunder Canyon Public Library," Katie answered, absurdly breathless. "May I help you?"

It was only someone wanting the library hours for the week. Katie repeated them and said goodbye.

Emelda shook her silver-gray head. "I swear you are jumpy as a frog on a hot rock today. I would have gotten that."

Katie hardly heard her. Her mind was full of Justin. What was he doing now? Had he gotten back to Bozeman safely? Well, of course he had. And it had barely been twenty-four hours since he left her at the town hall—well, okay, twenty-six hours, thirty-plus minutes, to be more exact. Not that long, not really. No doubt he had a mountain of work to catch up on. He probably wouldn't be able to get away to see her until the weekend. He'd be calling—soon—to set something up.

"Katie? Did you hear a single word I said?"

"Oh. Emelda. Sorry, I..." She was saved from having to make some lame excuse for her distracted behavior when a little girl with a towering stack of picture books, her mother right behind her, stepped up to the counter.

After that, Katie managed to keep herself from rushing to grab the phone every time it rang.

Besides, by then she was feeling more and more certain that Justin would be calling her house, not the library. There was probably a message waiting for her at home right now.

When she got home at five-fifteen there were two messages, but neither was from Justin.

She simply had to stop obsessing over this. He'd said he'd call and he would. Justin was an honest man.

That night she hosted the Historical Society meeting at her house. As she served up the coffee and cookies and listened to everyone bemoan the storm that had ruined their museum reception, and trade news on Ben Saunders's rapidly improving health, she couldn't help expecting the phone to ring.

It didn't. Not that night, not Thursday morning, not during her prelunch hours at the library, either.

She met Addy for their usual Thursday lunch date at the Hitching Post. Addy mentioned that she thought Katie seemed distracted.

Katie met Addy's eyes across the table and longed to tell her everything—of the magic time she'd known with Justin when they were marooned in the museum, of the shattering beauty of the one night she'd spent in his arms.

Of how she couldn't stop longing, every second of the day, for his call.

But no. It was all too new. She didn't want to share what she was feeling with anyone. Not yet. Not until...

Well, soon. But not now.

She reassured Addy that she was fine.

And then Justin didn't call the rest of the day, or in the evening, either.

By Friday morning she was beginning to wonder if something really might have happened to him, if he'd had some kind of accident on the way home to Bozeman. Whatever had kept him from calling her, she prayed he was all right.

She pored over the special edition of the *Thunder Canyon Nugget* that had come out Wednesday. It was chock-full of great stories of how folks had weathered the big storm. Two storm-related accidents were reported. One had occurred after the roads were cleared, when a pickup going too fast rolled on Thunder Canyon Road. The other concerned a high-schooler who'd driven his snowmobile into a tree while the snow was still falling on Sunday afternoon. Injuries were surprisingly minor in both cases. She found no mention of any accident on the road to Bozeman, nothing about a black Escalade or an out-of-towner named Caldwell.

Before she left for the library, she called Bozeman information. His home phone wasn't listed. But they did have a number for Red Rock Developers. She dialed it and a service picked up. The offices opened at nine. She could leave her number and Mr. Caldwell's secretary would get back to her during business hours.

"Uh, no thanks. I'll call later."

She hung up and considered calling Caleb, asking him if maybe he had Justin's home number. But she found herself hesitating to do that. Caleb would be curious. He'd tease her about her "groom," and ask her why she thought she needed his number. And then Caleb would tell Adele that Katie was trying to get ahold of Justin—and Addy would tell Caleb how distracted Katie had been at lunch the day before...

Oh, not right now, she thought. She wanted to find out how Justin was, wanted to *talk* to him, wanted to be reassured that everything was all right, with him and between the two of them, before she said anything to Caleb or Addy.

She went to work and tried to keep her mind on her job, a difficult task when every thought kept tracking right back around to Justin. Where was he? Was he okay? Why hadn't he called?

By lunchtime, after Lindy had asked her twice what was wrong with her and Emelda had expressed concern over whether she might be coming down with something, Katie realized she had to snap out of it.

Worrying about Justin wasn't going to do anybody any good. She'd track him down that evening, one way or another. Until then, she was keeping her thoughts strictly on her work.

At four-fifteen, the kids started arriving for Emelda's story hour, which started at four-thirty. They all gathered around the low round table in the center of the children's section, where Emelda would keep them spellbound with fairy tales and stories by the best contemporary children's authors—and sometimes true-life accounts from Montana history.

Cameron Stevenson, one of the two men Katie and Justin had found shoveling out the town hall parking lot on Tuesday, brought his seven-year-old, Erik, as always. Often the parents would leave their kids and come back at five-thirty to collect them.

Not Cam. The tall, athletic auburn-haired teacher

was a single dad and he took fatherhood seriously. He stuck around, even though he coached at the high school and would have to rush back there the minute the story hour ended to get his team ready for the evening's home game. As he waited, he read sports magazines from the periodicals section and browsed the fiction stacks.

After five, as Katie was wrapping things up for the day, Cam wandered over to her workstation at the central reference counter and he and Katie chatted about nothing in particular: how good the varsity basketball team was looking this year and how Cam and Erik had barely made it home Saturday before the snow shut them in.

Cam joked that he'd heard how she and her ''groom'' had been stuck at the museum alone for the duration. ''Some honeymoon, huh?'' he asked with an easy grin.

''It was...quite an experience,'' she replied in a library-level whisper, mentally congratulating herself on how offhand she sounded. ''Poor Buttercup.''

''That old mare of Caleb's, you mean?''

She nodded. ''The old sweetheart was stuck out in the shed all that time, no exercise and nothing but hay to...'' She didn't finish.

How could she? Her throat had clamped tight. Joy and relief went exploding through her.

Justin!

He must have just come in. He stood over by the check-out counter, wearing a sweater that matched his eyes and a gorgeous coffee-brown suede jacket. He was scanning the room.

He spotted her. Her heart froze in midbeat and then started galloping. Somehow, she managed to lift a hand and wave.

He headed toward her, long strides eating up the all-weather gray carpet under his boots. She was vaguely aware that Cam had turned to see what—or who—had stolen the words right out of her mouth.

"I had a feeling I might find you here," Justin said.

Good gravy, he really was the best-looking man in the whole of Montana! She had to swallow to make her throat relax before she could speak. "Uh. Good guess. And, um, great to see you."

It was the understatement of the decade.

She collected her scattered wits enough to introduce him to Cam. The two men exchanged greetings and then Cam left them alone.

The second the coach was out of earshot, Justin asked low, "When do you finish here?"

She ordered her crazy heart to stop racing. "Give me a minute. I'm almost ready to go."

As they passed the check-out desk, Lindy called out, "Have a nice night." Plump and pretty and very curious, the clerk gave them a big grin and wiggled her eyebrows at Katie.

Katie, getting the message, stopped to introduce them.

"Terrific to meet you!" Lindy enthused. Sheesh. She was practically drooling.

Then again, who could blame her?

Justin made a few cordial noises and at last they were out of there.

They walked down the library steps into a winter sunset. The cloudless sky was shades of salmon above the white-topped mountains and the melting snow at their feet sent rivulets trickling, down the steps, along the parking lot. A hundred miniature streams gleamed in the gathering dark.

She sent a quick glance toward the silent man at her side. He hadn't touched her—hadn't taken her arm. She longed to take his, but didn't feel comfortable enough with him at that moment, with the way he'd popped up out of nowhere, with the strange, shadowed look in his eyes and the hard set to his square jaw.

"Where's your car?" he asked flatly when they reached the big, black Escalade.

"I walked. It's only a few blocks and it was nice to get out." She almost said more. Meaningless chatter. About the warming trend. About how she liked to walk whenever the weather permitted. But she didn't. His eyes didn't invite chitchat. "Justin, what—?"

He cut in before she finished. "Who was that guy you were talking to inside?"

Her heart warmed. So that was the problem. He was *jealous.* "Cam? He's only a friend. Honestly. A friend…"

His mouth twisted into something meant to look like a smile. "Not that I had any damn right to ask."

She looked at him levelly. "If you were wondering, then I'm *glad* you asked. It's important that we both feel we can say whatever's on our minds."

"Is it?" He lifted a dark brow at her.

She blinked. "Now what is *that* supposed to mean?"

He shrugged. "Nothing."

Untrue and she knew it. It was very much *something*. She could see it in his eyes.

But before she could open her mouth to pursue the issue, he spoke again. "Will you have dinner with me?"

There was only one answer to that one. "I'd love to."

"Where would you like to go?"

He sounded so...formal. As if she was some stranger.

It came to her that she didn't want to go and sit in a restaurant with him. Surrounded by other people, she wouldn't feel she could really talk to him. And she needed that, to feel free to talk. This new distance between them scared her a little. She wanted, with all her heart, to bridge it.

And then again, was this feeling of distance really all that surprising? They'd found a rare and thrilling intimacy, just the two of them, in the museum. But she had to remember that they'd known each other less than a week. The attraction had been immediate and the forced proximity had made it possible for them to grow close very fast.

And then he'd returned to his life and she'd gone back to hers.

No. She had to expect that things would be a little awkward, now they found themselves face-to-face again at last.

She intended to eliminate the awkwardness, to

break down any and all barriers between them. That would be easier if they were alone.

"Tell you what? Let's just go to my place. How about fried chicken and oven-browned red potatoes, would that be all right?"

He frowned. "You're sure?"

She stepped back, a half laugh escaping her. "Justin. What's not to be sure of?"

He hesitated a moment longer. But finally, he agreed. "Well, all right, then. Let's go."

Chapter Eleven

''**B**ig place,'' Justin said, when Katie ushered him into a high-ceilinged foyer, where a walnut staircase rose gracefully from the far end, curving upward toward the second floor.

She set her purse on the long marble table by the door and turned to knock the breath out of him with a glowing smile. ''It was in bad shape when I bought it, but I've had a lot of work done. It was built in 1910, by the owner of the town dry goods store. Cedar Street used to be where all the town merchants lived. A lot of them were well-to-do.''

''Clearly.'' Beneath his boots, the fine, old wood of the parquet floor gave off a polished shine in the glow from the antique light fixture overhead. Carved walnut moldings crowned the walls.

She teased, ''Take a good look around. Just in case

you're thinking of making me an offer.'' He met those brown eyes again and a shock of sensual awareness ricocheted through him.

He wanted to grab her and carry her up the curving staircase, to find a nice, big bed up there and never let her out of it. ''I'm tempted,'' he muttered, and they both knew damn well he wasn't talking about her house.

He ached. All over. His damn skin felt too tight. He had only himself to blame for the state he was in. Not only for starting up with her in the first place, but for not taking care of his physical needs since he'd left her on Tuesday.

There were a couple of women he knew: willing, bright, beautiful women, who didn't expect—or even want—anything beyond a nice evening and a good time in bed. But he hadn't been able to make himself pick up the phone and call one of them.

His body burned for the satisfaction he hadn't allowed himself to take four nights ago in that big, old bed in the museum. But he'd done nothing to ease the ache. The thought of touching some other woman for the sake of a much-needed release…

It made him feel vaguely ill.

His mistake. To add to all the others. He should have at least taken a few minutes in the shower to get the edge off, but he hadn't even had sense enough to do that.

Somehow, he couldn't. He wanted Katie. His *body* wanted Katie. Only Katie.

Though he knew damn well he was never going to have her.

"Oh, Justin..." Her voice was so soft, like the rest of her. His arms itched to hold her. With monumental effort, he kept his hands at his sides. She seemed to shake herself and then, shyly, she offered, "May I take your jacket?"

He shrugged out of it and handed it over. She hung it on the antique claw-footed rack by the door, along with her heavy coat. Then she turned to him again, those amber eyes alight, her smile so bright it could chase away the darkness of the blackest night.

Damn. He was gone. Gone, gone, gone. He kept trying to remember why he'd come here, what he needed to say to her. He should say it.

And go.

But he said nothing as she gestured toward a door at the back, past the foot of that impressive staircase. "This way..." He fell in behind her and she led him to a big kitchen with acres of granite-topped counters and cherrywood cabinets fronted in beveled glass. "Have a seat." She nodded toward the cherry table in the breakfast area. "I'll get the dinner started."

He didn't want to sit there at the table while she bustled around across a jut of counter fifteen feet away. "Let me help."

"Well, sure." She was already at the sink, washing her hands. "If you want to..."

He followed her lead at the sink and then turned to watch her as she tied on an apron, set the oven and began assembling the stuff she needed. He scrubbed the potatoes for her. She cut them into quarters and shook spices on them, then drizzled them with olive oil and stirred them with a wooden spoon.

In spite of the constant, burning ache to grab her and hold her, to kiss her and feel her body go soft and warm and achingly willing against his, in spite of the nagging awareness that he had a grim purpose here and once he accomplished it, he'd have to walk out the door.

And never see her again.

In spite of all of it, a strange sort of peace settled on him, just to be there, with her, in the big, well-appointed kitchen, handing her a spoon or an oven mitt when she asked for it, watching as she prepared their meal.

She battered the chicken, her soft mouth curved in a happy smile. "So. What have you been up to since we broke out of the museum Tuesday?"

He told her how busy he'd been, catching up, getting back on top of the job again. As he talked, she put the chicken on to fry and checked the potatoes.

As she shut the oven door, she asked, "How about some wine?"

"Sounds good."

She went to the chef-quality fridge and brought out a bottle of Pinot Grigio. "Do the honors?"

He opened the wine and poured them each a glass. Then she started on the salad, keeping an eye on the chicken as she worked, and chattering away about the happenings at the library, about the Historical Society meeting she'd held on Wednesday.

"There was much concern over how the storm had ruined our 'wedding reception.' The society members were hoping the event would generate a few generous donations."

"Understandable. Did you tell them how grateful we were that they left all those sandwiches—and what they're collecting for a rummage sale?"

"I didn't," she confessed. "But I guess I should have."

He knocked back a big slug of the excellent wine to keep himself from flinging the glass to the hard-wood floor and hauling her into his arms. "Speaking of the rummage sale, I should have brought back that reindeer sweater—not to mention the ugly coat, the jeans and those beat-up sneakers. Sorry. I completely forgot." His mind had been filled with her, with the shining central fact that he'd see her face again. One more time.

Before the end.

"No one's even going to notice that stuff is miss-ing, believe me." She sipped from her own glass—much more daintily than he had. "But if you're feel-ing *really* guilty, you could make a donation."

"I'll do that."

"It doesn't have to be much. And you'll have the society's undying gratitude."

"Never hurts to build goodwill." He knew he should have choked on those words. After next Tues-day, he'd be the lowest of the low in her eyes. No amount of goodwill would help him then.

She nodded. "Never hurts."

Never.

The word got stuck in his mind.

Never to hold her again...

Never to see her smile at him...

Never to look into those wide brown eyes...

He set his wineglass on the counter—a stupid move, and he knew it. With both hands empty, the urge to fill them with her softness was nearly overpowering.

She watched him, her eyes tracking from his face, to his glass and back to his face again. After an endless few seconds of that, she set down her glass, too.

Behind her at the stove, the chicken sizzled in the pan, giving off a mouthwatering, savory smell. The salad sat, half-made, beside her glass.

And he couldn't stop himself from thinking...

If she were someone different, or if he was.

If those vows they'd exchanged Saturday in the town hall had been the real thing.

If she were truly his wife.

This would be their life, here, in this graceful old house, her in her apron, the chicken on the stove, the salad on the counter and the potatoes in the oven.

The two of them, talking about what had happened at work, sharing the little details of their separate days, before they sat down to dinner.

Together.

And later, he'd take her to bed—*their* bed.

He'd hold her and kiss her—kiss every last inch of her. Until she was pliant and heated and ready to have him. He'd enter her slowly, by aching degrees....

"Oh," she said quietly, the word like a yearning sigh between them. "Oh, I did miss you."

It was too much. More than he could bear. His need to touch her took over. He reached out.

With a cry, she swayed toward him. And he wrapped his arms around a miracle.

Katie. Right here. In his hungry arms.

He rained kisses on her soft, flushed cheeks. "I missed you, too. So damn much."

"Oh, me, too. I missed *you*." She let out a giggle and a sweet blush stained her cheeks. "But I already said that, I know I did. I— Oh, Justin. You should kiss me." She tipped up that plump mouth. "You should kiss me right now."

"You're right."

He took her lifted mouth. And she gave it, eagerly, sending a blast of heat exploding through him. She opened for him, so he could plunge his tongue inside and taste her—so sweet, so eager, flavored with wine.

She wore a kitten-soft sweater over a skinny wool skirt. It wasn't enough, to feel her through that fluffy sweater. He eased it up—just a little. He wasn't going to go too far.

He put his hands on the velvety, warm flesh at the small of her back. She moaned into his mouth. He sucked in the sound, breathing in her breath, letting it back out so she could take breath from him.

He muttered her name, between deep kisses on her open lips. "Katie, Katie, Katie…" And his hands…

He couldn't stop them. They wandered up her back, found the place where her bra hooked and eased those tiny hooks apart.

Yes! He brought his hands around, both of them, between them, and he cradled her small, round breasts, groaning at the feel of them, the soft, slight weight against his palms. He scraped her nipples with his thumbs and then caught them, each one, between thumb and forefinger, rolling, pinching a little, just enough to make her push her hips against him, just enough to make her moan.

More.

He had to have more of her.

He had to have *all* of her. Stark need pounded through him as his blood spurted, thick and hot and hungry, through his veins.

He raked that sweater up, losing her mouth so he could kiss her chin, scrape his teeth along her throat, nipping and licking as he went. He nuzzled the fluffy sweater, but only briefly. And then he found her breast.

He latched on and she cried out, clutching his head. He drew on the sweet peak, working his teeth against it, making her cry out again.

As he suckled her, he let his hands slide downward, over the glorious inward curve of her waist and out, along the warm shape of her hips beneath the nubby wool of her skirt.

The skirt was in his way and he wanted it gone.

He grabbed two handfuls of it and eased it upward, over those warm, slim, waiting thighs.

Her panty hose stopped him. His fingers brushed them, and sheer as they were, the slight barrier of nylon reminded him.

He shouldn't be doing this.

He had no damn right to do this.

It took every last ounce of determination he possessed, but he lifted his head. She tried, at first— raising her body to his, pleading sounds rising from her throat—to pull him back to her.

But no.

He couldn't. He had no right to give in to her tender urging.

He lifted his head and her soft hands fell away.

Gently, he smoothed down her skirt as she looked at him, dazed, flushed and dreamy-eyed. "Justin?" She whispered his name on a yearning, slow breath.

He didn't answer. *Couldn't* answer. He took her by the waist and carefully turned her around, taking the loose ends of her bra straps and hooking them together again.

He smoothed the sweater back down.

Only then, when those tempting bare inches of skin were safely covered, did he guide her back around.

Lazily, she raised her arms and rested them on his shoulders. "Oh, my." She let out a long, sweet sigh. "I think the chicken's burning."

He gritted his teeth to keep from taking her kiss-swollen mouth again. "Better see to it."

"Yes." She looked adorably regretful. "I suppose I'd better."

He let go of her—yet another impossible task somehow accomplished—and she turned for the stove.

The wine was right there and his glass was empty. He needed more. A river of it, to wash the tempting taste of her from his mouth—to numb the reality of what he was here to do. He filled his glass and topped off hers, too.

I could…just drop the whole thing with Caleb, he found himself thinking as he stood a few feet behind her, sipping more wine, his gaze tracking the length of her. From her gleaming, thick brown hair that curled sweetly at her shoulders, down to her trim waist, and lower still, over the smooth swell of her hips, along the shape of her thighs outlined beneath the slim skirt, and lower, to the backs of her slim calves. She sent him a smile over her shoulder as she moved from the stove to the oven again. From there, she came closer and set to work finishing the salad.

He watched her hands, narrow and smooth, clear polish on her short-trimmed nails.

I could just never make my move, he thought. *Let it all go ahead as Caleb believes it will. Give it up. At this point, no one would even have to know what I had meant to do.*

But then what?

Try to make his dream of a life with Katie come true?

And if he tried for that—what? Tell her the truth about himself? That basic fact that he'd lied—a whopping lie—in the first place, could ruin it between them.

So if not the truth, then what?

To hold forever within himself the central lie of his very existence? Seeing Caleb and his wife and their son all the time, becoming, in a sense, a part of the family?

No.

It was impossible.

He had to remember his mother. Remember Ramona Lovett, who called herself Ramona Caldwell. Remember the life they'd had. Barely holding on too much of the time. He had to remember, all of it.

Like that night when he was twelve. The night

she'd locked herself in the bathroom. Remember breaking down the door to find her limp in the bathtub, her forearms slit, bleeding out on the white tiles of the bathroom floor.

He'd slipped in her blood as he plowed through the medicine cabinet looking for something to staunch the flow.

After that, the Child Protective Services people had come sniffing around, so they'd moved. Again.

And then, always, he would have to live with the night she died.

She'd come to find him in Bozeman when she learned she wouldn't make it, come and let him take care of her for those final months. Once or twice, in the last weeks, she'd remarked that it was strange— maybe even meant to be. That he'd ended up here, in Western Montana, when she'd never once so much as brought him here the whole time he was growing up.

"I thought I raised you to live anywhere *but* here. And look. Here you are. Must be fate. Oh, yeah. Must be fate. When I'm gone you'll get your chance to make it all right."

He would ask her what she was getting at. What did Montana have to do with anything? And she would turn her head away.

Until the last. Until the night she died in the hospital, where he'd taken her once she couldn't get along without round-the-clock care.

"I know I never told you, who he was…your father. Maybe I should have." Her skeletal hand, tubes running from the back of it, weakly clutched his fingers. "Caleb. That's his name. Caleb Douglas. Wife,

Adele. They had one son. All they *could* have. Riley. In Thunder Canyon.''

"Thunder Canyon. That's right here. In Montana.''

She'd swallowed, sucked in another breath that wheezed like she was dragging it in through a flattened straw. Even the oxygen didn't help her by then. Nothing helped. "Yes. Twenty miles from here. In Montana. Caleb...'' she'd whispered, her eyes closing on a final sigh. "Caleb...''

And with that name on her lips, she was gone.

"Justin? Are you in there?'' Katie laughed, a light, happy sound. A sound from another world, a world of possibilities he couldn't let himself explore. "You should see your face. A million miles away.''

He shook himself. "Sorry.''

"Nothing to apologize for.'' She handed him the big wooden salad bowl. "Put this on the table? We'll just eat right here, in the breakfast nook, if that's okay?'' She handed him the salad tongs.

"Sounds good.'' He carried the bowl and tongs to the table, then helped her set it for two.

A few minutes later, she took out the potatoes, spooned them into a bowl, and transferred the chicken to a serving platter.

They sat down to eat. He looked at the food, and wondered if he'd be able to get anything down, though the chicken was crispy-brown and the potatoes perfectly cooked. The salad was crisp and green.

No. It wasn't the food.

It was the wrongness of being here, of holding her, of touching her soft body, kissing her lips, of drinking her wine and letting her cook for him.

Yeah. It was all wrong, to steal these last perfect moments with her, when in the end he could do nothing but continue on the course he'd set two years ago, on the day of his mother's death. In the end, his choice wouldn't change. He would get his payback—for Ramona Lovett Caldwell's sake, above all.

And that meant he had no right to sit here with Katie, in her house, at her table, pretending that there was some hope for the two of them.

There wasn't.

There never could be.

Katie set down her fork with a bite of potato still on the end of it. Justin had been much too quiet for several minutes now—ever since that kiss, as a matter of fact, a kiss that had almost ended with the two of them rushing to the bedroom.

But he had stopped it.

And ever since then…

"Justin, what is it?" She forced a joking laugh. "The food can't be that bad."

He pushed his plate away. "It's not the food." He really didn't look right.

Alarm skittered through her. His face was set. Kind of…closed against her. Why? "Was it something I said?" She tried to make the question light and playful, but didn't fully succeed. There was an edge to her voice. She couldn't help it.

She had the most powerful feeling that something had gone wrong.

Something major.

Something she had a sinking feeling she wasn't going to be able to make right.

Which was crazy. What could have gone wrong in the space of a few minutes? Hardly anything had been said.

"Justin, was it that you kissed me? But no. I don't see how it could be that." She raised both hands, palms up. "Did I do something to upset you? I just don't get it. I don't underst—"

He grabbed her hand. "Listen." He stood, pulling her up with him.

"Justin, I don't—"

"No. Hear me out. It's nothing you did." His eyes gleamed at her with a strange, wild kind of light.

"But if you—"

"No." He squeezed her fingers. Hard. "Wait. Listen."

She pulled her hand free of his, dread moving through her, dragging at her body, like an awful gravity from within. "All right." She folded her hands in front of herself, twining them together to keep from reaching out for him. He wouldn't like it if she tried to touch him now, she knew it, knew it in a deep and undeniable way.

Oh, what was up with him? How could something so right suddenly veer off into something so strange and wrong? It made no sense. And he still wasn't talking, in spite of telling her twice to listen. How could she listen if he had nothing to say?

"Justin, you're acting so strangely. Is something wrong? I'd appreciate it if you'd just tell me what's bothering—"

He interrupted. "Nothing." The single word was far too curt. Not to mention a whopping lie.

"But if you'd only—"

"Listen." He reached out as if he would grab her, then jerked his hand back as though he'd been burned.

"But I've *been* listening. You're not talking."

"It's only...I couldn't stay away. I missed you. I missed you like hell."

She would have smiled in relief and delight, if only he hadn't sounded so angry about it. She made another feeble attempt at lightness. "And this is a problem?"

He stared at her for a long, sizzling moment. She had the sense that he was going to spin on his heel and slam out the door. Why?

The word screamed in her mind.

Why, why, why?

"I shouldn't have come here. It was wrong."

This was making no sense. No sense at all. "Wrong? I don't see how. I invited you here. I wanted to make our dinner. I wanted to...be with you. I'm so glad you came."

He stepped back abruptly, knocking over his chair, catching it at the last minute, righting it—and then turning, backing away from her, toward the door to the foyer. "I should never have come. I only..."

She waited for him to finish, to say something that made sense. When he didn't, she prodded, "You only, what?"

"I couldn't stay away." He hung his dark head. He looked so lost. So alone.

Her yearning heart went out to him. But when she

took a step toward him, he put up both hands, palms out, to keep her at bay. "No," he said, and, "No," again.

She stepped back, to show him she wouldn't come closer.

Oh, what was happening here? "It doesn't make sense. You say you couldn't stay away, that you missed me so much." It was like a sharp knife, turning in her belly, in her heart, in the very center of her, to admit it. But it had to be said. "I just don't see it. The way you're acting now, well, what am I supposed to think but that I've had it all wrong, about you and me?"

"No," he said flatly, his mouth twisting. "No. You weren't wrong. Not about that. Never about that."

"Then what?"

"Listen." He said that word again and he reached for her—again. Every atom in her body cried out to move toward him. But she made herself stay right where she was.

And, as before, his hands dropped to his sides. "I came here to tell you something." His voice was infinitely weary. "To tell you, and leave. I thought I'd do it over dinner, in a restaurant, where I wouldn't be tempted to..." The words trailed off. They both knew what he meant.

Tempted to kiss her.

Tempted to hold her.

Tempted to make sweet, passionate love with her.

They stared at each other across a short distance that felt like a million miles.

Finally, she made herself speak. "Do you still plan to say it, whatever it is?"

There was a slight hesitation, but then he nodded. "Yeah. I do."

She felt weary, too, now. Weary and sick at heart. Still, she straightened her spine and lifted her chin. "Then I guess you'd better say it, don't you think?"

He drew in a long breath and let it out hard. And, at last, he came out with it. "You're going to hate me, soon enough. But when you do, remember. None of it was about you. You shouldn't have been involved. It was one rotten step too far, what I did with you. A gross error in judgment on my part. You are exactly the woman a man like me never finds."

"But then I don't see why—"

"It's simple. I'm not who you think I am."

Her legs felt achy and rubbery. And her heart was a big lump of lead in her chest. She felt for the chair behind her. Slowly, with great care, she lowered herself into it. "I don't understand you. *What* wasn't about me? And if you're not who I think you are, well, who are you, then?"

There was a long, ugly silence. Finally, he muttered, "I can't say any more. Goodbye, Katie."

And that was it.

That was all.

Without another word, he turned and went out through the door to the foyer. She didn't follow him. She knew, in an awful, final kind of way that there was no point. A moment or two later, she heard the front door open—and close.

Chapter Twelve

He had said she would hate him.

But she didn't.

She felt numb, as if she were floating, as if none of this was real.

The meal still waited, his plate untouched, hers almost the same, right there beside her on the table. She probably ought to go ahead and eat.

Through the numbness, she felt a touch of nausea.

No. No food. Not now.

She rose, very slowly, her legs wobbly and uncertain. Once she was on her feet, she leaned on the table for a moment or two, getting her bearings.

When she felt more certain her legs would hold her up, she calmly cleared the table and put the food away. She rinsed the dishes and put them in the dishwasher, washed the frying pan and hung it back on the overhead rack.

Once everything was cleaned up, all evidence of the meal they should have shared out of sight, once the sink was empty and the counters wiped down, she went through the door to the foyer, the same way he had gone. There, she locked the front door.

That taken care of, she turned for the stairs. As she climbed, she felt like someone very old and stiff, doggedly dragging herself up to bed. She held on to the polished railing, taking one careful step at a time.

What had happened, the things he'd said to her—none of it made any sense.

She only knew that it was over between them. Over before it had even really gotten started.

Beneath the ugly numbness, she knew she was going to have to get over him, get over a man who'd managed to fill up her world, to change everything, in the space of six days.

She hoped the numbness lasted awhile, bleakly aware that when it faded, she would have to deal with the pain of losing him, have to somehow learn to mend her shattered heart.

At eleven-thirty the next morning, Addy showed up at her door. "I came into town to pick up a few things and I thought we might go out and grab a bite of..." She peered at Katie closer. "Darling, what's happened? What's the matter with you?"

Squinting against the bright morning sun, Katie put her hand up to her tangled hair. "I..." She looked down at the pajamas she was still wearing. "I...well, I slept a little late."

Addy wasn't buying. She stepped over the threshold and closed the door firmly behind her. Quickly, she slipped out of her coat and hung it on the rack, then turned to face Katie again. "Something bad has happened. I can see it in your eyes." She grabbed Katie's hand and towed her into the living room, where she sat on the sofa and pulled Katie down beside her. "Now..." She seemed unsure of how to continue. "Oh, my dear. Please. Tell me what's happened."

Katie hadn't the faintest idea how to answer. She looked at the woman who'd been the mother she'd needed so much, the woman who'd come for her when she had no one else, the woman who'd been there, ever since, whenever Katie needed a listening ear or loving arms to hold her.

Katie realized she needed that now—Addy's loving arms around her. "Oh, Addy..."

Addy reached for her with a worried cry. "Now, now. Oh, honey."

Katie sagged into Addy's embrace, breathing in the faint scent of Addy's subtle perfume, feeling at least a little less numb.

Which maybe, on second thought, wasn't such a great thing. Something loosened in her chest. Without the numbness to keep them down, she felt the sudden tears rising. "Oh, Addy..."

"It's okay. It will be okay."

It wouldn't, and Katie knew it. Not for a long time. And that seemed so awful, so infinitely sad, that the tears rose high enough to burn her throat, to fill her eyes with scalding wetness. "Oh, I don't think so…oh, Addy, it won't. Not for a long time."

Her shoulders started shaking as the sobs took over, deep, wrenching ones. The tears dribbled down her cheeks and kept on coming, a river of them. Addy held her, not caring the least that Katie was soaking the front of her angora sweater. She whispered comforting words as Katie sobbed for the love—for the future with Justin—that was never going to be.

Finally, Katie spoke against Addy's warm, willing shoulder, the words fractured, broken—just like her heart. "It was…oh, Addy, I don't know how it happened, that I ended up caring so much. It shouldn't hurt like this, should it? It was only a few short days."

Addy stroked her hair. "Now, now…"

With another shuddering sob, Katie pulled free so she could meet Addy's eyes. "I—I think I love him," she said in terrified wonder. In complete disbelief. "But that can't be, can it? Not after so short a time, not after what happened last night—"

Addy asked the pertinent question. "Who, darling? Who do you love?"

Katie bit her lip. Suddenly she remembered: Caleb's ski resort project. It was so important to him. And this…what had happened, well, this was strictly personal. Between her and Justin. It had nothing to do with Caleb's business. But somehow, at that moment, she feared…

If Caleb found out how deeply Justin had wounded her, how she'd sobbed out her hurt and bewilderment in Addy's arms, he might confront Justin. He might even decide he couldn't allow Justin to be involved in his project.

She hadn't any idea what would happen then—maybe nothing. Or maybe Justin would back out and everything would have to be put on hold.

She didn't want that.

This wasn't about that.

"Addy, you have to promise me that you won't say a word to Caleb. I don't want him upset over this."

"Honey. Say a word about what?"

"You just have to promise me."

Addy's mouth pinched up tight. "It's that Justin Caldwell, isn't it?" When Katie only stared at her, she asked, outraged, "Well, who else could it be?"

Katie looked away.

Addy didn't allow that. "Look at me." Reluctantly, Katie did. Addy said, "It *is* Caldwell, isn't it?"

Katie only shut her eyes and wilted into Addy's arms again.

Addy held on tight. "There, there. Whatever he's done, I can see you're better off without him. You know that, don't you?"

The really awful, hopeless thing was that she didn't know it. She *still* didn't know it—oh, maybe in her head, she did. But not in her shattered heart, where it mattered. Even after he'd made it perfectly clear that she'd better learn to live without him, that he wouldn't be back, her hungry heart refused to believe it.

Somehow, though, she made herself nod against

Addy's shoulder. "Yes. I'm better off. I really am."
She pulled free of Addy's hold again and took the
tissue Addy handed her. She dried her tears and blew
her nose and drew herself up straight. "He broke it
off last night."

"You grew close in the museum?"

"Oh, Addy. It was a beautiful time. I felt as if I
knew him so well. It's so hard to explain. I felt this
powerful connection to him. I was so sure I'd found
the right guy."

"And then, out of nowhere last night, he told you
he wouldn't be seeing you anymore?"

"That's right."

"But why?"

It was the million-dollar question and Katie still
had no answer to it. "He didn't explain."

Addy grunted in pure disgust. "Some other
woman, no doubt."

"No. I really don't think so."

"Then what?"

"He just said it was over."

"But it makes no sense."

"That's what I've been thinking—*all* I've been
thinking. I've been trying to accept the fact that I'll
probably never know why he broke it off. I don't feel
very accepting, though. I really don't." She forced a
wobbly smile. "But, Addy. You're right. I'll be okay.
Eventually. I know I will."

Addy gave her a game grin. "That's the spirit."
Her grin became an angry frown. "And as for that
Caldwell fellow—"

Katie interrupted. "No. Listen. What happened was

strictly personal, between him and me. I shouldn't even have told you.''

''Of course you should have,'' Addy huffed. ''What affects you affects the people who love you. Never forget that.'' Addy sighed and took Katie's hand again, enclosing it between the two of hers. ''Sometimes, when you're suffering terribly, it's hard to keep from cutting yourself off from the people who matter. Promise me you won't do that now.''

There was something in Addy's voice, in her eyes. Something sad. And heavy with regret. Katie had to ask. ''Have you done that? Cut yourself off from the ones who love you? Is that what you're saying?''

Addy patted her hand. ''Am I so obvious?''

''Oh, no. Not at all. But I know you and love you. How you feel doesn't have to be obvious, for me to pick up on it—and it did seem to me as if you were talking about yourself just now.''

There was a moment of silence. Then Addy admitted, ''Well, yes. Maybe I was. I...well, I had a tough time when Riley was born. I almost didn't make it. And then they told me there would be no more children. I came from a big family and I always wanted, oh, ten or twelve or so of my own. I was cut to the heart by the news. I couldn't eat. Couldn't...love my husband. Or my new baby. The doctors said it was a serious case of postpartum depression.''

''But...?''

''I don't know. I think maybe it was the death of my most cherished dream. To have a big family, to someday be surrounded by an adorable crowd of happy grandchildren. It hurt so much to lose that dream, I lost sight of all the wonderful things I *did* have. It was a terrible time. I almost drove Caleb away.''

''Impossible. He loves you so much.''

''I know. But he's a man who needs a lot of attention. You know him, full of life and energy. Always on to the next big plan. He needs a wife to help him live his dreams, a woman who's there, right beside him, while he makes those dreams come true. After Riley was born, I was like a shadow of myself, for much too long. And a man like Caleb can't live with a shadow for a wife. And certainly it wasn't any good for Riley, either. He was an innocent baby, then, a baby who needed his mother's love.''

''But you worked through it.''

''Yes. Barely. I should have reached out. But instead, I disengaged from the two people who needed me the most.'' Addy smoothed a wild strand of Katie's uncombed hair, guiding it back behind her ear. ''Don't make the same mistake yourself. Please.''

''I won't,'' Katie promised. ''But I do need a little time, you know? Addy, I really cared for him. It was sudden, yes. But somehow, being sudden and short-lived doesn't make it any less powerful.''

''I understand. I truly do. Just don't hold it all in. Just remember that we're here, Caleb and Riley and I, any time you need us.''

Addy stayed for lunch. As the two of them fixed sandwiches and heated up some soup, Addy asked more questions. She pressed for specifics about Justin, about what had gone wrong.

But Katie only shook her head. "It's over, that's all. All the little details don't matter." *Except to me.*

She couldn't get Addy to promise not to say anything about Justin to Caleb. "Business is business," Addy said. "But Caleb certainly has a right to know the kind of man he's dealing with."

Katie tried to argue that Addy didn't really know what kind of man Justin was. "You've just been complaining that I haven't told you anything. Remember that. I haven't. I didn't say anything against Justin, and I won't. All you know is there was…something. And now it's over."

"I know that he hurt you, and that's enough for me. Unless you're ready to tell me a little more about what happened?"

It was too much. "Let's just let it go for now. Please."

Addy looked slightly put out, but she did drop the subject. They ate lunch and Addy hung around for an extra cup of hot tea and then said she had to get back to the ranch. "Come for dinner tonight. Let us cheer you up."

"I can't. Not tonight. I need a few days. A little time to myself, to…lick my wounds, I guess. Maybe that's self-indulgent, but—"

"Oh, of course it's not," Addy cut in tartly. "You get through this however you need to. Just remember what I said before. Don't shut us out for *too* long."

"I won't. I promise you."

After Addy left, Katie wandered back upstairs to

her bedroom. She climbed into bed and closed her eyes. Sleep wouldn't come, so she simply lay there, wishing the numbness would return, feeling broken and much, much too sad.

Eventually, she dragged herself from bed, took a shower and forced herself to go out for a walk through Old Town. The snow lay in patches on the wet ground by then. It was hard to believe that it had been a deep, unbroken blanket of white just four days before. She waved at friends and neighbors she saw on the street and even stopped to chat with Emelda, who emerged from Super Savers Mart, the grocery store that had once been known as the Thunder Canyon Mercantile and had been owned and run by the Douglas family for generations.

"Will you look at this weather?" Emelda shifted her bag of groceries to one arm and stuck out the other in a gesture intended to include the wide, sunny sky and the melting patches of snow just beyond the covered sidewalk. "Amazing, isn't it? Snow past my eyeballs one day, dirty patches on the bare ground in no time at all—are you all right, dear? You do look a tad under the weather, and I know you didn't feel all that well last week." She leaned closer to Katie and kept on talking, saving Katie the discomfort of having to answer the question about how she was feeling. "One thing I did like about that nice, deep snow pack. Kept trespassers away from that erosion hole behind my back fence."

The hole in question was a caved-in section of tunnel from Caleb's played out mine, the Queen of Hearts. Riley had seen to boarding it over, but someone kept pushing the boards aside. Probably adventurous kids, Katie thought, kids wanting to holler down the hole and pitch rocks into the dark puddles of stagnant water at the bottom. Emelda worried constantly that someone was going to fall in. She'd called the Thunder Canyon police department more than once to report that she'd spotted trespassers around the hole.

"Those boards were moved again this morning," Emelda reported with a fretful cluck of her tongue. "I hope you'll speak to Riley about it. I worry, I do."

What else could she say? "I'll call Riley today."

"Thank you, dear. It's just that it's so dangerous."

Katie made a few more reassuring noises and then, at last, Emelda toddled off, headed up Pine, toward her tidy little house at the west end of State Street.

Katie walked on, trying to remember to smile and wave when folks said hi, though her mind kept tracking back to last night, to the way Justin had kissed her, so hungrily, as if he would never let her go, the way he had unhooked her bra and cupped her breasts, putting his hot mouth to them, the way his hands had stroked her, the way he'd gathered up her skirt, as if he had to touch her all over or die.

And then, not twenty minutes later, for no reason she could see, he was saying goodbye forever and walking out the door.

None of it was about you. You shouldn't have been involved. What did that *mean?*

You are exactly the woman a man like me never finds....

If she was so special, then *why* had he left her?

I'm not who you think I am....

It made no sense. None of it.

It made no sense and it hurt.

A lot.

When she got home, she resisted the temptation to put on her pj's again and climb back in bed. She went to the kitchen, thinking she'd try focusing on what to have for dinner.

Easily handled. She had plenty of leftovers.

But when she pulled open the refrigerator door and looked at the covered dish full of chicken, at the plastic containers with the salad and potatoes inside, the bittersweet memory of last night overwhelmed her.

She saw him at the sink, scrubbing the potatoes; at the counter, handing her the slotted spoon. She could almost hear their voices, talking of everyday things, could see his smile and the warmth and admiration in his eyes.

Swiftly, before she could feel guilty for wasting good food, she took out the covered dish and the plastic containers and emptied them into the trash.

There. Now didn't that help a lot?

Hardly. Still, she would never eat that food and she was glad it was gone.

And there was still Riley. She'd promised Emelda she'd give him a call, though she didn't really feel like talking to anyone right at that moment. Reluctantly, she dialed his number. His machine picked up and relief flowed through her. She left a quick message about the problem at the erosion hole and hung up. There. She'd kept her word to Emelda and she hadn't had to listen to Riley's dear deep voice, hadn't been faced with the possibility he might pick up on her misery and want to know if something was bothering her.

She went upstairs early and lay in bed forever, pretending to sleep.

Sunday, Addy called after church. "We missed you at the service."

"I just felt like staying home today."

"Honey, now remember what we talked about. You can't let yourself—"

"Addy. It's only been two days."

"I know, I know. I guess I just, well, I want to make things all better."

Katie suppressed a sigh. "You can't. Not right now. I'm okay. Really." As okay as could be expected, anyway, given the circumstances.

"You're right. Of course you're right. I couldn't possibly talk you into coming on out to the ranch for dinner, now could I?"

"Next Friday. How's that?"

"And our usual lunch on Thursday."

"Of course."

"You call me. I mean it. If you need anything."

"Oh, Addy. You make it sound as if I've got some terrible disease."

"Sorry. Remember. I'm here."

Katie almost chuckled. "As if I could forget."

Addy clucked over her and urged her to take care of herself and finally said goodbye.

Katie spent a peaceful day, reading, taking a long

walk, watching television in the evening. She told herself she was feeling better, and she was.

Maybe. In a way.

Monday she went to work at nine, as usual.

Lindy was waiting for her, an avid gleam in her eyes. "Katie. Wow. That Justin Caldwell...total hunk. So did you have a great time Friday night, or what?"

It hurt—that cruel knife, twisting—just to hear his name. "Yes," she said flatly. "Great." And it had been, until the end. "And don't you have work to do?"

Lindy stepped back. "Well, excuse me for breathing."

Katie knew she'd skirted the borderline of rudeness, but somehow, right then, she didn't have it in her to smooth things over. She turned for her workstation in the center of the room.

The whole day, she did her very best to keep her mind on task. Neither Lindy nor Emelda asked if there was anything wrong with her. But she caught both of them looking at her, sideways looks of confusion and concern.

That night, at home, she tried to read, but it was no good. She didn't have the concentration for it, not right then. So she turned on the television and stared at the changing images, hardly aware of what she was watching.

Her mind kept circling back to the central question, kept worrying at it, trying to make sense of it....

Not for another woman. She would have bet every cent she had on that. And not for her money, either.

If it had been about her money, he'd still be there, he wouldn't have left. He'd be busy sweeping her off her feet, getting ready to propose marriage for real, paving the way at a chance for a big payoff when it came time for a divorce.

And if not for another woman, or for the money, then *why?*

She simply could not understand.

Why?

Chapter Thirteen

The meeting of the Thunder Canyon Ski Resort Investor Group was scheduled for ten on Tuesday morning, in the conference room at the back of the project offices on Main Street.

It was to be a strictly routine proceeding. As project manager, Caleb would sit at the head of the table and run the meeting, explaining the current status of the project to any investors who happened to show up. He would list the contractors who would supervise construction and assure everyone that the financing was in order and building would be ready to begin in May, right after the gala groundbreaking ceremonies.

Justin arrived at fifteen before the hour—which was fifteen minutes too early. When it came to dropping bombs, it was always advisable not to hang around the water cooler making casual chitchat beforehand.

The wrong subject might come up. He'd have to evade or lie outright and that could lead to questions he didn't want to answer—at least not before the crucial moment.

No. Better to be right on time, go straight to the conference room, ready to blow them all—Caleb most especially—out of their fat leather chairs.

In the lot behind the town hall, Justin parked and turned off the engine and sat behind the wheel, ready to dig into his briefcase and look busy if anyone noticed him just sitting there.

As he waited, he tried to keep his thoughts where they belonged: on the final stroke ahead. On his payback, at last.

Instead, his mind kept wandering to the one subject he had sworn to himself he would avoid.

Katie.

He stared out the windshield and saw nothing but her face: those wide amber eyes, that soft mouth, the shining brown hair.

She'd be at the library now, wouldn't she? Standing behind that central counter, ready to help any reader who needed to know where to find a certain book. She'd be—

A tapping sound on the driver's door window cut into his self-indulgent reverie. He turned his head.

Caleb. Damn it.

The older man swept off his big white Stetson and signaled with a jerk of his head.

No way to fake being busy now. Justin grabbed his briefcase and got out of the SUV.

"We've got a minute or two before the meeting,"

Caleb said, without any of the back-slapping how-you-been-and-good-to-see-you routine that was his usual style. "I want a word with you."

"What's up?" Alarm bells jangling along every nerve, Justin tried to keep it casual, despite the cold look on Caleb's tanned, creased face.

But even if the silver-haired wheeler-dealer had somehow found out what was up, there wasn't a thing he could do about it now. It was, in the truest sense, a done deal. Justin had the needed proxies in his brief-case and he *would* make his move.

Caleb didn't answer his question. "Let's go inside, to my office."

They went in the back way, Caleb ushering Justin ahead. The door to Caleb's private office stood open and Justin led the way in.

"Have a seat." Caleb shut the door.

Justin stayed on his feet. "Is there a problem?"

Caleb sent the white Stetson flying. It landed on a sofa in the small sitting area. He strode around Justin and pulled out the studded leather chair behind his wide inlaid desk. But he didn't sit down. He moved in front of the chair, pressed his knuckles to the desk-top and loomed toward Justin. "What's this I hear about you breaking my little girl's heart?"

Katie.

Damn it to hell. He should have known. "She... went to you?"

Caleb snorted. It was not a friendly sound. "Hell, no. Adele got it out of her. But it doesn't make a damn how I know. The point is, whatever you thought you were up to with her, you've messed her over and I want to know why."

Justin stared at the stranger who had fathered him. This was exactly the way it was supposed to go.

So why didn't he feel the least bit triumphant? Why didn't he feel righteous and eager to deal the final blow instead of fed up with this whole thing, fed up and sick at heart, an ashy taste in his mouth?

"I asked you a question." Caleb craned farther across the big desk.

The words came to Justin, the ones he'd once imagined himself saying. He went ahead and spoke them. He had nothing else to say. "It's interesting how concerned you are for the tender feelings of your wife's goddaughter, when you never spared a thought for the woman who did nothing wrong but to love you—and bear your son."

Caleb blinked. "Never spared a thought. For Addy? I don't know what the hell you're blathering about."

"You'll understand everything. I promise you. Soon enough."

"I don't know what you think is going on here. But I'll tell you this. You hurt my Katie—for no damn reason that anyone can see. And I'm not going to forget it."

Justin glanced at his Rolex. "Time for the meeting. I think we should go in."

Prior to the formal start of the meeting, the investors milled around, exchanging greetings, while Caleb's secretary bustled up and down the big table, carrying coffee to anyone who asked for it and bringing extra water glasses. A thick blue file imprinted with the ski resort logo of a downhill racer crouched and flying along a snowy slope waited at every seat.

Eventually, Caleb cleared his throat and suggested that everyone sit down. He settled into his seat at the head of the long table and glanced around at the investors. "Well. We have a pretty nice turnout." There were a few empty seats, including the ones that should have been filled by Verlin Parks and Josh Levitt. Verlin and Josh had thirteen and fifteen percent of the project, respectively. With Justin's twenty-six percent, that made a total of fifty-four. Three percent more than he needed, as a matter of fact. Caleb added, "Let's begin."

Up and down the table there were murmurs of agreement.

And so they began.

Caleb led them through the file. He was pleased—though he sent a hard look Justin's way as he said it—to announce that the project was a definite go. The financing was taken care of, and the contractors lined up. Justin sat and pretended to listen. He was only waiting for the proper moment.

Waiting and wishing that he even gave a damn anymore. Longing to get up and walk out and let Caleb have his damn project.

But he didn't get up. He would do what he'd come to do. He would make Caleb Douglas pay in the way that mattered most to him: Justin would take away control.

And *wishing* was an activity for fools, anyway.

He kept having to remind himself of that.

Ever since he'd met a certain amber-eyed brunette who'd made him start *wishing* for what he was never going to have.

Finally, it was time. Caleb asked, "Well, gentlemen. Is there any other business we need to discuss?"

And Justin said, "Yes, as a matter of fact, there is. There's the question of who's going to manage the project."

The room went dead silent—until Caleb boomed out, "What the hell are you talking about? I'm project manager. We're all in agreement on that. I'm listed as manager on the limited partnership contract that everyone here has signed."

There were murmurs and nods down the table.

Justin spoke again. "I have another man in mind. He's got the experience. Much more so than you, Caleb."

Beneath his deep tan, a hot flush rushed up the older man's neck. "I *have* the experience. And I have everyone's support but yours." There were more nods and whispers of agreement. Caleb blustered on, "It's been a given from the first that this was my baby and I would be in charge. The financing was arranged with that understanding. If anyone tries to change horses in midstream, the money could fall through."

Justin didn't waver. "If the current financing becomes a problem, I'll see that we find another lender. It's not going to be a problem. As you just spent an hour telling us, the project is in excellent shape. And as to your holding majority support..." He reached in his briefcase and pulled out the two proxies. He tossed them down on the table. "Joshua Levitt and Verlin Parks are in support of any decision I make. Here are their proxies to prove it."

The flush had left Caleb's face. Now he looked a little green. Justin could see in his eyes that until that moment, he hadn't guessed that Verlin and Josh were longtime business associates of Justin's—or that Justin had sent them in ahead to buy in for specific amounts. Caleb spoke low and furiously. "All right, Caldwell. What the hell is going on?"

Justin only shrugged. "As I said, Verlin and Josh have given me their proxies. I now speak for them. Look the proxies over. Please. You'll see they're in order. Between Parks, Levitt and me, we hold fifty-four percent. More than enough to choose a new project manager—according to the terms of the partnership."

Again, the room was pin-drop silent.

Then Darrell Smart spoke up. "Let's have a look." Darrell was one of Caleb's good buddies, and legal counsel for the project. Justin shoved the proxies toward the lawyer. Smart picked them up and studied them in a silence so total, the crackling of the papers as he handled them sounded loud as gunshots.

Finally, the attorney glanced over the top of his reading glasses at Caleb. "Sorry. Looks in order to me."

Caleb barely seemed to hear him. He was too busy glaring at Justin. Justin could read what he was thinking as if the older man had spoken aloud. *Why are you doing this? What the hell does it prove?*

Justin dealt the telling blow. "All right, then. I

move that we put in my man as manager. Since I hold control of fifty-four percent of this partnership, what I move, goes.'' He granted Caleb a frosty smile. ''And since these offices are part of the project, I'll expect you to turn them over. My man will be here next Monday, ready to get to work.''

There was some discussion—heated, but pointless. In the end, everyone conceded that Justin had the power to bring in his own manager. Caleb was finished as project head.

Finally, after sending Justin lethal looks and offering regrets to the by-then silent Caleb for the dirty trick that had been played on him, the others filed out.

Caleb remained in his chair, his gray head lowered, as the others took their leave. His left arm lay lax on the tabletop, his thick gold wedding ring gleaming in the shaft of winter sunlight that slanted in the room's one tall, narrow window.

Finally, it was just the older man, slumped in his big chair, Justin, still seated in his, and the secretary.

''Alice, you can go now,'' Caleb said quietly, not bothering to glance up. The secretary, looking wide-eyed behind her thick glasses, rose. ''Shut the door on the way out, will you?''

Alice did as she was told, pulling the door quietly closed as she left.

There was a long moment where Caleb simply sat there, head lowered as before, arm still outstretched on the table, wedding ring catching the light, giving back that eerie gleam.

Eventually, he rested his other arm beside the first, folded his beefy hands together and lifted his head. His green eyes had a lost look in them, one of shock and dazed confusion. He said one word. "Why?"

The question echoed in the silent room.

And Justin had his answer ready. "Because being the big dog, running everything in sight—that's what matters to you the most. I wanted to take away something you'd miss. And I have, haven't I?"

Caleb still wasn't satisfied. "Why?" he asked again. "Why would you want that? What the hell have I ever done to you?"

Justin reached in his briefcase again and brought out an envelope. From the envelope, he removed two snapshots. He pushed his chair back, rose to walk down the table and stood over the other man.

Shoving the ski resort file aside, he laid the pictures down, one beside the other, in front of Caleb. He pointed. "That's my mother, thirty-five years ago, before she met you."

Caleb stared down at the old, dog-eared snapshot. "Ramona…" It came out a bare husk of sound.

Relentless now, determined to finish this and get out, Justin pointed at the other picture. "That one was taken a month before she died. She came to me, returned to Montana at the end, so I could take care of her, when it was too late for anything else—too late for you to do anything to her that cancer wasn't going to do, anyway. She doesn't look much like the woman you knew, does she?"

Caleb raised his eyes then. He'd moved beyond dazed confusion. Now he looked like a man who'd seen a ghost—which, in a way, Justin supposed, he had. His face had a gray cast beneath the tan. "But…her last name was Lovett."

"That's right. But after you told her you wanted nothing more to do with her—or the baby you'd made with her—she left the state, just the way you wanted her to. She left Montana and she never returned until she knew she was dying. When she left, she took the name Caldwell. She went by that name for the rest of her life. She put it on my birth certificate. So that's who I am."

Caleb shut his eyes and slowly opened them. "You're…my son." He said it in a kind of horrified understanding. "My son…"

"By blood, yes. By blood only. You broke her, do you know that? She never could make a real life for herself, after what you did to her, after you threatened to do her serious damage if she ever came near you again, if she ever dared to let anyone know whose child she was carrying."

Caleb jerked back as if Justin had struck him. "No. You've got it—"

Justin cut the air with an arm, a brutal, final gesture. "I don't want to hear it."

"But you have to listen for a moment. You have to let me—"

"That's where you're wrong. I don't have to listen to you. Who are you to me, besides the man who destroyed the woman who gave me life, the woman who raised me the best she knew how?" He scooped up the two snapshots and turned for the door, stopping before he went out to deliver one last command.

"Clear out your office. My man will be in Monday morning, nine sharp."

Chapter Fourteen

Katie's phone rang at nine Tuesday night. She picked up the remote extension and checked the display before she answered it: Addy.

"No, thanks. Not right now," she muttered, and let her machine get it. She settled back in her favorite chair, and heard the sound of Addy's voice coming from the kitchen, as she recorded her message.

Katie couldn't make out the words, but there was something in the tone, something agitated. Something not right.

With a sigh, she picked it up. "Addy? Are you okay?"

"Oh, thank God."

Whatever it was, it wasn't good. Grim images invaded Katie's mind: Riley, in an accident. Caleb having a heart attack. "What? What's the matter?"

"Darling, it's Caleb."

She felt a hollowness below her ribs. "Has he been hurt?"

"Not physically. No. It's nothing like that. He... Well, he's locked himself in his study. He's been in there since noon. Nine hours. He won't come out and he won't let anyone else in."

"But why?"

"Sweetheart, if I only knew. I called Riley over here a couple of hours ago, when I couldn't get Caleb to open the door myself. Riley's tried. Caleb wouldn't let him in, either. Honey, it's just not like him. He came home from that meeting and he walked right by me. He looked so awful. Not sick, exactly. But sick at heart. Kind of beaten down and gray in the face, his shoulders slumped and sagging. I asked him what was wrong, but he only shook his head and headed for his study."

"Addy, what meeting?"

"The one for the ski resort project."

"Something bad happened at the meeting?"

"Well, if it did, he's just not acting his usual self over it. You know how he is. When things don't go his way, he paces. He gets loud and he lays down the law. But he never locks himself in a room somewhere and refuses to come out. Plus, I'm sure he's drinking. The times he barked at me through the door to go away, he was slurring his words."

"Have Riley call someone who was at the meeting and ask them what went on there."

"Oh, honey. Yes. Good idea." Katie heard her

speaking to Riley. Then she came back on the line. "All right. Riley's taking care of that."

"I'll be over as soon as I can get there."

"Darling, would you? I'm so worried. And you know how he adores you. Maybe he'll open that door for you."

Addy greeted her at the front door, her face drawn, eyes grim with worry. She helped Katie out of her coat and hung it in the front closet of the huge two-story foyer as she blurted out what she knew. "Riley got through to Darrell Smart. At the meeting, Justin Caldwell took the job of project manager away from Caleb."

Katie's heart lurched. "Justin...but how?"

"Oh, it was something about proxies. And percentages of the partnership. Somehow, that Caldwell fellow got control over enough of the investors to be able to kick Caleb out. Caleb has until Monday to vacate the offices so the new man can take over."

Could this really be happening? Justin. Breaking her heart, then stealing Caleb's dream.

The question was there again, echoing through her mind. She said it out loud that time. "Why would he do such a thing?"

"I haven't the foggiest. But if that man were in this room right now, I'd go get Caleb's best hunting rifle and shoot him straight through his evil heart. What did Caleb ever do to him, that he would treat my husband so shabbily—and for that matter, what did *you* ever do to him?" Addy answered her own questions. "Nothing. Absolutely nothing, that's what.

And now Riley's in a fury over it. He's insisting he's going to Bozeman to confront Caldwell. Oh, I don't know where we're headed, I don't know what to do."

Katie took the older woman by the upper arms, to steady her. "Slow down. We're going to get to the bottom of this, I promise you."

"Oh, Katie. I'm sorry to drag you into this, but I must admit, I'm so relieved you're here. I'm…well, I'm just a wreck."

Katie pulled her close and hugged her hard, then she took her arms again and met her eyes. "First, I'll talk to Riley, get him to slow down a little. And then we'll see if I can get Caleb to let me in."

Katie found Riley in Caleb's den, off the study, pacing back and forth. He was hot under the collar and far from willing to slow down.

"Good. You're here," he said at the sight of her. "Look after Mom, will you? I'm heading for Bozeman."

Katie grabbed one of his big, tanned hands and wouldn't let go. "Please. Let me try to talk to Caleb first. Let me see if I can find out what's really happened here."

Riley's green eyes shone hard as emeralds. "I know what's happened. That bastard worked you over, and now he's done this. If there's a reason he's decided to come after my family, I want to find out what it is."

So, Katie thought glumly. Riley knew about her and Justin, too. She supposed she shouldn't be surprised. Adele had never agreed not to tell Caleb. And once Caleb knew, Riley was bound to hear. "We all want answers." She squeezed Riley's hand between both of hers. "I beg you. Give me a chance to get to the bottom of this first. Then, if you still think you have to, you can go deal with Justin."

Riley made a low, angry sound. "Face it. Dad's not letting you through that door."

"Just give me a chance. Please."

Riley swore low. "All right. But if he won't let you in, I'm out of here."

"Thank you."

"No reason to thank me. He's not letting you in."

She gave his hand one more reassuring squeeze and then relinquished it.

Riley gestured at the shut door to the study. "Go for it." He stood back and folded his muscular arms over his broad chest, his mouth set in a grim line.

Riley was probably right. If Caleb wouldn't open the door for his wife or his son, there was no reason to believe he'd let Katie in, either. But she had to try. She didn't like the look in Riley's eyes. If Riley took off after Justin now, who could say what might happen when the two met up. One of them—or both—could get hurt. She didn't want that. Not for Riley. And, God help her, not for Justin, either.

She marched over, raised her hand and rapped sharply on the door.

Nothing. Complete silence from the room beyond. She glanced back at Riley. He still had his arms folded over his chest—and an I-told-you-so look in his eyes. She tried the door: locked.

Riley muttered, "See, I told—"

Katie put up a hand to silence him and called to the man on the other side of the door. "Caleb. It's me, Katie. Won't you let me in, please?"

Dead silence from beyond the door. Riley uncrossed his arms. "That does it. I'm—"

"Wait." She pressed her ear to the door, heard heavy footsteps on the other side. She put up her hand again, for Riley to be still.

The footsteps stopped. Caleb spoke from right beyond the door. "Katie? That you?"

"Yes. Oh, yes. It's me."

"Katie, I don—" He didn't seem to know how to go on. And Adele had been right. It sounded as if he'd been drinking. His words came slow and slurred-sounding.

"Oh, Caleb. Won't you let me in?"

Another pause, then Caleb growled, "Riley still out there?"

She glanced at Riley again. He looked as if he wanted to break something, to pick up one of the bronze cowboy sculptures that decorated the den and hurl it at the wood-paneled wall. "Yes. He's here."

"Tell him to go 'way. Can't talk to 'im now. Only you, Katie. Jus' you, 'kay?"

Riley muttered more swear words. Katie only looked at him, pleading with her eyes.

With another low, furious oath, Riley strode from the room.

"Katie?" Caleb asked again.

"It's all right. Riley's left. Now, won't you please let me in?"

Almost before she finished asking the question, the door swung inward.

She gasped at the sight of the man on the other side. "Oh, Caleb..." His green eyes were droopy and bloodshot. His mouth hung lax. He looked a decade older than the last time she'd seen him. And the smell of too much Tennessee whisky came off him in waves.

He gave her the saddest, most hangdog sort of look, and then he turned and trudged to his wide burled walnut desk and around to the back of it. With a heavy grunt, he dropped into his studded buckskin swivel chair and stared down at the papers spread on the desktop in front of him. A telltale half-empty bottle of whisky stood uncapped at his elbow. "I been...busy. Thinkin'. Thinkin' and drinkin'..." He looked up, let out a low, rough bark of humorless laughter, and then leaned back in the chair. His chin drooped on his chest. He gazed mournfully at the scatter of papers in front of him. "How, I keep askin' mysel'...how did it all go so wrong...?" Behind him, a picture hung askew on the wood-paneled wall, revealing his private safe, the door to which stood open. All the blinds were drawn and the only light came from the lamp on Caleb's desk.

Katie hovered before him, a million dismayed questions spinning through her mind. She pressed her mouth shut and kept quiet. She knew, in the end, he would tell her what she needed to know. There was no other reason for him to have let her in here when he refused to open the door to Adele or to Riley.

He *wanted* to talk. And he'd chosen her to do his

talking to. It was only a matter of waiting and listening—and applying gentle pressure at the right moment.

Gingerly, she lowered herself to one of the two carved, leather-seated guest chairs that faced the big desk. Once she was in the chair, she realized she'd been holding her breath. She let it out with great care.

Caleb shook his head. "Katie, Katie, Katie. Where the hell did it all go so wrong?" He raised his hanging head enough that she could look into those bleary eyes.

"Tell me," she said softly. "Just tell me. Everything. And then we can talk about what to do next."

He kept shaking his head. "Bad idea. To tell you. Yeah. Pro'ly a bad idea…"

"Just tell me. We can't work this out until you do."

"Hell. I don't know…"

"Oh, yes, you do. You know. It's time to talk about it—whatever it is."

"Maybe."

"Uh-uh. No maybes. It's time. You know it is."

He regarded her woozily. She looked back at him, waiting.

At last, haltingly, he began to speak. "I was…a true husban'. I swear it to you. Never looked at another woman…"

Suddenly she was recalling what Addy had told her a few days before and prompted gently, "But then Riley was born…"

He grunted. "Tha's right. Riley. Af'er Riley was born, they tol' Adele she couldn't have any more chil'ren. It broke her heart. Lo's o' kids. She always wanted that. For the longes' time, she was...like a stranger in our house...in our bed. She jus' ignored me. An' Riley, too. Poor little fella. He was cryin' all the time. I couldn'...take it. It got so I, well, I jus' needed someone.''

He said he'd met Ramona one night when he went out to a roadhouse to get his mind off his vacant-eyed wife and their poor, screaming baby. ''Ramona was a waitress. A tall, black-haired beauty.'' He heaved a heavy sigh. ''Ramona. Damn my soul. Ramona.''

For over an hour, his voice low and whisky-rough, the words sometimes slurring together, he told her the sad story of his own folly and betrayal. When the tale was told, Katie sat silent, hardly able to believe what she'd just heard.

Justin was Caleb's son. His *son*.

Suddenly, everything was making sense. A hideous, awful, ugly kind of sense, but sense nonetheless.

Caleb threw out a hand—missing the whisky bottle by an inch. In a sweeping, unsteady gesture, he indicated the papers scattered on his desk. ''I's all here. Righ' here...you jus' see for yourself.''

Katie stood and bent over the desk.

''See. Look here.'' He waved a snapshot. ''Ramona an' me.'' He dropped the picture and picked up what looked like a letter. ''Her love letters. She wro'e me a hundred of 'em. Sen' 'em here, to the house. Addy never knew. She wasn' up for checkin' the mail. She jus' stayed in our room, then. Alone. I hardly saw her. Ramona wro'e me, love letters first.

And then there were the ones that came later, the ones with the threats.'' He scanned the desk and snatched up a small scrap of paper. ''An' this. The check I gave 'er. Jus' like I tol' you, cancelled. See?''

Katie took it from his fingers. ''Yes. I see.'' It came to her, right then, as she stared at all those zeroes. She knew what she had to do.

''I—I did care for her, for Ramona,'' Caleb muttered. ''But...she wasn' Addy. Addy is...my love, my life. Never should have started up with Ramona. I know it, I do. And then, well, after Ramona disappeared, Addy got better. The years went by an'...I started thinkin' it was maybe for the bes', jus' to let it be, not go stirrin' up ol' trouble.''

A large yellow envelope lay at the edge of the desk. Katie took it and dropped the cancelled check into it. Then she gathered up the letters and the photographs and put them in the envelope, too.

''What d'you think you're doin'?'' Caleb demanded.

She hooked the envelope's metal clasp. ''I'm taking these to Justin.''

He regarded her blearily. ''Wha' for?''

''Because he doesn't know the whole truth, and it's time he did.''

Caleb rubbed his eyes. ''Hell. What good's that gonna do now?'' He was shaking his head again. ''No point. Too late.''

''Caleb,'' she said softly. ''It's never too late to do the right thing.'' Turning, she set the envelope on her chair, then she went around the desk and put her hand on Caleb's sagging shoulder.

He looked up at her, a lost look. "I...don' know what to do."

She squeezed his shoulder. "First, and foremost, you have to remember that Adele loves you. And, though I know you've had your rough patches, Riley loves you, too."

"They'll hate me. After this."

"No," she said firmly. "They love you. I'm not saying it will be easy, getting past this. You've done wrong. Very wrong. Not only because you betrayed your wife, but also because of the way you handled it when Ramona told you she was having your baby. But now you've got to clean up the mess you made, as best you can. You've got to tell Adele everything. You've got to take the first steps toward making things right."

"Oh, no. I can't." His head hung down again.

"Look at me," she commanded. Slowly, he raised his bloodshot eyes. "Caleb, you can't let this break you, can't let the bad things you did once destroy your family now."

"But I—"

"No buts. It's the only way."

He tried to bluster. "I didn' let you in here so you could tell me what to do."

"Yes, you did. That's exactly why you let me in here."

He let out a hard breath that reeked of too much whisky. "Oh, no..."

"Oh, yes. You need to do the right thing and you know it. You let me in here so I could help you to do it." She touched his silver hair, pressed his shoulder again. "I'm going to go get Addy now. And you're going to tell her. Everything."

He said nothing and she figured that was acceptance enough. She turned for the door.

"Katie?"

She glanced back at his hangdog face, his haunted eyes. "You're a good girl, my bes' girl."

"I love you, too. Put the cap on that bottle. I'll be right back."

A half an hour later, Riley walked her to her Suburban. She had the envelope in hand, Justin's home address and phone number scrawled across the front of it.

"Thanks," Riley said, and gave her a hug.

"Any time." She hugged him back, good and hard.

When he pulled away, he looked doubtful. "You sure you don't want me to go with you, to see Caldwell?"

"Nope. I'll be fine."

"Damn." He raked a hand back through his dark hair. "What a mess, huh? And I've got a half brother…"

"Yes. You do."

"That'll be something to get used to—after I get through telling Dad just what I think of him."

She suggested gently, "Wait 'til he's sober. For tonight, Addy's going to need your strong shoulder to lean on once she's through dealing with Caleb."

Riley swore. "At least what Caldwell did to Dad is more understandable now. If I were in his position, I might have done a lot worse." He scowled. "But there's still no excuse for what he did to you. I could bust his face in for that.''

She put her hand on his arm. ''No need to go hitting anyone. I can handle this. You watch me.''

He almost grinned. ''You know, I believe that you can.'' He chucked her under the chin. ''You're a tough little tenderfoot.''

''That's me. Tough as they come.''

He grew more serious. ''When will you go?''

She looked up into his face and for the first time, she saw the resemblance to Justin. In the shape of his brow and the strong, aggressively masculine jut of his jaw. So strange. Why hadn't she noticed before?

Riley was frowning. ''Katie. You okay?''

She drew herself up. ''I'm fine. And I'm going to go see Justin right now. It'll be near midnight when I get there. I'm figuring that's late enough on a weeknight he'll probably be at his house.'' Plus, if she went right away, there was less of a chance she'd lose her nerve.

Riley gave her a sideways look. ''You sure about this?''

''Riley, he needs to know and, given the circumstances, I think I'm the best one to tell him.''

Justin was sitting in his study at the front of the house when the doorbell rang.

His laptop waited, open and ignored, on the desk before him. His mind was far away from the spreadsheet on the screen, stuck on a brown-haired woman and a silver-haired man and why he didn't feel the sense of triumph and vindication he'd always expected to feel after finally making his move.

The doorbell chimed and Justin ignored it.

He wasn't expecting anyone; he didn't want to see anyone—and anybody who came ringing his bell at midnight could damn well go away and come back at a decent hour.

But then, a minute later, the doorbell rang again. "Get lost," he muttered, and stared blindly at the computer screen in which he had no interest at all.

But then it rang a third time.

That did it. He swore, low and crudely, and pushed himself to his feet. Whoever was out there was going to get an earful.

He strode, fast, through the door to his study and across the hardwood floor of the entry hall. When he got to the door, he flung it wide.

"Hello, Justin."

The breath fled his lungs. He felt as if an iron hand had just punched him a good one square in the solar plexus. He blinked and stepped back. "Katie."

"May I come in?"

"What—?"

She cut him off, sweetly but firmly. "I said, may I come in?"

He fell back another step. He just wasn't getting this. What reason could she possibly have to seek him out now?

It made no sense. Katie, here. At his door.

And still, though it gained him nothing but more pain, he couldn't help drinking in the sight of her, of her shining hair and angel's face, of the grim set to her soft mouth and the strange, determined gleam in those beautiful brown eyes. The scent of her taunted him—warm and temptingly sweet.

Katie. All his senses seemed to call out her name.

"I'll take that as a yes." She stepped over the threshold. She had a big envelope in one hand. She waved it at him. "I have a few things I need to say to you. Is there somewhere we can talk?"

Quelling the urge to sputter out more exclamations of disbelief that she was standing right there, in front of him, he muttered, "Yeah. All right."

She slipped out of her coat, switching the envelope from hand to hand as she shrugged free of the sleeves.

"Here." He reached for it.

But she held on. "No. I'll keep it. This shouldn't take long."

The more he looked at her, the more certain he was that he didn't like the strange gleam in her eyes.

But why should he like it? No way she'd come here to tell him she loved him and couldn't live without him.

Any chance he'd had for that, he'd blown Friday night—and doubly, at the meeting fourteen hours before. Which meant it was going to be something he didn't want to hear.

Might as well get it over with. "Suit yourself." He turned on his heel. "This way."

He led her to the great room at the back of the house, where the ceiling soared up two stories high and two walls of windows looked out on the night. She perched on a chair in one of the sitting areas and folded her coat in her lap. He hovered a few feet from her.

"Please," she said. "Sit down."

He wanted to refuse, felt he'd be better off to stay on his feet. But she looked up at him, mouth set, amber eyes afire with a steely sort of purpose. He gave in and dropped into the chair across from her.

She bit her lip. "I...hardly know where to begin."

He said nothing. It was her damn show, after all.

She sat up straighter and cleared her throat. "Okay. To start, I know about what you did to Caleb this— or rather yesterday—morning. I also know why, at last. I know that you're his son, that he had an affair with your mother when Addy suffered a serious bout of depression after Riley was born. Caleb couldn't take it, watching Addy suffer—her continued rejection of him. He met your mother and they had an affair."

Impatience curled through Justin, coiling like a spring. He wanted her out of there. Every moment in her presence brought it more clearly home to him that he had lost her.

Hell, lost her? He'd never *had* her.

And he never would.

He demanded, "Is there some reason you imagined I needed—much less, *wanted*—to hear all this?"

Her sweet mouth got a pinched look about it. "Be a little patient. Please. I'm getting to the part you need to know."

"Speed it up."

She outright glared at him. "Fine," she said. "It went like this. Caleb and your mother had an affair.

When your mother got pregnant, Caleb told her he did care for her, but he still loved Adele. He wouldn't marry your mother, but he offered to give her a half million dollars. For you.''

He couldn't stay in his seat. He shot to a standing position. ''That's ridiculous. It never happened.''

A hot flush flowed up her neck and over her soft cheeks. ''Will you let me finish?''

He turned from her, stared at his own shadowed reflection in the dark window opposite where she sat. ''Make it fast.''

She picked up the pace, each word emerging clipped and cold. ''Caleb offered your mother five hundred thousand dollars if she'd give you up, if she'd give you to him—so he and Adele could raise you. Somehow, he hoped to make Adele understand and accept you into their family. It might even have worked. Addy wanted more children so badly.''

He whirled on her. ''So what? It doesn't matter. My mother turned him down and then he started threatening her. She had to run away.''

''No. She didn't turn him down. And she was the one who made the threats.''

He refused to believe that. ''No.''

''Yes. She threatened all sorts of wild things—to kill Adele, to kill Riley. To tell the world that she was carrying Caleb's child and what a rotten bastard he was. But then, in the end, she agreed to Caleb's terms. She took the check.'' He was shaking his head, but Katie just went on talking. ''She took the check when she was eight months along. But instead of sticking around to give you to Caleb when you were born, she ran off. She cashed that check. And she raised you on her own—just as you told me she did, always moving from one place to another, keeping ahead of any chance that Caleb might find her—and you.''

"No.''

She threw the envelope on the table between them. ''It's all in there. Her threatening letters, what Caleb offered, what she refused—and then eventually accepted. There's even the cancelled check for a half million dollars, complete with her endorsement on the back.''

''No. I don't believe you.'' He glared down at her.

And her face softened, suddenly, with something that might have been pity. ''It's all there. Look it over. Come to grips with the truth.'' She stood. ''We can all use a little more truth around here, and that's a plain fact. And the truth is, your mother took Caleb's money and she ran off. Where do you think she got the start-up funds for those businesses you mentioned to me once—you know, the ones that failed?''

''No,'' he said. Again. He couldn't say it enough. ''No, no...''

Katie refused to back down. ''I'm sorry, Justin. I truly am. Sorry for you, for what you've become. I think, if there's ever going to be any hope for you, you're going to have face what your mother did. And accept it. You're going to have to admit how angry you are at her. Because I know, just from the few things you said to me about her, that she made your childhood a living hell.''

It wasn't her fault, he thought, as he'd been think-ing for his whole life. *She did the best she could....*

Too bad his old excuses for the woman who'd raised him rang so hollow now.

And Katie wasn't finished. "What Caleb did was wrong. All wrong. Using your mother, and then trying to buy her off, to cut her out of your life, to take you away from her. He was so wrong. And now he's pay-ing for it. But don't imagine he didn't want you. Don't even try to tell yourself he walked away from *you.* He would have claimed you, would have possi-bly lost Adele for your sake, would have taken the chance of putting Riley's childhood in jeopardy, if your mother had kept her end of their bargain."

Justin couldn't stay upright. He sank to a chair, muttered, one last time, "No. It can't be...."

"Justin. It *is.*"

He stared up at her—at the matchless woman he'd lost to his own blindness and pride. Right then, as he began to fully understand the depths to which he'd sunk, his mother's words came to him.

When I'm gone, you'll get your chance to make it all right.

He saw it all then, in a blinding burst of terrible clarity that had his stomach churning, and acid rising to his throat: the truth Katie spoke of.

He'd made nothing right. He'd only made a bad situation worse.

Yes. Katie was right. His anger with his mother went deeper than he'd ever realized.

But that anger was nothing against how much he was finding he despised himself.

"Go," he said. "Please. Go now."

Katie looked uncertain. A miracle, that woman. *His*
miracle, lost forever to him now. He saw in her sweet
face that, in spite of everything, she was afraid. For
him.

He sat up straighter. "I'm not going to do anything...drastic. I'm going to sit here and read over the
stuff in this envelope. I'm going to think about what
you've said to me. I need to do that alone."

She swallowed. "All right, then. You may not believe this. But I do wish you well. And I hope that,
somehow, you'll find a way to make peace. With
Caleb. And with your mother's memory."

He forced a twisted smile. "Goodbye, Katie."

A shudder went through her. But she lifted her head
high. "Yes. All right. Goodbye."

Chapter Fifteen

The next day, Justin Caldwell did something he'd never before done in his adult life. He called his office and said he had personal business to see to and he wouldn't be in.

Strange, now he thought of it. He really didn't have a personal life to speak of. He could think of only one other time when he might have needed a personal day and that was when his mother died.

But as it turned out, Ramona had died on a Saturday afternoon, so Justin had his "personal" days on the weekend and showed up at the office at nine Monday morning.

This time, the personal business in question consisted mostly of wandering around in his bathrobe, reading and rereading the letters in the envelope Katie had left with him—reading the letters and staring at the photographs of his father and mother, together.

And occasionally, picking up that cancelled check with his mother's signature on the back of it and wondering...

At his blind, thoughtless and pigheaded father.

At the selfish vengefulness of his mother.

Really, when it came down to it, blood did tell. Hadn't their son turned out to be all those things?

Blind, thoughtless, pigheaded, selfish—and vengeful.

Justin Caldwell. Biggest SOB on the planet, bar none.

The question now was: what the hell could he do about that?

All day long, wandering around his gorgeous, empty house in his bathrobe, he pondered that question. All day long, and into the evening.

It was a little after seven and he was starting to think that maybe he should make himself go into the kitchen and microwave something to put in his stomach, when the doorbell rang.

Katie...

His pulse started racing and his heart did something acrobatic inside his chest.

But the thrill quickly faded. It wouldn't be her. It *couldn't* be her. It was over between them. He knew it. At least in his mind. Over time, he hoped the rest of him—body, heart, soul—would learn to accept it.

Shaking his head at his own foolish yearning, he got up and went to the door.

"Mr. Caldwell. How are you?" Josiah Green stuck out a hand.

Baffled, Justin took it. They shook. "Er. What can I do for you?"

Green took in Justin's unshaved face and the bathrobe he'd never gotten around to changing out of. "Oh, my. I see I've come at an inopportune time."

It was the perfect excuse—but for some weird reason, Justin didn't take it. "Come on in."

After a moment's hesitation, Green came through the door and Justin shut it behind him. The tall, somber fellow wore a long black coat over what appeared to be the same ministerial black getup he'd worn the day Justin and Katie exchanged their fake vows. "Well. Can I take your coat?"

"Thank you." He had an envelope in his hand— an envelope like the one Katie had brought the night before. Bizarre. "Hold this, please."

Justin took the envelope and Green removed his coat and laid it over one of the two entrance hall chairs. When Justin tried to hand the envelope back, Green put up a lean, long-fingered hand. "No. That's yours."

"I don't understand."

"Ahem. Well. We shall get to it." Weirder by the minute. Green said, "Right now, I'd so enjoy a cup of nice, hot coffee."

Justin blinked. "Coffee."

"Yes. Please." Green gave him a tight little smile.

"Uh. Well, okay. This way."

They proceeded to the kitchen, where Justin set the envelope on the table and Green took a seat.

"I'll just get the coffee going."

"Bless you."

While the coffee dripped, they spoke of the weather—the warming trend had ended; snow was predicted for tomorrow—and of how Green admired Justin's lovely home.

"And, may I ask," the older man inquired with some delicacy, "where is your charming bride?"

Katie.

Didn't he have it bad enough, trying not to think of her, without some crazy old guy showing up at his door and asking where she was? He peered more closely at the old guy in question. "I have one question."

"Certainly. Ask away."

"What's going on here?"

Green did a little throat-clearing. "Well. Sadly, I must inform you that, while you and your bride are married in the eyes of Our Lord, the state of Montana has its own rules."

"Rules?" Justin repeated, for lack of anything better to say. He sincerely was not following.

Green tapped the envelope. "I've brought you your marriage license. I'm afraid I was somewhat remiss when I stepped forward to lead you through your vows a week ago last Saturday."

"Uh. Remiss?"

Green chided, "It appears the two of you never applied for this license. When I attempted to file it, I was told they had no record of your application. Nowadays, I regret to inform you, the blessing of a man of God is simply not enough."

Without a doubt. Weirder by the minute. "You mean you actually are…a minister?"

Green snapped his thin shoulders back. "Well, of course I'm a minister."

Justin put up a hand. "Look. Sorry."

"Ahem. Well. All right, then. Your apology is graciously accepted."

"Thanks. But I thought you understood. That 'wedding' was a reenactment. It wasn't—"

"There are no reenactments in the eyes of heaven," Green cut in reprovingly before Justin could finish. "One does. Or one doesn't. You did. So don't mistake me, young man, Katherine *is* your wife in the eyes of the Lord, and those eyes, as you should very well know, are the ones that truly matter. Ahem." He frowned. "Now, where was I?"

As if Justin had a clue. "Something about applying for a license, I think…."

"Yes. Well, and that is the crux of it. You and Katherine must go immediately to the county clerk's office and apply for a valid license, then the marriage can be resolemnified and all will be well. I will be pleased to perform the ceremony for you, if you would like me to do so. But any ordained minister will certainly suffice. Legally, you can simply say your vows at the courthouse, if that's your bent." Green put a dark emphasis on the word, *bent,* making it crystal clear that he felt all marriages should be *solemnified* by a man of God.

And Justin hadn't the faintest idea what to say to all this. It seemed to him that the old guy might be a little off in the head—in a harmless sort of way. So he simply announced, "Coffee's ready."

"Wonderful. Two sugars. No cream."

Fifteen minutes later, after handing Justin a card, "In case you should wish to request my services for the ceremony," Green put on his big, black coat and went out the door.

He left the envelope on the kitchen table.

Justin tried to ignore it. But it was like his mother's letters, like the photographs of her and Caleb, like that damn cancelled check.

The envelope on the kitchen table would not be ignored.

He microwaved some canned spaghetti and sat at the table to eat it, his gaze tracking to the waiting envelope after every bite.

Finally, muttering a string of very bad words, he pushed his plate away and grabbed the damn thing.

He pulled out the license and stared down at it. "Katie…" he whispered to the empty room. With a shaking finger, he traced the letters in her name. "I love you."

He said the three impossible words and he knew they were true.

Out of all the lies, all the dirty tricks, out of everything he'd done so very wrong.

This one truth remained.

He loved Katie Fenton.

He loved her.

It was all wrong and it was too late.

But that didn't change the basic truth.

He loved Katie.

And now it was up to him do what he could—though it would never be enough—to make the wrongs he'd done right.

He loved Katie, and... Nothing he could say
somehow it was... to him, do what he could...
though he would... never... he counted... to... find's the
wrong he'd deliberately...

Chapter Sixteen

At eight-thirty on Monday morning, Justin entered the Thunder Canyon Ski Resort Project offices through the front door.

He found Caleb's secretary standing behind her desk in the reception area, packing a large cardboard box. She glanced up and gasped.

He tried a friendly smile. "Alice, isn't it?"

Alice didn't smile back. Instead, in a clear attempt to show the evil man before her exactly how she felt about the current situation, she adjusted her thick-lensed glasses more firmly on the bridge of her pointed nose and dropped a bronze paperweight into the box—hard. "We have until nine," she announced loftily. "Certainly you can wait until then."

He spoke gently. "Alice. You were never asked to leave."

"I prefer *Ms.* Pockstead—and I'm Mr. Douglas's assistant. He goes, I go."

Justin nodded. "Ms. Pockstead, I completely understand." He waited while she threw a stapler and a red coffee mug with dancing white hearts on it into the box. Then he cautiously cleared his throat. She sent him a hot glare. "What *is* it?"

"I wonder, is Caleb in?"

For that, he got another gasp of outrage and a tightly muttered, "The unmitigated nerve of some people..." She tossed some pencils and a ruler in the box, simmering where she stood.

Justin moved a step closer and injected a note of command into his next question. "I asked you, is he in?"

Ms. Pockstead picked up a letter opener and stabbed the air in the direction of the hallway that led to Caleb's private office. "See for yourself."

"Thank you."

She muttered something. It wasn't, *You're welcome.*

The door to Caleb's office stood slightly ajar. Justin hesitated in front of it. There was silence from inside the room beyond.

But he couldn't stand there forever. With some reluctance, he lifted a hand and tapped lightly.

"What the hell now?" grumbled the gruff voice from the other side. "It's open."

Justin flattened his palm against the door and pushed it inward.

Caleb sat at his desk surrounded by open, half-packed boxes. He appeared, at the moment, to be doing nothing about filling them.

He glanced up. Something sparked in his eyes—and then went cold. ''Justin.''

''Hello, Caleb.''

They regarded each other. Justin had no idea what, exactly, he should say. He got the impression Caleb was having the same problem.

Finally, Caleb put out a hand at the guest chairs facing the desk. ''Sit. If you've a mind to.''

It seemed like as good a suggestion as any. Justin strode over, moved a box to the floor, and took one of the chairs.

They looked at each other some more. Eventually, Caleb inclined his head at the boxes surrounding him. ''Sitting down on the job, I'm afraid. But I'm working on it.''

How to begin, Justin was thinking.

Hell. *Where* to begin…

Caleb must have been pondering the same questions, because, again, he spoke first. ''Katie said she told you…everything.''

Justin found the best he could manage right then was a nod.

Caleb nodded, too. A lot of nodding going on. Oh, yeah. They were a couple of nodding fools.

Caleb said, ''Well, then. It's all out in the open.'' He grunted. ''I have to keep reminding myself how that's good. I…'' He paused, seeming to seek the right words. Evidently he found them, or close enough. He said, ''I understand now, why you did what you did at the meeting last week. Given the circumstances, I've got no damn problem with it.'' He raised both hands, indicating the office—the whole ski resort project. ''In a half an hour or so, it's all yours.'' Justin started to speak, but Caleb cut him off before he got a word out. ''What you did to Katie, though. No damn excuse for that.''

''I know,'' Justin said.

Caleb stared at him, narrowed-eyed. And then he grunted again. ''Hope you do. You threw away a good one. The very best, as a matter of fact.''

''You don't have to tell me.''

''Hell. I guess I don't. I can see it in your eyes.'' He sat back. ''You love my girl, don't you?''

Justin reminded himself that he was through with lies. He gave Caleb the painful truth. ''Yes. I do. I love her.''

Caleb pondered that for a moment, then he shrugged. ''Well. Evidently you're not as big of a fool as I'd been thinking—and don't go imagining you're the only one who's trifled with a good and loving heart. I've done the same thing, as you damn well know.''

Justin said nothing. He was realizing that here was another way he was like this man who'd fathered him.

''Your mother,'' Caleb said softly. ''She was a good woman. A good woman done wrong. She couldn't…get past that, what I did to her, that's all.''

Justin waved a hand. ''She's gone now.''

''Don't judge her.''

''I'm working on it. Your…wife?''

It took Caleb a moment to answer that one. ''Addy and me, we've been together too long to give up now.

She's not happy with me. But I've got hopes that someday…'' He let that sentence finish itself. "Riley, though. I don't know. He's not in a mood for forgiving.''

"Give him time.''

"Time.'' Caleb chuckled, a dry sound with no real laughter in it. "Well.'' He stood. "Better get this junk packed up.''

Justin stood, too. "Put it back where it came from.'' Caleb blinked. And Justin continued, "I put my man on something else. This is your project and you're fully capable of seeing it through to a successful conclusion. I'm leaving it to you, where it always belonged. And I'll be pulling out completely, as soon as I find some other solid investors to step in and fill the gap.''

Caleb sank to his chair again. "You don't have to do this.''

"Yeah. Yeah, I do—and don't even think of trying to turn me down. I'm out. And you're going to be needed here.''

Caleb looked up at him. "Don't pull out. Stay in.''

Justin frowned. "That's probably a bad idea.''

"No. It's a good one. An excellent one. Stay in. We'll make a little money together. We'll give a shot in the arm to the local economy and we'll…start getting to know each other.''

"You want that?''

"Yeah, I do. I want that a lot.''

"Let me think about it.''

"Take as long as you need. Just be sure the answer's yes.''

* * *

Caleb called him at home at seven that night. Skipping right over anything resembling hello, he said, "So. You made up your mind yet?"

Justin couldn't hold back a chuckle. "I thought I was supposed to take all the time I needed."

"You've had time enough. Say yes."

He'd already decided, anyway. "All right. I'm in."

"Good. You have a nice night, now." And the line went dead.

Justin took the phone away from his ear and stared at it, shaking his head. Then, gently, he set it down.

He turned for the table where the remains of his solitary dinner waited to be cleared off. The job only took a few minutes.

Then he went out to his study, where he booted up his laptop and settled in for a few hours of work on a new project he was putting together.

The doorbell rang at five to eight. He hit the save key and got up to answer.

The last person in the world he'd ever expected to see was waiting beyond the front door.

"Katie." Damned if his heart didn't do a forward roll.

She looked up at him, brown eyes gleaming, soft cheeks flushed. There was snow on her shoulders, sparkling in her chestnut hair. She brushed at it. "Caleb said you wanted to see me."

His mind was a fog of hope and yearning. "Caleb..."

Her sweet face fell. "He...was wrong?"

"No," he said—so forcefully that she jumped back.

He tried again, more gently. "No. Caleb was absolutely right."

"Well. So, then?" She managed a hopeful smile. "Do you think maybe I might come in?"

He gaped at her, and then, at last, he remembered to speak. "Yeah. Absolutely. Come in."

Chapter Seventeen

He took her coat, his heart racing like a runaway train at the mere fact that she'd handed it over.

Because, after all, if she let him take her coat, that meant she would stay, didn't it? At least for a little while.

He shook the remaining snow off it, set it on the entry hall chair and led her through to the great room. "Sit down. Please."

She perched on a long sofa. "I..." She seemed to be doing a lot of swallowing. He understood. His throat kept locking up, too. She tried again. "Emelda tells me you made a generous donation to the Historical Society—very generous, is what she said."

He looked down at her, astounded. Amazed. Was there ever a woman so damned, incredibly beautiful?

No. He was sure of it. She was one of a kind.

"Justin?"

"Yeah?"

"You're staring."

He gulped again. "Uh. Sorry. Listen, want some coffee? I made it an hour ago, but it should still be okay."

Her gaze scanned his face, sweetly. Hungrily.

Or was that just him seeing what he wanted to see?

"Coffee," she repeated.

"Yeah. You think?"

"Yes. Okay. I'll have some."

"Stay right there."

She let out a nervous little giggle. "Well, Justin. Where would I go?"

He raced for the kitchen, poured the damn coffee— two mugfuls, since it seemed a little rude to let her drink hers alone. He remembered she liked cream and splashed some into hers. Then he rushed back to the great room, coffee sloshing across the Kelim area rugs as he went.

When he got back to her, she was standing at a narrow section of wall between two wide windows, looking at…

Damn. She was never supposed to see that.

He'd never dared to imagine she'd set foot in his house again, or he wouldn't have put the thing up.

She turned to him. "Justin? That's the fake license. From that day at the town hall."

"Uh…" He scooted over and plunked the mugs down on a low table. Coffee, still sloshing, dribbled down the sides.

"It is, isn't it?"

He rubbed his hands together, brushing off the coffee he'd spilled on them. "Well, yeah. That's what it is."

She came toward him. He watched her as she moved, devouring her with his eyes. When she stood about a foot from him, she asked, "Where did you get it?"

Her scent swam around him. His fingers itched to grab for her. To keep them busy, he gestured at the table. "Coffee. There you go."

"Justin." Her voice was so soft. And the tiniest, most radiant smile had begun at the corners of that mouth he wanted so badly to kiss. She touched his arm. He felt that touch all the way down to the center of his soul. "Where did you get it?"

"Josiah Green."

"Our fake minister?"

"Turns out he wasn't a fake. A little eccentric maybe, but not a fake."

"You're kidding. The real thing?"

He managed a nod.

"He gave you the license?"

"He did."

"But why?"

His throat loosened a little and he told her about Green's visit, about the things the old guy had said.

She hadn't removed her hand from his arm. Her touch burned him. He was going up in flames.

She said, "Caleb says you love me. Is that true?"

Struck mute again, he could only nod.

"Oh, Justin…"

He knew she needed more than that. Hell, *he* needed more than that. "I... Katie, I know the things I did were wrong. Unforgivable, even. I know I blew it. Lost you. Lost the best thing that ever happened to me. That's why I had that fake license framed. I hung it on the wall, where I'd see it all the time. Where I'd remember, what might have been. If only I hadn't—"

"Justin."

"What, damn it?"

"Close your eyes."

"I don't—"

"Just do it. Close your eyes."

"Hell." But he did what she asked.

And as he stood there, blind before her, he felt her warm breath against his neck, felt the living, sweet-scented heat of her.

She whispered, "Personally, I *believe*. In forgiveness. I believe in hope. And faith. And..."

"Wishes," he whispered. He didn't know where that word came from. Or maybe he did.

"Yes." It came out on a gentle breath. "Yes." That *yes* shivered through him. He felt it echo, in the beating of his heart. "Wishes," she said. "Wishes that can come true. If you..."

"Make them."

"If you're—"

"Done with lying. With dirty tricks."

"Oh, yes. That's right. Wishes and hope and faith. And forgiveness. I do believe in them, Justin. I believe in *you*."

It was too much.

It was everything.

Every wish he never dared to make.

Every dream he'd never known how to believe in.

All of it. Right here.

Everything. Katie.

She put her hands on his shoulders. A shudder went through him. And he felt her lift up, on tiptoe, to place a kiss on each of his lowered eyelids, one and then the other.

And that did it. He couldn't keep still one second longer.

He opened his eyes and he reached for her.

With a happy, willing cry, she came into his arms.

He lifted her high against his chest and, holding her close, knowing he'd never, ever let her go, he carried her out of the high-ceilinged room, away from all those dark windows, down a long hallway to his bedroom.

They undressed each other, quickly, hands shaking, sharing kisses and nervous, eager glances—soft whispers, and yet more kisses.

At last she stood before him, slim and proud, her body gleaming, pale and pearly, in the dimness.

"Katie…"

She held her head high, and she looked right back at him. "Justin."

He swept her up again, carried her to the bed and laid her down on it.

And he kissed her. Kissed every fragrant, smooth,

beautiful inch of her, lingering at her breasts, her belly, her thighs.

He kissed his way up them, and then he parted her and he kissed her some more, there, at the wet, hot feminine heart of her, as she called out his name, her soft fingers tangled in his hair.

When she came, he drank her, taking her release inside of him. So sweet. So exactly what he'd never dared, till now, to dream of.

She touched his shoulders, reaching, urging him up over her. He settled—so carefully, his body aching for her—between her open thighs.

He looked down at her, met those shining eyes. "Your first time?"

She pressed her lips together and nodded. "It's what I want, though. You. You're what I want."

He didn't want to leave her. Not even for a moment. But there was protection to consider. "I should..." Her sweet heat was all around him, her body pliant, ready. "We need to..."

She caught his face between her hands. "What Reverend Green said...we're married. Right? How did you say he said it?"

He groaned. "In the eyes of heaven."

"Oh, yes. I...well, don't say I'm crazy. But I like that. I *believe* in that. And if there was a baby..."

A baby. Incredible.

She asked, so softly, "Would that be all right with you?"

It *was* crazy. Absolutely insane. But he found that it would. He swallowed. Hard. And he managed to croak out, "Yeah."

And she wrapped her satiny legs around him. "Then it's okay...it's all right."

He made himself go slowly, pushing in just a little, holding still...waiting.

It was the sweetest kind of agony—the pleasure, within the pain. He held still and he kissed her—eyes, cheeks, nose, chin. He whispered, "Slowly...slowly..."

She moaned and held him, her sleek body moving, then going still. He pushed in farther—felt resistance and then, at last, the slow, gentle opening.

Welcoming.

It took forever. An eternity of slow, controlled degrees.

Until at last, he felt himself fully within her. "Don't...move..." he pleaded on a ragged sigh.

But she had other ideas. "I...I have to. Oh, Justin. I need..." And her hips began to rock him. "I need...you. You. Only."

He kissed the words from her lips and gave them back to her. "Only you."

The pleasure took over, all the words flew away. They rode an endless, swirling river of it, of pleasure. It sucked him into a whirlpool. He went spinning...

Spinning.

And then it centered down.

Down into Katie. Into the soft pulsing of her heat and wetness all around him.

He let out a cry, tossing his head back. And she cried out in answer.

The rest was soft sighs, tender caresses.

"I love you," she whispered.

And he could only smile.

* * *

It was an hour later when he dared to suggest, "Marry me. Again."

She looked up at him from under the sable fringe of her lashes. "Yes. I will."

"Soon," he demanded.

"Oh, absolutely. And in the town hall. With everyone in Thunder Canyon invited. And the Reverend Green presiding. What do you think?"

"I think, yes. Beyond a shadow of a doubt. No conditions. Yes."

"Just one thing."

"Anything. Everything."

She laughed then, and the sound banished all darkness. It filled up the world with golden light.

"Promise me," she said. "No free beer."

So he promised, sealing it—and all the other, more important promises—with a tender kiss.

Epilogue

On the first Saturday in February, Katie and Justin said their vows for the second time, in the town hall. In spite of the blizzard gathering force outside, the old hall was packed. The bride, radiant in white satin, had asked Caleb to give her away. Riley stood up as Justin's best man. The eccentric Reverend Green, looking pleased with himself *and* the proceedings, officiated.

When the reverend asked Katie if she would take Justin to be her lawfully wedded husband—to love him, to honor and to cherish him for as long as they both should live—Katie, so often soft-spoken, especially in crowds, answered loud and clear.

"I will." Her brown eyes shone. Her face was suffused with a glow of pure joy.

After the vow-sealing kiss, the party began, right

there in the hall. Montana Gold, a band of local boys, took the stage and a generous buffet, laid out on long tables, eased the appetites of the assembled guests. Beer was limited, as per the bride's instructions.

But there was champagne, and it flowed freely. When the band took its first break, the toasting began. Caleb was delivering a long speech about true love and happiness and getting through the tough times, when Cameron Stevenson's seven-year-old, Erik, sneaked up on the stage and started banging on the keyboards. Caleb sent a quelling look over his shoulder at the boy, who quickly moved on to the drums. With a crashing sound, the high hat tumbled to the stage.

Cam went after Erik, then, and led him off, but everyone laughed and burst into raucous clapping and catcalls.

After the toasts and speeches, Katie and Justin cut the enormous cake. As Adele supervised the cake distribution, the band took over again for a second set.

Several men pitched in to push the tables back against the wall and Caleb led Katie out on the floor. They danced, but not for long. Justin cut in.

As the citizens of Thunder Canyon applauded the bride and groom's first dance, Justin whispered, "Happy?"

Katie looked up at him, all her love shining in her eyes. "Happy doesn't even begin to describe it."

He pulled her closer. She settled her head against his shoulder. Other couples joined them, filling the floor.

When that dance ended, the band swung into another number. Katie stayed where she wanted to be: held close in Justin's loving arms. The band played on. They danced every dance.

It was no time at all until Montana Gold announced their second break. Justin took Katie's hand and led her to the sidelines, where a special table had been set up specifically for the bride and groom and family.

Adele was just serving them each a piece of cake, when Cam Stevenson edged his way toward them through the milling crowd.

One look at Cam's too-pale face, and Katie knew there was trouble.

Cam bent down to ask her, "Have you seen Erik?"

She shook her head. "But he's probably out in the foyer. I saw a bunch of the kids heading that way."

"No. He's not there. I looked."

"Did you look—?"

"Everywhere, damn it. I've been all through the building."

Justin was already on his feet. "Come on. Let's look again. He can't have gone far...."

* * * * *

ALL HE EVER WANTED

BY
ALLISON LEIGH

Allison Leigh started early by writing a Halloween play that her class performed for her school. Since then, though her tastes have changed, her love for reading has not. And her writing appetite simply grows more voracious by the day.

Born in Southern California, she has lived in eight different cities in four different states. She has been, at one time or another, a cosmetologist, a computer programmer and an administrative assistant. Allison and her husband currently make their home in Arizona, where their time is thoroughly filled with two very active daughters, full-time jobs, pets, church, family and friends.

In order to give herself the precious writing time she craves, she burns a lot of midnight oil. A great believer in the power of love—her parents still hold hands—she cannot imagine anything more exciting to write about than the miracle of two hearts coming together.

For Chris, Pam, Judy, Karen and Cheryl, fellow "Gold Rush Groomers" and for Susan who kept us on track. It's been a pleasure.

Chapter One

"How long has it been since you last saw your son?"

Cameron Stevenson eyed the police officer. Impatience clawed at him. He wanted to be out *looking* for Erik, not answering Bobby Romano's incessant questions. "Almost two hours. The band was taking their second break."

The officer's pencil scratched on his small notepad. "How do you know it was their second? Maybe it was their first. Their last."

Romano's neck was looking more appealing by the minute and Cam's hands itched to strangle it. But it wasn't Romano's fault that Erik was missing.

It was Cam's.

So instead of throttling the officer for detaining

him when he would otherwise have been scouring the buildings surrounding the Thunder Canyon Town Hall—usually known as The Hall—Cameron's fist tightened around the leather coat that Laura had given him their first winter together in Thunder Canyon.

Their only winter.

"It was Montana Gold's second break," he said flatly. "As soon as I saw the band members putting down their instruments, I started hunting for Erik. He'd already messed with the instruments after the band's first set. I didn't want him getting into mischief on the stage again." The first time, Erik's focus had been the drum set. The end result had been a crash of cymbals when the hi-hat tumbled off the stage. "It was around eight. I was gonna take him home."

Romano scratched his jaw and then made a few more notes. "And you're sure he's not just hiding? We all know how Erik can get. Kid was probably bored out of his skull coming to a wedding and reception."

Since it seemed as if everyone in town had crammed into The Hall to celebrate with the bridal couple—Katie Fenton and Justin Caldwell—Cam couldn't have very well come to the event without his son. None of the regular baby-sitters had been available. So he'd dragged Erik—not quite kicking and screaming—along with him.

Now he wished they both had stayed home. He hadn't wanted to come to the wedding in the first place, but Katie had been pretty insistent.

And he'd had the notion that Laura was standing behind him, silently pushing him to take part in the town's activities. So he'd accepted the invitation, and he'd lassoed Erik into accompanying him.

"He's not just hiding," he assured. The door to The Hall opened yet again, letting in a spit of snow along with the arrival. The evening had not only marked a second wedding for Katie to Justin in as many months, but it seemed to be capped by another blizzard as well.

Which only thinned out his control to a translucent veneer.

Most of the wedding guests had already departed because of the weather. Many of them were even now out looking for his son *despite* the weather.

While he was stuck in the lobby of the town hall answering Romano's damn questions.

"How do you know?" Romano was plodding.

Cam exhaled roughly. His fingers flexed. Tightened on the coat. "Because Rhonda Culpepper was here at the wedding, too." Rhonda manned the information desk for The Hall. She knew every nook and cranny of the place. "She had her keys. We checked all the offices upstairs. We checked the archives in the basement. We checked the damn elevator shaft. We checked every damn hiding hole in this entire damn place!" His voice rose, and there was little he could do to stop it. He towered over Romano, wanting to smash the man for hindering him.

"Here." A hand, holding a cup of water, appeared from one side, pushing between him and the police officer. A physical barrier. He looked at the cup for a moment, and the slender hand—then at the woman who'd offered it.

Faith Taylor.

He knew her only by sight.

Which was more than he wanted…and not because he didn't like the look of her.

He just didn't like the effect she had on him.

But she was SAR. Search and Rescue. The fact that his son might need her, though, or any other member of the county-wide team, made that veneer of control even thinner.

Don't panic.

"I don't want any water. I don't want to answer any more questions about how tall Erik is, or what he was wearing." Questions from Romano that had eroded Cam's nerves and pulverized his ability to remain calm. "I want to find my son. He's probably playing down on Main Street somewhere. He likes pretending he's an outlaw from the Old West."

"And the old-fashioned Western buildings all along Main provide the perfect setting." Faith's voice was calm enough. "Let's just hope that he's doing exactly that. And if he is, he'll be found quickly enough. There are officers and volunteers right now out canvassing the area, doing a door-to-door."

"And I should be out there with them. It's only getting later and that snow doesn't look like it's gonna lighten up anytime soon."

Her soft lips pressed together. Earlier in the evening, she'd worn a deep blue dress that had flowed around her slender ankles whenever she took a step. But since word had gotten out that Erik was missing, she'd changed. Now, she wore a coat similar to the one

Bobby Romano wore, only hers didn't bear the insignia of the Thunder Canyon police. It shouted Search and Rescue in nauseatingly bright orange letters across the back of the slick green fabric. She looked official.

Except for her eyes.

But looking at those eyes that were neither brown nor green but somewhere...distracting...in between was something he'd tried to avoid since the first time he'd seen her months ago sitting quietly in the rear of one of the town council meetings.

"Have you called your son's friends? Would he have tried walking home without you?"

"Erik tries anything," he said grimly. Despite Cam's concerted efforts otherwise. "And yes, I've called all of his friends. Most of the families were already here anyway."

There must have been three hundred people crowded into The Hall. And if Cam hadn't been cornered by the troublesome threesome—a term he'd privately applied to the trio of high school girls who were forever trying to practice their budding wiles on him—he'd have never lost sight of Erik in the first place.

"Yet you didn't call in the police right away," Romano observed. "Any particular reason for that, Coach?"

Cam narrowed his eyes. He didn't care for Romano's tone. He didn't care for Romano, for that matter. "Maybe because I was combing every square inch of this building, because I figured Erik *was* just hiding out. Only he's not. He's not *in* this building. Get it?"

He looked down at the coat his wife had given him.

God.

He couldn't lose Erik, too.

He shoved his arms into the coat.

Don't panic.

"I'm going to find my son."

He ignored Romano and Faith and turned on his heel. His boots rang out hollow on the wood floor of the nearly empty lobby and the wind ripped the door out of his grip when he stepped onto the wooden sidewalk outside the entrance. The awning that stretched across the front of The Hall, as well as the adjacent buildings butting up against it, didn't offer much protection against the swirl of snow.

He flipped up his collar and set off across the street. The town square held plenty of hiding places for a seven-year-old boy. "Erik," he yelled, his feet moving faster.

He shouldn't have made Erik go to the wedding and reception. Shouldn't have made him put on his best clothes—even a damned tie. His son had been nearly apoplectic.

Rightfully so, Cam had realized, as soon as they'd walked into The Hall and had seen just how casually many of the guests were dressed, given the short notice of Katie and Justin's "do." Erik had slanted a look up at Cam and immediately started fiddling with his tie, despite Cam's warning. Ten minutes later, he'd caught his son in the bathroom, wrapping toilet paper around his head like a turban. The turban had been ditched, but the tie had come off and Erik had returned to his seat with Cam.

"Erik!"

He rounded a slow-moving car and nearly hurdled an old-fashioned bench sitting outside a Western-themed storefront.

Don't panic.

"Mr. Stevenson. Wait."

He very nearly ignored the raised voice. But he stopped, impatience coiling inside him, and turned to see Faith Taylor jogging across the road, her sturdy boots kicking up puffs of snow.

"Don't mind Bobby." She skidded a little on the slippery road as she reached him. "He really is trying to help."

Cam steadied her and just as quickly released her. "He's pissed that I've still got his son benched," he said bluntly. Danny Romano—Romance, as he was called—was one of the strongest players on the high school basketball team Cam coached. He was also carrying the worst grades. But that didn't matter to his dad, Bobby, who was more interested in his son being spotted by a scout than whether or not his son had decent enough grades to even be accepted into college.

Faith's long blond hair—confined in a ponytail—rippled and lifted in the harsh wind, reflecting the dim glow from a nearby lamppost. "He's going back to the police station to make the report. A broadcast will go out on the local television station. Did you have a picture to give him?"

Cam nodded, his gaze scanning the white-dark shadows of the town square. He could hear the shouts of his son's name, and through the swirling snow, could see the bob of flashlights. "Erik's school picture." It had been in his wallet, next to the photo of Laura when she'd been pregnant.

"Good. The more people who see it, the better. The radio station here will also be making the announcement. And there's no one who might have taken Erik? Your wife, or—"

"My wife is dead. And there are no other family members in the area."

Her lips parted for the briefest moment. "I'm sorry. I, um, I didn't know that." She hesitated, as if she were adjusting her thought processes. "I assume Bobby told you the process for issuing an AMBER alert?"

He nodded. The very notion of a nationwide alert being issued for his missing son was more than he could stand, because it would mean that Erik hadn't just wandered off. It would mean that his son had been abducted. That he could be facing serious injury. Or death.

His head felt ready to explode.

Don't panic.

How many times had he issued that advice to Laura?

Erik would be fine. He was probably sitting in someone's living room, drinking hot chocolate and talking about the impossibility of two snowflakes being identical as he watched them hurtle from the sky.

"Okay. Well, we're not at that point, which is a good thing." She shifted from one foot to the other, her legs looking long and slender in her heavy, tan pants. "I'll head out in just a few minutes, too. I've been in contact with the other members of my team. Unfortunately, thanks to this snow, it'll be a while before any of them can make it here to Thunder Canyon. And, of course, while the search is still confined to the town limits, the police are in charge of coordinating the search."

"Erik is still in town," he said. Because he had to believe it.

"You're probably right," she agreed evenly. "And you need to go home. It's likely that your son will show up there."

She clearly didn't know Erik. "He won't."

"Mr. Stevenson—"

"Cam."

She exhaled in a visible puff. "Mr. Stevenson. Let us do *our* job. Go home."

"What you really mean is that you don't think I've done *my* job," he countered.

Another gust of wind blew over them and she flipped up the lined collar of her coat, deftly fastening it around her neck. She didn't deny his words, either. "Let's just find Erik," she said. "The quicker the better, considering the way this storm is picking up. Has he run off like this before?"

"No. Yes." He shook his head sharply. "Dammit. I have to find him. This is wasting more—"

"Don't." She touched her gloved hand to his sleeve. "I know you're worried. Upset. But the best thing that you can do is try to stay calm, and go home. Make a list of Erik's friends. The places he likes to go. Was he upset about anything? Did you argue?"

"Being forced into a monkey suit," Cam muttered.

"And Erik doesn't run off because he's angry. He runs off because he sees a bug he's interested in, or a rabbit he wants to follow. He's seven. He's got more energy and curiosity than either one of us knows what to do with." Attention deficit wasn't his son's problem, either. He just had an insatiable curiosity toward life.

In that regard, he was like Laura.

And Cam hadn't been able to protect Laura.

He *would* protect their son.

If he could only find him.

"Okay." Faith nodded. "So go home. Call the station and give them just that kind of information once you're there. And wait for Erik."

"I'll do better looking."

"But—"

"I've already told Todd Gilmore to go over to my place in case Erik shows," he interrupted. "The Gilmores live next door to me." Todd was the star center on the team. He was also one of the more reliable students at Thunder Canyon High School where Cam taught math and coached the men's athletic teams—football, basketball and baseball, depending on the season.

The information didn't seem to please Faith Taylor any, though. She still looked at him with something not quite veiled in her expression.

Judgment.

Well, nobody could judge Cam more harshly than he judged himself and he wasn't going to stand there—useless—on that cold sidewalk any longer. "I appreciate whatever help you can give." He pushed out the words, meaning them. He just didn't like having to mean them.

Asking for—or accepting—help from others didn't sit comfortably on his shoulders.

But when it came to Erik, Cam would do whatever it took.

Faith shoved her gloved hands in her pockets and watched Cameron Stevenson turn on his booted heel. In moments, his tall body seemed swallowed by the swirling, snowy shadows filling the darkened town square. There was no point in trying to call him back. Or to ask him to wait.

The truth was, Erik Stevenson probably *would* be located quickly enough—right here in this old section of Thunder Canyon—now that folks knew to keep an eye out for the boy. It was a far more likely scenario than that the child had met with any foul play.

Even though Thunder Canyon possessed a population of ten thousand, the crime rate was so low it was nearly nonexistent.

She chewed the inside of her lip. Closed her eyes for a moment when she heard Cameron Stevenson's deep voice calling his son's name.

If she were lucky enough to have a son, she wouldn't be so careless as to lose sight of him.

And that was a thought that wouldn't lead anywhere but to depression. So she opened her eyes, dashing snowflakes away from her eyelashes, and headed back to her SUV, which she'd left double-parked in front of the brightly lit town hall.

She climbed in and drove as quickly as the weather

permitted back to her office at the fire station. She'd
make yet another attempt at raising another member
of the SAR team, but she had no plans to sit on her
thumbs if she couldn't. There were only six of them
on the team, and they covered the entire county. It was
only on rare occasions that they were all called in to
one case at one time.

Erik Stevenson probably *would* be located safe and
sound somewhere nearby. And she'd be one of the
people out looking for him, until he was home again
with his father.

And maybe next time, Cameron Stevenson would
keep his thick-lashed brooding brown eyes more
clearly focused on his innocent little boy.

When she reached the public service building, a big
brick complex that housed both the Thunder Canyon
police and fire departments, she parked in her usual
spot and hurried inside, grateful to get out of the bitter wind.

She didn't have an office assigned for her use in the
portion of the building used by the fire department, but
had a serviceable metal desk, a few filing cabinets and
a computer, all situated off to one side of the open office area. She yanked off her coat and sat down at her
desk, then dialed her co-workers' numbers with one
hand and punched up her computer with the other.

A grainy image of young Erik Stevenson immediately came up and for a moment she sat there, looking into his impossibly young face.

He looked like a miniature version of his dad, right
down to the squarely cut jaw, dark auburn hair and

deep brown eyes. For a moment, she wondered if Cameron would have the same cowlick that Erik possessed if his hair weren't cut so conservatively short.

"Hey there, Blondie." Derek Winters, one of the members of Fire's C Company and the husband of her best friend, Tanya, tugged at the end of her ponytail and sat on the corner of her desk. "Any news on the Stevenson kid?"

"Not yet."

"He's a cute one." He jerked his chin toward the small television that sat atop one of the tall filing cabinets across the room. "His picture's been all over the news for the past thirty minutes."

"Good." She gave up on the phone and quickly typed out a report and posted it to the county system where the rest of her team could access the information. "The more exposure, the better."

"Well, talking about exposure—" Derek's face looked serious "—the weather service has issued a severe weather alert for the next seven hours. They're expecting road closures all the way to Bozeman."

Dismay settled cold and heavy inside her. "The father said Erik has his parka and gloves with him." Which would be sufficient under *normal* circumstances. She propped her elbows on her desk and pressed her chin to her linked fingers, sternly marshalling her thoughts. "I've heard that a lot of people think this boy is pretty mischievous." She looked up at Derek. "What was Toby like when he was seven?" Her honorary nephew was now twelve.

Derek's lips curled. "Hell on wheels one minute.

Too angelic for belief the next." He shook his head. "If I were in Cam Stevenson's position right now, I'd be ready to rip apart the whole world until I knew my kid was safe."

Which pretty much described Faith's impression of Cameron Stevenson's state of mind.

She rose and grabbed her coat again. She had spare gloves and scarves in her truck. She checked the batteries in her flashlight and took a freshly charged radio from the row of them on the rear counter. "Cam spent half the evening at the reception tonight surrounded by women." She wasn't sure what made her admit the observation. It wasn't as if she'd sat at the table alongside Tanya watching the man the entire while.

Derek was grinning. "Poor guy. We can't all be beautiful like me. And it doesn't mean that he wasn't watching his kid properly," he added more seriously.

Faith couldn't make a call on that particular point, no matter which way she instinctively leaned. All she knew was that the few times she'd seen Cameron Stevenson since she'd returned to Thunder Canyon last year, he'd almost always had a bevy of females flocking around him. Didn't matter if it was at a town council meeting, where he often posed incredibly pointed questions to the council members, or at The Hitching Post for hamburgers and shakes following a Friday night high school ball game.

She could understand why the man wouldn't take a child to a council meeting. But she hadn't yet seen Erik in The Hitching Post following one of the games.

Maybe Cameron Stevenson did watch his son properly.

And maybe he didn't.

She'd barely seen the boy amid the mad crush attending Katie and Justin's wedding.

"I'm going out. The rest of the search is concentrated around Old Town. It's unlikely that he would have gone so far, but I told Romano that I'd check out White Water Drive and the houses down that way. Then I'll work my way around the edge of town and up Thunder Canyon Road."

"You think he could have headed out to the ice rink?"

She shook her head. "A unit already checked it out. He wasn't there. And he hasn't been seen on Lazy-D property, either." The ranch owned by the prosperous Douglas family bordered the entire western side of town.

She waved the radio in her hand and headed out the door. The snow was steady. Her SUV was already coated in white. She swiped her arm across the windshield as far as she could reach and then climbed inside. The heater blasted warm and comforting almost immediately as she backed out of her space and drove slowly through the town where she'd been born and raised. She hoped to heaven that Erik was somewhere warm.

As she drove, she could see the steady track of Thunder Canyon police vehicles moving carefully up and down the streets.

Wherever Erik Stevenson had gotten to, they *would* find him.

She refused to even consider the alternative.

She drove back up Main Street, past the town square and The Hall. When she reached White Water Drive, she turned south. Drove past the hospital, where her brother Chris was probably still on duty in the E.R.

The farther out she went, the heavier the snow seemed to fall, until her SUV was virtually crawling. She'd flipped on both her spotlights, but the powerful beams went only so far through the wall of white. When she reached the last of the houses, a little past the Lone Pine Medical Building, she got out and started door-to-door, working her way back up toward the hospital. When she reached it, she took a few precious minutes to grab a hot coffee from the cafeteria. She also radioed in to the station.

Still no news.

And now, it was nearly midnight.

There was a steady chatter coming from the police scanner in her SUV. Officers reporting in. The search grids of the town being slowly and steadily ticked off, yielding no sign of Erik.

She continued her way back toward the center of Old Town—driving a few feet, knocking on doors, waking people up, tramping around their houses, their yards, calling Erik's name, only to drive a few more feet and repeat the process. It was freezing, tedious work, but she never once gave a thought to stopping.

At twelve-thirty, the snow picked up even more, but it was hardly noticeable since the wind had also picked up, throwing whatever fell right back up again and swirling it around twice as hard. She ignored the command over the scanner that all searchers were to seek immediate shelter from the blizzard.

And when those commands were directed squarely at her, she turned off the scanner and still continued. She didn't take her orders from the police. She took them from the senior member of the search and rescue team, and *he* was over in Bozeman.

Not that Jim Shepherd would be pleased with her when he found out, but she couldn't get the image of Erik's face out of her head.

She'd grown up in this town. She'd learned to drive on its streets. And when it came to Old Town, she knew every corner like the back of her hand. So as long as she could still make her way from one house to the next, she was going to.

Which was fine, until she nearly drove her crawling truck right over the figure hunched against the wind outside The Hitching Post.

She sat there in her truck, her gloved hands curling tightly around the steering wheel as she stared at the person barely a foot from her front bumper.

There was no question who it was.

Erik's father.

The wind buffeted the SUV, and Cameron swayed.

She shoved the truck into Park, grabbed the blanket from her back seat and raced around to him, her boots sliding on the ice. Reaching up, she yanked the blanket around his shoulders.

"Are you crazy?" Her raised voice, muffled by her scarf and whipped away by the wind, was barely audible. The man was stiff with cold, his leather coat no match for the elements. "You're not supposed to be out here still!"

His head ducked toward hers. "*You* are!"

Bitter wind shot needles of cold into her, nearly shoving her off her feet. She grabbed his waist, as much to keep herself steady as him. "Get in the truck," she yelled.

He was already moving, and she wasn't sure if she pushed him or if he pulled her. He went to the passenger door. Dragged it open, and nearly lifted her inside. He was close behind, the door slamming closed on them.

The protection from that awful, bitter wind was immediate and she blew out a long breath.

"Jesus," he muttered, as the air howled and the SUV rocked. From the glow of the dashboard, his eyes looked ravaged. "You haven't found him, either."

She wanted to look away from those eyes of his. Wanted to, but couldn't.

And she loathed the feeling that engulfed her.

Failure.

She wasn't used to it in her professional life.

Personal? That was a different story.

So she stared up at him, unconsciously cataloging the creases—deeper now than they'd been hours earlier—that fanned out from his eyes.

"No," she said quietly. "Not yet." She was half perched on the console between the seats, half perched on his thigh, and she awkwardly maneuvered herself into the driver's seat, anxious to put some distance between them.

She tried closing herself off from the desperation seeping from him and turned on the scanner again, only to hear her name being furiously called. She lifted the mike and reported in.

Beside her, Cameron was still. He had to have been freezing, but he didn't pull the blanket tighter around himself, or redirect the heater vents more in his direction.

Sighing faintly, she leaned over again, pulling the blanket around him more fully, then simply reached even further to grab his safety belt and snap it in place.

She squeezed his arm. "We'll find him," she whispered.

His jaw worked and when his voice finally emerged, it was raw.

"When?"

Chapter Two

*W*hen?

Faith slowly sat back in her seat. "Soon," she promised, her voice husky.

The station was just as close as trying to get either one of them home. And at the station, there was still some hope that she'd be able to do some good where little Erik Stevenson was concerned.

Closer or not, her nerves were strung tighter than a wire and her eyes ached by the time her tires slid to a wobbly stop outside the fire station. She felt as if she'd been driving for hours, but knew it had been a fraction of it.

Outside her windshield, beyond the frenzied slap of the wipers, she could just make out the familiar brick wall of the public service building. "Can you make it inside?" She handed him her spare scarf.

He didn't answer. Merely wound it around his neck and face, and shoved himself out of the vehicle.

She pulled her own scarf up higher around her nose and followed suit, heading straight for the wall that was made elusive by the undulating curtain of snowfall.

When her gloved hands hit solid surface, she didn't dawdle with relief, but ducked her head even more against the vicious wind and felt her way along the wall until she found the entrance. Cameron's shoulder brushed hers all the while.

The wind nearly picked them up and tossed them inside.

Breathing hard, she sat down on the nearest object. The floor.

Cameron folded his arms across the top of a tall filing cabinet. His head bowed wearily, and the blanket fell from his shoulders, unheeded. After a long moment, he shrugged out of his coat and placed it with inordinate care over the back of a desk chair.

She sat there, still trying to catch her breath while sympathy shoved hard against the knot inside her that wanted to blame him for being careless with his child.

She looked away from him, unwinding her heavy scarf. It crunched as chunks of snow and ice fell from it, only to melt when they rained onto the floor.

She leaned her head back. Felt the unyielding metal of a desk drawer behind her. And wanted to rail at the weather gods for throwing the nastiest of curveballs their way.

"Here." Cam crouched down before her and began tugging off her thick gloves. He said nothing else.

His expression was enough to let her know where his thoughts dwelled.

She looked like the abominable snowman, and he wasn't much better. And his son was still missing.

Cameron Stevenson was a big man with shoulders that had undoubtedly filled a football uniform at some point in his past. Not brawny. But definitely muscular. Strong.

She had the impossible urge to put her arms around him as if he were a harmless child nursing a hurt.

She swallowed hard, until she got rid of the knot in her throat that would do nobody any good right now.

"The weather will ease up," she assured, her voice not quite as calm as she'd have preferred. "We'll all go back out again."

His jaw was white. He rose and his movements were slow, as if moving caused him pain. He began to pace.

Her iced-over pants had thawed sufficiently thanks to the warm interior of the building, and she pushed to her feet as well. She went back to the locker room and changed into the spare clothes she kept there. She wouldn't win any fashion awards, but the olive-drab cargo pants and fleece sweatshirt were warm and dry.

She returned to her desk, giving Cameron—whose expression was closed and unwelcoming—a wide berth. He'd exchanged the well-cut black suit he'd been wearing when she'd seen him at The Hall for a thick gray sweater and blue jeans. A dark shadow blurred his blunt jaw and his hair looked as if it had been raked by claws. His tension, however, *was* terribly familiar. Only now it was worse.

She checked her computer, amazed to find the Internet connection still running.

But there was no news about Erik there, either. No sightings. And no help from any other members of her team coming anytime soon, since the roads had officially been closed and they were dealing with their own local emergencies.

Stifling a sigh, she crossed the hallway that divided the building and went over to the police station. There were a handful of officers sitting at their desks, looking busy. All except Bobby Romano, who was leaning back in his chair, his boots propped on the corner of his desk.

The sight irritated her.

She went over to him and shoved his feet off the desk.

"Hey!" The cup of coffee he held splashed over his uniformed stomach. "What the hell?"

"At least pretend to be on duty, Bobby." Her voice was flat. She ignored the muffled snickers coming from the others and went past his desk to the dispatcher's office.

When she stuck her head in, she saw that Cheryl Lansky held the fort. "I'm here. You can call off the dogs."

"Taking chances, Faith." Cheryl tsked and shook her head. "I'll let the chief know you've come in, though."

"I nearly ran down Cameron Stevenson," she admitted. "Any reports?"

"Aside from the usual panics over a blizzard, only call we've gotten is the weekly from Emelda Ross."

Bobby came up behind Faith, sopping at his shirt with a paper towel. "Woman needs to be put in a home somewhere."

Cheryl looked disgusted.

"Is she still doing the story hour at the library?" Faith asked.

Cheryl nodded. "My grandson loves her just as much as his mother did."

"She told the best stories," Faith murmured. "But what'd she call in for tonight?"

"Same thing she calls in for every week," Bobby grumbled. He tossed the soaked towel in the small metal wastebasket beside Cheryl's desk and her array of computers, phones and radios, and missed. "Attention."

Cheryl leaned over and deposited the trash where it belonged. "Suspected trespasser." She shrugged a little. "Same complaint she always makes."

"Did someone check it out?" Faith looked at Bobby.

"We did a drive-by, before the storm settled in after the Coach decided to announce his kid was missing," he defended. "That old house of hers was quiet as a tomb. There isn't gonna be any trespassers going anywhere tonight. Not with that white soup coming down out there."

"And don't you go thinking you're going back out in this storm yet, either, Faith." Cheryl's voice was firm. She might smooth things over with the chief on Faith's behalf, but she was drawing a line. "I'll let you know if anything useful comes in."

It would have to do. Faith nodded. "Thanks."

"Been compiling the results of the search areas," Bobby told her grudgingly. "Copy of the report for you is in the folder on my desk."

Faith nodded. It was strictly courtesy that had him giving her the report, and she was glad that she hadn't had to wrangle it out of him. She picked up the folder on her way back to her own work area.

Instead of pacing, Cameron was now sitting by her desk, staring at the faint specks of color in the serviceable tile beneath his squarely planted boots.

She slid into her desk chair and flipped open the folder, scanning the results of the police search. The tension emanating from Cam was palpable.

On the television screen across the room the blurb about the missing boy was being repeated. Erik's engaging grin gleamed out from the small screen. Then a snowy shot of volunteers searching, including many members of Cameron Stevenson's own basketball team. The jolting, bouncing video showed them going door-to-door, canvassing the town, before the weather had been deemed too dangerous for anyone's efforts.

She looked back to see Cameron, his thumb and forefinger digging into his closed eyes.

"Why don't you try and get some sleep," she suggested softly.

His lips twisted. "Right."

Since she wouldn't be able to sleep in his position either, she dropped it.

The last thing she wanted to do was finish up paperwork, but she forced herself through the motions. The minutes ticked by. Excruciatingly slow.

Please, God, let that boy be somewhere safe and warm.

The knot in her stomach wouldn't let her find comfort in the silent plea.

Cameron rose again. Paced. Cursed. He moved from the fire department side to the police department side, and in his absence Faith propped her elbows on her desk and raked back her hair, struggling against the worst of the thoughts they'd all been willing Cameron Stevenson not to even think. And when he returned, she had herself once more under control while he paced some more. Made phone calls. Stared hard out the window.

"Is it still snowing?"

"Can't tell." He pressed his palm against the wind-rattled windowpane for a moment.

No matter what she did or didn't think about him, the action broke her heart.

"The sun will be up soon."

"If it breaks through the clouds."

"Don't lose hope, Mr. Stevenson. The sun always comes out eventually."

His face was tight when he turned and looked at her. "If that's a metaphor that my son will be found, save it."

"It's a simple fact," she said evenly. "With daylight, we'll resume the search."

"How many missing kids have you found?"

"Enough." And then, because she didn't want him asking if all of them had been found unharmed, she turned back to her desk and started shuffling papers together. When her telephone rang, she started.

Cam's dark gaze crawled from the ringing telephone to Faith's face. She swallowed and lifted the receiver. "Taylor."

It was Cheryl. But as soon as the dispatcher mentioned that she was calling about Emelda Ross, Faith's shoulders relaxed. Lowered.

From the corner of her eye, she saw Cameron's hands curl into fists, then slowly, deliberately relax.

She'd dealt with a lot of families and friends who were concerned when someone they cared about went missing…on a hike, while camping, while rock hunting. Something about Cam's worry hit her in a spot she tried hard to keep under wraps. What good was a search-and-rescue worker too emotionally wrought to do her job?

She smoothed back her hair. Murmured some excuse and crossed the hall again. Ignored Romano and stuck her head in Cheryl's office once more.

"What exactly did Miss Emelda say?"

"Listen for yourself." Cheryl had the recording already queued up. "Think the poor woman is as nervous as a cat with the storm. Weather service said the front is moving out more quickly than they'd expected though. That's good news."

Miss Emelda's voice didn't sound particularly frail or frightened to Faith. What she sounded was mighty irritated at the lack of attention her *first* call had received.

When the recording finished, Cheryl just looked at her with a shrug. "Romano wasn't exaggerating. She calls in every week like clockwork."

"Where does she live?"

Cheryl leaned over and tapped the large map of Thunder Canyon that was affixed to her wall. "Same place as always. Don't know why she doesn't move to one of the newer homes in town considering how many nervous calls she puts in to us. But she's still in that sprawling old place out past Elk."

Faith eyed the map. Emelda Ross's home was located on the western outskirts of town. The only thing further out than her place was the ice rink and Douglas property. Her gaze traced along the road, backtracking toward town. Cheryl hadn't been given a chance to ask the elderly woman about Erik during the second phone call, because Miss Emelda hadn't let her get in a word edgewise.

"What did Romano say? About Miss Emelda calling again?"

"I haven't told him." Cheryl's lips pursed. "You know what he'd say. Fact is, though, the whole squad is benched 'cause of the blizzard and this was a nonemergency call. If she were really scared, she'd have better luck complaining of shortness of breath, because we'd dispatch a fire unit out to her, and she knows that."

Faith fiddled with the sturdy watch she wore, still studying the map. Emelda Ross's house was barely in the town limits. But as the crow flew, it was definitely within walking distance of The Hall. Question was, whether or not it was walking distance for young Erik. "But *I* could go out there."

"If Erik Stevenson somehow found his way from The Hall to Miss Emelda's place, she would have said so in her call."

Cheryl was only saying what Faith was already thinking. "Yes. I know."

"The snowplows haven't been out yet. The roads are impassable."

"I'll take the snowmobile. You can break the news to Romano if you'd like."

Cheryl's lips quirked. "My pleasure." There was little that Cheryl enjoyed more than needling the officer. He barely tolerated Faith's presence. Cooperated with her only because the Chief would come down on him if he didn't. But he never liked the notion that Faith and her team accomplished anything that the police didn't.

Glancing at the big wall map one more time, Faith crossed the hall again and quickly nixed the half-formed notion of asking Cameron if he wanted to go with her.

He was sitting beside her desk again, still as a sigh, his arms folded tightly over his chest.

He was asleep.

She was glad Derek and the other members of Company C were all snoozing, some in the sleeping quarters of the building, some sprawled on the massive recliners crowded into the station's recreation room.

Because without the fire crew present, she didn't have to worry about anyone noticing the way her feet dragged to a halt, or her hand pressed hard to her chest for a moment.

There was something wrong with her in that she was somewhat undone by the sight of that tense father finally dozing.

Moving quietly, she keyed in a report of her plans to her team and collected a fresh radio and the keys to one of the snowmobiles that were garaged in a smaller building on the other side of the parking lot. She went back to the locker room and added a pair of thermal underwear beneath her clothes, then bundled up in her coat and gloves again.

Outside, the wind was still blowing, but not quite as severely. And the snow *had* stopped. Visibility was considerably improved. Still, there was no way she'd be able to maneuver her SUV through the drifts of snow filling the streets. She unlocked the garage housing the small fleet of snowmobiles and other off-road equipment. Minutes later, the whine of the engine filled the odd quiet, and she slowly steered the massive machine out of the lot.

There was no point worrying about the roads, so she went south, then west, cutting across snowy fields and empty lots in a sloppy, loose arc. When she got to Thunder Canyon Road, she dropped down into the ditch that ran alongside it. The headlight gleamed ahead of her in a wide sweep and she opened the throttle.

The powerful cat sped over the thick powder and

in minutes she'd made it to Miss Emelda's ancient home. Tucking her radio in her lapel pocket, she approached the house. Before she'd even reached the steps, the front porch light snapped on and the door creaked open. "Who's there?"

Faith's boots crunched to a stop in the snow. "Miss Emelda? It's Faith Taylor. Cheryl Lansky told me you called in again and I just wanted to come by and make sure you were all right."

"All right?" The woman pushed the door wider and Faith saw the business end of a shotgun slowly lower, to be enfolded by yards of flower-sprigged flannel and a dark, calf-length coat. "Of course I'm all right. Not that those idiots down at the police station—who can't find their way out of a paper bag, mind you—care whether or not I am. Well, come on up, girl. You're probably half-frozen."

She wasn't, but she went up the steps anyway, then stomped the snow off her boots before entering. Miss Emelda was locking the shotgun in a glass-fronted gun display. "Should know better than to call the police," she said when she turned. "Bunch of young pups, thinking I'm just a lonely old woman jumping at shadows." She waved her hand toward the chintz couch. "Sit down. Sit down."

Faith reluctantly sat. "Miss Emelda, perhaps you could—"

"Do you still read the classics?" The elderly woman settled herself on a chair with crocheted antimacassars covering the arms. Judging by the ball of thread and long needle on the coffee table, Miss

Emelda had crocheted the delicate arm coverings herself.

"I...excuse me?"

"The classics, girl. You were reading Dumas before any other child in your class."

"The Man in the Iron Mask," Faith murmured. "I'm surprised you remember that."

"Of course I remember." Miss Emelda smiled. "I remember all my children. And now you're back in Thunder Canyon despite the adventures you set off to find."

Adventures wasn't exactly the term Faith would have used to describe her time away from Thunder Canyon. "Well, I remember you talking about a lot of adventures during story hour at the library when I was little. Miss Emelda, what made you think you might have a trespasser out here last night?"

"Dog was going crazy." She raised her voice. "Dog!" A small Jack Russell terrier trotted into the room. "He doesn't bark unless someone's out in the yard."

Faith held out her hand for the curious dog. He gave her wrist an experimental sniff, then slopped his tongue over her fingers.

"He started barking before I heard your snowmobile," she said surely.

"Would you mind if I took a look around?"

Miss Emelda looked surprised. "Why would you want to do that? This was a job for the police. Like I told them. Someone wanted to break into my garage out back. My father's Model T is parked out there, you know. Only reason I called again is because Dog kept whining. I was afraid whoever it was might've gotten stuck in my garage from the storm."

Faith honestly wasn't certain what sort of market there was for stolen Model Ts, particularly in Thunder Canyon. And Miss Emelda undoubtedly did know better than anyone else whether or not her garage was being broken into. "Do you think it might be possible that it was Erik Stevenson, rather than a trespasser?"

"Erik? Good gracious, why would I think that?"

"He went missing from Katie's reception last night."

Miss Emelda pressed her hand to her chest, her delicately wrinkled visage fading. "Well…when? I saw him at The Hall with his daddy. He was as much a live wire as ever. The darling can hardly manage to sit still during story hour on Friday afternoons. Reminds me of your brother, Christopher, actually, when he was that age. Always asking questions. Wanting to know how things work. Such a shame what happened with his mother."

Now was not the time to indulge Faith's own insatiable curiosity. "I'd like to look around your property if you don't mind."

"Of course." Her hands fluttered. "Of course, dear, you do anything you want. Oh, my, that poor boy. I left the reception when the music first started playing. I'm afraid these ears are too old to acquire a taste for anything other than big band. How did I not know?"

"If you haven't had on your television or radio you wouldn't have," Faith murmured. Undoubtedly, Miss

Emelda wasn't the only one. And she could still hold out hope that Erik was snug as a bug in one of those households that hadn't been reached by the broadcasts, or the door-to-doors.

It was possible.

But unlikely, a worried voice whispered.

Faith headed to the door. Miss Emelda followed after her, her nightgown and coat flapping around her. "He's so curious," she fretted.

Faith was gaining a pretty detailed impression of young Erik. "That's what I hear." She smiled reassuringly at Miss Emelda as she pulled open the door. "Look. The sky is starting to lighten up already." It wasn't entirely an exaggeration. The sky had gone from pitch to a dark, charcoal gray.

"Well, you watch your step anyway," Miss Emelda called after her. "Particularly if you go out past the windmill at the edge of my property." She gestured at some distant point beyond her house. "The snow's likely to cover over any holes in the ground and there are still tunnels out there from the Queen of Hearts mine."

Faith froze for a moment, and it had nothing whatsoever to do with the frigid temperature. "The mine?" How could she have forgotten the Douglas's defunct gold mine?

"Played out almost before it began." Illuminated by the lights behind her, Emelda's white curls looked like a halo. "Folks tend to think the only thing left of it are memories and geegaws over at the museum. But the tunnels are still there. Ground's eroded in a few places.

Some holes are covered over. Some aren't. So you watch your step."

Faith nodded. "I'll be careful. It's cold. Stay inside."

Miss Emelda nodded and closed the door, her movements reluctant. Faith returned to the snowmobile and radioed in to Cheryl. Any minute, she knew the first rays of sunlight would start sending experimental fingers over the horizon. But for now, it was still dark. The wind still howled. And the air still smelled of snow.

The snowmobile cut a clean swath through the sea of snow as Faith steered it past Miss Emelda's house. She directed her powerful searchlight in a slow sweep. Whether Erik had been there or not, the snowstorm had obliterated whatever footprints might have been left behind.

She carefully circled the gabled garage. Tried to pull open the double door. There was a lot of play, but ultimately, the wide wooden doors stayed put. Still, she crouched down, peering through the separation. "Erik?"

She heard a soft shuffling and her nerves went into overdrive. She pulled out her penlight and directed the narrow beam of light through the opening, trying to make heads or tails of what she could see. "Erik, are you in there?"

She heard the crunch of snow, then felt a hand fall on her shoulder. She jerked around, tumbling onto her rear. Her penlight rolled out of her fingers and landed end-up in the snow, the narrow light shining up a long, denim-clad leg.

Her heart dropped out of her throat and returned to its usual spot in her chest as recognition settled. "Mr.

Stevenson. What are you doing here?" She couldn't believe she hadn't heard his truck, which she could see behind him. It looked as if it were half-stuck in the deep snow near the house. She thought about commenting on how dangerous the driving conditions were, but thought better of it.

He crouched down, plucking the penlight from the snow, and handed it to her. "I'm doing the same thing you are. Looking for my son. Cheryl Lansky told me you came out here." He pulled at the ancient wooden doors, the same way she had. "Erik? Come on, bud, if you're in there, it's time to come out."

But Faith realized that the only sounds she'd thought she'd heard hadn't come from the inside of the locked garage. They'd come from Cameron Stevenson. "He's not in there."

"Erik!"

Cameron pulled harder on the door and it groaned so violently, Faith feared the frozen hinges would pop right out of the wood. She pushed to her feet and closed her gloved hands around his arm. "Mr. Stevenson. Erik is *not* in the garage!"

Even through the layers of gloves, coats and sweaters, she could feel his muscles bunch. Could feel the resistance in him, the need to believe his son was so close. "We need to keep looking," she said quietly.

She could feel, more than see, his glare. By slow degrees, his grip on the doors eased. He let go, and the wood all but sighed in relief as the door settled.

"I can't lose him, too." His voice was barely audible, yet its rawness tore at her.

Her fingers curled against the thickness of his coat. "You can't give up."

His voice dropped even lower. "It's been more than ten hours."

She was well aware of that. Painfully so.

Maybe the man hadn't watched his son properly, but he was suffering now.

Then her radio crackled with life and she started just as badly as he did. But it was just Cheryl, dispatching a fire unit out to a woman in labor.

The noise was enough to rally her focus away from the father back to the boy, where it belonged. "I don't suppose it'll do me any good to tell you to go inside with Miss Emelda." She looked pointedly at his truck. "You could call for a tow truck to pull that loose, and then *go home.*"

He shook his head.

"Then come with me." She tugged her knitted cap down around her ears and mounted the snowmobile again. When he climbed on behind her, taking up more than his share of the seat, she closed her mind off to everything but Erik. She headed out toward the stark windmill that seemed little more than a skeletal shadow against the sky, as it turned ever so slowly in the still morning.

She pulled up next to it, and cut her engine. The silence was overwhelming.

"What are you doing?"

She tilted her head, closing her eyes, concentrating on the silence. Had she heard something? "Listening."

The only thing answering her was a soft creak from

the windmill. She turned off the searchlight and pulled out the penlight. When she started to tuck it between her teeth, he took it from her and directed it at the map she spread out.

"What are we looking for?" His voice was so near her ear, she felt the warmth of his breath on her cheek.

"These are known erosion holes into the Queen of Hearts." She tapped the marks she'd made courtesy of her conversation with Cheryl. "Those that are marked have been boarded over."

"And the ones that aren't marked?"

She didn't answer and he swore beneath his breath. She could only silently concur. There wasn't a soul living in these parts of Montana who wouldn't be familiar with the "Stay Out, Stay Alive" motto when it came to abandoned mines. It was taught in school, splashed across early Sunday morning public service announcements on television and painted on bus-stop benches.

All of which might mean absolutely nothing to an adventurous, curious young boy.

She folded the map and he handed her the penlight, which she pocketed. Then she started the snowmobile again and drove slowly along Miss Emelda's property line, her powerful searchlight steady thanks to Cameron's guidance. The entrance proper to the Queen of Hearts was a good two miles away. But the tunnels were surprisingly extensive, according to Cheryl, who had a grandfather several generations back who'd worked the Douglas-owned mine.

She nearly drove right over the first hole since the planks covering it were almost obscured by snow. Cameron swung off the cat and dropped to his knees, tunneling his hands through the snow to yank at the planks. They budged even less than Miss Emelda's garage doors had.

The wind skidded over them, lifting the dark hair on his unprotected head as he strode back to the snowmobile and climbed on behind her.

Did Erik's parka have a hood?

The snowmobile jumped forward, her anxiety unfortunately finding its way to the throttle, and Cameron's hands abruptly closed over her hips as he steadied himself. Ignoring him was impossible, but at least the sudden heat streaking through her helped hold the cold at bay. "What does Erik know about the mine?" She raised her voice so he could hear.

The entire length of her back felt the press of him as he leaned over her shoulder. "Nothing beyond what Emelda Ross talks about at the library."

If Miss Emelda were spinning her tales as enticingly now as she had when Faith was a child, she could only imagine the effect on an impressionable, adventurous boy. "Does he ever talk about it?"

"No."

Well. Okay. No wiggle room there.

She found the second site. Long, narrow and securely boarded over, though the board looked as if it had taken its share of potshots from a pellet gun or two.

The third site was also a bust.

Discouraged, Faith pulled out her map again. The sun was finally peeking over the horizon, but as it often did at dawn, the temperature seemed to drop several degrees in the process. There was also a low-lying layer of gray cloud that practically screamed *snow*. And she was glad for the solid warmth of the man behind her. "We had to have missed one." She studied the map. Turned and studied the physical land-marks around them.

"There." Cam reached around her and pointed at the map. "That would be, what? About fifty yards north."

He was right. She traced her gaze in that direction. There was an ebb and flow of snowdrifts along the fence line, in some places completely obscuring the wood rails. It was anybody's guess whose property it was. She figured they'd long passed Emelda Ross's land, which meant it was probably Douglas property, as was most of the open land.

The back of her neck prickled and she quickly folded the map. "Call for him." Her voice was practically hoarse from all the calling she had done.

The man needed no second urging. His deep voice boomed out as she maneuvered the cat around once more. Up, over the hills, fairly flying across the little valleys. And then she spotted the haphazard point of upended planks poking out of the snow.

Snow spewed from beneath the runners when she pulled to a stop nearby. Cam was off the cat before she could even form a warning to be cautious. He went flat on his stomach, his head disappearing below a jagged, splintered board that stuck up from the snow like some ancient spear. "Erik!"

Faith's knees went weak when they both heard the faint response.

At last. Thank you, God.

They'd found him.

Chapter Three

"*Erik!*" Cam stared into the dark pit. His eyes burned. "Are you hurt?" He could hear his son's muffled sobs. His fingers tightened on the board, oblivious to the dagger-sharp splinters that tore through his gloves. "We're gonna get you out in a sec," he promised roughly.

He looked back to see Faith speaking into her radio even as she dragged equipment out of the cargo beneath the seat of the snowmobile. Rope. Harness. Shovel.

She ran over to him, surprisingly adept even though her legs sunk into the snow nearly to her knees with each step, and dumped the items beside him. "I need to see down there." She waited until he'd moved back and she leaned carefully over the narrow opening, peering down. "Erik, I'm going to throw down some light sticks, okay?"

His answer was too long in coming. But eventually, his young voice floated upward. "'Kay."

She quickly shook a few sticks—pulled from one of her many pockets—to activate them and tossed them down. "Fire's sending a truck," she said without looking back at Cam. "My boss, Jim, is going to try to get here, but it's gonna take at least an hour before he can get a chopper free. We need to get some of this snow cleared." She grabbed the shovel and began attacking the white weight.

Cam helped, scooping away snow with his hands, then his arm, until they could see the full scope of the boarded-over hole.

Nausea curled its nasty fingers into him.

Faith sat back, the short shovel resting on her thighs. "He was probably looking down where those boards are pulled away, and this one gave way beneath him." They both eyed the freshly split plank.

There'd only been four planks to start with. About eight feet long, covering the opening that was—at best—half that long and even less than that wide. Only one board remained intact, but when she tested its solidity, dirt and snow rained down into the crevice.

"Daddy!" Erik's voice howled up.

"It's okay, Erik," he yelled down. Then he eyed Faith. "I'm not waiting."

"Yes, you are." She caught him in a surprisingly

strong grip when he reached for the rope. "Your son didn't climb down there. He fell. We're going to need help to get him out."

He shrugged her off. "I am *not* waiting." He stood up, grabbing the rope, eyeing the best place to tie it off. The old snow fence with boards as ruinous as what was supposed to have protected the erosion hole, or the snowmobile that was massive only if he compared it to Faith Taylor's size rather than his own? "He's down there, crying, and there's no way a fire crew can get across that snow."

The sunlight was even stronger now—he saw the flicker in her hazel eyes and knew she'd thought the same thing. They'd been able to traverse the deep snow only because of the snowmobile. If a fire crew were to make it to them, they'd either need to be following a snowplow, have a fleet of snowmobiles—which they didn't exactly have considering half of it had already been used by Faith—or be on foot with cross-country skies or snowshoes.

"There's no way you can even *fit*," she countered, her voice flat as she eyed his shoulders.

"Daddy!" Erik's wail was faint. "Iwannagetoutta heeeere!"

Ignoring Faith, Cam headed toward the snowmobile. As an anchor, it was the best they had. He cinched the rope around it, and started carrying the rest of the coiled rope back toward the hole, only to be side-swiped by a hundred and twenty pounds of irate female.

The snow cushioned their fall but the impact still

knocked him for six. He stared up at the sky, at the blonde nearly sitting on his chest. "What the hell are you doing?"

"Maybe football tackles are the only thing you understand." Her voice was tight and her eyes flashed. "I am *not* letting you endanger yourself, too."

He lifted her bodily from him and dumped her on her backside. "And you obviously don't know what it's like to have a child in danger."

The high color in her cheeks drained right back out. "That doesn't mean I don't care about the child who *is*," she said stiffly. "For your son's sake, let me do my job!"

"What? *You're* going to go down there?"

She pushed to her feet and stomped through the deep snow back to the snowmobile, where she began untying his knot.

"Faith, dammit—"

She shot him a killing glare and he realized she was tying a fresh one. "At least learn how to tie a knot that won't slip." Her voice was cutting. "I may be the only female SAR in this county, Mr. Stevenson, but I've earned my place on this team." She shouldered the rest of the coiled rope and kicked her way through the snow past him toward the hole. "Do you know how many times we end up having to get *two* people out of difficulties because someone was foolhardy enough to enter a situation they weren't prepared or qualified for because they were so intent on solving the problem themselves?" As she spoke, she was working the rope through the harness and a series of pulleys. "Too many. Frankly—" she shot him a dark look "—I have better things to do with my time than rescue a father whose concern for his son comes a little late."

"What the hell is *that* supposed to mean?"

Faith shook her head and carefully stepped over the one remaining undamaged board, ignoring Cameron's furious voice. Looking down, she could see the faint, green glow of the light sticks. She was going down because she couldn't stand to listen to Erik's woeful cries a moment longer, and for no other reason. "I'm coming down there, Erik," she called loudly.

And when Jim showed up and found out she'd acted without backup, she'd probably lose her hard-won spot on the SAR team.

She stepped off the board, and the rope whizzed as she descended into the narrow crevice. The farther she went, the more obvious it became that Cameron—even if he'd tried—would never have managed to fit. Not when it was so close around her.

"Erik?" She braced her legs against the dirt walls on either side of her, and slowly began maneuvering out of her coat. "My name is Faith Taylor. How ya' doing down there?"

"I'm cold."

She was sweating. And his voice was definitely weak. "I'll bet you are." She finally worked out of the sleeves and simply let the thing fall. She needed the extra few inches of space she'd gain without it. "My coat is coming down. If you can grab it, go ahead. Did you hurt anything when you fell?"

"I dunno." His crying abated a little. "Oh. There goes your coat. I, um, I missed it."

"That's okay. It's just a coat." She lowered a few more inches, carefully working her shoulders past an embedded rock that had already painfully caught her hip. "Did you hit your head when you fell?"

"I think so. It hurts a lot. Where's my dad?"

"He's waiting for you up top," she assured gently as she worked a little faster. His words were slurring. Concussion? Exposure? Both?

Regardless, she wanted to keep him talking and alert. "Erik, are you on a ledge or something?"

"'S wood. I got splinters in my bu—rear."

And she was mighty grateful he was in fair enough shape to sound indignant about it. "What were you doing all the way out here?"

"Dad's gonna ground me for a year."

"Maybe." Her voice was cheerful, masking her tension. "My parents grounded me once for six months." She finally cleared the rock, only to duck her head when a cascade of dirt rained down on her. When it stopped, she looked up. She could see Cameron leaning over the hole. "Don't suppose Fire is here yet?" she called up to him.

"No."

And Jim obviously wasn't, either, or he'd be haranguing her.

"What'd they ground ya' for?"

Faith slid down another foot. She figured she was about thirty feet down. "I went climbing in the canyon without permission. And I ended up breaking my arm.

And since nobody knew where I was…well, once they found me and had finished hugging me, they grounded me."

Erik had no reply to that. He might only be seven, but she hoped he was grasping her point and not falling unconscious. "Erik? You still with me?"

"Uh-huh."

The hole widened again and she tugged a flashlight out of the cargo pocket on her calf. She flipped it on, shining it around, then down. She could see Erik's feet another fifteen feet or so below her and she lowered herself the rest of the way.

Her flashlight danced over him, catching his dirt-smudged face. She caught her toes over the wood beam and steadied herself. "Hey there. Think you can hold my light?"

"Yeah."

She reached out, handing the light to him. "Shine it downward, though. Okay?"

The beam redirected away from her eyes.

"Kinda scary down here, huh?"

"I think there might be bats or something."

Faith doubted it, but she wanted to keep the boy talking. The rough beam was incredibly unstable and she didn't dare use it to take her weight. Only problem was, she couldn't ascend with him, because there wasn't enough space, and she couldn't rig her second harness around him unless she had a steady foothold. Which meant she'd have to take him down lower with her, before she could get him up.

"You're a girl."

She grinned. "'Fraid so. Only seven-year-olds and girls could fit down that hole up there. Think you can scoot closer to me, Erik?"

He started to, but the wood moaned and debris tumbled loose. She held up her hand. "Okay. So that's not gonna work."

"I want my dad," he whispered.

Her heart squeezed. "I know you do, sweetie. Here's the deal. I'm going to swing over closer to you in a minute, and you're gonna grab onto me good and tight, then we'll lower down into the mine shaft below us, okay?"

"I don't wanna go down *more!*" Panic riddled his words.

"Believe me, you've come down the worst of it, already," she assured calmly. "I just need to know if you can grab onto me. Really fast. I'll catch you, too, at the same time."

"What if I fall?"

"I won't let you."

"But—"

"Erik? The quicker we do this, the quicker I can get you up top again. Or we can wait until one of my friends gets here." Not that Jim would fit down the hole any easier than Cameron would have.

"How long's that gonna take?"

"I don't know, sweetie. Might be an hour or so."

"I gotta pee," he whispered. "And my head hurts really, really bad."

Her throat tightened. "I can't do anything about your head just yet, but you could go down here. I won't tell anyone."

"Dad said I'm not s'posed to do that 'cause it's bad manners, just like I'm not s'posed to call grown-ups by their first name."

She bit back a smile at the odd pairing of rules. "Ordinarily I'd agree," she murmured. "But I think this would be considered extenuating circumstances. I'll turn my back. Give you some privacy. And you can call me Faith. It's okay, when you've gotten permission from an adult."

He looked torn. "I'll jus' catch you."

"All rightee then." She reached forward and took the flashlight back and returned it to her calf pocket. "I don't want you to move your legs or anything. Just reach out with your arms." She was too afraid of the beam toppling if he did more than that. "When I count to three, you be ready, okay?"

"'Kay." His voice was breathless. She hoped it was only from formulating the stories he'd be able to share after this was all over.

"One." She adjusted her grip on the rope, prepared to pull up or let down depending on what the beam did. "Two." She pressed the toe of her boot against the wall of dirt for leverage. "Three."

She swung toward him and a set of young arms grabbed onto her like a lifeline and she scooped him up, taking on his fifty pounds as the rope whizzed and they descended into the mineshaft.

Her feet hit solid ground with a jolt and she carefully knelt, settling him on the earth. "I don't want you to move, okay? Just in case you *have* hurt something you don't know about." She waited until he focused on her, then stood and unhooked the second harness from her belt.

She walked a few feet until she could see daylight at the top of the hole. "I've got him," she called up. "He'll be coming up in a few minutes."

She saw Cameron's arm lift. The man was probably too choked up to speak. Her conscience bit at her some for speaking so harshly to him, but she ignored it and turned her focus back to Erik.

"So." She tugged off her gloves and pulled out her flashlight again to shine it over him as she crouched next to him. "Seriously. What *were* you doing coming out here by yourself?"

"Wasn't by myself," he defended. "I was with Tommy Bodecker, 'cause it was his dare."

Good Lord. Save her from boyhood dares. She slowly felt along his arms and legs. "Is Tommy in your class at school?"

"Nah. He's ten already."

"And where's Tommy now?" She wasn't familiar with the Bodecker family.

Erik made a face. "He went home 'cause it started to snow."

"I see. And you didn't go with him, because... *why?*"

"'Cause of the dare," he said as if it should be perfectly obvious. "He said I was ascared of ghosts an' I told him I was not. And he said if I wasn't then how come I never came out here and saw 'em for myself."

"Ghosts. I see. Tommy Bodecker thinks there are ghosts here in the mine?"

"Yeah." Erik flinched a little when she ran her fingers over his shoulder, but he didn't complain.

"So when he left you out here by yourself, you figured you had to stay." She discovered the enormous goose egg behind his ear. "And prove you weren't scared."

His expression was approving. "Yeah."

She'd have a few things to say to Tommy Bodecker if and when she caught up to him. "I think I might have heard of it if Tommy had ever spent the night in the Queen of Hearts," she murmured. "So if anyone's the authority on ghosts here, that'd be you."

"Oh." A dimple snuck out from his cheeks. "Yeah."

"So? Were there any ghosts?"

He shook his head.

"Just bats?"

He nodded.

He was adorable. "Think you can stand up so I can get you into this harness?"

He scrambled to his feet, hunching over a little, definitely off balance. She steadied him as she helped him into the rescue harness, adjusting the webbing, fastening off her rope to him.

"What do I gotta do?"

"Not a thing," she promised. "I've got you roped off up top. I'm just going to pull on this end, and you're going to lift out. Simple as can be." She suited actions to words and his feet left the ground.

"Cool."

"It's cool that I can get you out of here," she said, bringing him eye-level with her. "If you want to learn how to climb, you should do it properly next time. Ever seen the rock climbing gym at Extension Sporting Goods?"

His eyes were enormous. "I seen it, but my dad's never let me do it."

"Tell him they give classes there. You ready to go?"

He nodded.

"Just tell me if you want me to slow you down or anything. If you feel sick to your stomach or anything."

His head bobbed yet again and he winced, going still. "I hurt."

She gently ran her hand over his tousled hair. "I know, sweetie. But you're going to be okay."

"Dad's mad."

"He's gladder that we found you," she promised. "Ready?"

His eyelashes were drooping. "Uh-huh."

She began working the rope, levering him upward. It took less time to raise him to the top than it had for her to make the descent. And she knew the moment he was close enough for Cameron to grab hold, because the weight of him was immediately lifted from her braced body. Moments later, the rope snaked back down to her again.

She let out a long breath and willed her legs to stop shaking. She could hear the high pitch of Erik's voice and the lower murmur of Cameron's and didn't have to work hard to imagine the relief that would be in the man's deep brown eyes.

Pulling out her flashlight again, she played its light

over her confines. In both directions, the tunnel had completely caved in. Directly above her was none too stable, either, considering the rotting timber on which Erik had managed to land.

It was considerably warmer below surface, though, which was a blessing. If Erik had been more exposed during the storm—

She cut off the thought. Her coat lay in a shadowy heap and she grabbed it, tying it off her belt. Her hip ached with a sharp throb where she'd connected with the embedded rock. She could only imagine the bumps Erik had sustained.

She moved until she could see sky again. "Use the radio," she called up. "Find out what's holding them up. Erik needs medical attention."

Cameron's head appeared. "Already called. Ambulance is on its way," he yelled back.

Well. She had to give the man credit for thinking.

And now that Erik was up top, the effects of the last day were definitely starting to wear on her. She wanted a hot bath and sleep.

Neither of which she was going to get if she didn't get herself out of the mine.

If the ambulance or Fire hadn't managed to make their way to them by the time Faith made it out, she'd tell Cam to take Erik to the hospital on the snowmobile. They could always send someone back for her.

In this section of the mine shaft, there was no wall to climb up, and the rotting beams that had caught Erik were too unstable to use as support. So she climbed the rope. Hand over hand, rope snaking between her twisted boots. For the first time in a long while, she actually felt grateful for the number of times her ex-husband had challenged her on the ropes while they'd been living in Albuquerque.

"How are you coming?"

Cameron's voice startled her and she jerked a little, knocking her knee on one of the beams. The wood creaked and debris fell. "Coming up," she told him, carefully pulling herself up the thick rope, beyond the treacherous wood. She was starting to feel light-headed and wasn't certain if it was simply hunger, the expulsion of her adrenaline, or the air quality in the mine. Whatever it was, it made her stop for a moment, suspended there on the rope, as she waited for the spinning to stop.

A lovely time to remember that neither rock climbing nor ropes had ever been her favorite pastime.

At last, she heard the whine of a siren coming closer.

She swallowed, and cautiously began again. But when she reached that same, particularly narrow patch with the rock her hip had already greeted intimately, she had to slow again.

Even though she'd tied the coat off and it hung harmlessly down behind her, it still created too much bulk. She pulled it loose and let it fall again. Pity. They had to buy their own uniforms and those coats didn't come cheap. Her sweatshirt wasn't much of a help, either, she discovered, and she inched down a bit on the rope, twining her legs tightly to keep her balance, and worked out of it, leaving her with only the thin waffle-weave of her thermal undershirt. But it gave her the quarter-inch she needed, and she started to squeeze past the obstruction, earning herself a fresh set of scrapes and bruises in the process.

But just when she thought she was within sight of passing it, another cascade of dirt rained down on her head, blinding her. She swore, ducking, and lost several precious inches. The dirt just kept coming, piling in around her, filling in the bare spaces between her body and the eroding walls.

Panic nipped at her with nasty teeth. The downfall eased and she finally lifted her head, squinting against the dust that wanted to attack her eyes.

"Cameron!" His name was a hoarse yell.

"I got you." His voice was audible, though she couldn't make him out beyond the swirling dirt. "The last board collapsed. Ground's caving in."

She wriggled, trying to turn her hipbone away from the rock. Something caught. A strap of her harness. A fold of her pants. Something. She coughed, spitting dirt out of her mouth. Freeing one hand to wipe at her face. "I'm stuck!"

She could hear him swearing. "I'm gonna pull you up."

The rope went tight as a wire. She could feel it dragging at her, as surely as she could feel the earth keeping her in its greedy grasp.

"Wait!" Tears burned her eyes. It felt like she was being split into two.

The rope eased. She tilted her head back. The hole up top was wider, yet it was filling up where she was pinned as if she were some thumb plugging up a dike. Cameron stared down at her. The siren was growing louder.

It felt as if hours had passed since she'd lifted the boy out of the mine, but she knew it was only minutes.

"Keep Erik away from the hole."

"He's sitting by the snowmobile."

There was still space for her feet to move. She felt around, seeking some leverage to push up, but found none. Her toes were getting numb and the pressure on her chest was making her dizzy. Her hand was trapped near her abdomen and she worked her fingers around until she found a buckle.

"What are you doing down there?"

"Having a tea party," she muttered. "I have to get out of my harness," she said as loudly as her compressed chest allowed.

"What do you need from me?"

"A shovel, if more dirt comes down here." She coughed. Every time she inhaled, she got a lungful of dust, and with her free hand, she stretched the collar of her thermal shirt up over her chin and nose.

"At least you've got a sense of humor," she heard him say.

At least he got the fact she'd been facetious.

Her fingers strained to work the webbed strap free. There was no question of when the buckle loosened, because she felt an immediate release of pressure pulling down on her hips. She held tightly to the rope with her free hand as she wriggled a little more, trying to gain more space. She could feel the warmth of blood where her skin was being torn away by the immovable rock. Her boots scrabbled and she finally managed to pull herself upward a few precious inches. She exhaled, sucked in her stomach, and scraped past the rock. At last, her other hand was free, and she grabbed the rope with it. "Okay, now pull." The siren was so loud now, she wasn't sure he'd even hear her.

Her voice was barely audible, but Cam heard. He braced himself and pulled on the rope. Not that she weighed much. But every time he moved his foot, he feared another cubic foot of earth was going to collapse in on her.

And he still had one eye on his son. Erik had lain on his side in the snow. "Erik!" His voice was rough.

His boy lifted his hand slightly, and relief eased the vise around his heart. But Faith was still hanging on to the end of the rope.

He dragged on it, hauling it upward. Faith's head appeared and he grabbed her shoulders, bodily lifting her the rest of the way just as the ambulance, preceded by a snowplow, arrived. Two police vehicles followed.

He pulled Faith clear of the crumbling hole, plunged several feet away and settled her in the snow. It seemed a better choice, rather than keeping her tightly against him. Her fingers were still locked around the rope and he carefully loosened them. Her knuckles were raw. Bloody. He'd tended plenty of banged up football players—broken noses, broken legs, split lips. The sight of blood had never bothered him before.

It did now. He didn't even have something clean and soft to wrap around her hands.

"See to Erik." Her voice was husky. She was caked with dirt, but he could still see the blood seeping through her skinny white thermal shirt. More blood.

"Can you walk?" He tore out of his coat and cautiously pulled it around her shoulders, shaking off the unwelcome urge to wrap his arms around her as well.

"I'm okay." The fuzziness in her hazel eyes was already starting to clear. She turned her head, looking back at the erosion hole. "Thank you."

Cam shoved his shaking hand through his hair. "Thank *you*," he said huskily. Then, because he couldn't leave her lying in the snow any more than he could leave his son for a moment longer, he scooped her up.

"I can walk," she muttered. But her head still fell tiredly to his shoulder. Ignoring her protest, he carried her over to where the paramedic was bending over Erik.

"She's bleeding," he announced, settling her on the seat of the snowmobile. Letting go was harder than it should have been, and he took a few steps away. As if he could step away from the knot she caused inside him.

The paramedic lifted his blond head and Cam realized the man wasn't a paramedic at all, but one of the doctors from the hospital.

"What're you doing here?" Faith asked the man.

"You kidding? The whole town's talking about you finding Erik down in the Queen of Hearts."

Faith's lips twisted a little. Her gaze flicked up to Cameron. "This is my brother. Dr. Christopher Taylor." Then she looked back at Erik, who was staring at her as if she'd sprouted wings. "How's he doing?"

"Good, considering." The doctor grinned at Cam's son, and the resemblance between the Taylors became even more apparent. "I want to run some tests, check him in for observation for a few days, just to be safe."

"I don't wanna."

"You hit your head pretty hard, pal," the doctor said smoothly. "We need to make sure you heal up okay from that."

"Daddy?"

Cam crouched down beside Erik. His hands shook as he smoothed back his son's hair. His boy had his coloring, but every time he looked at Erik, he saw so much of Laura looking back at him. How would he have gone on if he'd lost Erik, too? "I'll go with you."

The ambulance driver and the snowplow driver stood by with a stretcher, and the doctor placed Erik on it. He'd already hooked up an IV to Erik's arm and he handed the bag to Cam to carry alongside. "For dehydration," he said.

They started for the ambulance, but Cam hesitated. "What about Faith?"

She waved her hand. "Go. I'll be fine."

The doctor snorted. "Hardly. You're going, too, Faith."

She lifted an eyebrow, clearly rallying. "Not today, Topher."

Judging by the tone in her voice, the nickname

wasn't one the doctor particularly enjoyed hearing. And the man obviously wanted to argue. But there was no hiding his urgency in getting Erik to the hospital. Cam was feeling pretty urgent, too.

"Go." Faith waved her hand. "I can bandage up my own scrapes."

The doctor leaned over and whipped Faith's shirt up above her waist. Cam winced even as Faith was jerking her shirt back down over the torn pants and raw flesh. "You need to go to the hospital," he said flatly. "And not on that snowmobile."

"I'll go by after I've had a shower," she said stiffly. "And I *won't* take the snowmobile."

"If you don't, Faith—" Doctor Taylor cut off his threat when Erik wretched.

"Go," Faith insisted to Cam as the doc tended his son. "There's not room in the ambulance for all of us. I'll grab a ride with the uniforms." She waved a hand toward the police officers who were struggling through the snow toward the dangerous hole. "I'll send someone back later for the cat. And Cam's truck."

Then, as if the matter was settled, Faith leaned over, grabbed her radio, and began speaking into it. She hardly seemed to notice her injured fingers.

The doctor quickly loaded Erik into the ambulance and Cam moved aside in the confined space to make room for Dr. Taylor. In seconds, the ambulance lurched and began crunching over the frozen ground.

Through the rear window, Cam watched Faith Taylor. She looked incredibly small inside the bulk of his coat.

If she hadn't gone down to get his son when she had, Erik might have still been down there when the hole caved in even more.

"Remarkable, isn't she?" Dr. Taylor's voice was quiet.

Cam dragged his gaze away from the woman. His fingers tightened around Erik's small hand. "Remarkable," he agreed after a moment.

And he owed his son's safety to her.

But that still didn't mean he welcomed the effect she had on him.

Chapter Four

The only thing holding Faith upright was the door-jamb of her front door against her spine. She waved at Teddy as he departed. She'd ended up riding back with the snowplow driver since it had quickly become clear that the police would be occupied for a while securing the erosion hole.

As soon as the snowplow lumbered down the street, however, she slunk inside her condo and nudged the door closed. Cameron Stevenson's coat slid off her shoulders and she left it where it lay, shuffling straight to the bathroom.

She flipped on the shower, letting the room fill with steam while she summoned enough stamina to peel out of her clothes. When she did, a cloud of dirt puffed out to settle on the pale green rug. She ignored that, too, and stepped under the hot spray, wincing as the water found her wounds and swirled around her feet in a cloud of dirt and blood. She rinsed the worst of the dirt from her hair and the moment she felt reasonably clean, she flipped the rush of water from the shower-head to the faucet, and filled the tub, sinking down with relief.

She soaked until her skin pruned and the water cooled. And then, because her muscles were stiffening beyond belief, she made herself get out of the tub before it got any worse. She gingerly spread antibiotic ointment over her cuts and scrapes, used up every bandage she managed to unearth in her medicine cabinet, then padded barefoot into her bedroom.

She was so tired she could barely keep her eyes open. She opened her closet and pulled a clean oversize T-shirt from a neat stack. As she did so, her gaze lifted, as it always did, to the pastel items folded on the top shelf.

Then she firmly closed the door and climbed into bed, pulling her quilt up to her ears. The phone rang, but she ignored it, knowing her answering machine would pick it up eventually.

Once she'd had a nap, she'd go check on Erik at the hospital.

But it wasn't the boy who was on her mind when she fell asleep moments later.

It was the boy's father.

"Pull a stunt like that again, Taylor, and you're off the team." Jim Shepherd's eyes were level as he stood smack-dab in the corridor outside Thunder Canyon General's pediatric unit. Faith hadn't managed to visit Erik at the hospital the prior day, simply because she'd slept clean through to the next morning. Now, after spending the morning at the fire station, it was lunchtime, and she simply was not going to be delayed any longer.

Not even by her boss, who'd been dogging her heels for ten minutes. He also hadn't made it to Thunder Canyon the previous day. But he was making up for not getting to the site of Erik's accident now by raking her over the coals.

"I'm serious, Faith. We don't enter abandoned mines without backup."

She didn't mind the raking when she'd earned it. But she couldn't—wouldn't—change the decision she'd made. "Well, as I've said about a dozen times now, the only backup I had handy was Cameron Stevenson. It would have taken a demo crew to get through to Erik from the mine shaft itself. Any access points had already collapsed."

"But you didn't know that beforehand, did you?"

She couldn't deny that point, so she just stood there, eyeing her boss.

After a moment, he sighed noisily, then looked around the hospital, with its pale walls and stark tile floors.

"*The Nugget* wants an interview about the rescue."

"Give 'em one if you want." Faith had already erased the message from the local reporter who'd called the previous day. "I don't have anything to say."

Jim wasn't particularly enamored with the publicity their team often garnered, but he was also aware of the fact that their salaries came from the same people who read those newspapers. "Evidently, during the cleanup, somebody found a small gold nugget."

Faith shrugged. "I didn't notice any gold," she said dryly. "I was a little busy."

He smiled a little. "So how's the kid?"

"Concussion. Dehydration." The answer didn't come from Faith, and she stiffened, looking past Jim to see Cameron standing there.

Her gaze roved over him before she could stop herself. The handsome man with the broad shoulders had hauled her out of a very sticky situation, she silently defended. Of course she had some...enhanced interest in him. It was gratitude.

Which didn't at all explain the odd curling sensation inside her stomach. Or the reason his coat was still laying on the couch in her living room like some welcome visitor.

His brown gaze was steady on her face and she was positively mortified to feel her cheeks warming. "Jim, this is Cameron Stevenson," she introduced hurriedly. Anything to restore normalcy. "Mr. Stevenson, this is Jim Shepherd, my boss."

The two men shook hands. "Glad things worked out okay," Jim said. He was probably ten years older than the mid-thirties in which she'd privately placed Cameron. Jim also was not as tall, nor as broad.

And comparing her boss to Cameron's wealth of physical attributes seemed a ridiculous waste of time.

"How is Erik today? I meant to get over here yesterday."

"He's terrorizing the nurses," he said. "He's been asking after you."

Her spurt of pleasure at that news dwindled quickly when Faith felt Jim's gaze silently travel from Cameron to her and back again. She wished she didn't know what the man was thinking. He'd been happily married for twenty years, and in the year since she'd been on the team, he'd made no secret that he figured she needed a man in her life again. Judging by his speculative expression, she could only imagine where his thoughts were going now.

"I hope you've made time to get yourself treated, too," Cameron said. "Since you didn't do it yesterday."

The palm of her hand snuck across her hip where several large gauze pads lurked beneath her clothing, and the way his sharp brown gaze veered down for a fraction of a moment told her that her self-conscious movement hadn't gone unnoticed. "How'd you know I didn't come in?"

"Dr. Taylor mentioned it."

"Treated?" Jim didn't look pleased. "You were injured? That wasn't in your report."

"A few bumps," Faith defended evenly. "Nothing that necessitates my brother's overdeveloped sense of protection."

"But since you're here at the hospital, you might as well let him take a look at you." Cameron's voice was smoothly reasonable. "You were bleeding a lot when you came out of the mine."

"You want me to put you on inactive?" Jim asked, knowing full well that she'd go bananas without work to occupy her time.

She really did not like feeling ganged up on. But how could she tell them just how much she loathed going to a doctor, any doctor, even for something as minor as patching up her scrapes? "I'll go after I've seen Erik." She mentally crossed her fingers. "Is he awake?"

In answer, Cameron pushed open the door to his son's private room. Faith hesitated for a moment, then stepped past him. And she did *not* notice how good he smelled, either.

She focused on the boy, who seemed to be nearly swallowed by the hospital bed, though she figured Erik was pretty average-size for his age. "Hey there, kiddo."

"Faith! You came."

Warmth filled her at the way Erik's expression lit. She put Erik's dad out of her mind as far as he would go—admittedly not very far, if she were honest—as she approached the bed and handed Erik the large box that was wrapped in bright blue paper patterned with footballs, basketballs and baseballs. "You can't use it until your doctor gives you the say-so, though," she warned when his hands grabbed onto the gift.

"Can I open it now?" There was such hope in his sparkling brown eyes that if he hadn't already charmed her, he would have done so now.

She laughed softly. "That's sort of the point," she assured. "Open away."

"Yessss." His fingers dragged at the wrapping, and paper flew. Then his jaw dropped a little, his eyes widening, when the neon green soft toboggan was revealed. "Kew-ell," he dragged out the word. "I always wanted one of these, but Dad wouldn't let me."

She felt a stab of guilt at that, wondering if she should have asked permission from Cameron before giving the gift to Erik. She had no nieces or nephews. Was there some sort of etiquette she should have known to follow?

On the table beside the bed were a stack of video games, and she had a qualm that she ought to have brought something similar. And judging by Cameron's expression, he wasn't all that pleased with the gift.

But all he said was, "What do you say, Erik?"

Erik looked chagrined. "Right. Thank you, Faith."

"Ms. Taylor," Cameron prompted.

"Uh-uh," Erik countered. "She told me I could call her Faith. Right?"

She nodded. "Yes, I did. When are they going to spring you?"

Erik rolled his eyes. "I just wanna leave now."

Behind Cameron, Jim lifted his hand in a wave, gesturing with his pager, before heading off. Cameron walked into the room, letting the door swish closed. "They told us he'll be ready to go home by Wednesday."

"Maybe Faith can come over and show me how to use the toboggan, huh, Dad?"

He didn't approach the bed where Faith was standing, she noticed, but remained closer to the door. Almost as if he couldn't wait to open it again and have her leave.

"I'd love to," she told the boy, though it seemed unfathomable to her that any child living in Thunder Canyon hadn't already had *some* experience with tobogganing. There was a hill near the ice-skating rink that was perfect for sledding and snowboarding, and during snow season, it was nearly always congested with children.

"We'll see," Cameron said.

Faith eyed him for a moment, but being well aware of Erik's avid attention, she held her tongue. Instead, she grinned at the boy. "Any word from Tommy Bodecker about ghosts?"

Erik started to speak, but Cameron was the one who answered. "Erik won't be hanging out with Tommy anymore." His voice was flat.

Faith could hardly blame the man for that. She resisted the urge to smooth the cowlick on Erik's forehead. "Guess maybe he won't be issuing dares anymore, eh?"

He started to smile, but it died as he shot his dad a wary look. "No, ma'am."

Ma'am. Ouch. "Well, you just let me know when you're up to trying out this puppy." She tapped the colorful sled. "And I'm glad you'll be getting out of here soon."

"Thanks." Erik's smile was ever so much easier than his father's.

She winked at the boy, and headed to the door. Her steps slowed, though, as she waited for Cameron to move out of the way, and when he followed her into the hall once more, she hoped the jumping in her stomach wasn't visible on her face.

"Did you get your truck back okay from Miss Emelda's place?"

He nodded once.

She brushed her palms down her thighs. "I, um, I hope you don't mind. You know. About the gift for Erik."

"It was nice of you to think of him."

"He's had other visitors?" She certainly hoped so. She could only imagine how tedious it would be if he didn't have some entertainment.

"A few of his school friends have come by. Adele Douglas came by yesterday, too. Said she wanted to see for her own eyes that he was going to be fine." It was Adele and Caleb Douglas who owned the mine.

Faith listened with half an ear. She noticed that Cameron didn't move out of the doorway to Erik's room. He was obviously keeping an eye on his son, inside.

"He's not going to disappear from the hospital room," she said softly. Did he think the boy was going to dash out the window and try out the unwelcome toboggan?

"First you think I don't watch him closely enough, and now you think I watch him too closely?" His voice was audible only to her ears.

Since his assessment was fairly accurate, she wasn't sure how to respond. And then there was the bungee jumping her stomach was doing. A decidedly unfamiliar sensation, but not one that she couldn't pinpoint to a very specific source—namely one six-foot-plus man. "It's none of my business," she finally settled on, which was also true enough.

Some of the lines had left his face, and his square jaw was again smooth-shaven and far too masculine and appealing.

She shifted, pushing her hands in the front pockets of her khakis. Learning that her libido was evidently alive and well wasn't necessarily a particularly welcome thing. "I, um, really should be going." She'd told Tanya that she'd help out at the sporting goods store that afternoon. "I'd like to come by and see Erik again." When he didn't tell her to stay away, she took it as a good sign. Nodding again, feeling awkward and not liking it one bit, she turned to go.

"The Bodeckers came by and apologized." His voice forestalled her. "Apparently, they didn't realize Tommy was missing at all from the reception, because he was back at The Hall before they even left."

She halted and looked back. It had to be her imagination that he was deliberately delaying her departure. "And when word got out that Erik was missing? Why didn't Tommy speak up *then?*"

Cam shook his head, keeping his fists from curling. But it took an effort. Just as it took an effort not to stare at her face—so female, so golden—as she looked up at him. "Evidently, he'd been grounded for a few weeks. No television. No radio. When his folks went to the wedding, they dragged him along with him." Same as he'd dragged Erik.

"Well." Faith's eyes didn't meet his. "This is one of those times to concentrate on the fact that everything turned out all right."

He made a noncommittal noise and then her gaze did lift to his, and it felt as if the collision jolted the ground right under him.

Dammit.

"*Is* it all right?" She lowered her voice even more. "If Erik's so fine, why does he have to stay two more days in the hospital?"

"Precaution. He had a pretty good concussion going."

Her lips pressed softly together. "But he'll be fine?"

How many times had Cam, himself, fired that question at Erik's doctor? He nodded, and there was no denying the relief that softened those brownish-green eyes of hers.

"Well, for once the rumor mill of Thunder Canyon General is on the mark. Heard you'd stepped foot on our holy grounds."

Faith's expression tightened a little as she turned to see her brother striding in their direction.

"Don't you have duties in the E.R.?" she asked pointedly.

Dr. Taylor grinned, but his blue eyes, when he glanced at Cam, were serious. "More patients than Carter's got pills," he agreed. "Your boss stopped by. Heard you're going on inactive until we give you a medical clearance."

"I came to see Erik, not get poked at by a sadist in a white lab coat."

"Hey. I resent that remark."

Judging by her expression, Cam figured she wasn't amused. "Chris—"

"Just a once-over," the doctor interrupted. "We've got a new crop of residents. You can take your pick of 'em."

The look she sent her brother was killing. "Fine." She nodded at Cam and strode off down the hall.

Realizing the doctor was watching him, Cam dragged his attention away from the impeccable fit of Faith's khaki pants. There was an unholy gleam in Christopher Taylor's eyes now, though, that told Cam the other man knew exactly what Cam had been eyeing.

And why.

"Town's buzzing about Friday's game," was all the other man said. "People wanting to know when you're gonna put Romance back on the court."

"When he's not failing every class but PE," Cam said evenly. He'd taken plenty of heat about the decision to bench the boy.

The younger man just nodded, though. "Fair decision. You've got eyes for my sister?"

He figured it was his own preoccupation over Erik's safety that Cam hadn't seen that one coming. "She saved my son's life," he hedged.

"Mmm. True enough." The doctor suddenly reached for his hip and the pager that hung on the waist of his scrubs. "Duty calls." He lifted his hand and waved at Erik inside the room, then strode away.

Cam wasn't sure quite what to make of either one of the blond Taylors.

He went back into Erik's room, resigned to an afternoon of his son's chatter about his favorite new toy...Faith Taylor.

Faith winced when the resident—a young guy who looked as if he were all of twelve years old—finished cleaning the worst of her cuts and spread antibiotic ointment over them, followed by fresh gauze pads.

The rattle of the blue-and-white striped curtain partitioning off the bed from the others in the E.R. gave her little warning before her brother appeared. She gave him a baleful look as he eyed the bandages covering most of her hip and nearly all of her abdomen, and deliberately pulled her shirt down before zipping up her loosened pants.

Chris, with his typical equanimity, ignored her and simply took the chart from the child-doctor, glancing over it. He scribbled his pen across it after a moment, and handed back the chart.

"Go," he said humorously, when the boy still hovered there.

The resident went.

Chris rolled his eyes. "Seems like they're getting younger every year," he murmured.

"Only because you're getting *older,*" Faith pointed out a trifle wickedly. At thirty-two, Chris was the eldest of the four Taylor children.

Chris merely lifted an eyebrow. "Someone looking thirty in the face ought to know enough to respect her elders," he pointed out. "So what's the deal with the Stevenson duo?"

Faith frowned and slid off the examining table. "Nothing."

"Right. *Nothing* got you past the cafeteria in this place."

"I just wanted to make sure he was doing all right." She fussed with the sleeves of her cotton shirt, folding them up her arms, then back down again.

"Which *he?*"

"Erik, of course." She hoped her cheeks weren't as fiery looking as they felt. "He's a cute boy. How, um, how long have they been in Thunder Canyon? Do you know?"

"Since the kid was an infant, I think." He thought about it a moment. "Cam didn't start teaching at the high school until after his wife died, though. He was some sort of financial whiz from Denver."

"I didn't ask for details."

"No. But you wanted to."

Faith snorted softly. "You're into reading minds now?"

"It's a big brother thing," he assured blandly. "If you'd come in yesterday when I wanted you to, we could have stitched up the worst of those cuts of yours. You'll probably have a helluva scar."

"It won't be the first one," she muttered. She had an assortment of old, fading scars on her elbows, her knees. All courtesy of never quite being the girly-girl daughter her mother had wanted. Fortunately, her two younger sisters, Hope and Jill, had been more than feminine enough to make up for Faith's failings.

They'd be the ones to provide the next generation

of Taylors, too. Unless Chris ever got off his duff and got serious about a woman himself.

She realized she was still fiddling with her sleeves and made herself stop. "I need to get over to Extension Sports. I promised Tanya I'd help out this afternoon."

"As long as you're sitting on a stool behind the counter, and not teaching climbing in the rock gym."

"Trust me," she assured as she stepped out of the curtained area, "I have *no* desire to get close to a rope right now." She sketched a wave and started to leave, but decided to swing by the cafeteria to grab a coffee on her way.

She was just fitting the lid on the tall cup when Cameron strode inside, heading straight for the hot-sandwich station. She hung back, not entirely certain why she didn't want to be noticed, but knowing that if she left now, he'd be sure to see her.

She cautiously sipped the strong brew, watching him over the top of the oversize cup.

The man did have a way of making plain blue jeans and an off-white fisherman's sweater look…extraordinary. And Faith knew she wasn't the only one who thought so, because there were plenty of female faces turning to watch Cameron's progress.

It was the middle of the afternoon, so the cafeteria was plenty busy, and several people spoke to him. Bits of conversation were audible above the clank of flatware and the hum of people's chatter. Everyone asked about Erik. Or the upcoming basketball game on Friday. He seemed to answer all comers, but he didn't exactly linger over them.

And that response wasn't altered whether or not the person to approach him was a man or a woman, she noted.

Then, when his tray was loaded with a plate of meat loaf, potatoes and salad, he didn't find a chair in the cafeteria, or head to the courtyard beyond the tall windows overlooking it. He simply pulled a thin wallet from his back pocket, flipped out a few bills for the cashier, and strode right back out of the cafeteria again, his demeanor neither welcoming nor standoffish.

She chewed the inside of her lip. What kind of a teacher would a man like that be? Stern, authoritative? Factual and removed? She certainly couldn't imagine him kicking back in his chair behind the large metal desk she remembered her high school teachers possessing, grinning in response to the rowdiness of a roomful of teenagers.

He was far too serious for that.

She walked out of the cafeteria, still watching him walking ahead of her, the tray held capably in his long-fingered hand.

She knew the man was strong. And she knew—having seen him in one of the worst situations a parent would ever find themselves—that he could be incredibly gentle with his son.

Realizing that she was still staring after him even when he'd entered the elevator for the second floor, she felt her cheeks heat and glanced around, hoping nobody noticed her hovering there in the corridor like some gawking groupie.

The fact was, she knew certain things about

Cameron and she was enormously curious to know more, and it wasn't *all* caused by the fact that her hormones had unfrozen with unseemly haste the first time she'd ever seen him.

But Cameron Stevenson was a family man, pure and simple.

So it didn't matter what sort of effect he had on her.

She wasn't going down *that* road ever again.

Chapter Five

"You came!"

There was a wealth of delight in Erik's young voice when Faith stuck her head in the door of his hospital room the next afternoon.

She pushed open the door wider, laughing a little. "Considering the way you've called me three times since this morning, did you think I'd forget?" Erik's first call had been at eight o'clock, and since then he'd gotten progressively more creative in his persuasive entreaty to visit him.

She hadn't had the heart to tell him that she'd planned to drop by all along. It might well have ruined his fun.

But her laugh hiccupped in her throat when she realized that Cameron was in the room, too. He was sitting in the corner, a stack of paper in his lap. For some reason, she'd expected him to be at the school.

"Hello."

"Ms. Taylor." He looked back down at the sheet, and began slashing his red pencil across it.

Faith pitied whoever the student was who'd completed that particular assignment. As for her, she felt pretty well dismissed, and didn't much care for the sensation.

But, she deliberately reminded herself, she hadn't come to see Cameron. She'd come to see Erik. So she focused on the boy. "How are you feeling today?"

He pulled a face. "They don't let me do nothing here. I don't see why I gotta stay here 'til tomorrow. I wanna go home now."

There were two chairs in the room, with Cameron occupying one. Yet she didn't feel comfortable enough to pull up the second, so she stood beside Erik's bed, instead. "They just want to make sure you're all healed up in here—" she lightly riffled her fingers through his mop of hair "—before you go climbing drainpipes."

"Drainpipes?"

"Don't give him ideas," Cam murmured from the corner.

"I'll tell you about 'em later," she whispered, sotto voce.

Erik grinned.

Cameron did not.

She eyed the video games still stacked beside Erik's

bed. "You have your games, at least, to keep you from getting bored."

"Dude, you got no idea how boring it is, though."

Dude? Her lips twitched. "I could bring you a book."

He looked askance and she laughed outright. "The horrors of it, huh? But I thought you liked going to the library for story time with Miss Emelda."

"I do. 'Cause she's got the best stories. But I don't gotta *read* them."

"Don't have to," Cameron corrected.

"Yeah. That."

Faith slid another surreptitious glance toward Cameron only to find his gaze *not* buried in his schoolwork, but firmly fixed on her. Wishing she would leave?

"Well. How do you feel about checkers?" She pulled out the travel game she'd stuck in her purse before coming to the hospital, and showed it to Erik.

"Cool." Erik scooted up on his pillows, folding his legs. "Can we play right now? Huh?"

She set the game on the mattress. "If it's all right with your dad." Cameron seemed to have gone very still and she lifted her eyebrows, giving the man plenty of opportunity to stop them. But he just nodded after a moment, then started scrawling with his red pencil again, his movements sharp.

Faith chewed the inside of her lip. His uncommonly stark expression tugged at her.

Erik noticed nothing amiss, though. His hands were busy as he unfolded the checkerboard right there on the bedding below his folded legs and doled out red and black checkers. "Come on, Faith."

She slowly perched her hip on the mattress. "I see you're not a novice, here."

"What's a novice?" His fingers rapidly placed the pieces—both hers and his.

"A beginner."

Erik laughed. "Me 'n' Dad play all the time."

"Guess it's a good thing we're not playing for money then." She couldn't help looking at Cameron again, adding another brushstroke to the painting of him in her mind. "Because I haven't played checkers in a really long time." Maybe Cameron didn't want anyone else playing the game with his son.

Yet that idea didn't feel right, either.

"You go first."

"I thought black went first?"

"Yeah, but you're the girl, so you gotta go first." Erik shook his head as if the matter were obvious.

"Well, I need all the help I can get against a regular player like you, so I'll take advantage of such chivalry." She slid a piece diagonally forward.

"What's chivalry?"

Dead, according to a good number of her friends. "It means being very courteous to women." She pushed another piece forward.

"Huh." Erik backed up his first piece with a second. "Dad says that's what we men gotta do."

Another unexpected brushstroke.

She blindly pushed another piece forward, which Erik immediately captured. He crowed and set her man on the blanket beside the board. After he made another capture, though, she decided she needed to pay a little closer attention. Erik's chivalry might have extended to allowing her the first move, but it certainly didn't extend to showing mercy once the game began.

Cameron watched Faith slowly fold up the sleeves of the khaki long-sleeved shirt that should have looked more official than appealing, and slide a little more fully onto the bed. He noticed her next move was made with far more deliberation than the previous ones.

He also noticed that Erik was thoroughly engrossed. His head hunched forward a little. Faith's blond head hunched forward a little. Their two heads didn't quite meet over the checkerboard, but it was close.

He set aside the math tests he was grading and rose, quietly leaving the room. Neither Faith nor Erik seemed to take note, and that was fine with him.

In the hall outside, he pressed his head back against the wall. There should've been an ache inside him. And because there wasn't, he found a new ache.

And he couldn't get the sight of their heads over the checkerboard out of his head no matter how hard he tried.

He wasn't sure how long he stood there when the door to Erik's room swished open and Faith touched his arm.

"Are you all right?"

He hadn't been all right since the day Laura died. "Needed to stretch my legs."

Her lashes lowered, hiding her expressive eyes. "I'm sorry if you think I've been...intrusive."

He straightened up at that. "Why would I think that?"

"Well—" she exhaled a little. "I can tell you don't really want me around here. But once Erik is released and back to normal, he'll quickly lose his fascination with me."

"I never said I didn't want you around." Irritation shortened his voice. If only that *were* the problem.

Her changeable eyes looked up at him at that. He could handle the curiosity and challenge glinting in them. But the vulnerability?

"Right," she returned. "That's why you glower every time I come within five feet of you and your son."

"I don't glower."

"You couldn't even say hello to me when I arrived."

"Erik gushed enough for both of us."

She huffed, skeptical. "Please. You also hated the toboggan yesterday. Thank goodness I didn't bring him a snowboard, which I strongly considered. Why don't you just admit it?"

"I don't hate it." He shoved his hands in his pockets. "I hate the fact that, no matter how hard I try to protect him, he still manages to get hurt. Okay?"

Her lips parted for a moment, then closed. "He's seven," she finally said. "He's bright and curious. Accidents can sometimes happen."

"And sometimes people don't survive them," he said flatly. "If you hadn't been there to get him out—" His throat closed. "I owe you. Okay? And I don't like owing anybody. Particularly when I should have prevented what happened in the first place. I should have known that Bodecker kid was filling Erik's head with stories. I shouldn't have taken Erik to the wedding in the first place. There're a lot of things I should have done, and I didn't." He wasn't speaking only of the past weekend, either. His should-haves went back a lot further than that.

She was silent, her eyes not entirely convinced.

"I used to play checkers with my wife. Erik's mother," he said abruptly. "In fact, on our first date, she prodded me into it." He'd come bearing tickets to the ballet, figuring the ethereal art lover whom he'd first spotted at a gallery showing would have been enchanted. Instead, they'd ended up sitting cross-legged on a checkered blanket in a city park, using the pattern on the blanket as the board, and torn pieces of French bread as their playing pieces, and he'd been the one enchanted.

"I'm sorry." Now, Faith looked stricken. "I had no idea."

How could she? And it wasn't the fact that another woman was playing checkers with his son that tore at him. It was the fact that looking at another woman playing checkers with his son had made him feel things he had no right to feel.

Even before the checkers, he'd felt things whenever Faith Taylor was in the vicinity. He didn't want to feel…anything.

"It's not you," he said gruffly. "I just—"

"—miss your wife," she finished softly.

He closed his eyes. He'd loved Laura. But he hadn't changed his life for her until after she was gone and it was too late.

Did he miss her?

He wasn't even sure of that anymore.

He scrubbed his hand down his face, leaving Faith to her assumption. "I need coffee."

"Frankly, you look like you need a good night's sleep more than you need caffeine," she countered evenly. "I suppose you don't want to *owe* the staff here at the hospital, either, for doing their jobs. What have you been doing? Staying with Erik around the clock?"

"Yeah. That's *my* job."

Her lips compressed. "And you'll be able to do it *so-o-o* well, when you're comatose from lack of sleep."

"I sleep."

"Where?"

"On a cot in Erik's room."

Her gaze drifted up and down his body, clearly taking a mental measurement. "Must be mighty comfortable," she said after a moment. "Is that why you had him put in a private room? So you could hover nearby 24/7?"

He'd requested a private room because that's what the Stevenson family did. Hell, when he'd been seven and getting his tonsils removed, his parents had not only had him in a private room, but with a private nurse, as well.

He pinched the bridge of his nose.

"Go get your coffee, Cameron," she murmured after a moment. "And some food. I'll stay here with Erik, if you think I can be trusted to keep him from harm, that is."

His breath hissed out between his teeth. "It's not a matter of trust, dammit."

Her eyebrows lifted. "Then what is it?"

How to admit to her reasonably posed question that he—a grown man—felt panicked nearly every time his son was out of eyeshot?

Faith waited, her heart squeezing at the shadows that darkened his eyes from melted chocolate to obsidian. "How do you take it?" she finally asked.

He looked at her. "What?"

"Your coffee." She lifted her hands when he started to shake his head. "Don't argue. I'm here. I might as well be of some use. And I'll bring back a milk shake or something for Erik, if that's all right."

The shadows slid behind sharp curiosity. "Why are you doing this?"

The question hovered between them for a moment. From down the hall, she could hear the rattle of a cart being rolled along the tile floor. Music was coming from a nearby room. The peds unit was decorated as cheerfully as any peds unit could be, but it was *still* a hospital.

Yet, as her brother had pointed out the other day, she'd entered the doors and ventured beyond the cafeteria.

Again.

Voluntarily.

"Truthfully," she said at length, "I have no idea. Maybe I just think Erik's a pretty terrific kid."

"He is." His jaw slanted. Centered. "Black. No sugar."

She should have guessed.

He started to pull out his wallet, but she waved her hand. "We'll settle up later." And before she could let her common sense tell her she was absolutely nuts for becoming even the slightest bit involved with the Stevenson men, she strode down the hall.

There was a faint itching at the base of her spine, and she knew that Cameron's gaze was following her.

Then she turned a corner and knowing she was out of range, she stopped. Drew in a deep breath and let it out slowly. Her heart was thudding.

It barely calmed down when she made it to the cafeteria and selected some items to take back to Erik's room. But, she figured wryly, if she were going to have a heart attack, at least she was in the right place to do it.

She thought she had herself more or less in control when she carried the tray back up to Erik's room. There was a good possibility her brother wouldn't much care for her bringing the boy the gargantuan chocolate milk shake, hamburger and French fries, but the boy's glee when she set them before him was worth any amount of trouble she might hear from Chris. And Cameron didn't put up any protests, either, when she handed him the tall coffee along with a plate of roast beef and all the fixin's.

"How'd you know I'd like roast beef?"

She lifted her shoulders. "Lucky guess," she demurred. There was no point in telling the man that she'd asked the cashier if Coach Stevenson had shown any particular preference beside the meat loaf that, if she hadn't been surreptitiously watching him the way she had the day before, she could have warned him to avoid.

"Eat up," she insisted when he didn't touch the food. "Before it gets cold."

"What about you, Faith?" Erik spoke around the French fry he was shoving into his mouth.

"Actually, I'm meeting a friend for an early dinner."

"Are you gonna go now then?" He eyed the checkerboard. "Or can we play another game?"

"You've already trounced me at two. But maybe we can play another time."

"Yeah. After you come t'bogganing with me. Can *you* toboggan?"

"Questioning my prowess because I'm a girl?"

He wrinkled his nose. "Huh?"

She laughed. "Yes, I can really toboggan. And snowboard, for that matter. Can't say I'm expert by any means, though. I'd actually rather have skis on my feet than do either."

"Dad likes to ski, doncha, Dad?"

"What about *you*?"

Erik shook his head. "Never gone. Dad went b'fore Christmas, though, huh, Dad?"

"What did you do while he skied?"

Erik rolled his eyes. "Visited Grandma and Grandpa in Denver. They had me go to a party."

Which sounded like a fate worse than death, judging by his tone. And Faith couldn't help but wonder if Cameron had skied alone, or if he'd had company that he hadn't wanted his son interfering with.

Her mood turned south.

"Well, like I said, I've got an early dinner. So I'll catch you on the flip side, 'kay?" She lifted her hand and Erik high-fived it. "Take care, sweetie." She winked at him, letting her gaze skate over the boy's father, and sped out the door.

She hurried through the pediatric wing before she could come up with some reason to stay. Her feet dragged a little when she passed the nursery with its wide window overlooking the collection of bassinets. A nurse sat in a rocking chair, crooning to the tiny baby in her arms.

Faith paused, watching. A frazzled-looking young man joined her at the window after a few minutes. He stared through the glass with disbelief and adoration all rolled into one.

"Which one is yours?"

He pointed. "Baby girl. Last one on the right." He shook his head. "Don't even have a girl's name picked out, because my wife was so convinced it would be a boy."

Judging by his expression, Faith figured the man was not in the least disappointed. "Congratulations."

"Thanks. What about you?"

She shook her head. "I'm just admiring."

"My wife used to do that, too, before she got pregnant." He pressed his hand against the window. The nurse noticed him and beckoned, and he practically tripped over his feet in his haste to go in and visit his daughter.

Sighing a little, Faith turned to go as he fumbled

into a protective gown and the nurse transferred the baby from the bassinet into his arms.

Admiring was all she would ever do.

"D'ya think she's got a boyfriend?"

Cameron propped his feet on the end of Erik's hospital bed. On the television hanging from the wall, college basketball was in full force. "Does who have a boyfriend?" The question was for show. He knew exactly whom Erik was referring to.

"Jeez, Dad. Get a clue."

He lifted an eyebrow. "I have no idea if Ms. Taylor has a boyfriend." Didn't mean he hadn't wondered plenty about it himself. Not that he intended to apprise his inquisitive seven-year-old of that fact.

"You could ask Dr. Taylor," Erik suggested. "He'd know 'cause she's his sister. I wonder what it's like to have a sister?"

Cam shrugged. "Can't help you there. Never had one." Nor a brother.

"Did my mom have a sister?"

Cam's gaze slid from the television to Erik. "No. Your mother was an only child, too." One of the things they'd had in common.

"Am I gonna get to go home for real tomorrow?"

Long used to his son's ping-pong method of bouncing from topic to topic, Cam nodded.

"Good." Erik's knees bounced. "I don't gotta go back to school yet, though?"

Cam gave Erik a dry stare that his boy interpreted just fine.

"If I see Tommy Bodecker in the halls, I'm gonna pound him."

Cam made a noncommittal sound. Truth was, his son didn't have a violent bone in him. Erik didn't even squash bugs. He was more interested in collecting them and giving them names.

"She's real pretty, huh?"

"Yeah."

"Not pretty like Mom."

Cam closed his eyes. The clear image of Laura that should've been there wasn't. He opened his eyes again, and stared blindly at the television. "Your mother had hair as black as midnight and eyes the color of lilacs." She'd been barely five feet tall, with an eye-popping hourglass figure. Kissing her had generally been most easily accomplished if he simply lifted her up to him.

That wouldn't be such a problem with Faith. Her head reached his shoulder. He'd just have to lean down a little. She'd lean up a little.

The thoughts snuck in. Grabbed hold, good and tight, not so willing to be shook.

"I know. I got Mom's picture in my bedroom," Erik said. "Just Faith's all…kinda…gold."

Cam's hand curled. Golden. She was that. "Yeah. You gonna finish that milk shake or not?"

Erik snatched up the oversize cup. "Yes," he said protectively, and tucked the straw between his teeth for good measure.

Relieved to have distracted his son, Cam focused once more on the ball game.

Too bad his mind wasn't as easily swayed as his son's.

Faith *was* golden. Gleaming blond hair, gleaming brown-green eyes. Gleaming golden skin, satin smooth and sleek with lean muscles and long limbs.

Dammit.

Chapter Six

Every inch of every bleacher inside Thunder Canyon High School's gymnasium was occupied that Friday night. The heat generated by all the bodies was more than enough to keep the enormous building warmed, as two teams battled it out on the hardwood for top spot in the state basketball semifinals.

Todd Gilmore, star center, stood on the foul line, bouncing the ball a few times, preparing to take his second free throw that would put his team in a tie game. Only ninety seconds remained on the clock.

Feet pounded collectively on the metal bleachers, creating a racket loud enough to wake the heavens. Gilmore's name was a throbbing chant on the air.

Faith, sitting in the nosebleed section—second row

from the top—peered down to the sideline where Cameron stood, his attention intently focused on his players. The long sleeves of his white shirt were folded up over his forearms. His narrow gray tie was pulled loose of his collar. His thick hair was slightly rumpled. He gave no indication whatsoever that he even noticed the raucous crowd.

Todd set up for his throw, the basketball rolling smoothly from the tips of his fingers in a graceful arc toward the basket.

It sank right through, and the crowd went ballistic.

The man to Faith's right crowed. "Nothing but net!"

Faith smiled, still watching Cameron.

Erik stood on the bench behind him, right behind the players on his father's team. He had an enormous foam finger on his hand that he waved about wildly. She knew he'd been released from the hospital on Wednesday as scheduled, because she'd seen him and Cameron leaving as *she* was leaving, having grabbed a sandwich with her brother for lunch that day in the cafeteria, and she'd watched their departure from her SUV parked in the lot.

She still wasn't sure if that had been cowardice on her part, or common sense.

But Erik had noticed her, and waved until she'd feared he'd fall out of the wheelchair he'd had to use until reaching Cameron's car.

Now, Faith couldn't tear her attention away from Erik's dad.

Cameron clapped his hands together as the game continued, frenzied. He called out to his players. Faith could see him glance up at the clock as if the depleting seconds were of no consequence. Up the court the players pounded. A bank shot, deflected. Down the court again.

The crowd was on its feet.

The noise was deafening.

How long could it take for ninety seconds to pass?

Faith pressed her fist to her mouth, her heart in her throat, just as caught up in the game as everyone else. She could see Bobby Romano in the stands, his expression dark as he looked at his son, Danny, on the sidelines, still benched.

The ball whizzed from player to player. The seconds cranked down. Twelve. Eleven. Ten.

"Come on. Come on." Her gaze slanted down again to Cameron. His hands were on his hips, his feet planted. She could practically see him willing his boys through their play.

Seven. Six. Five.

The ball flew. Hit the backboard. Bounced off the rim.

Players scrambled, rebounded.

Slammed the ball home.

The buzzer sounded.

And the crowd erupted, people pouring onto the court.

Cam's team had won.

Faith blew out a long breath, her heart pounding. She sat down, her legs weak.

"Helluva game!" The man beside her was positively gleeful. "Helluva game! First time we've made it to the state championship in seventeen years!"

She laughed. Her gaze kept sliding down to where Cameron stood. He'd lifted Erik up onto his shoulder and the boy was waving his foam finger over his head. Parents and players milled around, a congestion of jubilation on their side of the court, while the opponent's side rapidly emptied. She gathered up her coat and started making her way down the steps.

"Faith. Faith!" Erik's voice managed to find form among the loud roar.

She waved at him and angled her steps diagonally toward him. Her heart thudded unevenly. The players were whooping and hollering, slapping each other on their backs, and she couldn't help but laugh at their exuberance. She also couldn't get any closer to Erik than the second to bottom bleacher. "Good game!"

Erik's smile practically reached around the back of his head. "When are you gonna come tobogganing?"

Faith lifted her shoulders. "Whenever your dad says you're up to it."

Erik wriggled around until he got his dad's attention. Cameron tipped him off his shoulder, making the boy giggle before his feet hit the bleacher next to Faith.

"Did you see me wave at you when I got outta the hospital?"

Faith bent her knee on the bleacher so she was closer to his level. "You saw me wave back, right?"

"How come you didn't come and see me?"

She pulled out her pager and held it up for him to see. "I was on call. A skier got lost." That was the truth. She'd hovered in the hospital parking lot longer than she ought to have, in fact.

"Did you rescue him like you did me?"

"Well, he was a lot easier to find than *you* were," she assured.

"Did ya' hear that there's *gold* in the mine? All 'cause of me falling in?"

Faith laughed. "Well, that ought to drive Tommy Bodecker clean out of his tree."

Erik grinned, grabbing her hand. He was still practically yelling to be heard over the din. "You gotta come with us to The Hitching Post. Dad *never* lets me go there, but he's gonna tonight, 'cause we won. Says I'm his good-luck charm, so he's gotta."

"Naturally, a good-luck charm should *always* be included in the after-game celebration."

"So, will you?"

She started to shake her head, but Cameron leaned over just then. "Come on along," he invited.

Her heart jolted. She tried to tell herself it was just surprise, but she wasn't convinced.

"Everybody's going," he continued.

Of course. She ordered her heart to settle right back down again. Fat lot of good it did, though.

"I know it's late, but I owe you a dinner," Cameron added unexpectedly. The people standing between them were finally shuffling out of the way and Cameron scooped up an enormous duffel bag packed with sports equipment. He looped the strap over his shoulder and looked up, his gaze meeting hers. "What do you say?"

Heat squiggled along her veins.

"Please?" Erik wriggled her arm.

He's a family man. A family man. A family man.

"I...sure." She exhaled the word, ignoring the frantic reminder circling inside her head.

Cameron nodded. "Meet you there. Hustle up, Erik."

Faith blinked as Erik scrambled down from the bleachers and hurried to catch up with his dad's long-legged stride. The squiggles were still squiggling, even though she couldn't have said whether or not Cameron was pleased she'd agreed.

"That is one seriously good-looking man."

Faith jerked around to see Tanya smirking at her. "I didn't know you were here."

"I didn't know *you* were here," her friend returned. "So...what gives?" Her eyebrows rose meaningfully.

"Nothing gives. Did you close the store tonight?"

"Yup. No point in staying open when all the sports fans were here. Derek's on duty and Toby is spending the night at a friend's. All of which I mentioned at dinner the other day. When you did not mention that you were coming to the game tonight."

Faith stepped off the bleachers. Tanya followed. "I wasn't planning to," she admitted.

"Just couldn't help yourself, huh?" Tanya bumped her shoulder to Faith's when she didn't reply. "Hey. I'm just teasing you, you know. Because it's pretty nice to see you showing some interest in a man. After you split up with Jess—"

"I'm not interested," Faith said hastily.

Tanya just eyed her and the defensiveness oozed out of Faith, leaving her feeling deflated.

They pushed through the gymnasium doors and followed the clusters of people heading to their cars. "He's not the kind of man for me," she said after a moment.

"Why on earth not?" Tanya sidled in front of her, and stopped, forcing Faith to stop as well. "Sweetie, you're my best friend. Talk to me."

Words welled up inside Faith, but they were held back by a dam of her own making. "I'm not interested in *any* kind of man," she rephrased. "Yet—" she added hastily, recognizing the glint in her friend's determined blue eyes.

Tanya tucked her arm through Faith's. "Well, that's something, at least. You want to come over and have coffee and cake? Derek was baking again on his day off. Death by Chocolate. Seriously good stuff."

"Tempting." It was. Derek's prowess in the kitchen was significant. And he had a way with chocolate that generally made him the designated chef at the fire station when he was on duty. "But I can't." They neared her SUV and she tugged out her keys.

"Early shift tomorrow?"

"Um, no." Though she was on call, as she usually was.

Tanya was eyeing her again. "Okay. What's up?"

Faith unlocked her truck and tossed her purse inside. She tugged on the scarf hanging around her neck. "I, um, I told Erik I'd drop by The Hitching Post after the game."

"Erik, or Erik's fine-looking daddy?"

"Tanya—"

Her friend grinned. "Oh, fine. I'll let you off the hook. But one of these days, you're just gonna have to admit to me that you've got the hots for Cameron Stevenson." Tanya squeezed her arm and stepped back from the vehicle. "It's okay, you know. You don't have to be ashamed of it. You're a healthy, twenty-nine-year-old woman. Enjoy it." She started to cross the lot, but turned back after a few feet. "By the way, I'm going to want details!"

Faith felt herself flush, and Tanya laughed, as she darted between the slow-moving cars. Faith climbed into her SUV, only to sit there for a good ten minutes before the congestion in the parking lot eased. Ten minutes during which she seriously considered turning left out of the lot and driving straight home.

But when she nosed out of the lot, the SUV seemed to turn right of its own accord.

The Hitching Post was located in Old Town, down the street from The Hall. The parking lot behind the building was already bulging with cars, so she parked down the block and walked back to the popular grill. As she walked beyond the old-fashioned hitching post outside the building, she couldn't help but remember the frantic night she'd spent searching for Erik.

But when she pushed through the door, she pushed aside those thoughts. Erik Stevenson was standing on a bar stool, near the original bar from when the establishment was once a saloon, putting him at the same height as his dad's tallest player, and making him easily visible through the crowd.

She crossed the hardwood floor, heading his way.

Country music throbbed through the place. She had to turn this way and that to slip between groups of people crowded around the bar tables, and nearly fell on her rear when a young man backed straight into her.

He hurriedly steadied her, and she smiled off his humorous apology, only to turn around and find Cameron standing two inches behind her.

And she felt truly unsteady in that moment as every nerve she possessed went on alert.

"I was beginning to wonder if you were going to show." His fingers wrapped around her arm and even through her coat she felt the jolt of it. "Come on. I've got a table over here." He guided her through the throng, his tall body close behind hers, and she dragged in a breath, surreptitiously pressing her palm to her swaying stomach.

The table was nearly in the corner, and an enormous basket of cheese-covered fries sat in the center of it. Cam scooped Erik off the bar stool and carried him—one arm around the waist—over to the table, and dumped him on a chair. The boy could hardly seem to stop laughing, and his high spirits were so infectious that she relaxed a little and managed to slide into the chair that Cameron pulled out for her without completely embarrassing herself.

Which didn't mean that she didn't nearly jump out of her skin when he touched her shoulders. She looked up at him.

"Your coat?"

Her cheeks heated. He was only trying to help her out of her coat. Her thoughts skidded and she hurriedly unbuttoned the big round buttons on the front and shrugged out of the navy wool peacoat. He tossed it on the fourth chair that already held an assortment of winter wear. Then he sat down in the chair to her right. The square table was spacious enough, but his legs brushed against hers as he scooted in.

"Sorry," he murmured, and angled his legs in another direction.

Faith hurriedly snatched up one of the menus sitting on the center of the table and studied it, even though she'd eaten at The Hitching Post often enough to have the entire thing memorized. "Have you and Erik already ordered?"

Cameron plucked a few crispy fries from the basket. "Only these." He pulled them free of the melted cheese topping them.

Her stomach dipped again as she watched him consume them, then lick his thumb before wiping his hands with his napkin.

"Get you something to drink?" The pregnant waitress who stopped by their table was young. Fairly new to town, too, Faith knew, courtesy of Tanya, who kept her finger pretty firmly on the town's pulse. The petite Latina looked busy, but her sparkling eyes and smile didn't show how harried she undoubtedly felt as she waited patiently.

Faith's gaze skated over Cameron's beer and Erik's soda. "I'll just have water, thanks."

"I'll be right back with that. Give you a chance to look over the menu." She hurried off.

Even though the place was crammed with people

and noise, Faith felt very alone there at the table with Cameron and Erik. It wasn't necessarily an unpleasant sensation. Erik was slurping his soda through his straw, blowing bubbles as much as drinking, and Cameron was working on the cheese fries with an oddly intense determination.

She wasn't going to blindly study the menu any longer, and she flipped it closed. "Amazing game tonight."

Cameron's eyes slanted her way for a moment. "Yeah. Haven't seen you at any of the games before."

She repositioned the napkin in her lap. "Guess I got caught up in the excitement like the rest of Thunder Canyon. It's on to the state championship now. Quite an accomplishment on your part." His lashes were unreasonably thick, she noticed, not for the first time.

"I'd feel more accomplished if the guys were pulling better grades in math." His lips twisted wryly. "Basketball's just a game."

She leaned forward a little. "Better keep your voice down when you say stuff like that. Lynching isn't too far in Thunder Canyon's past, you know."

His head tilted and she sucked in her breath, painfully aware of how close they sat. Fortunately, the waitress returned with her water, and Faith sat back, wrapping her unsteady hand around the glass as they gave their orders and the waitress headed off once more. "So, is the championship on Friday?"

He shook his head. "We'll have next week off. Game's the following week. Superstition or something, but nobody wanted to schedule a game on Friday the thirteenth."

She'd forgotten all about the date. She was due to have lunch on Valentine's Day with a bunch of girlfriends. "I imagine you must have played basketball yourself?"

He nodded, and looked up when Mayor Brookhurst stopped by, clapping him on the back for the great game. He stood and shook the man's hand. "Tell that to the team." Cam easily deflected the mayor's praise. "They're the ones who worked their tails off for it."

The mayor smiled broadly, obviously feeling expansive. "Don't be modest now, Coach. Considering what you've accomplished with a bunch of teenagers, imagine what we could do if you were on the town council."

Cameron's smile stayed put, but Faith could tell it was forced. She'd seen for herself that Cam didn't always agree with mayoral opinions. "I'm considering it," he admitted, without giving away much.

The mayor nodded, satisfied enough, and moved along, evidently happy to keep greeting the elated crowd as if he were personally responsible for the night's outcome.

Erik was wriggling in his seat, his soda already gone.

Faith laughed a little, watching him. "You're like a Mexican jumping bean over there, Mister Erik. I think I may need to start calling you Juan or something."

"I never had Mexican jumping beans. But Susie in school did. But she got 'em taken away 'cause the teacher said she was playing with 'em during class. They're so-o-o cool. Dad, have we ever been to Mexico?"

Cameron shook his head as he sat down again. He handed Erik a handful of coins. "Here. Go play a video game."

"Aw-w-wright." Erik scooped up the coins and dashed off to the arcade area behind their table.

Cameron's gaze followed after his son, then he looked back at Faith. "Be nice to bottle some of that energy. I could use it to perk up my sixth-hour class every day." He nudged the basket of fries toward her. "Have some."

Her mouth was pretty much watering and it was easier to blame it on the cheese fries than anything else, so she took advantage of the offer.

"What were you like in school?"

Faith shrugged, and wiped her fingers on her napkin. "Anxious to graduate," she supplied wryly.

His lips tilted and the crease in his cheek deepened.

She took a quick drink of water. Set down the glass, only to rotate it between her thumb and forefinger. "I couldn't wait to leave Thunder Canyon, actually. I didn't really think anybody could have any sort of real life here."

His gaze centered on the fries, hiding his expression. "You were young, and the town is pretty small. What'd you do?"

"I went off to New Mexico for college. Met someone. Graduated. Got married. Got divorced." She shrugged. "Nothing particularly interesting." *Just life-altering,* the voice inside her head whispered.

He was silent for a moment and she looked up from her water glass to find his gaze on her. "What about you?" she asked somewhat desperately. "What brought you to Thunder Canyon? I think I heard that you were from Colorado, right?"

"Denver. My wife drove through here once and fell in love with the place."

She bent her elbow on the table, and propped her chin on her hand. Jess had never done anything simply because *she'd* loved it. "And you moved here because of that?" How much he must have loved his wife.

"She'd just had Erik. She wanted to raise him here, rather than in the city."

"I guess I've never thought of Denver as being all that major of a city."

His lips twitched. "Better not let any of the Denver power brokers hear you say that."

She lifted her glass, amused. "I think I might be safe all the way over here in Thunder Canyon. Are you really going to run for town council? You're always at the meetings."

"So are you."

"Ah, but I'm a county employee who has to report back to her team anything that might affect our ability to scrounge space from the town services. Only reason we can afford to have the team spread out the way we are is through cooperation with the local agencies that share their resources—and office space—with us. Every time the budget gets looked at, we sweat it."

"The council supports your presence, though."

She nodded. "True. Some members of the police department aren't so enamored of my presence, but it usually works out in the end."

"Well." His hand closed over hers, and her heart simply stopped for a moment. "I, for one, am damn glad you were here." His thumb brushed over the back of her hand and the chaos surrounding them seemed to fade away.

Then he let go of her, reaching for the cheese fries again, and the chaos returned, loud and rambunctious as ever.

Faith dropped her hands to her lap, rubbing one hand over the tingling in the other. A happy father stopped by to pound Cameron on the back, then Erik dashed over, and a slightly shorter boy followed hard in his wake.

"Hey, Dad. Can I spend the night at Josh's? His mom's over there. She said I could."

Cameron shook his head without even seeming to think about the matter. "Tell Mrs. Lampson thanks, but no."

Faith felt the disappointment sweeping through Erik even before his shoulders sank. "Come on, Dad."

Cameron merely lifted an eyebrow, and Erik's pleading stopped before it had barely begun. "Have you spent all of your change?"

"No, sir."

"Better do it now before the food gets served, then."

Erik nodded. He turned and shuffled off with Josh at his side.

Cameron didn't look at her, but pulled another few fries free of the web of cheese.

"Excuse me." Faith stood and dropped her napkin on her seat. "I'll be right back."

She felt Cameron's gaze on her spine as she went after Erik. He was feeding coins into a video game, his expression sulky, when she crouched down beside him. "I have some free time tomorrow," she told him. "Around ten. I could come by and we can check out that toboggan of yours. What do you say, Juan?"

His eyes, so similar to his father's, brightened. "Honest?"

She stuck out her hand. "Honest."

He slapped his palm against hers. The game beside them chirped and gurgled. And Faith resumed her seat at the table with Cameron.

"What was that about?"

"I told Erik I'd come tobogganing with him tomorrow." She eyed him. "Unless that's something you're going to say no to as well?"

He sat back in his seat. "You think I should've let him spend the night at the Lampsons'."

"Would it have been so terrible?"

"Maria Lampson works a swing shift every night at a convenience store. She leaves Josh home alone with his twelve-year-old sister from midnight to 8:00 a.m. So, no, I'm not going to feel badly for disappointing Erik."

"I didn't realize."

"Now you do."

They sat there, eyeing each other.

Then the waitress, Juliet, appeared with a laden tray and began unloading their dinner.

Erik darted back to the table, and slid onto his seat, nearly diving headfirst into his hamburger. "Faith's gonna come tobogganing with me," he announced. A drop of ketchup dripped onto his chin.

Cam watched Faith lean over and hand Erik's napkin to him. His son took it and wiped his face without breaking stride for a second, and without adding his usual complaints whenever Cam told him to use his napkin.

"We could use the hill behind our house, right, Dad? It's big enough."

The hill was steep as hell. And he really didn't want his son going near it. But Faith's gaze was fixed on his face as if waiting for him to deny Erik another pleasure, and he choked down the misgivings. "It's big enough," he finally said.

Faith's long, soft lashes swept down and her lips looked ready to soften into a smile.

He'd spent more than enough time being preoccupied over Faith Taylor's lips.

It wasn't as if he was going to do something about his curiosity over whether they were as supple as they looked.

He made himself look away, only to realize the troublesome threesome were bearing down on him, intent glinting in their overly made-up eyes. Tiffany Scherer, Amber Wells and Krista Decker. Pretty girls with too much time on their hands.

He stifled an oath.

Faith leaned a little closer. "What's wrong?"

He grabbed her hand and hauled her out of her chair. "Dance with me."

"What?" Her napkin slid to the hardwood floor.

He knew Erik was staring at them, goggle-eyed. "Dance with me," he repeated, and nearly lifted her off her feet to get her onto the dance floor that was only sparsely occupied. He swung her into his arms, glancing over her head.

The teenaged girls had halted their progress, expressions of surprise etched in triplicate across their faces.

"God help their fathers," he muttered.

Faith was staring at him as if he'd lost his mind. And maybe he had lost it. Because he could feel every inch of her lithe body—clad in a bronze turtleneck that made her hair look more golden than ever and narrow brown jeans that made her legs look longer than ever—against his body. "*Whose* fathers?"

He shuffled, turning her so she could see the girls. "Their fathers. You know what it's like to be chased by three seventeen-year-old girls? It's a bloody nightmare."

A soft laugh erupted from her and he felt the ripple of it through his chest. "They have a crush on you, I take it."

He could feel his neck heating. "I don't know. Just every time I turn around, there they are. It's becoming…a problem."

"Because you like them?"

He glared at her. "Give me a break. They're children."

She shifted against him, her hand slipping up over his shoulder. Their legs brushed against each other as they slowly moved over the postage stamp of a dance area. "Poor guy."

"You wouldn't find it so amusing if it were *you*. They've been bringing me cranberry muffins every school day lately. I don't even like cranberries."

She considered that. "Romantic gestures. Well, I suppose if it were me, I probably wouldn't find it funny, either. But since I've never had young men falling over themselves for me—or grown men, for that matter—I can't be entirely certain."

That seemed inconceivable to Cam. He was vaguely aware of the girls turning on their collective heels. "At least they're not in any of my classes this semester. I don't know how to discourage them anymore than I already have."

"Get a girlfriend," she said smoothly.

"I'm—" he broke off. Married, he'd almost said.

Only he wasn't married. He was alone.

And he had a beautiful woman who was very much alive in his arms, her body warming his.

"You're what?"

"Hungry," he said abruptly. "And our food's getting cold." He stopped doing the shuffle-disguised-as-a-dance, and nudged her back toward the table.

He'd accomplished one thing at least—diverting the trio of girls, even if it was momentary.

Too bad he'd also accomplished something else.

Awakening a hunger of another sort that, up until now, he'd managed to keep under control.

He sat down in the seat, dropping the napkin over his jeans that had gone painfully tight.

"I never seen you dance before, Dad."

"Finish your hamburger, Erik."

"But—"

"Then you can order dessert."

Erik nearly shoved the rest of the hamburger into his mouth, his eyes gleaming at the prospect.

Cam, however, couldn't look at Faith without wishing he were feasting on *her.*

As soon as she'd picked up her fork, though, she jumped a little. "My pager," she said, and pulled it off her belt, peering at the display.

Erik craned around, trying to get a look. Faith flashed him the display, and cast Cameron a look that was too hard to read. "I'm sorry. I'm going to have to run."

"Everything okay?"

"Yeah. Just duty calling." She rose and started pulling on her coat. He stood also, helping her despite the surprised look she gave him. She gestured at the table. "Sorry about the meal."

If he hadn't dragged her onto the dance floor, she'd have had a chance to eat more of the mammoth salad she'd ordered than just a few bites. "We could get it packed for you to take."

"I won't have a chance to get to it," she murmured. "But thanks. I'm...sorry about this."

So was he, he thought, watching her walk out of The Hitching Post.

More sorry than he had any right to be.

Chapter Seven

Faith sat in her car, looking up at Cameron and Erik's home. There were only two other homes on the hillside, set well apart from each other. And it reminded her all over again that Cameron hadn't always been a high school coach and math teacher. He'd had an entirely different career before he'd come to Thunder Canyon. One that, judging by the spacious size and rugged beauty of the house, must have paid pretty darn well.

She had a fleeting urge to put the car in gear and turn around and run. But Erik had already thrown open the wide front door and was racing pell-mell down the shoveled walkway toward her, the toboggan clutched under his arm. He ran all the way to the street and looked fit to vibrate out of his skin as he waited for her to join him on the sidewalk.

"Hello," she greeted. "What's your name again?"

Erik's dimples flashed. "Juan."

She nodded. "Right. I remember. And that thing?" She tapped the end of the rolled sled. "That's a mechanical bull, isn't it?"

"A *real* one," Erik corrected.

"Erik." Cameron stood on the front porch. "Invite Ms. Taylor in."

Faith's stomach jittered. Nerves soothed by Erik came back in full force with the presence of his father. "That's okay," she raised her voice so he could hear. "The hill behind your house should be perfect for this puppy." He could hover as close as he needed.

"Master Juan?" She looked at Erik as she pulled her gloves out of her coat pocket, and snugged her scarf tighter around her neck. "Think you'd better put some boots on those feet of yours."

He looked down. Giggled. Flew back up the walk in his stockinged feet, darting past his dad into the house.

Faith retrieved Cam's coat from her car and slowly followed, since Cameron was still standing there. She took her time pulling on her gloves. Maybe if she didn't look at him, she wouldn't spend another night plagued with dreams about him.

Right.

"Nice place you have," she commented, stopping near the base of the five stone steps leading up to a front door that could have accommodated her car it was so wide. She tossed the coat to him.

"It's a roof." He neatly caught the garment.

She wriggled her toes inside her boots. From inside the house, she heard Erik's yell, asking where his snow boots were.

Cameron's gaze met hers and his lips tilted. "Better come inside," he suggested dryly. "Based on previous experience, this may take a while. He was supposed to have gathered up his stuff before you got here."

He stepped back, waiting.

It was just a house, she told herself. And he was just a tall man in blue jeans and a thick wheat-colored sweater.

Didn't make going up the steps and walking past him any less disturbing, though.

And he smelled good. Again.

She swallowed and focused somewhat desperately on the house. From the foyer was a wide-open view of the land behind the house, courtesy of the plate glass windows that seemed to take the place of walls. Her feet rooted into place at the magnificence of it. "A little *more* than a roof."

His hand lightly touched the small of her back and she nearly jumped forward a foot. "It's the view that sold us on the house."

Now, her spine was tingling. "I'll bet."

"Da-ad!"

He let out a breath. "Excuse me." He dumped the coat on the already-laden coatrack near the door.

She nodded and he disappeared down a hall. She could hear the low tone of his voice as he directed Erik's search. She could have stood there looking out those windows for hours. The snowy hillside looked pristine, the white powder glittering like jewels beneath the clear, afternoon sun.

Beyond the foyer and the soaring great room furnished with oversize, rustic pine, the floor plan split, going down a half-dozen steps to the kitchen with a built-in breakfast nook, and a less formal family room. Looked like Cam used it more for an office though, judging by the textbooks and papers strewn across a desk that floated in the middle of the room, facing out the windows.

She wondered how he accomplished any work. If she had a view like his, she'd have to face away from it, because there was no way she could have concentrated.

Erik and Cam were still searching, evidently, and she passed the desk, hoping her intense interest was masked by casual glances. There were a few framed photos of Erik sitting on a bookshelf. And no photos of his mother as far as she could tell.

Her curiosity over the woman who still held Cameron's heart would have to go unquenched.

"Okay. He's ready." Cameron stepped into view, closely followed by Erik. The boy ran across the room and shoved at one of the windows. It slid silently aside, then started to close as soon as Erik reached the covered deck right outside. Cam stopped it from closing altogether, though, holding it open with the palm of his hand.

Faith went outside. She couldn't see a single fingerprint on the glass pane and couldn't help but wonder how they managed that. "You coming?"

He jerked his chin at the mess on his desk. "Kids complain about homework, but it's the teachers who really get socked with it."

She nodded. But a glance at his hand told her he wasn't as calm as he seemed.

His knuckles were white.

"It's just a sled. We'll be careful," she said quietly.

His gaze was focused beyond her, and she wondered what he was seeing. "If I thought otherwise, you wouldn't be here," he assured.

She supposed that was a compliment, and went to the side of the deck where a short staircase led to the ground and Erik waited, standing on top of the toboggan.

Faith studied the lie of the hill. The tree line didn't pick up until well beyond the base of the hill, and beyond the trees was the road. It couldn't have been a more perfect location if she'd taken Erik out to the hill behind the skating rink where most kids congregated for sledding.

"Alrighty, Juan. Let's take a crack at this, shall we? We'll go down together until you get the knack of steering, and then you can fly solo. Right?"

Cam was grateful there were no witnesses nearby when he broke out in a sweat at Erik's first faltering attempt on the toboggan. Faith had already accompanied him down the hill more than once, with Erik tucked securely in front of her, and her sleek ponytail streaming behind them until they disappeared from his line of vision.

He went into the kitchen, shoving the bench in the breakfast nook out of his way. The angle was different there, and he could see clear to the snow-filled ravine at the base of the hill.

On Erik's solo attempt, his son made it about ten feet before he tipped sideways, rolling like some human snowball in the snow. Faith, perched farther down the hill, darted upward, her boots sinking into the snow, and when she caught Erik up, Cam could hear their laughter ringing on the afternoon. She flipped a handful of loose snow into his son's face and settled him back on his feet, pointing to the top of the hill again.

Cam slid back a foot, not necessarily wanting to be seen with his nose pressed against the window like some starving kid at a candy store. Erik plodded back up the hill, dragging the sled behind him by the nylon cord.

On his third attempt, he made it all the way to the base of the hill, and the *whoop* his son made could've been heard in the next county. Cam could see him pumping his arm in the air, strutting around victoriously. Then Erik grabbed the toboggan again and raced up the hill.

He spotted Cam watching and waved wildly. "Dad. Watch me!"

Cam lifted his hand in return. At the base of the hill, Faith looked up in his direction.

Then she smiled.

He was vaguely surprised the warmth of it didn't melt the snow all around her.

"Watch me," Erik cried again, and was off in a blur of neon green. Again, when he made it to the base, he bounded to his feet to dance around like he'd won Olympic gold. Then some lively discussion ensued, and Faith trudged to the top of the hill, the sled tucked under her arm.

She didn't look toward the window, where she had to know he was still watching, and he wondered if it was deliberate or not.

She arranged her lithe form on the toboggan, long legs crossed in front of her. Cam caught a flash of her grin in the moment gravity took hold and she went flying down the hill.

Cam turned his back on the sight and returned to his work, but it wasn't so easy to turn his back on the feelings churning inside him.

He stared at the textbooks in front of him. At the rate he was going, he'd be using the same final exam this year as he'd given to his students last.

Through the insulated windows, he could still hear Erik's and Faith's laughter.

He abruptly shut the books, went out to the mudroom located below the kitchen, shrugged into a down vest, and went outside.

The snowball smacked him in the center of his chest, and exploded into powder.

"Bull's-eye," Erik crowed. He pranced around victoriously in the snow. "I told you he'd come out here, Faith. Dad *loves* the snow."

"Good thing." She waved her arm at the snowy landscape. "Because this isn't exactly the Mojave Desert."

Cam straightened, a snowball in his hand. He lobbed it at his son, catching Erik in the shoulder. His boy laughed, and dove down. And Cam realized belatedly that Erik and Faith had already prepared an arsenal.

The snowballs came fast and furious. Almost as fast as Erik's laughter.

Faith was no help, either. She was most definitely in his son's corner.

And she had a hell of an arm on her, though she left most of the work to Erik.

"You're gonna regret this," he warned, deflecting a hail of snowballs with his arm.

She laughed, and handed Erik another snowball.

Cam ducked his head and dove straight toward them, tackling them both into the soft snow.

Erik wriggled out from beneath his arm and jumped on his back, trying to shove snow down the collar of his shirt. Cam yelped, twisting around. He grabbed Erik and tipped him upside down.

Erik laughed so hard he looked ready to bust. "Get him, Faith. Help me!"

But Faith was still lying on her back in the snow, her legs and arms splayed, laughing herself.

Cam shoveled a handful of snow down his son's collar and let the boy go. Erik jumped around screaming like a banshee, trying to shake the snow out.

"Monkey," Cam said and turned to extend a hand to Faith.

She took it and he pulled her to her feet, only to have her shove a handful of snow into his face.

Erik sat down on his butt and howled. "She did it, she did it!"

Cam swiped a hand down his face. "You two planned this, then? If one of you couldn't get me, the other one would?" He bared his teeth, holding back his own laughter.

Faith was backing away, her palms held out peaceably. "Just some good, clean fun," she assured, breathlessly.

"Good *cold* fun, more like."

Erik got to his feet and grabbed the toboggan. "I'm going down again." He sat on the sled and pushed himself over the hill.

Cam watched him fly down from the corner of his eye as he advanced on Faith. "I see how you are," he murmured. "Ganging up on the old guy."

"Old." She snorted. "Get over yourself." She sidled sideways, ducking under an angled brace for the deck overhead. "That's why you've got teenaged girls oohing and ahhing all over you." She darted to the side, avoiding the snowball he tossed at her.

"Seems to me the only person who hasn't had snow down her back is you." He sidestepped, following her easily even as he scooped up another handful of snow.

"Proving the superiority of the female species," she said blithely, and ducked again, as elusive as a sprite.

He snorted and some part of him gaped at the easy laughter coming out of him.

How long had it been?

"Doesn't mean a thing," he assured. "Except that your time *is* coming."

Her lips twitched. "I think it's time I be going now. I, um, I have things I need to do."

"Things."

"Yes. Things." Her boots brushed through the snow, wisely widening the distance between them. From down the hill, they could hear Erik still whooping and hollering. Her bright gaze slanted, obviously gauging the distance to the deck steps.

"You won't make it," he murmured.

Her eyebrow peaked, Faith clearly taking that as a challenge. "I used to run a Memorial Day marathon every year when I lived in New Mexico."

"Used to."

She lifted her shoulder. "I moved back home."

He thought that was an interesting turn of phrase. Hadn't she considered New Mexico her home? "A marathon is for endurance. Sprinting is for speed."

"I suppose you ran track, too."

"Oh, yeah."

"Any sport you *didn't* participate in?"

"Gymnastics."

"Not macho enough?"

He grunted. "Not flexible enough. Not fast enough for tennis, either."

Her gaze drifted down his body. "Really," she murmured. Then, while he was stomping down hard on the effect of that unexpected look of hers, she launched herself toward the deck stairs.

In two steps, Cam caught her, and they tumbled into the snow bank angling up the wall. He flipped her scarf loose and grabbed a handful of snow, holding it up, threatening.

She tilted her head back, laughing. She tried to grab

his arm with her hands and he shackled her wrists with one hand, pinning them over her head.

"No. Really. Don't," she begged breathlessly.

His gaze caught on her slender throat. The smooth, long grace of it.

He let the snow fall from his hand.

Her lips parted, eyes flaring.

And rather than pushing snow against that long, slender column, he pressed his lips against it, instead.

She tasted as golden as she looked. And he felt the hitch in her breath as she inhaled sharply.

Her captive wrists jerked against his hold, then went still, and he lifted his head.

She stared up at him, her eyes wide. A living, breathing snow angel, with rosy color riding her cheekbones and unmistakable desire turning her eyes mossy green.

He released her, and she slowly lowered her arms. Her gloved fingers flexed against his shoulders, but didn't push him away. Her lips slowly formed his name, soundless.

He lowered his head. Grazed the coolness of her lips with his.

His down vest crinkled softly as she touched his chest. He lifted his head. Stared down at her, need ripping up his spine.

Her pupils dilated. A swallow worked down her lovely, bared throat.

He swore. And slammed his mouth on hers.

She gasped and he swallowed it. He knew he was too rough, tried to temper himself, only to realize she was right there with him, her mouth open, and her tongue tangling as desperately as his.

Then there was nothing but sensation.

The heat of her.

The softness.

The crunch of snow beneath them when her arms twined around his neck and he caught her waist, hauling her hips against his.

He'd never wanted anything in his life as badly as he wanted her.

The realization yanked him back.

He let go of her, and shot to his feet.

She lay there, swollen lips parted, eyes glazed. Her breath was an audible hiss. Her hair was coming loose of her ponytail. Her coat was open, the waist of her sweater pushed up beneath the swell of her breasts, displaying the bandages that had been necessitated by her rescue of his son.

God.

What the hell was he doing?

She slowly drew her sweater down her stomach. Pushed up with one hand until she was sitting in the snow. "Cameron?" Her voice was low. Husky.

Laura's voice had been higher pitched. More…fragile.

Guilt clawed at him, and *still* the want didn't abate. "I'm sorry." His voice was harsh. Flat. "I shouldn't have done that. I'm not interested in—" The lie only went so far.

It didn't matter. His tone had done the job.

"I see." Her chin angled away. She looked down.

Slowly pulled her coat together and adjusted her gloves. "Please tell Erik goodbye for me." Her voice sounded thick. She rolled gracefully to her feet before he could even offer a hand.

He didn't think it was possible to feel lower than he did. Apparently, it was. "Faith—" But he didn't know what to say to her.

So he said nothing.

He just watched her walk away from him.

And still, he wanted her.

"There's an order of baseball gloves in the back that needs to be checked, if you have a chance to get to it."

Tanya's voice sounded harried over the phone and Faith glanced around the interior of Extension Sporting Goods. "There's only been two customers this afternoon," she commented. "I think I'll probably get to the order. Are Monday evenings always this slow?" She was filling in for Tanya only because her friend was home with a sick Toby.

"It'll pick up when baseball season starts. I really appreciate you coming in. Are you sure you didn't have something else to do?"

Faith closed off the image of Cameron standing over her, his regret for touching her nearly flashing neon from his face. "I'm sure. Take care of your son. Everything here will be fine. I'll drop off the day's receipts in the night deposit at the bank on my way home after I close up."

"You're the best."

"That's what I tell all my friends and relations,"

Faith assured dryly and Tanya chuckled as she hung up, as Faith had intended.

She replaced the phone and picked up the towel she'd been using to polish the glass display case that served as the checkout counter. The customer who had been browsing came over with his ski wax selection, and once Faith rang him up and the man left, the store was silent, except for the low music coming from the radio. The Beach Boys singing about California girls.

It was going to be a slow evening, which was unfortunate. Faith had hoped—when she'd offered to help out Tanya—that she'd be kept busy enough to keep what had happened between her and Cameron the other morning *off* her mind.

So much for that.

She went to the back room and began unloading the new shipment, taking extraordinary care to check every label, every detail.

Still, she couldn't get it out of her head. It had been that way all weekend.

The unspeakable feeling of Cam's kiss, followed by him jumping away from her as if he'd found her poisonous.

Even now, humiliation burned inside her. And she hated it just as much now as she had when Jess had found her wanting, too.

She gathered up an armload of baseball mitts and carried them out to the front just as the door jingled.

Cameron and Erik entered.

The mitts tumbled from her arms, spilling over the

countertop and thudding onto the sturdy brown carpet. "Faith!" Erik's face lit up. "I didn't know you'd be here."

That was painfully evident, given Cameron's frozen expression. "I'm friends with Tanya Winters. She owns this place."

"Cool."

Try as she might, she couldn't keep herself from sneaking a look at Cameron. Not that it mattered, since he was most assuredly *not* looking at her.

But Tanya trusted her to fill in for her, and no matter how much she'd have preferred to go hide in the back room, she made herself round the counter and approach them. "Can I help you find something?"

Erik had shrugged out of his parka and shoved it into his dad's hands as he raced across the spacious store toward the display of climbing gear hanging on one wall. "Cool. Can I climb up it?" He pointed at the mock rocks.

Faith shook her head. "Not that one, I'm afraid. It's just for looks."

"He needs a tennis racket." Cameron's voice was abrupt.

Faith lifted her eyebrows. "Tennis?"

"It's for school." Erik's hands were exploring the display. "I gotta play *summer* in the chorus. Dumb, huh?" He hefted up an enormous coil of nylon rope above his head and nearly tipped over.

"Erik." Cameron grabbed the rope with one hand and hooked it back over the heavy-duty hook. "Leave the stuff alone."

"Tennis rackets are in that aisle." Faith pointed toward a rear corner. "Not a very large selection right now, though."

"I'm sure we'll find something." Cameron stepped around her, heading toward the display.

Faith's teeth sank into the inside of her lip, watching. But her thought wouldn't be contained. "Be less expensive to borrow a racket from someone. The school, even."

Cameron slid one of the three racket styles out of the rack. The grip seemed eclipsed by his long fingers. "Erik." He extended the racket to his son.

Erik barely glanced at it. He was still fascinated with the climbing display. "Whatever."

"It's for *your* play, buddy," Cameron reminded.

Erik made a face. Dragged his feet across the carpet and gave the racket a close-up once-over. "It's pink."

"It has a red stripe," Cameron countered.

Erik grimaced. "Da-ad. It's pink!"

"Magenta, actually," Faith put in. She reached carefully past Cameron and pulled down the second style. It was a slightly larger racket. "What about this one?"

Erik's expression looked no happier. "I don't see why I gotta be in a dumb old program, anyhow. Just 'cause I ain't tone-deaf like—"

"Erik," Cameron prompted blandly. "Pick a racket and be done with it."

"It's *yellow,* Dad. I'll look like a geek."

"Well, your only other choice is this one." Cameron pulled out the last style. "And since it has little pink kittens on the grip, I figured you wouldn't be interested."

"Plenty of guys use these two styles, even with the magenta or yellow," Faith said peaceably.

Erik's head lolled back on his neck. He looked as put upon as any person in the history of the world. "Whatever."

Cameron looked like he was gritting his teeth. "Erik." His tone said volumes.

Faith quickly slid the rackets back in place. "I have a black one at home. He could borrow it."

"No, thank you," Cameron said over Erik's suddenly interested "cool."

"Aw, *Dad.*"

"Pick a racket."

The two males looked at each other, clearly in some battle of wills. The best thing for her to do would be to stay out of it. "I really don't mind," she said, proving she had never learned her lesson about doing what was best. "It seems a shame to spend this much on a racket that he's only going to use for one school program. Unless you're planning to learn tennis?"

Erik looked askance.

Cam looked irritated. "You don't have to go out of your way."

She had her own share of irritation rippling down her spine. She eyed him. "Believe me. I won't. If you want the racket, you'll have to come by and pick it up." She waited a beat. "I'll leave it on my front porch for you."

If she'd expected Cameron to be bothered by her dig

at his seeming lack of graciousness, she was wrong. If anything, the man looked as if he'd rather purchase a hundred tennis rackets than avail himself of her simple offer.

"You didn't wanna buy a racket in the first place," Erik said suddenly. His head appeared from the inside of a round rack holding skiwear, then just as quickly disappeared. A moment later, he was crouched down near the floor, looking at a bookcase full of books and local maps.

"It'd just be for the one evening," Cameron said after a moment.

Faith tucked her fingers in the front pockets of her black jeans. "See that it is," she said evenly. "Since the weather is so nice, I figure the town's tennis courts are due to be open any day."

At last, his lips quirked. "You've got a smart mouth on you."

Her shoulder lifted a little. At least he'd stopped looking as if she'd offered to chop off his foot rather than lend his son a tennis racket.

She moved back to the glass checkout counter and found a piece of paper. She scribbled her address on it and handed it to him. "I really will set it out for you, though," she murmured. "Then it won't matter if I'm out on a call or not and you can get it whenever you want."

"My show is tomorrow night." Erik popped up next to her, a thick picture book on bug collecting in his hands. "You wanna come?"

How could anyone not be enamored of this boy? "I can't," she said regretfully. "I already have plans."

"With who?"

"It's none of your business," Cam told Erik. He folded the paper with her address and tucked it in his lapel pocket. "We need to let Ms. Taylor get back to her work."

She was back to *Ms. Taylor.*

Faith stifled a sigh and wished it didn't hurt quite so much. She looked at Erik, deliberately ignoring the fact that Cameron was clearly ready to leave. "I'll be in Bozeman all day tomorrow."

"You won't get back in time?"

She crouched down and shook her head. "I don't think so. I'm sorry." And she was. Surprisingly so. She'd have thought that she'd rather be anywhere else other than an elementary school.

"That's okay," he said after a moment. "Maybe next time."

Her heart squeezed. "Right."

Erik pointed at the climbing display. "Sometime will you teach me how to do that?"

"I'd like that. But if you want to learn climbing *really* well, you should take a class. The guy who teaches it here—Rick—is phenomenal. Much better than I am. The climbing gym is through that door right there." She pointed to the glass doorway on the right side of the store.

"Can I, Dad? Take a class? When is it?"

"Rick comes every other weekend." Faith rose. One glance at Cameron's set expression told her that the boy was doomed to disappointment.

"No," Cameron said evenly. "You climb enough without adding classes in it."

"Da-ad."

"I said no, Erik."

The boy's head fell back and he stomped off around the rack of ski boots.

Faith pressed her hands together. "Rick focuses on safety first, Cameron. Erik could very well benefit from that." She kept her voice low.

"Always so nice when people who *don't* have kids go around passing advice to those who do."

He might as well have slapped her. "Well, pardon me."

He exhaled noisily. "Look. If you want to go to Erik's thing, go. Don't let me stop you. I won't be trying to kiss you or anything."

"Trust me, Cameron—" her voice shook slightly "—I *am* busy. And contrary to the opinion of the female population of Thunder Canyon High School— all who seem to think you hung the moon—not everything is about *you*. You couldn't have made your disinterest in me more plain."

A crash sounded, followed by Erik's plaintive "Oh, man," and Faith darted around the ski boots to find Erik standing on a shelf, shoeboxes tumbled around him.

Cameron swiftly moved past her and swept Erik off the shelf, setting him on the ground. "When I said you climbed enough already, did you think that was an invitation? Do I need to ground you again?"

Erik looked abashed. His chin tucked down into his chest. "No, sir."

Faith gathered up a few boxes and slid them back into place. "Nothing's broken."

"Small mercies." Cameron handed him his coat and pointed to the door. "Move it."

Erik shrugged into his parka. "See ya', Faith."

"See you, Juan."

Erik's lips barely moved into a smile. He pushed out the door, dejection in every movement.

Faith looked at Cameron.

"Sorry about the mess," he said.

"It'll clean up," she said flatly. "You know, maybe if you'd let Erik *do* more of the things he's interested in—like climbing lessons—he wouldn't need to focus his energies on being mischievous. And *no,* I don't need a child of my own to be able to figure that out."

He grabbed the door that Erik had opened before it could swing closed. "When you *do* have a child of your own, then we'll talk." He strode out and the door sighed shut.

Faith closed her eyes.

Then she and Cameron would *never* be talking.

Because having a child of her own was the one thing she would never be able to do.

Chapter Eight

When Faith drove back into Thunder Canyon the following evening from her trip to Bozeman, she could see the line of cars parked up and down the street around the elementary school before she even drove past.

She tapped her thumb on the steering wheel and slowed even more. The parking lot itself looked wall-to-wall with cars. The high windows on the building where the auditorium was located were brightly lit against the night sky.

The building looked welcoming. As if it exuded a physical aura.

Or maybe it was her own longing that was causing the sensation.

She rubbed her forehead. The day had seemed unending with meetings with Jim Shepherd and the rest of the team. Then lunch, celebrating the engagement of Nathan—the youngest of their group. And after that had come Faith's annual doctor's appointment. She'd been poked and prodded and pronounced fit enough—healing scrapes notwithstanding. Nothing had changed since her last visit, a year earlier. Not that she expected otherwise. She'd already been picked apart, medically speaking. There were no surprises left.

She reached the end of the block and braked at the stop sign. There were no oncoming cars, yet she still didn't proceed.

The engine idled. Warm air whispered from the heater vents. Slow, lazy jazz hummed softly from the CD player.

She reached up and nudged the rearview mirror until it was angled enough to see the reflection of the school behind her.

The toot of a horn warned her that another car had pulled up behind her. She hurriedly adjusted her mirror and drove through the empty intersection, letting the impatient car pass her by.

It wasn't all that late. Not even eight o'clock. And the idea of going home to her dark, empty condominium was suddenly more than she could bear.

So she turned her truck around and drove back toward the cheerfully lit, crowded school. She found a parking spot—well, made herself one at any rate—beneath a streetlight, and strode quickly to the auditorium. She could hear the high pip of youthful voices even before she quietly slipped into the rear of the room.

Folding chairs were set up in neat rows, filling nearly all of the floor space. The children stood on risers on the low stage at one end of the room.

A quartet stood in front of the chorus, Erik among them. A little blond girl about his size was singing a solo at the moment. She was dressed in skiwear and her voice shook a little as she sang about the beauty of winter. Then she took a step back while parental applause rocked the house, and another girl took her place, this one decked out like spring flowers. Faith stepped a little closer, still keeping well to the shadows in the rear of the room. She wasn't altogether surprised to see how Erik stood so still and serious while "Spring" sang her solo. Even though the boy was an utter ball of energy, she knew he was perfectly capable of focusing it when he chose. She'd experienced it herself when he'd pitted his prowess at checkers against her.

She didn't realize that her gaze was methodically working along the rows of chairs until it stopped.

Cameron sat in the third row from the front. Dead center.

And he held a small video recorder in his hand.

It wasn't as if he were the only parent present capturing the event on video. From where she stood, she could see dozens of faintly lit video camera screens in varying sizes. But the sight of Cameron—

She blew out a soft breath, and tugged nervously at her ponytail.

The sight of Cameron taping his son definitely did something to her insides. And it didn't matter at all that inside her head, she could still hear his words to her the previous night.

And even though *that* should have been warning enough, she stayed there, rapt, through the rest of the performance, only managing to drag her attention from Cameron when Erik stepped forward for his solo.

His voice shook a little, just as the others had, but with each stanza, he gained confidence, until he was belting out his lines, and by the time he and the other soloists stepped back into their spots on the risers, the audience was practically cheering. The children's smiles beamed out, and along with everyone else, Faith clapped until her palms ached when the performance ended a few songs later.

She fully intended to disappear again before Erik saw her, but that plan was foiled when the parents made beelines for the door the moment the rest of the lights came up. Unprepared for the mass exodus, Faith found herself stuck behind the row of chairs.

Cameron spotted her first.

His footsteps didn't falter, but even across the distance of a dozen rows of chairs, she felt the sharpness of his gaze fastening on her face.

He'd tasted of coffee.

Her face heated. She looped her long scarf around her neck, which regrettably only made her feel warmer. But she refused to fidget. Particularly when he was watching her so steadily, and providing no hint whatsoever as to what his thoughts were.

While hers, on the other hand, kept running down the same paths until they'd made deep enough ruts that she could have sailed a ship in them.

What was she doing here?

Was it Erik that drew her, or Erik's dad?

Or both?

Did it even matter? The sly whisper worked through her, ringing in her thoughts as Cameron stopped a foot away from her. His big hand eclipsed the camera he held, and the child's backpack—probably fat with books and goodness knew what else— slung over one shoulder looked rather minuscule.

His jaw was blurred by a five o'clock shadow, but she could still see the muscle ticking there.

And everything female inside her went foolishly soft.

"Thought you were busy," he said after a moment. He took another step forward to allow a woman with a stroller to get past them.

"I was. I finished."

His lids drooped and her lips suddenly tingled. She pulled off her scarf. "Erik's quite the performer," she said cautiously. She didn't want a repeat of the previous night.

He nodded slowly. "Just give him an audience."

Her hands bunched the scarf. "When I was his age I could never have done a solo like that." She swallowed. "Well, I couldn't do it *now* for that matter."

His lips tilted slightly. "His mother liked an audience, too." Apparently, Cameron didn't want to have an argument, either.

"And...you?"

"I prefer a more private production."

She nearly choked and whipped the scarf back around her neck. She was so far out of her element it was a wonder she wasn't drowning in her own rutted thoughts.

She simply could not figure the man out, and it was better if she'd stop trying.

"I, um, I should be going. Tell Erik I thought he was great."

"Tell him yourself." His gaze skipped past her and he lifted his chin a little.

Faith turned to see Erik coming into the auditorium from the entrance. Two little girls, the soloists, were hard on his heels.

"Hey, Faith." Erik grinned, but seemed to take her presence without surprise. As if he'd half expected her to show up no matter what she'd said to the contrary.

Since she *was* there, perhaps Erik was on to something.

"You and Dad gotta come to our classroom now," he said blithely. "You gotta see our *work*. We been pinning it up on the bulletin boards for a whole week."

Faith's gaze darted up to Cameron's. "Oh, I really should get home." Her voice strangled when Cameron closed his hand over her elbow.

"Lead the way," he told his son.

"She's the lady who rescued you, huh," Spring whispered not so quietly to Erik, casting a curious look up at Faith.

"Uh-huh."

The other girl wasn't so shy. She tilted her blond head and addressed Faith directly. "Do you get to keep the gold you found?"

Faith's eyebrows shot up. "Only gold *I* found in the mine was named Erik. It's been other people who are catching gold fever, I think."

The boy rolled his eyes, but giggled a little as the kids scurried ahead. "Hurry up, Dad. Or there's not gonna be any cookies left by the time we get there."

Faith still hung back when Cameron started to follow. "I really should go."

"Go where?"

Through her long-sleeved sweater, she felt his thumb smooth over her elbow.

An empty home? An elementary school packed with lively children?

Both caused their share of pain.

"Faith?"

She swallowed, knowing her hesitation went on too long. Too obvious, yet unable to do one single thing about it now. The man's kiss had hinted at heaven, all wrapped up in sinful temptation. But he'd pushed her away as if she'd turned vile. And now...now she didn't know what he was doing.

Or what she was doing there.

It all came back to that.

And for some reason, it made her want to sit down and cry. But she hadn't cried in a very, very long time. And she'd be darned if she'd start now.

"Maybe for a few minutes," she said finally.

He nodded, not smiling. "Erik'll be pleased."

"And you?" The words were out before she could think twice. His eyes narrowed a fraction. And she quickly waved her hand. "Never mind. Probably better if we leave that one alone." Proving that cowardice was alive and well and dwelling inside her, she hurriedly turned and followed after Erik.

The classroom, when they got there, seemed packed with people. But like a determined fish, Erik wriggled between them and latched onto Faith's hand the moment she stepped through the doorway. She didn't have to look back to see if Cameron was there. She could feel him in the sparks of energy tickling her spine even when he was yards behind her.

"Come and see my desk." Erik tugged at her as he dove back into the fray.

There was little Faith could do but follow. She admired his desk and the neat journal that was taped to the top surface. When he lifted the lid, she was suitably impressed with the order of his supplies inside.

"We all hadda clean our desks during class today," he admitted, grinning. "I had a whole bag of trash."

Cameron's hand closed over the back of her neck as he leaned over them both, looking at the desk as well.

How was it possible to freeze and melt all at the same time?

Yet that's exactly how she felt.

She stared blindly at a vocabulary workbook and tried to pretend there was nothing more extraordinary going on than Erik's pencils being lined up like a half-dozen dutiful soldiers.

Fortunately, Erik's teacher was trying to call order to the group.

"Sit here," Erik hissed and pushed her to his under-size chair.

Faith sat, which was good since her legs felt oddly insubstantial. Once the room was more or less quiet, the teacher—a humorous, middle-aged woman whom Faith had never met—welcomed the parents, and briefly outlined the work the students had been doing for the past semester. She pointed out the various projects that were displayed around the room, and then invited everyone to continue drinking punch and eating the cookies.

Erik, along with a dozen other seven-year-olds, darted toward the refreshments that were set up on a short table beneath the blackboard. He was back before Faith could even start to make noises about leaving again, bearing a napkin loaded with several cookies. He dumped it on her lap, then was off again.

Faith looked up at Cameron, half afraid that she'd find him looking at her and wishing it were his beloved wife sitting there, instead. But his eyes were only amused as he leaned over and plucked a chocolate-chip cookie from her lap. "Have a cookie," he said blandly.

Erik had left them with at least a half-dozen of them, and Faith found herself smiling, too.

"Does he like cookies?"

"Don't all seven-year-old boys?"

She watched Cameron finish off his cookie in two bites. "Don't all grown men?"

"We never had homemade cookies when I was growing up," he said. He dumped Erik's backpack on the floor near her feet, set the video camera on the desk, and hunkered down on his heels next to her chair. He studied the selection remaining, then reached. His knuckle brushed her knee as he picked up a sugar cookie sprinkled with red crystalline sugar.

Sheer effort kept her from shifting in the chair. "Why not? Your mom didn't bake?"

"I doubt my mother even knows how to turn on an oven," he said dryly. "Might mess up her hundred-dollar manicure."

"Your parents are wealthy?"

"Oh, yeah." He finished the cookie. Brushed the crumbs from his fingertip on his thigh.

A muscular thigh that looked hard and solid as it bulged against his well-cut charcoal gray trousers.

She quickly looked back at the napkin and cookies in her own lap.

"We had cookies, of course. Beautifully prepared by Denver's finest pastry chefs." He shifted a little, putting one arm behind her on the back of the chair.

She was finding it difficult to breathe. She'd spent many an afternoon in the kitchen with her mom and sisters baking cookies. For holidays. For fun. "My parents live in Arizona," she announced baldly.

"Were you close to them?"

She nodded. "Still are. They still hold hands. It's great." An enduring marriage like her parents' is what she'd thought she'd have when she'd said her vows to Jess.

So much for that.

"Any other siblings beside the doc?"

"Sisters. Both younger." She picked up a cookie. Nibbled a corner of it. Oatmeal raisin.

Figures. She loathed oatmeal raisin. That's what she got for letting herself be so distracted by a man. By *Cameron*.

"How long were you married?"

She started. "Six years. You?"

"Five. You still love him?"

Her fingers went lax and the cookie tumbled to the sturdy green-flecked carpet. "That's a very personal question."

"Yeah." His head nearly brushed her thigh as he leaned over and retrieved the cookie. He set it on the corner of the desk and looked back at her. "Are you?"

"No." She'd called Erik a jumping bean, but it was *her* nerves that were jumping all over the place now. "Are you?" she challenged.

"In love with your ex? Not likely."

Her lips pressed together. "Ha-ha."

His gaze was on the cookies again. "Yes."

Her jumping nerves collided and collapsed into wreckage. Well. She'd asked, hadn't she? "I'm sorry."

His gaze slanted to her face. "For what?"

"I don't know."

He slowly took another cookie. "This is what Laura wanted," he said after a moment.

"Broken gingerbread?"

His lips twisted. "A regular life like this." He lifted his chin, encompassing the families who milled around the room. The children who raced back and forth. "She wanted to move here so damned bad. Had a vision in her head of the kind of childhood Erik would have. The kind of home we'd have. How we'd be part of the whole small-town deal."

She could see each individual lash of his thick, sooty eyelashes. Could see the fine lines barely webbing out from the corners of his dark eyes. "Then she'd be pleased," Faith said quietly. "That you have what she'd wanted for you."

"Yeah." His gaze roved over the room and she could practically feel the restlessness seeping out of his pores. "Too late, though," he added grimly.

She curled her fingers, realizing that she'd actually begun lifting her hand as if to touch his hair. And wouldn't that be the height of folly? "Because she... died."

"Because I didn't start living the life she wanted until *after* she died." He pushed to his feet. "Don't think Erik's coming with punch anytime soon. I'll be back." He headed toward the line of people at the refreshment table.

Faith watched him go. He wasn't necessarily the tallest, or even the biggest man there. He did have height and mile-wide shoulders on his side, true. But the thing about Cameron that made him stand out from the others was not his physicality. It was something...deeper. Something that came up from his soul.

And rather than being put off by his confirmation that he still loved his wife, she feared she was only more intrigued than ever.

Realizing she was staring—and probably drooling on herself as well—she looked down at Erik's journal. It was displayed in a manner clearly meant to be read, so she flipped open the thick paper that served as the cover, and looked at the first page. Erik's writing was slapdash, as if he could hardly be bothered with penmanship when there were more interesting things in the world to attend to. But it improved as she paged through, reading the weekly entries that covered a span of about three months.

At the end was his recounting of his adventure down the mine shaft. He'd even drawn a picture—a well-drawn picture for that matter—of himself, being drawn up the shaft by the safety harness and rope, with Faith down below him.

"He inherited his mother's ability to draw, too."

She looked up, already aware of Cameron's presence before he'd spoken. He held out a clear plastic cup filled with red punch. She took it, carefully avoiding his long fingers, and sipped. "You don't draw?"

"Stick figures are more my speed," he assured dryly. "Toss in a little calculus, trig and math analysis, and that's my art."

"And high school sports."

"Yeah." He drank from his own cup. "I think Erik's permanently camped out at the refreshment table. He doesn't usually get homemade cookies, either."

"Maybe I'll have to get out my cookie sheets," she murmured.

"You bake?"

"I'm not all about the search and rescue," she said dryly.

His lashes dropped. "Yeah. I know. I need to apologize. For last night."

At least he hadn't apologized for the kiss.

Again.

She wasn't sure she'd have been able to take it, if he had. "We both said things we probably shouldn't have."

His index finger tapped his plastic cup. "Truth is, you'll make a great mom. When you decide to have a family." He looked around the room. "There are at least six people here who don't have the interest in their own child that you have in Erik. Who would rather be anywhere other than here."

Faith was grateful his attention was elsewhere. She choked down her punch in a huge gulp, then transferred the napkin and remains of the cookies to the desktop and stood. "I don't suppose school functions are everyone's cup of tea."

"They weren't my parents'." His voice was matter-of-fact. "Only time they came was when it was time to pick me up from boarding school at the end of each term."

She tugged her scarf back into place and picked up her coat. He'd gone to a boarding school? Sounded lonely.

"I have to go," she said. "I'll just sneak by and tell Erik. If I can get his attention away from his girl-friends there."

"*Girl*friends?" His head snapped around.

There was nothing blasé in his expression now. And if Faith weren't feeling so off-kilter, she might have found his surprise amusing. "Also known as Winter and Spring. They've barely let him out of their sight since we came in the classroom." She headed toward the refreshment table and worked her way toward Erik.

"Can we go tobogganing again soon?" he asked after she'd told him it was time for her to leave.

"Depends on my schedule," she said honestly. He had a smear of chocolate on his chin and the front of his hair stood up in a cowlick.

Her head told her she would be better off staying far, far away from either of the Stevensons.

But her heart?

She tweaked Erik's tumbled hair and crouched down to his level. "I'll see what I can arrange, okay?"

"Cool." He smiled. And even though he was surrounded by classmates, he leaned forward. His hug was brief, but tight.

And it stole her heart.

She rose and turned. Felt the slam of Cameron's brown gaze when she saw him standing just behind them, and had to look down, unable to withstand the intensity of it.

"I'll walk you to your car," he told her. "Erik, you stay in this classroom until I get back."

Erik looked surprised. But he nodded. "'Bye, Faith."

She winked, though what she wanted to do was hug the boy again. "'Bye, Juan."

"How come she calls you Juan?" she heard Spring whisper as she and Cameron headed toward the door. Before they left the building, she stopped to pull on her coat. Cameron took it from her and held it up for her.

She tucked her tongue between her teeth and silently slid her arms into the sleeves. Then he closed his hands over her shoulders and turned her to face him. His fingers brushed her chin when he buttoned it.

"Faith! Wait!"

She drew in an unsteady breath and looked back to see Erik racing down the hall.

"Erik, I told you to wait in the classroom."

"I know, Dad. But I forgot this." He pushed an oversize sheet of paper at Faith. "I made this for you. I had to get it down off the bulletin board."

Faith took the paper and turned it until she could see the front. It was a watercolor painting and the sturdy brick lines of the fire station were clearly recognizable.

"That's you," he stabbed his finger at the slightly blurry figure astride a snowmobile outside the building.

"I figured." She couldn't stand it. She leaned down and kissed his forehead. "Thank you. I'm going to hang it up at home when I get there."

He rolled his eyes a little, but grinned, then he was racing back down the hallway toward his classroom.

"Yeah," Cameron murmured. "You'll be a great mom." His hand touched the small of her back even as he reached forward to push open the heavy door.

Cold air washed over her hot face as she stepped outside. "Actually," her fingers tightened unconsciously on the corner of Erik's painting. "I really don't plan to have kids."

She felt his sidelong look at that and quickened her step. Cameron's long legs easily kept pace, however. And when they reached her SUV, he snorted softly. "Think making your own parking space where there is none might just be worse than double-parking."

"There's a foot of snow between my wheels and the grass," she defended lightly. "I'm not damaging anything. And the only one who'd delight in giving me another ticket would be Bobby Romano."

"*Another* ticket. Wild woman." He pulled open the driver's side door. "You didn't lock it."

"Not much point." She'd never been called a wild woman before. She thought she might just like it. "Thunder Canyon isn't a hotbed of criminal activity." She climbed up into the vehicle.

He stepped closer, inside the open door. "Maybe not. But it'd be safer for you."

"I think I'm pretty safe," she demurred.

The streetlight overhead shined down on his bare head, casting his dark auburn head with a gilded sheen. He stood close enough that she could feel the warmth of him. His coat hung open, and it would only take one small move and she could slide her hand over the pale gray shirt that draped his hard chest.

"Are you?"

Her lips were tingling again. "Hmm?"

His deep voice seemed to drop even more. "Safe."

She curled her hand tightly around the steering wheel. A much *safer* alternative than touching him. The only one in danger of anything was her. But maybe it was better that Cameron was still in love with his wife. There was no danger of her being hurt again, the way she had been when Jess walked out, if Cameron found out just how much she was lacking.

"I'm safe as houses," she finally whispered.

He leaned down, his mouth hovering inches above hers.

A car drove by, tooting its horn. "Hey, Coach! G'luck on Friday!"

Cameron straightened. He lifted his hand in acknowledgment of the drive-by well-wisher. "Parking under a streetlight." His voice was dry. "Perfect."

She stuck the key in the ignition, rather amazed that she managed it on the first try. "It's *safer*," she said.

He was silent for a long heartbeat. Then he smiled. He backed up, out of the way of the door. "Drive carefully."

"Always."

But he wasn't so breezy. "I mean it, Faith. Be careful."

She nodded slowly. "I'll be careful, Cameron."

He studied her for a moment longer then, apparently satisfied, he nodded once and pushed her door closed. He stepped away from the truck so she'd have room to back out of her impromptu parking slot.

She drove away, with the reflection of him in her rearview mirror.

He stood there until she turned out of sight and she continued on home.

Safe?

Who was she kidding?

Chapter Nine

"We forgot to get your tennis racket back to you last night."

Faith's hand tightened around the telephone and she managed to scatter the pages of the budget she'd been working on for Jim across her desk.

The last voice she'd expected to hear on the other end of the phone when it rang was Cameron's.

"And here I was about to put in a missing racket report." Her voice was deliberately light.

"I still owe you a dinner."

"You don't *owe* me anything."

"You didn't have a chance to eat last Friday at The Hitching Post. I'm tossing some steaks on the grill tonight. If you're interested."

She *was* interested. That was the problem.

"Erik's been practicing with the toboggan, too. Think he has some trick he wants to show you."

She pressed her fingertips against her forehead. Shifts had just changed and there was a lot of commotion inside the station. "I'll be on call this evening. I wouldn't want to disappoint Erik if I get called out."

"He'd just have something new to brag about at school tomorrow."

In his background, she could hear a school bell. It sounded even noisier on his end than it did at the fire station. And it took no effort at all on her part to envision Cameron at his desk, students pouring into his classroom. "Cameron—"

"Erik's not the only one who'd like you to come."

She swallowed. Hard.

"You still there?"

"Yes." She pushed out the word. "All right. Um... can I bring anything?"

"Just yourself. Come by around seven. We've got a practice game after school. *Romance*," his voice sharpened. "If you want to avoid the principal's office, get off the desk." His tone changed again. "See you tonight."

"Okay." She'd barely gotten the word out when he'd hung up, and she sat there for a long moment staring at the receiver in her hand.

"Works better when you talk *into* it, Blondie." Derek stopped by her desk. He dropped a plastic container by her elbow. "Cake."

She finally hung up the telephone. Glanced at the

container. "Thanks." She shifted it to the side, off the budget papers.

His eyebrows shot up. "Okay. Tanya was right. Something's up with you."

"Nothing's up with me."

He leaned way over, crossing his arms on the desk, to peer into her face. "That's chocolate cake in there, and you're *not* diving into it? Something is up all right. Wanna tell Uncle Derek about it?"

She rolled her eyes. "Don't be ridiculous."

"Have anything to do with the coach?"

Faith's cheeks warmed. "No."

"Even though he was kissing you last night at the elementary school?"

She gaped. "How…he was not." He hadn't kissed her, because of the car that had driven by.

Derek was grinning, looking knowing. Faith bunched up the papers and tapped them against the desk, squaring the edges. "He's just still feeling grateful."

"Keep telling yourself that, Blondie." He nudged the container. "Better eat this up before word gets out that I didn't bring anyone else any dessert. You might find yourself in a dogfight or something."

She snatched the container, protective, and tucked it in her desk drawer. "Nobody gets between me and chocolate," she assured him.

But Faith didn't get a chance to eat the chocolate cake that afternoon. Nor did she make it to Cameron's for dinner.

The entire team was called out just after noon, when an AMBER alert was issued for a three-year-old girl who'd gone missing just outside of Bozeman.

And it was well after midnight when she finally dragged herself home, where the only thing to welcome her was the flashing red light on her answering machine. She hit the Play button on her way into the kitchen.

Her mother's voice trilled out, talking about the beautiful weather they were having in Arizona, and when was Faith going to take a vacation and come see them?

Faith opened the refrigerator door. Stared at the unexciting contents. Derek's chocolate masterpiece was still tucked away in her desk drawer at work. She closed the door and leaned wearily back against it. Listened to her brother's message, calling to see if she wanted to have lunch later that week. Then a third call.

Cameron.

She pushed herself away from the refrigerator and left the kitchen to eye the message machine, which sat next to the phone on a small maple telephone stand that her mom had passed on to her years earlier. She pressed the Stop button. Rewound it a few seconds. Pressed Play.

Faith. This is Cam. Practice ran late. But you're not here, anyway. Heard the AMBER alert on the radio. Figured you're out on it. Guess I'll have to feed you another time.

She crossed her arms, avoiding the temptation to rewind the message and listen to it again.

But the messages weren't finished.

Faith. Cam. It's after eleven. Just saw the news. Call me when you get in. I don't care how late. Call. He reeled off the number.

The machine's red light stopped flashing. All of the new messages had been played.

She unfolded her arms, feeling just tired and weak enough to actually dial that number. But something held her back. Cowardice? Sensibility?

She went into her bedroom and replaced the uniform she'd been wearing for so many hours with her thick, comfortable robe. She pulled off the clasp holding back her ponytail, and dropped the gold loop on her dresser, rubbing her hand against her tired scalp.

The phone rang, sounding sharp and imperious. And she knew, just glancing at the extension, who would be calling her at this hour.

She sat on the side of the bed and slowly picked it up. "Hello?"

"You didn't call." Cameron's voice was low. Deep.

A frisson rippled through her. "I just got in a few minutes ago. I'm sorry. I didn't get a chance to call you before dinner. We were pretty busy."

"Are you okay?"

She reached out for a pillow and pulled it over her lap. "It was a...tough night." Her throat felt tight. "You saw the news?"

"Yeah."

So he knew the child had been found too late. Three tiny years of innocence obliterated in an instant because of one man's malevolent insanity.

"Have you had to deal with other cases like this?"

Where a child was killed by an abductor? "No. We've had more than a few that ended up being a recovery rather than rescue." And it never got any easier. "But nothing like this." Accidents versus heinous intention. "The FBI was there. Police crawling all over the place. Local, county, state. Must've been around seventy-five searchers." Her eyes ached, dry and so tired. "It was…awful, Cameron. We found her poor little body stuck under a bush near a highway rest stop."

"Where were you?"

She pinched her eyes closed. "On the other side of the highway. A witness had called in a report of a driver pitching something out their car window—a car similar in description to one used by the suspected abductor—in that area. We were in tight critical spacing. Nathan—he's the youngest SAR—found the body. He's pretty wrecked."

"Jesus."

She wished she could get the image out of her head. "I'm sorry I didn't call and cancel dinner."

He made a rough noise. "Come on, Faith. Do you think that really matters?"

"It always had to Jess." She hadn't meant to admit that.

"Your ex? He was a firefighter, wasn't he?"

"Yes." She didn't recall ever telling him that fact.

"You'd think he'd have had a better grasp on priorities."

Faith carefully exhaled. "He didn't figure I needed to be out saving anything when he was already doing it himself." No. Jess had wanted her home having his babies. And when she'd failed in that regard, he'd traded her in for a better model.

"Do you want me to come over?"

Forget carefully exhaling. She felt as if her breath were knocked right out of her. "Why?" she croaked.

"Because you've had a tough night. You shouldn't be alone."

She rubbed her eyes a little harder. "You can't leave Erik alone. Particularly at this hour."

"Then call someone. Your brother. Or your friend who owns the sporting goods store. Tanya, right?"

It undid her that he recalled such specifics. "Chris is undoubtedly on duty, and if he's not, he's grabbing what little sleep he manages to get between the hospital and the ranch. And Tanya's still dealing with Toby, her son. He's had the flu for the past few days." She opened her eyes, but the image of that poor toddler seemed seared into her brain, overriding the pale, sage green bedroom wall she'd painted just a few months earlier. "I appreciate the concern. But I'm fine."

He made a soft, disbelieving sound. "Right."

Her spine stiffened a little. "I'm not some fragile thing, Cameron."

"No. You're human," he countered evenly. "And this has nothing to do with your competence or abilities. Which, frankly, might intimidate the hell out of some people."

"But not you?" Some portion of her mind realized that she was shaking. "Never mind. I didn't mean that."

"You make me feel a lot of things, Faith. Intimidated isn't one of them."

Her eyes stung unmercifully. "Cameron—"

He swore softly. "What the hell are we doing here, Faith?"

She trembled harder. "I don't know. I, um, I'm going to take a shower." Maybe she'd be able to warm up, then. "And go to bed. Where you should be. You have school tomorrow." The clock face mocked her. "Today," she amended.

"Faith—"

"I'm *fine,*" she spoke quickly, over him. "Good night, Cameron." She quickly leaned over and hung up the phone.

Then she stayed there, hunched over the pillow bunched against her abdomen. But he didn't call back.

And after several minutes of silence, she finally stopped expecting the phone to ring again. She went into her bathroom and took her shower, just as she'd said she was going to do. And even though the room was dripping with steam when she finally stepped out a long while later, she still felt cold inside.

She pulled on an ancient pair of sweats, wrapped herself in her thick robe for good measure, and went back into the living room. She flipped on the television. But the only things on were an infomercial touting the miraculous effects of a hair tonic and all-night news.

She wasn't up to seeing a news report of that night's horror so she settled for the infomercial, even though she didn't think she was going bald anytime soon. But the low noise was better than silence and she went into the kitchen. She hadn't eaten since breakfast and her stomach was protesting, but the thought of food was more than she could stand. She eyed the bottle of wine Tanya had brought over when they'd had dinner together last week. But when she reached into the refrigerator, she pulled out the jug of milk instead.

Hot chocolate was a better choice.

She pulled out a saucepan, sloshed milk into it and stuck it on the stove to heat.

Her head was pounding.

In a bowl, she mixed up real cocoa with sugar, a dash of salt and a splash of vanilla, the way her mom had always done when she was little.

The bottle of aspirin sitting on the kitchen table was empty. Her silent reminder to buy another when she managed to get herself to the store. Fortunately, she had a stash in her first-aid kit in the SUV. She turned down the heat under the milk, pushed her feet into the fur-lined boots sitting by the door and went outside to retrieve it.

She found the bottle just where it was supposed to be, and shook out a few pills into her palm. Cold night air whisked over her wet head so she hurriedly locked up the SUV again and turned back to the sidewalk.

Cameron stood in her path.

She swayed. God. Now she was seeing him in her mind, too.

Only hallucinations didn't reach out and grab your elbows with strong, remarkably gentle hands.

Did they?

"What the hell are you doing out here?" His voice was rough.

She opened her palm. "Aspirin."

He exhaled noisily, and closed his arm over her shoulder. "Let's get you inside. You don't even have on a coat."

She found herself hustled up the walk. She wasn't sure he hadn't just lifted her right off her feet, when it came down to it. And she was still staring at him when he let go of her to close her front door.

He set the tennis racket he'd been holding in one hand on the narrow table by the door where she always dropped her keys and mail, and shrugged off his shearling coat, which he dumped over the top of her weighted-down coat tree. "What do I smell?"

As if he'd been there a dozen times, he walked right past her into her small kitchen. She followed, seeing him pull the saucepan off the heat in just enough time to keep it from bubbling over. He turned the heat off.

In her preoccupation, she hadn't turned the heat down. She'd turned it too high.

"What are you doing here? Where's Erik?"

He opened one cupboard. Then another. Found a glass that he filled with water and handed it to her.

She stupidly remembered the aspirin in her hand, and swallowed it quickly. Then he took the glass back and set it in her sink.

"Erik's still asleep in his bed at home," he finally answered, apparently satisfied now that she'd swallowed her aspirin. "Todd Gilmore came over to stay with him."

"Todd Gilmore. As in your student, Todd."

"Yeah. He watches Erik now and then for me."

"In the middle of the night?"

"No. This is a first. Gilmore's a night owl, though. Brags about it every day when he's falling asleep in my second-hour math class. I knew he'd still be up when I called him, and he was. Plus, he lives in the house next door to me," he reminded her.

She could feel her face heating under the steady weight of his gaze. "Does he know you were coming over here?"

"He knows."

"Great." She could just imagine the gossip that would fly now. "I told you I was fine, Cameron. I don't need your...coddling."

He was standing with his back to her stove, a good ten feet from her. "What *do* you need, Faith?"

She stared at him, mute, while too many things tangled inside her head, her chest, to be let free.

He made a rough sound, and crossed the kitchen in two strides. "Think you may be a harder case than I am," he muttered, and pulled her against him, tucking her head against his chest.

She shuddered. His warmth, his strength, his... *comfort*...nearly more than she could bear. "Cameron." She didn't know what else to say.

He just held her.

And a tear leaked down her cheek. She rubbed her cheek against his soft beige shirt. His fingers slowly threaded through her hair. And another tear fell.

"I don't even know if they've caught the guy," she murmured at last.

"They did. News was full of it." His lips pressed against the top of her head. Her forehead. Then he cupped her face and tilted it back to his gaze. His thumb slowly brushed over her damp cheek.

"I hope they hang him," she said thickly.

His palms were warm on her face. And there was no judgment in his dark gaze. He just slowly tucked her back against his chest, rocking ever so slightly. "How'd you ever end up in search and rescue?"

She curled her hands over his biceps and closed her eyes. "Because of Jess," she admitted. "My ex-husband." She was silent for a long moment, soaking in the warmth of Cameron's body through her completely unappealing robe and sweats. "I was actually going for a teaching degree."

"In?"

"Elementary education." She sighed when his fingers started threading through her hair again then rubbed gently against her scalp.

"Then what?"

She lowered her head a little when his fingers found her nape and massaged there. Heaven. "Jess was with the fire department already. We were out on a departmental picnic and a child got separated from his folks." She sighed, angling her head a little more. Oh, he was good at that. "I'd always been into outdoor activities. Camping. Sports. It's one of the things Jess and I had in common." Things that hadn't been enough to hold them together. "After that picnic...I don't know. I saw what SAR was all about, up close and personal. I changed course a little."

"Was the kid found?"

She nodded. "Safe and sound and sunburned as all get-out."

"Were you and Jess already married?"

"About six months by then." No matter how good Cameron's hands felt on her, she didn't particularly want to discuss her marriage. She shifted, lifting her head and his hands fell away, but only to transfer to her shoulders.

Where he found a whole new set of tired muscles.

She closed her eyes, her lips curving despite herself. "You could have a second career," she murmured after a moment. "Cameron Stevenson. Master masseur."

"Third career."

"Right." Her head had found its way back to his chest. "What was it you did in Denver?"

"Made rich people richer." His palms slid beneath the robe and the soft, worn terry cloth slid off her shoulders. It bunched loosely around her waist, still held in place by the tie. The collar of her faded gray sweatshirt had long been cut out and his fingers slid beneath it, finding the bare skin of her shoulders.

Her hands slid down his sides, finding purchase in the empty belt loops of his blue jeans. "And you, too?"

"And me." His voice dropped even lower.

"So, you, um…" She hesitated, then let out a long sigh when his fingertips pressed firmly against her back. He'd reached up beneath her sweatshirt, she realized dimly.

"I…what?"

The robe's tie finally gave up the ghost and the once-pink terry cloth slid to her feet. His fingers swept down her spine. Found the ache at the small of her back even through the worn-thin fabric of her sweatpants.

What had she been going to say? "Ah...right. Didn't go into teaching to make your fortune."

He laughed softly. "Who does?"

She wasn't cold anymore. She was melting. From the inside out. "But you changed...oh, that feels good...your, um, mind about making rich people richer?"

"Mmm-hmm."

"Why?"

His fingers hesitated for a moment and she held her breath, yearning for him not to stop.

His fingers pressed again, moving in a tight circle right above her rear, and she let out an appreciative sigh.

"I had more degrees than anyone could ever need," he murmured. "And a client list longer than my arm. I couldn't keep up with them from here—not when they were spread out all over the states. I was traveling all the time. Gone more than I was here. And after Laura...died—" he exhaled "—not working wasn't an option. I had to find something to do. And it wasn't hard to add a teaching certificate to my other credentials."

He hadn't turned to teaching until after his wife had passed away. Her hands slid up his torso, exploring the hard ridges of muscle and sinew. "How did she die?"

For a long moment she feared he wouldn't answer.

His head brushed hers. His mouth touched her shoulder and she felt his lips moving against her skin. "She was out antique hunting. It was raining. Her SUV hydroplaned into a tree. She never had a chance."

Her hands slid behind him.

"She was always on me about traveling too much. Was afraid with all the flying I was doing that something would happen." He sighed again. "And she was the one who—" His voice broke off and he lifted his head. His eyes were shadowed. "She wasn't even fifty miles away from Thunder Canyon. Erik was with her."

She sucked in a hard breath. "Oh, Cam."

"He was belted in his safety seat. Laura had always been rabid about that."

And ever since, he'd been afraid of losing his son, too. No wonder the man was so protective where Erik was concerned.

"I didn't give her what she wanted while she was alive. So I'm doing it now," he said gruffly. His hands lowered to his sides and he stepped back. "Living the life she'd wanted."

She frowned a little. "And what about what you want?"

He was backing up. Until he planted his hands on the kitchen counter on either side of him. "It doesn't matter what I want. This is what I'm doing."

She looked at the floor tiles, measuring them off between her feet and his. He couldn't put more distance between them unless he left the room. "Which doesn't include doing this," she concluded. Her voice was barely audible. "Doing…me."

"Don't." In contrast to hers, his voice was sharp. Harsh. "Don't reduce this."

She pressed her lips together for a long moment, until she felt vaguely certain that her vocal chords might work. "Have you—" Did she even want to know the answer to this? "Have you been with…anyone since she died?"

His fingertips were pressing so hard against the countertop that they looked white.

And she chickened out. "I'm sorry. It's none of my business." She of all people should know there were some things too private for discussion.

His lips twisted. "If not your business, then whose?"

Which she didn't know how to take. "I don't know what you want from me." She swallowed, and tugged the sagging collar of her sweatshirt back up her shoulder. She had to look a fright.

But his gaze, when it ran over her, told her differently.

A fact that only added to the confusion mired inside of her.

"I want to know that you're all right," he said after a moment. "I *need* to know that."

Her heart squeezed. "Why?"

He just eyed her. "I don't know."

She absorbed that. "I'm…tired." To-the-bone tired. She bent down and picked up her robe, pulling it securely around her shoulders. "I'm going to bed. I'm fine. And you can lock the door on your way out."

Chapter Ten

"And you're telling me that Cameron came over just to make sure you were okay after the search, and then *left* without…?" Tanya's head was close to Faith's, her voice barely a whisper.

Faith dabbed the end of her French fry into the puddle of ketchup on the side of her plate. "He just came to make sure I was okay," she said evenly. There were four other women seated around the table at The Hitching Post that Saturday afternoon. They were there for their official no-hearts Valentine's Day lunch.

Tanya had been included only because her husband was still on duty at the station. *She* wasn't officially manless, as the rest were.

Frannie Waters, Becka Townsend, Sharona Miles

and Diana Crocker had all graduated from high school the same year as Faith and Tanya. Ever since, every Valentine's Day, those without significant others had gotten together for lunch. Not a single year had passed without at least two of them meeting.

"My soon-to-be-ex golfs with Theo Gilmore," Frannie said. Her hand was wrapped firmly around a strawberry daiquiri. Her second, and she vowed it would be her last for the day. "And he told me—as he was dropping off our final papers, mind you—that the coach called Todd over to watch that little hooligan after *midnight*."

"Erik isn't a hooligan," Faith defended, only to wish she'd kept her mouth shut when she saw Frannie elbow Diana, knowingly. That was the problem with old high school friends. They never forgot how to push your buttons.

"Told you she liked the coach," Frannie singsonged.

"What does it matter," Becka goaded. "You've just spent the past hour claiming that romance is truly dead."

"Yeah, well, it is." Frannie lifted her drink. "The trick to keeping romance alive is *not* to marry the guy when he asks. After the wedding gifts have been put away, it's *all* downhill." Her gaze rounded the table, resting on everyone's faces. "Am I right?"

"Honey, what you are," Diana murmured, "is over your limit."

Frannie looked as if she were going to take exception to that. But then she laughed. And nodded. "One drink's all it takes," she agreed. "I know. Call me bitter. It'll pass. Right, Faith? How long ago was your divorce?"

"Two years." Faith caught the waitress's attention, and signaled for a refill for their iced teas.

"Do you ever talk to Jess?" That came from Sharona.

"No." Faith handed over her glass when Juliet returned with the pitcher of tea. When she realized she was staring at the waitress's pregnant abdomen, she quickly averted her eyes. "Nothing to talk to him about. He remarried about two minutes after the ink was dry on our divorce papers." In the two years since, she figured her ex-husband's new wife had probably capably produced at least one child, if not more.

"When does it stop hurting?" Frannie stared at her over her fruity drink.

Faith murmured her thanks to Juliet after she'd finished filling the glasses, and the waitress flashed a pretty smile before moving off, her thick dark hair bouncing behind her shoulders. She thought about Frannie's question. "I don't know that I hurt about Jess anymore," she admitted. Jess had done what was best for him. And she hadn't been part of that package any longer.

It was the *reason* she wasn't suitable that hurt. She'd had a staph infection when she was a teenager. But not until she had failed to conceive with Jess and had grown concerned enough to seek a medical opinion had she learned the infection had left her so damaged.

"Puhleeze," Sharona drawled. "If you weren't still

hurting over that jerk's defection, then why on earth aren't you seeing other people by now?"

Faith eyed the other woman. "Maybe because I've been busy?"

"Not all of us have alimony settlements the size of yours," Becka added dryly, and the women laughed again. "Some of us actually have to work for a living."

"I'm dragging us all down," Frannie admitted. "Aren't I?"

"Yes," Diana agreed. But she winked. "We still love you anyway."

Frannie made a face. "Well, at least there's that."

Juliet returned with the check. "Anything else I can get you this afternoon?"

"You look like you should be sitting down here with *us* waiting on you." Tanya nodded her head at Juliet's expanding waistline. "I'll bet your feet are just killing you after your shift here."

Juliet's cheeks flushed a little, which seemed to make her liquid dark eyes sparkle even more. Her palm curved over the thrust of her abdomen. "Sometimes, a little," she admitted. "But everyone who comes in here is always so nice."

"Honey, I used to wait tables here—"

"—about a hundred years ago."

"—and I *know* not everyone who comes in here is nice," Becka continued, ignoring Sharona's interruption. She pointed at the painting hanging over the bar of a woman wearing nothing but strategically placed gauze. "And the Shady Lady there could attest to it."

Faith glanced up at the painting. She was so used

to seeing it there that she hardly noticed it anymore. But it did remind her that the bar and grill had once had a considerably more spicy reputation. "She probably shocked the hell out of the good townspeople in her day," she murmured. The painting wasn't lurid. But it was…suggestive.

Sharona reached out and took the check from Juliet. "Ladies. This lunch is on my third ex-husband." She produced a gleaming gold credit card. "God love him. My bank certainly does." She laughed.

Faith knew the laughter wasn't completely true, though. Every time Sharona married, she did it believing that it would last forever and a day.

Juliet took the credit card and check and disappeared again.

Becka lifted her iced tea. "Here's to another Valentine's Day sans a loving Valentine. Let's hope next year at least one or two of us is missing."

They all clinked glasses. Faith wondered if they were all wondering which of them would be there to share the day with old girlfriends.

She would probably be at the top of the list.

Which was just a little too much of a pity party to tolerate. She took a last drink of iced tea and stood. Hugged all of her friends, who were also gathering up purses and shopping bags and cell phones. Juliet returned, and Sharona was busy signing the charge slip.

Tanya hooked her arm through Faith's as they left the restaurant and headed to their cars. "So. *Are* you okay?" She clearly hadn't lost the thread of their whispered conversation.

"I didn't have nightmares about the search," Faith admitted as she reached her SUV and pulled open the door. She'd had dreams about Cameron *not* pulling back from her. And wasn't that the ultimate fantasy? "So, yeah. I guess I'm okay."

"Glad you came?"

Faith nodded. Tanya had goaded her into it, promising that if Faith didn't show at The Hitching Post, Sharona had threatened to come and haul Faith out of her condo by her toes. "I still have to make those cookies I promised Chris, though," she said. "I think he's planning to use 'em with the new residents. He told me yesterday that things are just going crazy at the hospital lately."

"I thought 'crazy' was standard operating procedure over there."

"Yeah. But he said it's been worse than usual." Faith shook her head a little. "You know, I've actually had two reporters come to me, wanting statements about the mine. *That* is what is crazy. I can't believe that gold fever is hitting this town. So, Toby's completely over his flu?"

Tanya nodded. "Thank goodness. I love that boy o' mine, but he isn't exactly the sweetest of patients."

"Give him a hug for me."

"Give Erik a hug for *me*." Tanya waited a beat, then laughed gently. "Oh, girl, you should see your face." She gave Faith a quick hug. "I'll talk to you later. I've gotta run into Bozeman. See if I can find some sexy lingerie that'll keep Derek awake for a few minutes tonight when he comes off duty." She wiggled her eyebrows and hurried toward her car.

Faith watched her go for a moment. Tanya was really lucky. She and Derek had fallen for each other the moment they'd laid eyes on one another when they were only seventeen years old. They'd married two weeks after graduating high school, throwing both sets of parents into fits. But here they were, fourteen years later—a child, a demanding career and a successful retail business later—still as giddy as newlyweds with one another.

Everyone should be so blessed.

She tilted back her head, looking up into the pristine blue sky. For the first time in weeks, she wasn't on call. She could have driven to Bozeman, too, if she'd wanted.

But she had a date with some flour and eggs and her oven.

And the fact that Erik and Cameron hadn't had much in the way of home-baked cookies didn't figure in at all to her unwarranted enthusiasm.

Four hours later, though, Faith's heart was in her throat and it irritated her to no end. So when she rapped her knuckles on the Stevensons' front door, the knock was a little louder than necessary.

She hoped Erik answered the door.

It would be *much* easier. She could hand over the frosted cookies to him, he'd probably be goggle-eyed over the prospect of a major sugar high, and she'd head on down the road again, giving her heart absolutely no reason to remain in her throat, threatening to make her pass out either from dizziness or from choking.

But the door wasn't yanked inward by the energetic boy.

It wasn't yanked inward at all.

She stood there staring at the firmly closed, heavy, dark wood-paneled door as her heart took a slow, anticlimactic slide back down where it belonged.

Well, what had she expected? It was Valentine's Day. Erik and Cam were probably out doing something...valentiney.

She smoothed her hand over the sealed box of cookies. She was *not* going to stand there and knock again. Not that there were any neighbors close enough to notice Faith loitering on the front porch. And even if there were, she figured her presence there on a Saturday afternoon was a lot less salacious than Cam calling for Todd to sit with Erik in the middle of the night.

She set the container on the slightly bedraggled welcome mat and went back down the steps to the snow-shoveled walk. She may have had plenty of fun at the grill that afternoon, and she may have enjoyed her baker stint, but now the evening stretched out in front of her with yawning emptiness.

She actually found herself wishing that her pager would go off, which was fine thinking, given that it took someone's safety being in jeopardy for her to be summoned.

And since she *wasn't* on call for once, why did she even have her pager on?

She fumbled with the car door, her bare fingers flinching from the cold metal. Maybe she'd take herself to a movie.

She abruptly nixed that idea. She ordinarily didn't mind going to a movie on her own. But on Valentine's Day? Major date night?

No thank you.

Two years ago, if she'd had time on her hands, she'd have kept them busy with crocheting. But she'd stopped crocheting when she'd started facing reality. Now, she just had a closet full of items that reminded her of what she couldn't have, that she used for baby shower gifts.

"Faith?"

Her fingers clenched around the edge of the door. She looked up. Cameron stood on his porch, the container of cookies in his hand. "I thought I heard the door," he said. "What's this?"

Her heart had taken its trip upstairs to her throat again.

She closed the car door and leaned against it. Maybe the chill penetrating her corduroy pants would keep some starch in her knees. "Cookies. You know. For Valentine's Day. I made too many. I could only pawn off so many on my brother. I thought maybe Erik would enjoy them." Which was a pretty blatant lie. Chris would happily have taken every single cookie. She just hadn't chosen to give them all to him.

Cam had flipped open the lid and was looking inside.

Her heart ached more than a little at the sight. Particularly when she knew good and well that she wouldn't be seeing him at all, if she hadn't taken this uncharacteristic step and approached him.

"He *will* love 'em," he said as he lifted out a bright pink-frosted heart and bit into it. "If there are any left by the time he gets home."

She realized she'd somehow traveled halfway up the walk again. "Gets home?"

"He's spending the night at Josh Lampson's."

Her jaw very nearly hit the concrete sidewalk. "He must be excited about that," she said cautiously.

Cameron shrugged, and something soft curled inside her because she knew the movement was not the casual thing he'd meant it to be. "I spoke with Josh's mom. She got switched the other day to a day shift. She'll be home all night tonight."

Faith took a few more steps. Cameron finished off the cookie in another bite, then licked his thumb, his glance sliding over her.

"Wanna come in?"

"Oh." She looked back at her car. "I, um—" Had nowhere else to go but home, she thought. And anywhere else to be that would be safer than being around him. "Sure. For a few minutes."

He cradled the container in his hand as if it were a football, and stood aside when she joined him on the porch, pushing the door inward. "After you."

She went inside, and silently chastised her foolish sense that entering his home felt different now than it had the other time she'd been there.

Just because Erik was gone—

She nearly jumped out of her skin when his fingers brushed her shoulders.

But he was only helping her out of her coat. She

quickly pulled her arms free and he hung it by the collar over the tree stand in the foyer that was already fat with several winter coats—some sized seven-year-old boy, and the rest sized full-grown man.

He passed her, his fingers poking inside the cookie container again. "Come on back. I was grading papers."

She realized he wore only socks on his feet. For some reason, it felt intimate seeing those scrupulously white, thick tube socks with a thin line of gold stitching over his toes.

"Seems you do a lot of that," she said very brightly, looking elsewhere. But "elsewhere" proved just as distracting. His hair had grown in the few weeks since the mine incident. Even in the few days since he'd come to her condo in the middle of the night because he'd *needed* to know she was okay.

And the rich, dark auburn strands did show a tendency to wave around his neck just as she'd suspected they would.

She surreptitiously rubbed her palms down the sides of her jeans. Cam slid the cookie container on the rectangular farmhouse-style table, and glanced back at her.

"Your hair's down."

She barely restrained lifting a self-conscious hand to her loose hair. "Guess it is. Is, um, that all stuff you have to grade?" She gestured toward the desk where papers were spread across the entire surface. A stack of folders, fat with assignments, she assumed, sat on one side. Two enormous textbooks were pushed to the other side. She also noticed a playbook among the mess.

"Yeah." His lips quirked a little. "And I used to complain about the massive amounts of paperwork back when I had my own finance firm." He picked up the slender bottle of beer he'd obviously been nursing, and tilted it. "Want one?"

She shook her head. His gaze was inscrutable, yet she still felt herself flushing at the steadiness of it on her face.

"That blue color's good on you," he said after a moment. "Got a date later?"

She *knew* she was blushing at that, which should have been ridiculous. "No."

"Why not? It's Valentine's Day. Evening," he corrected, as his gaze slid to the windows, which clearly showed the purposeful descent of the sun in a truly glorious display of fiery color.

"So?" She crossed her arms. Uncrossed them. "You're here doing schoolwork. Unless you're going out later," she added belatedly. He *had* let Erik spend the night at a friend's, after all. Which was highly unusual. Maybe he'd had a personal motivation behind that decision.

After all. He hadn't exactly answered her question about whether or not he'd been involved with anyone since his wife's death. Just because *she* couldn't think beyond him to another person, didn't mean he felt similarly toward her.

She was such a head case.

He plucked another pink cookie out of the container and demolished half of it in one bite, then followed it with a beer chaser and still his gaze stayed on her.

He'd looked at her that way the afternoon he'd kissed her, too. Before he'd backed away as if she were some sort of biohazardous material, that was. And he'd looked at her that way in her kitchen the other night. Before he'd put twelve feet of kitchen tiles between them.

"Do I have dirt on my face or something?" she finally asked, vaguely exasperated, as much from those particular memories as anything.

His lips quirked again, a little stronger this time. Enough to hint at the slash of a dimple he'd passed on to his son. He placed his bottle on the table, taking his time. "No. You don't have dirt on your face. No, I didn't ship off Erik for the night so I could go out later and score." His gaze burned over her face for a moment. "With anyone."

Her cheeks heated.

His lips tilted a little more. "You just look different."

"Great," she murmured. "That either means I'm barely presentable ordinarily, or I'm barely presentable now."

"Fishing for compliments?"

"No!"

He smiled outright, and the power of it bathed over her like seductive summer sunshine. "And do you know how to handle a compliment when it's given?"

"When I can tell it's a compliment," she countered.

So she'd changed into her brand-new blue turtleneck after her close encounter with her oven. So she'd dashed a little more makeup on than her usual smear of clear lip gloss. Next time, she wouldn't bother.

Next time?

What was she thinking?

"You look as beautiful as you always do." His deep voice had turned matter-of-fact. "Just different. So I figured you must have a reason. A date."

"I don't date." Which he undoubtedly had figured out for himself.

"Why is that?"

"Why do *you* care?"

"*You* asked me."

No. What she'd asked was whether he'd been with anyone in the years since Laura died. Definitely a different question. At least to her. But maybe not to him. And did it matter anyway?

Either way, the answer was *no*.

Silence ticked between them. She shook her head. "I should go." Before she made more of a fool of herself than she already had.

"What're you going to do?"

"I don't know." She wouldn't think about how she'd manage to fill the empty hours until she was on duty again. "Maybe make another batch of cookies so Erik might actually get one." She added some starch to her tone.

His lips tilted and he finished off the one still in his hand. "Wouldn't have taken you for a pastry chef."

She narrowed her eyes. "I told you I used to bake

with my mother and sisters. So, if that's an example of your compliments—"

He lifted his hand peaceably. "No. They're great. Which is clearly obvious. But to save you the extra work—" he deftly snapped the lid back on the container "—I'll preserve the rest for Erik. Good enough?"

"I like baking. It's nice to have a reason to do it." Her mind flitted to Erik's open house and she knew Cam was thinking about the same thing. Maybe his steady gaze wasn't quite as inscrutable as she'd thought. Which made all manner of warmth stir right back up inside her. "Well. I should let you get back to your work. Tell Erik I said happy Valentine's Day."

He nodded and she turned to go. She was halfway to the door when he spoke.

"I never did get a chance to give you that dinner. Why don't you stay and eat? I've got a couple of steaks ready to go."

She closed her eyes for a moment, blocking out the sight of his well-loaded coat tree that seemed to shout the fact it belonged to a family man. "I'm not sure that's a good idea," she admitted.

It wasn't his stockinged feet that alerted her to the fact that he was walking up behind her. It was the shiver that danced down her spine. The knot of breathless…waiting…that formed in her chest.

"Because Erik's not here?" His voice was as quiet as hers, and the low timbre dragged velvet-soft over her senses.

She exhaled carefully and turned to face him, only

to find him standing closer than she'd expected. Her nose practically grazed the thick, ivory knit of his bulky sweater. She slid back her foot, needing space. "Yes."

"If he were here, would you have stayed?"

She was trapped in his eyes, as surely as if he'd lassoed her. "I don't know," she admitted.

"He can wear a person out."

"He's energetic. And he undoubtedly got that from you, just like he got your hair and your eyes."

"Then why the hesitation?"

She wasn't even sure what they were talking about anymore. It was problematic, looking at a man who made one's ability for coherent thought fall right out the window.

"Not enough appeal unless my son is around?"

She shook her head. "You know that's not so." Her voice had gone husky again.

"Do I?"

Her entire body felt flushed. "I'm not the one who regrets kissing…touching…me." She pushed out the words.

His slashing eyebrows rose. "Regret. Believe me, darlin', I'm on intimate terms with regret, and that *isn't* what I've been feeling where you're concerned."

"Well, you could have fooled me." She hated that her voice wasn't steady. "Considering the way you—"

The rest of her words died under the swoop of his mouth catching hers.

Shock rocked through her, as deep and encompassing as it had the first time. Her fingers flexed. Grazed thick, cable knit. In shock's wake flowed need and pleasure. It spread through her, achingly warm, finding crevices that had been cold and empty.

His fingers tangled in her hair and her head fell back, her mouth opening under his. He made a low sound that rippled her nerve endings and her fingers curled around his forearms, kneading.

When he finally lifted his head, she sucked in a sharp breath, willing away the dizziness clouding her judgment. But she might just as well have tried jumping over the moon.

His hand surrounding the nape of her neck anchored her in place. "*This* is not regret," he rasped.

Faith trembled. "Cam—"

He kissed her again. Harder. More urgently. Only to break away again. His breathing was rough. "I want you. And you were right. It's been a long time. I haven't felt this way since my wife. And maybe I convinced myself that leaving you alone the other night was the right thing to do, but today I'm not feeling so generous. So if you really want to leave, do it now. Otherwise—" he grazed his thumb over her lips "—don't."

Chapter Eleven

Leave.

Don't leave.

A million thoughts whipped through Faith's head, but none of them stuck around long enough to gain form. "It would be smarter for me to go."

His thumb swirled over her chin. "Definitely."

"But I don't want to leave." The words were more exhale than form, but he seemed to understand all the same.

He stepped closer, his thumb raising her chin. His head dipped. But the racing urgency she'd expected didn't come. Instead, he brushed his lips over hers, a light exploration, a gentle discovering.

Her heart lurched. Her fingers twisted in his sweater.

When had she moved her hands to his chest?

She could feel the race of his heartbeat and it went to her head faster than the daiquiris had gone to Frannie's head that afternoon.

He kissed the corner of her mouth, the point of her chin, the line of her jaw.

She twisted her head, desperate for his mouth on hers. "Cam—"

His lips caught her earlobe and she shivered. His hand flattened over her spine, bringing her flush against him and a moan rose in her throat, her knees going soft.

He laughed silently, sounding so pleased with himself that she started to push at him, but he just covered her mouth again, tsking against her lips, and lifted her right off her feet, pulling her up his body until her mouth was even with his.

She clutched his shoulders and stared into his eyes. With no seeming effort at all, he held her there, his hands slowly sliding from her waist to her rear, her thighs.

Her legs circled his waist seemingly with a mind of their own and they both went still.

The only sound in the room was the rasp of her denim jeans against his, underscored by harsh breaths.

Then he swore under his breath, muttering an apology almost simultaneously, as he backed her against the knotty pine table right there in the foyer.

Envelopes and car keys flew under the haphazard swipe of his hand and he lifted his mouth only long enough to drag her sweater over her head. When it was gone, his palm covered her bare breast. His lips swallowed her gasping delight.

She pulled at his sweater, desperate to feel his skin against hers, and he obliged by tugging it off himself. Her blood hummed in her veins. Her mouth pressed against the satin warmth of his shoulder. Her breasts nestled against the crisp-soft swirl of hair on his chest. Her fingers blindly fumbled with the button at his waist, only to knock into his as he slid down *her* zipper.

"Hurry," she gasped.

And he swore, removing his hands from her altogether. And if she weren't pressed up against him so tightly, he'd have been inside her if not for a few layers of fabric.

She froze. "No. Not again. Don't pull away from me again."

His fingers circled her wrists, keeping her from touching him. "Dammit. I have to. What was I thinking?"

"Maybe I like you not thinking," she admitted unevenly. "Maybe I like you just...*being*. With me."

His jaw worked for a moment. "I want to. God. I want to. But I wasn't prepared... I—" he broke off, swearing. "No condom," he finally said, bluntly.

She stared. Felt the blood drain out of her face, only to return, double-speed. Hesitation niggled at her, but she stomped down hard on it. He might have her hands subdued, but he didn't have her legs.

She twined them more tightly around his hips and pulled him back. "We don't need one. Safe as houses, remember? Please, Cam. Do you want me to beg here?" She was so afraid she'd do just that. Hadn't she come bearing cookies in some barely disguised, antiquated gesture?

Her reserve was nil, and pride hadn't kept her from waking night after night from dreams of his hands touching her. So even though he'd pushed her away more than once, she'd still had to try.

His shackling grip had loosened just enough for her to slip one hand free, and she tugged at his jeans, popping the strained fly the rest of the way.

He groaned when she slid her hand over him. Touched him. Shaped him.

"Lift up," he rasped. She tilted her hips and he pulled the rest of her clothing free, dragging jeans and boots and socks off in one fierce motion. Then his hands, warm and so strong, slid up her thighs. "Are you sure, Faith?"

He'd called her Faith. She was shuddering wildly. "I'm sure." The words were little more than a moan, and she pressed her mouth against the hot column of his throat.

She felt—tasted—the groan he gave.

And then he sank into her.

Harder. Deeper. *More* than anything she'd ever experienced.

She cried out. Her head fell back, knocking the wall, but she barely noticed for the wild pleasure streaking through her.

His forehead fell to her shoulder, his hands like iron as he lifted her to him. "I don't want to hurt you."

She barely heard him. Her hands swept over his back, holding tight. "You're not," she promised. "Oh, Cameron."

His heartbeat felt like a locomotive pulsing against her breast. Her fingers flexed against him and she arched, mindlessly greedy, shocked in some small, tidy corner of her mind at the gasping moans coming out of her mouth, at the feral growl rising from him as he took.

And took.

And took.

He slapped a hand against the wall above her head. His mouth devoured hers, swallowing her cry. Everything inside her screamed for release.

The foyer table rocked precariously.

His mouth tore from hers. Burned to her temple. Her ear. His breath was harsh. "Faith."

Just that. Her name, so raw, so...perfect as she felt everything he was explode inside her.

And she shattered, too, flying apart.

She wasn't sure who was holding whom together more.

But in the end, it didn't really matter.

They were both destroyed, baptized in the fire of each other.

It wasn't really an eon of soul-deep pleasure, though it felt that way before Cam felt Faith go boneless against him, their bodies still fused. It was hardly a testament to his masculinity, but his damned legs were marshmallows. He blew out a shaking breath. Cautiously pushed his hand against the wall again, straightening away.

She clung like a limpet, her head tucked against his neck. "Don't go," she whispered hoarsely.

And damned if he didn't want her all over again, right then and there. "I'm not going anywhere." He sounded as if he'd run a marathon.

Maybe that's what happened when a man was out-running his past.

He lifted her with him, managing to more or less collapse on the carpet without bruising either one of them.

He hoped.

She still had her head tucked against the crook of his neck, as if he'd been grown specifically for that purpose. Her long legs tangled with his.

And it all felt…right.

He tossed his arm over his eyes, slowly stroking her hair. "I still have on my pants," he muttered, feeling like a complete, lumbering jackass. It wasn't a sensation he was accustomed to, or one that he relished.

But *she* giggled. "I know."

Of all the sounds he'd elicited from her, it was the giggle that was the most unexpected.

And something inside him loosened. Unfurled. "I—"

"Wait." Her hand snuck up and covered his mouth. She lifted her head and looked at him. Her honey-colored hair drifted over them in silky sheaves. "If you apologize *now,* Cameron Stevenson, I'm very much afraid I might have to hurt you."

Her voice was humorous. But her eyes—more green than brown, and decidedly slumberous at the moment—were starkly vulnerable.

He stroked his knuckles over her smooth cheek.

Golden.

Touching her was like stepping into the warmest, most inviting, molten sunshine.

And he was so damn tired of being out in the cold.

Her lashes had flicked down, hiding her gaze when he'd touched her cheek.

"No. I can't apologize for that. Unless I left bruises or something." He moved his hand. Cupped her arms where he knew he'd grabbed her—probably too hard, too tight—and gently rubbed her satiny skin.

Her lashes lifted. "I don't bruise that easily," she whispered.

But he knew otherwise. Faith Taylor, competent, strong, beautiful Faith Taylor, just carried her bruises—whatever their cause—on the inside.

And he knew, the same way he'd known his life was forever changed the day he'd played checkers on a woolen blanket in a park, that he never wanted this woman bruised by anything. Ever.

He turned, settling her carefully on the carpet, and reached past her for his sweater. Then he held it out for her. She looked at him for a long moment before silently tucking her head through it.

For some reason, it seemed as trusting a gesture as what they'd done together in his foyer.

He pulled the sweater down around her. The ivory knit enfolded her past her hips. Then he rose. Fastened his jeans, fumbling a little at the avid way she watched him, and held out his hands. "Come on."

Her eyes narrowed a little. "Where?" But she settled her palms on his.

He pulled her to her feet. "So suspicious." And he'd given her plenty of reason to be. "I want to show you something."

"What? Your etchings? Think maybe we've covered that already."

He gave a bark of laughter at that. "You'll see."

He drew her back down the hall to the great room. Past his desk, past the windows that looked over the hill where she'd tobogganed with Erik, and into the den beyond. "I was in here when you knocked," he told her. "That's why I didn't hear you."

Her gaze was traveling over the burgundy leather couches and the massive bookcase built into the wall that was already overflowing with books. The fire he'd built earlier that day was nothing but a smolder now, and he tossed another log on, jabbing it with the poker, making sparks fly up the chimney. A fresh scent of wood smoke curled into the room.

He replaced the black iron screen and turned to Faith. "I was watching that." He gestured at the big-screen television mounted on the wall, but she'd already noticed the frozen image of Erik from the night of the school's chorus program. He picked up the remote and pushed Rewind. "You were there only long enough to see the last ten minutes or so."

Her fingertips were curled around the edges of his sweater sleeves. She cast him a sideways look. "How'd you know when I came in? I was in the back."

He handed her the remote and slid a long lock of her hair free of the sweater collar. "I noticed. Same way I always noticed when you'd come in the council meetings. When you snuck out a few minutes before it ended. When you climbed up in the bleachers at the last game. I noticed."

Her lips parted softly. Her thumb roved restlessly over the buttons on the remote, not pushing any of them. "Oh."

His lips twitched. "Yeah. *Oh.*" He gestured at the furniture. "Make yourself comfortable. I'm just gonna heat up the grill."

She looked thoroughly bemused and he wondered how long he'd be able to keep her in that state. She sat down on the corner of the couch, curling her long legs beneath the hem of his sweater, and pointed the remote to start the video playing again.

He went into the mudroom and grabbed a shirt off the pile of laundry he'd yet to put away, and pushed his feet into his boots, then went out on the deck to flip on the grill. He left it to heat and went back inside. Steaks were a no-brainer, fortunately. And these days the salad came conveniently out of a bag.

Thank God for modern conveniences.

He dumped it into a bowl, scooping what he spilled on the counter into the trash. Then he hastily scrubbed a few potatoes, stabbed 'em a couple of times and tossed them in the microwave, punching the button that said…ta daa…*potato.* Another major convenience, since the only way he'd learned his way around the kitchen was by trial and error. He pulled out the steaks, went back to the deck and slapped them on the grill, then closed the domed lid over them and went back inside.

"Gourmet touches." Faith stood in his kitchen looking more edible than anything he could have imagined. She held up the emptied bag from the salad between two fingers. "I've never had a man cook for me before."

"Oh yeah?" He dropped the long-handled fork he'd used with the steaks onto the counter and headed for her. "Stand around looking like that, Faith, and I'll be happy to cook *any*time."

Her eyes widened and her lips curved. "Cam—"

"Keep saying my name," he suggested gruffly as he slid an arm around her waist, delving oh-so-easily beneath the sweater. He pushed his other hand through her silky hair and her head fell willingly to the side, letting him taste the skin right below her ear.

"Cam." That came a little more breathlessly.

He caught her earlobe gently between his teeth.

"Cah…ham." Her hands grazed his chest. "The, um, the video is rewound."

He heard her. He just didn't hear her. "I'm not ever going to get enough of you." He widened his stance, pulled her closer. Tighter.

She wriggled against him, pushing at his shoulders. "The, um, the *video?*"

He exhaled. Pressed his forehead to hers. "Right." He took in another long breath. Let it out even more slowly. Reluctantly let go of her. "Bright idea of mine," he muttered. "You deserve candlelight and champagne. I serve up nuked potatoes and home movies."

Her eyes softened even more. "I've never had much of a head for champagne, actually. And I don't…expect romantic gestures."

He looked at her. "You said something like that before," he remembered. When he'd conveniently used her to derail the threesome at The Hitching Post. "Don't you believe in romance?"

"Of course I do." She dropped the empty sack on the counter. "I just don't think I'm the kind of woman who brings that out in anyone."

He nearly laughed out loud until he realized she was serious. "You must have been married to a prize idiot," he murmured, slipping his hands along her neck. Watching the way her lips parted unconsciously as he pressed his thumb against the pulse fluttering at the base.

"I suppose you treated your wife to grand gestures all the time."

"No," he said, and for once the honesty didn't scrape raw and painful at his insides. "She was the one who was into gestures. I was the practical one who cleaned up the mess afterward."

"Mess. Ah. Well. There you go. Grand gestures *must* be overrated if they leave a mess."

He closed in on her, following her as she backed up, until she was caught between him and the undoubtedly cool front of his stainless steel fridge. "Yeah, darlin', but I've learned that some things are worth a mess." He leaned down and nipped at her lower lip, watching her face.

Her eyes glazed, turning more green than brown again in the moment before they started to close.

"Come on," he whispered. "Let's go watch the video."

Faith pressed her lips together, scrambling for composure. "You enjoy keeping me off balance, don't you?"

He nibbled her lip again. "Gotta take my advantages where I can...against the superior species."

She started to smile, remembering the snowball fight when she'd jokingly assured him females *were* superior. But the fact of the matter was Cam needed no special effort to throw her off balance. All he had to do was *be*.

Thank heavens his heart was still tied to his wife.

If it weren't, Faith could never let herself be with him this way. It would just be too dangerous. Too painful when he ended it. And end it he would, if he knew about her infertility.

She lifted her mouth more fully to his, pushing the thoughts away. Hard. "How long are those steaks going to take?"

"Not long enough," he murmured.

Still, he kissed her slowly.

Thoroughly.

Until she was in danger of melting right into the floor beneath her bare feet. Then he walked her back to his den. Settled her on that sinfully soft leather couch.

Picked up the remote.

Hit Play.

And sat in the chair opposite her. His eyes were sharp. Amused. Aroused.

She exhaled. Focused on the mammoth television set.

In minutes, she was entranced all over again by the children and managed to forget—mostly—the fact that Cam watched her far more than he watched the video.

When it came time for Erik's solo, she hit Rewind twice. Fortunately, Cam had gone to the kitchen again to attend to dinner, after giving her strict instructions to stay put.

She did, with one quick foray to find a bathroom.

In her exploration, though, she found Cam's bedroom.

The bed was mammoth. No real surprise there. Cam would need a good-size bed. He was a good-size man, after all. It was covered with a thick, caramel-colored comforter with a few brown pillows tossed haphazardly on top. And it was made.

Which was more than she could say for her own considerably smaller, full-size bed at home, which she'd left in kicked-about disarray from her restless nights of late.

It was the photographs on the dresser as she crossed to the attached bathroom that grabbed her attention, though.

They gave Faith her first look at Laura Stevenson.

And Cam's wife had been stunning.

There was just no other word for her. Clouds of black hair. Violet eyes so vivid they seemed to leap from the photographs. She'd had curves where Faith had never had them, and the adoration between her and the man beside her was tangible.

But as curious—and yes, daunted—as she'd been about Laura, it was Cam's image that really stopped

Faith in her tracks, making her actually pick up the sterling-framed photograph to look closer.

His hair had been brutally short, but the severe style simply played up his carved features. Maybe made him look a little older than he would actually have been at the time the photograph was probably taken. And the suit he wore looked as if it belonged on the cover of *GQ*.

It was Cameron. Yet…it wasn't the Cam she knew.

The Cam who padded around his house in tube socks and jeans and—her hand drifted down the front of his thick sweater that was all she still wore—who'd pelted his son with snowballs.

She settled the photograph carefully back in place, well aware that she was intruding in his personal space, no matter *what* they'd done together in his foyer, and quickly used his bathroom. She was hurrying back to the den when he appeared in the hallway opposite her, a large wooden tray held in his hands.

She froze, feeling ridiculously guilty. "I, um, used your bathroom. Hope you don't mind."

His eyebrows drew together a little bit, almost as if he were curious why she'd even have to ask. "Better mine than Erik's," he said after a moment. "Kid's a slob no matter what I tell him." He gestured a little with the laden tray. "Come on. We'll eat by the fire."

She went into the den. He set the tray on the iron coffee table in front of the couch and then sat down beside her. He grabbed the remote and punched a few buttons. The video turned off. The television slid down, disappearing into the rustic pine cabinet beneath it.

She slid a glance his way. "You definitely don't live like any other teachers I know."

He smiled a little. "Nice to know the law, business and accounting degrees went to *some* good."

She tugged at her ear a little. "So, um, what are your parents like?"

He handed her a plate buried under by steak, salad and potato. "Conservative. Old money." His lips quirked. "As old as Denver goes, at any rate. They had me when they were both over forty. No brothers or sisters, either. By mutual agreement, we see as little of each other as humanly possible, and mostly only for holidays. Dad didn't take too kindly to it when I didn't join his brokerage, but put out my own shingle. I actually became his competition." He sliced off a corner of steak and studied the pink center for a moment. "They raised me to have my own brain, and didn't want me to use it." He shook his head a little, then ate the meat. "Last time I heard from him, it was to tell me he'd gotten Erik accepted into my old private school."

Alarm halted her fork as she stabbed it into the fluffy potato. "You're not going to send him to boarding school, are you?"

He shook his head. "No. That was never the plan."

Relieved, she poked at the potato a little more, letting some of the heat escape. "And that plan is to raise him in Thunder Canyon," she confirmed quietly. "Laura's plan."

His gaze was suddenly inscrutable. "Yeah."

"Do you like living here, Cam?" She couldn't bear to think that maybe he did not.

"Do you?"

She nodded immediately. "There was a time when I was perfectly anxious to leave it, of course." She grinned wryly. "I was eighteen and ready to grab the world by the tail and swing it around my head a few times."

"And now?"

She tasted a corner of steak, and stared into the fire across from them for a moment as she savored the bite. A little crispy on the outside. A lot juicy on the inside.

"Now," she said eventually, "I can't really imagine living anywhere else." Thunder Canyon had welcomed her home when her world had been in tatters. It had healed her.

Had it?

She ignored the unwelcome query and caught Cameron watching her when she looked at him. "And you still haven't answered the question," she pointed out.

"I don't know."

She lifted her eyebrows. "You must have some opinion. You're not exactly without one when it comes to most matters. I've heard you at those council meetings, remember?"

He smiled wryly at the jab. "I haven't thought a lot about what I feel about Thunder Canyon," he said after a moment. "I've been…going through the motions."

"Doing what you believed Laura would have wanted you to do," she finished quietly.

"Yeah."

His gaze shifted to the fire and Faith wondered if he was envisioning his beautiful, black-haired wife.

She set down her fork, her ravenous appetite suddenly gone. "You know, maybe it's none of my business, but it seems to me that for a guy who's living his life to someone else's desires, you're doing an awfully good job of it."

"What?"

"Well." She turned sideways on the couch, tugging the sweater over her knees. "Just that you could have stayed here in Thunder Canyon, raising Erik here and all, without going to the measures that you have. I mean, you don't *have* to be the coach at school. You clearly didn't even *have* to become a teacher, for that matter. And the mayor wants you to run for town council. You actually told him you'd consider it. Pretty involving stuff, that's all." And she wasn't at all sure how he'd react to her opinion.

He turned a little on the couch, too, his arm stretching across the back of it. He lifted a lock of her hair and slowly flipped it through his fingers. And all he said in response to her observation was a low "hmm."

But the glint in his eyes was unmistakable and heat slid through her with the subtlety of a bulldozer. "I, um, I should probably be going."

He shook his head once. "It's cold out."

"It's February," she said dryly.

His lips twitched. "And you brought Valentine's Day dessert."

She shot a look at his plate. He'd eaten more than she had, but his plate was still half full. "I'm sure you'd tell Erik that he had to eat more of his supper before you'd let *him* have a cookie."

His smile widened. He leaned forward, grasping her arms and easily pulling her right over to him. She caught her breath as he swept his hands beneath the sweater.

"Who mentioned cookies? I was talking about you."

He kissed her, and didn't stop until they were both breathless.

Then he pushed to his feet, lifting her right along with him, and carried her down the hall to his bedroom. When he reached the bed, he leaned over, swept back the comforter, sending the pillows bouncing to parts unknown, and settled her in the center.

The room was dimmer now. The sun had set. The only illumination came from the hallway. But there was enough that she could see the look on his face as he slowly pulled off his clothes.

Faith tucked her tongue between her teeth, unable to look away from him. He was so incredibly beautiful.

"Something wrong?" His voice was amused.

"Not a thing," she assured faintly.

He smiled a little, then knelt next to the bed. He curled his warm hands around her ankles and slowly pulled her back across the bed toward him. She moved. The sweater, however, stayed put, until it rode up above her waist. Her breasts.

"I'll never unwrap another present and not think of you," he murmured, watching the progress of the sweater.

She swallowed, steeped in the warmth of his gaze as he pressed his lips to the curve of her knee.

His palms slid over her thighs. Reached up to her hips. The nearly healed scrapes. "Do they still hurt?"

She slowly shook her head. "Not anymore."

His right eyebrow peaked. "Supposed to say that they do," he murmured, sin and temptation wrapped up in that low, husky tone. "So I'd have to kiss 'em better."

She exhaled. "Oh." Then swallowed as he moved. "I…ah…think you're doing that anyway."

He lifted his head for a moment, his brown gaze colliding with hers. "Observant, aren't you?"

Her legs shifted, restless as his lips roved over the point of her hipbone. She pulled at his shoulders, but the man was immovable. "Cameron."

He leisurely pressed his mouth against her navel. "Mmm?"

He was maddening. Playing her as skillfully as if he'd written a playbook designed just for her. "Cam."

"Yeah." His lips moved against her. His palms pushed on her thighs as he slid forward.

Her head fell back against the mattress as he found her. Took her. Just that smoothly.

Just that easily.

Just that perfectly.

Her arms circled him, and she opened her mouth against his. His name sighed through her mind.

And then she thought no more.

Chapter Twelve

Faith wasn't aware of falling asleep. Not until she woke when the cool dawn light curled into the room and the warm weight of Cam shifted beside her.

She turned on her back. His elbow was bent on the mattress beside her head, his chin propped on his hand and she reached up, smoothing back the hair that was falling over his forehead. "Hi," she whispered.

"I was watching you sleep."

She let her hand trail down his face, his jaw. Rub against the hair on his chest for the sheer pleasure of feeling it against her palm. "Hope I wasn't drooling."

He chuckled softly. Leaned down and kissed the tip of her nose. "That would've been me, looking at you."

She smiled faintly.

Then he touched her hand and warmth crept up her arm, soothing. Seductive. She couldn't have moved if her life depended on it. Nor did she want to move. Her palm slowly flattened, barely grazing against his.

The warmth reached her shoulders. Drifted through her bloodstream, thawing. Steeping. "Cameron—"

"Shh." His thumb slid along hers. Traced up her index finger. Pressed gently against her fingertip, then slid down, and up her middle finger.

Her heart thudded heavily. She turned toward him, her leg sliding over his. "We probably shouldn't have done this," she whispered.

"Regrets already?" His fingers slowly slid through hers, bringing their palms flush against each other, snug and warm, steady and strong.

Did she regret being with him? She slowly shook her head. "No."

His fingers slowly released hers, only to run down the inside of her wrist. She swallowed. His fingers dipped to the inside of her elbow, then retraced the burning path back to her wrist. Her pulse thudded erratically against his fingers when he paused over it.

"Your skin is so soft." His low, deep voice rolled over her, as sensitizing as his fingertips. "Here." He dragged the palm of his hand back down her arm, then up to her shoulder.

Her breathing stalled.

"And here." He smoothed over her collarbone. Cupped the base of her neck. "Here." Her breasts tightened when he flattened his hand against her chest, thumb and little finger grazing the inner swell of them as he followed a straight line down to her navel.

Her abdominal muscles jumped. He sucked in an audible breath and his fingers slid again. Tightened against her waist, turning her toward him more fully.

A soft sound escaped her lips. She pressed her forehead against the hot curve between his shoulder and neck. Her hands drifted over the supple skin stretching over his ribs. His hand cupped the base of her neck, tilting her head back until his mouth found hers, lingered, then moved on to her temple. Her ear.

She sighed, lost in pleasure.

"I could get used to this."

His voice was a low murmur through the haze clouding her senses. "Mmm-hmm."

He tipped her onto her back again, and threaded his hands through her hair, spreading it out around her shoulders. She finally opened her eyes only to find him looking at her. "What? I'm drooling now?"

He shook his head. "I could get used to this," he repeated. "Not just you in my bed. But you. In my life."

Her breath stuttered. Stopped. She flattened her palms against the mattress, and pushed herself up against the rough-hewn headboard. "Cam—"

"No. Let me get this out." He caught her hands in his. Even in the dim light, she could see the muscle that had begun to tick in his jaw. "I never thought I'd be able to say that to another woman, Faith. But you—"

"You don't have to say anything, Cameron." Her voice was quick. Nervous. And there seemed nothing she could do to modulate it. "I haven't…had sex since my divorce. You haven't had sex since Laura died."

His eyes narrowed. "I've had plenty of *sex* since she died," he said flatly.

"But you said you hadn't felt this way since your wife."

"Felt," he said evenly. "Not just working off some sexual steam. But that's what you thought this was, didn't you? Scratching some damn itch? Fulfilling some damn need?"

She flinched at the hard note in his voice. She couldn't back up any more than she had, since her spine was already plastered against his headboard. "No." She struggled with words, knowing none of them would be right. "You know you're special to me, Cam." A monstrous understatement, but all she was capable of uttering when panic was turning her inside out. "You have to know that by now. This isn't…typical of me."

His gaze didn't waver from her face. His tone gentled. "Well…maybe we need to make this more typical. You. Me. Together."

His hands curled more tightly around hers, as if he'd read the frantic, futile messages screaming inside her head for her to pull her hands free. She stared at him, mute.

"Faith, until you, I never thought I'd even be able to contemplate a future that included another woman. That I'd ever consider marriage again. More children."

Her breath suddenly whistled between her teeth. She was actually getting dizzy. She concentrated hard on his face, but it was the only thing in her vision that didn't seem blurry. "No. No. This isn't… You're just—" she wheezed "—overreacting."

"Holy Chri—" He bit off the curse. "You're hyperventilating." He was off the bed in a flash.

She leaned over, gasping, struggling for breath. *This could not be happening.*

He returned almost immediately, a small paper lunch sack in his hand, and stuck it over her mouth. "Breathe." His hand smoothed over her spine.

Tears burned out the corners of her eyes. She cupped the bag to her mouth. Breathed into it.

"There you go. Slow and easy." His hand swept down her bowed spine.

Her dizziness slowly faded, only to leave exhaustion in its wake.

"That's it. Just relax." He kept stroking her back. Again. And again.

And the fact that she wanted to stay there, wanted to have him touching her, in passion, in tenderness, in…anything and everything, made her slowly lift her head.

To sit up.

To face him.

His hand slowly fell away.

There were faint red marks on his shoulders. Not scratches. But definitely marks from her own fingers. His bed—the bed he'd undoubtedly shared with the beloved wife he'd lost—was more than tumbled. The bottom sheet was hanging on to the mattress by little more than a prayer.

Panic had ripped through her.

Exhaustion now dragged at her.

And, as she looked at Cameron, her gaze taking in the rest of the room beyond him—complete with the collection of family photographs on his dresser—she could feel a great wave of grief building on the horizon.

He's a family man.

You knew it, and you didn't stay away.

She shook her head, even as her hand crept up and grazed the soft bristles blurring his hard jaw. "I can't do this, Cam."

His jaw flexed against her palm and she went to draw away, but he grabbed her hand, holding it there. Tight. "Why?" His voice was raw. As raw as she felt inside.

Oh, what a fool she was. She was supposed to help keep people safe. And now she was only causing pain. To her. To him.

But it was better to do it now, rather than later.

Wasn't it?

"I'm not cut out for…you know. Relationships."

He snorted and swore. "That's bull."

She felt the blood drain out of her head again, and worked her hand free of his. "I don't have to convince you."

If she could only convince herself.

She slid off the mattress, away from him, and blindly swept around for her clothes only to realize they were still lying near the front door. She bunched the sheet around her body, and headed for the doorway.

"Don't."

She tripped a little. Snatched up the offending edge and moved faster.

"Faith."

She couldn't look back to see if Cam followed her.

If she looked back, she'd weaken. And if she weakened, she'd agree to anything he suggested. Anything, as long as she had him in her life.

One step at a time.

She just had to get through one step at a time.

Yank on her jeans.

Pull her sweater over her head.

She made the mistake of glancing up.

Cam stood there. His eyes narrowed. His arms crossed over his wide chest. He'd pulled on his jeans, too, but they were only half-fastened.

She left the sheet on the floor where it lay. Grabbed up her purse. Fumbled with her boots, only to give up and just clasp them to her chest.

She scrambled with the door, and tore out into the frozen dawn as if the devil was at her heels.

But it was just a man who was behind her. A good, decent, family man, who had the tools in his very being to break her heart.

And if she stayed—oh, God, if she stayed—when that day came, she wouldn't survive it.

Not this time.

The sidewalk burned so cold against her feet as she ran to her SUV. When she climbed behind the wheel, she dropped the keys twice in her fumbling attempt to get them in the ignition.

Then the engine caught. Roared like some beast in pain.

She looked back at the house.

He stood on the porch.

She hauled in a breath, only it sounded more like a sob.

And the sight of him wavered because of the tears flooding her eyes.

She shoved the SUV into drive and flattened her foot on the gas pedal. The vehicle shot forward.

Some portion of her mind was coherent enough to be grateful for the empty streets courtesy of the early hour on a Sunday morning. Because she managed to make it to her condo without mishap.

The phone was ringing even before she made it inside. Had obviously been ringing a number of times. And the message light was already blinking.

The ringing stopped. Cam's voice came on. "I don't know what's going on, Faith, but you better damn well tell me you made it home safely, or I'm coming over even though you've made it *more* than plain that you don't want to see me." His voice was tight. Angry.

Hurt.

She picked up the phone. "I'm home."

"Good."

He hung up.

She cupped the phone against her stomach and slowly slid down the wall until she was sitting on the floor. Eventually, the phone started beeping.

She pressed the button, disconnecting the call.

Then she lay down on her side.

And cried.

Cameron stared at the phone sitting on his desk.

His hand reached out to pick it up again. To call her again. To tell her anything that would get her back.

Might as well try to rewind the past twenty-four hours. He'd have as good a chance of success.

He shoved himself out of his chair and it rolled back, tipping on two wheels and crashing over, knocking hard into the wall. A framed oil painting Laura had picked up at an estate sale the first year they were married slid straight down, bouncing off the base of the chair and landing flat on the floor.

He exhaled roughly. Started to just leave it there. He'd never liked the painting, with its fussy strokes and jarring colors. But Laura had loved it.

And he'd loved her.

Loved.

He raked his hands through his hair and slowly went over to the painting. Crouched down and set it upright against the wall.

He'd *loved* Laura.

He'd made a life here in Thunder Canyon that would have made her happy.

But that was all in the past.

She'd died. And he was finally starting to feel alive again.

He pinched the bridge of his nose, digging his fingers into the pain that squatted malevolently behind his eyes.

And the woman responsible for shoving him into the land of the living couldn't face the mere idea of a relationship with him without coming unglued.

He straightened and left the painting leaning against the wall.

Living again sucked.

Chris Taylor stared at his sister's blond head and struggled hard to keep the worry out of his voice as he leaned his hip against the corner of her desk at the fire station. "You going to drive in to Bozeman for the basketball game tonight?"

She didn't look up from the report she was typing. "I'm on call," she finally answered. "And half the town is heading over there, anyway." She finally cast him a look. "Is that the pressing question that dragged you over here?"

"We were supposed to have lunch today remember?"

Her expression told him clearly enough that she hadn't. "Sorry," she mumbled, and looked back at her computer screen.

He sighed mightily. He'd waited for her at The Hitching Post for twenty minutes before realizing she wasn't going to show. Only thing he'd accomplished while he was there was getting Juliet Rivera off her feet for about ten minutes. As far as he was concerned, the young woman needed to be off her feet permanently until her baby made its appearance.

He straightened off Faith's desk and grabbed the side chair nearby to pull it up closer. He sat down.

Grabbed the arms of her chair and physically turned her until she was facing him. "Talk."

"There's nothing to talk about."

"Yeah. Right." He kept her from turning her chair back toward her desk. "Not so easy. I want to know what's going on. Mom called me last night. Said you sounded weird on the phone the other day when she tried calling you. Jill called me this morning to complain about you forgetting to mail her one of those crocheted baby blankets of yours for her girlfriend's shower, and she said you hung up on her when she bitched at you about it. So what gives?"

"Nothing is going on." She reached forward and pinched the inside of his arm, hard. He yelped and let go of her seat. She turned back to her desk. "Absolutely nothing, and that is exactly the way I want it."

"This is about the coach."

She typed, but he could see on the screen that it was more gobbledygook than words. "This is about *nothing*."

"Yeah, that washes real well, kiddo."

She glared at him.

Chris saw the glisten in his sister's eyes, though, and stifled a sigh. "They're just worried about you," he said quietly. *They,* hell. *He* was worried, too. But telling Faith that wouldn't do him any good. "Saw Erik Stevenson today," he said deliberately.

At that, her eyes widened, her attention definitely on him. "Is he okay?"

"Yeah. Just a follow-up visit."

Her relief was palpable.

"He was full of talk about how his dad signed him up for rock climbing over at Tanya's place," he added.

Her eyebrows shot up. "He did?"

"Haven't talked to Tanya much this week, either, have you?"

Her eyebrows lowered. "It's been a busy week."

And his sister was hiding out from the world. "He's also signed the kid up for Little League baseball," he informed her. "You know, Faith, I'm sorry about what Jess put you through. But he was a selfish jerk. He was selfish before you married him. And he was selfish after you were unmarried. You can't have kids. I know. I'm sorry. But there are a lot of people a helluva lot worse off than you."

Her brows drew together, stricken. "I know that."

"Do you?" He dragged her chair around again. "Word around town is that you and the coach haven't been seen in the same five-block radius since last week."

Her lashes swept down, but not quickly enough to hide the stark pain in them, and his irritation dissolved. "Do you love him?"

"*What? No!* Of course not."

Methinks she doth protest too much, he thought. "Okay. Just asking."

She slid her attention back to her computer. "Stop asking. There's nothing to say."

He rubbed his thumb down her arm. "You still haven't told anyone, have you. About the infertility."

Her face turned red. She eyed him. "No, but if you don't keep your voice down, anyone passing through the station here will know."

"It's nothing to be ashamed of. You had a staph infection, Faith. When you were a teenager. Nobody could have predicted the effect it left behind."

"Nobody could have predicted," she agreed tightly. "And I'm not infertile. I'm sterile. A revelation that made Jess immediately start looking for a new wife who *could* produce kids. End of story. And Cam..."

He waited.

She exhaled through her teeth. "Sooner or later—probably sooner, given the things he said—he's going to want more children. And I can't give that to him. And I can't watch another man I lo—*care* about, walk away from me because of *my* failure."

He wanted to latch on to the word she wouldn't let herself say just as much as he wanted to throttle her for the word she *had* said. Failure. "You're physically incapable of producing a child," he said—quietly, because he wouldn't entirely put it past Faith to pound him if he didn't. "It's a fact, not a failure." And it was a fact *he* knew, only because at her most desperate, she'd sought his professional opinion.

"Well, I've dealt with it as much as I intend to."

He stood. "Honey, you haven't dealt with it, at all. If you had, you wouldn't still be keeping it a secret." He glanced around the station house where a half-dozen firefighters were moving around doing various tasks from filing to polishing the inside of the windows. "And I don't mean from these guys. I mean from Mom and Dad. From our sisters. From the man you lo—" He hesitated deliberately, watching her eyes widen as if daring him to say it. The pager at his waist buzzed, and he automatically pulled it free to check the display.

Lunchtime was over.

"How're the new residents coming along?"

He took pity, allowing her dogged change of subject. "I'm surviving them. One's got an attitude that Thunder Canyon isn't exactly the pinnacle of medical achievements."

"Too bad you can't tell him to take a hike."

"Her." A damned pretty her, at that.

He leaned down and kissed the top of Faith's head, putting Dr. Zoe Hart *out* of his head. "Don't let Jess's failure where you two were concerned control your future, Faith. Maybe you might think about that."

He left, sketching a wave at the fire truck that was just pulling in from a call.

His pager buzzed again.

He sighed a little and quickened his step.

The E.R. seemed to be getting busier with each passing day, and every other person who came through seemed to be running a temperature fueled by gold fever.

The distinctive yellow school buses passed Faith on the highway between Bozeman and Thunder Canyon shortly after midnight.

Standing well off the side of the road next to her SUV with Jim Shepherd, she stared after the taillights until they dwindled to nothing in the dark.

"Probably your basketball team," Jim murmured, handing a coil of nylon rope over to her.

She nodded and tucked it away in the back of her SUV. She didn't want to wonder how the team had done.

She wondered anyway.

So she focused harder on the task at hand. They'd already loaded up Jim's equipment. Their engines were running, sending wisps of white exhaust curling into the night. "Maybe it'll help cut down on lost cross-country skiers when Caleb Douglas gets that ski resort of his up and running. At this point, I think we're close to breaking a record on this kind of call."

"Might be." Jim tugged at his ear for a moment. "You doing okay?"

The slick fabric of the SAR jacket she'd bought to replace the one she'd had to leave in the Queen of Hearts rustled as she closed her tailgate. "Why wouldn't I be?"

Her boss shrugged. "You just seemed preoccupied."

"I'm sorry. Won't happen again."

He let out a breath. "Faith, it wasn't a judgment on your performance. In another year, you'll probably be the ranking member. I was just asking."

She hesitated. "I'm fine. Really. I just…have a few personal issues to deal with."

"Well. If you want to talk, you know where I am."

She nodded. Watched him walk toward his truck and climb in. But he waited until she'd gotten into her own vehicle and turned it toward Thunder Canyon before he set off in the opposite direction.

Her hands tightened around the steering wheel. Talk. Maybe it made her the biggest coward on the planet, but she just didn't want to talk. What was the point of talking about something that could not be changed?

Her foot pressed harder on the accelerator, and intentionally or not, she soon had the three buses within eyesight, again.

She hung back, though, just following along. She had the scanner turned down low, but not so low that she didn't hear Cheryl's chatter about the game.

Cam's team had won.

Faith's hands tightened around the wheel a little more. She had no difficulty imagining the celebration that would occur upon their return. It was a wonder the buses weren't simply floating home.

The highway headed uphill and the buses slowed some, laboring against the grade while her SUV ate it up. She flicked her blinker and passed the first bus. Through the windows, she could see arms waving, hats flying.

The same was true of the second bus, and the one in the lead, when she passed that one, too.

She even saw Erik, who noticed her. He pulled down the window as far as it would go and stuck his head right out, waving madly, his hair whipping around his head like mad.

Aching inside, she waved, too.

Then a long arm scooped Erik's head back inside the window. Faith caught a glimpse of Cam's face. He eyed her for a moment.

Then slid the window up.

Headlights were in the oncoming lane and Faith accelerated, passing the bus and moving back into her own lane.

But she was shaking.

Cam hadn't even smiled.

What did you expect?

She drove the rest of the way back to town, feeling as if Cam's dark eyes were boring into the back of her spine. It wasn't on her way, but she found herself passing The Hitching Post, all the same. The place was still lit up. Cars lined the street and filled the lot.

She fully intended to drive on by. To go home. To fold herself in a blanket in the corner of her couch and pretend that she would be able to sleep, the same way she'd done for the past five nights.

She drove around the lot. Made herself a parking spot where there was none.

Inside, the grill was already packed. Many had clearly already returned from the game. If there was a patron in the grill who *wasn't* a basketball fan, she figured they would quickly become one, or they'd quickly be escorted to the door.

"Hey." Tanya grabbed her elbow. "Didn't expect to see you. Toby and I are over in the corner, but we can make some room for you. Did you find the skier?"

Faith shrugged out of her slick coat and followed her friend. "Yeah. Safe and sound, but cold. We sent him to the hospital for a look-see." She pointed at an empty bar stool near a group of people. They waved at it, and she carried it over to Tanya's small round table. If she craned her neck a little, she could see the door. She'd see when the team came in and escape through the back.

"Oh, man." Toby's sparkling brown eyes were fastened on someone across the room. "Look at Polly Caruthers. She is so suh-wheet." He slid off his stool, all long legs and gangling arms. "Gotta go, Ma."

Tanya rolled her eyes. "I'm Ma, now. Lovely, huh?" But she was smiling. "Kids. Gotta love 'em. Even when they're twelve-year-old boys who've discovered girls don't have cooties after all."

Faith toyed with one of the round cardboard coasters sitting in the center of the table. "Speaking of kids," she said slowly.

A tall waitress rushed by the table, settling a glass of water in front of Faith. "What can I get you?"

A vat of courage?

She ordered a diet cola. Figured it would be easier to obtain.

"Speaking of kids," Tanya prompted after the woman scurried off, menus tucked under her arm and an empty tray in her hand. "What about them?"

Faith flipped the coaster over. Took a deep breath. Expelled it in a rush. "I can't have any," she said bluntly.

Tanya blinked. "Excuse me?"

"Don't make me repeat it," Faith said thickly.

"Oh, honey." Tanya covered her hand with hers. "Just because you and Jess didn't..." Her voice trailed off at the look Faith gave her. Realization hit. "Oh. *Oh.*" She grimaced. "Well, that schmuck. He never was good enough for you."

The last thing Faith expected to do was to laugh. But she did. It came out a little rusty, but it still came. "Sure. You say that now."

"Well, you should have met some fine boy here in Thunder Canyon instead of going off to foreign parts like New Mexico," Tanya said wryly. But her eyes were sympathetic. "Why didn't you say something before now?"

She lifted her shoulder. Tugged the length of her ponytail over her shoulder, only to toss it back again. "I don't know. I guess...the more people I tell, the more real it is. And believe me, I felt like it was pretty real already."

Tanya squeezed her hand. "And it doesn't have anything to do with the fact your SUV was outside of the coach's house last weekend? Never mind. Your expression is plain enough." A loud commotion sounded near the front of the grill.

The team had arrived.

And despite Faith's intention to leave, she couldn't make herself do it.

She sat there, her vision pinpointing on the door as the players trooped in, one after another. Todd Gilmore had Erik on his shoulder and both of them ducked way down to get through the doorway.

Cameron and his assistant coaches came in last.

Faith's heart chugged.

In seconds, though, he was surrounded by a crowd of people, whooping and hollering and chanting.

"I have to go," she whispered to her friend. "I can't do this."

"If it feels wrong," Tanya murmured, "then you shouldn't." She leaned forward and hugged her quickly. "Question is, what feels wrong?"

Faith slid off her bar stool. She fumbled with her coat. She could go out through the kitchen. Cameron would never know she'd been there. She stepped behind a table. Scooted around a high chair that held a sleeping toddler.

Made it to the kitchen.

And looked over her shoulder.

It was *all* wrong.

Why could she swing on the end of a rope in a canyon if she had to, but not face up to the man who held her heart in his hands, whether he knew it or not?

She squared her shoulders.

Swallowed the panic that wanted to nip at her.

And turned around.

She made her way to the front entrance. The door was still open, and cold air swept in around the cluster of people surrounding Cameron. Faith slid her arms into her coat. Her heart was in her throat. She sidestepped, and there he was.

The smile was on his face. But it wasn't evident in his deep brown eyes.

And when he saw her standing there, she knew down in her very bones that *she* was the reason for that.

And it made her want to weep all over again.

She moistened her lips. Stepped a little closer. "Congratulations on the win." It seemed silly to offer her hand. And hugging him was too painful to contemplate. So instead, she pushed her hands in her coat pockets. "You're going to be a hero in this town for the next few decades."

"The kids are the heroes," he said smoothly. He

nodded at someone's laughing comment, then closed his hand over Faith's elbow. "Excuse us for a minute." He drew her outside onto the wooden sidewalk and let go of her the second they were clear of the doorway.

Faith swallowed, but the knot in her throat remained, nearly suffocating her.

"Are you going to hyperventilate if I ask how you're doing?" His voice was even. Cool.

She flushed. Shook her head. "I'm fine." Miserable, more like. "And...I'm sorry. For the way I ran out like that."

"Not a problem." His voice was as bland as it had ever been. "I got the message. I just wanted you to know that Erik's still expecting you to go tobogganing with him again. Your choice whether you do or not."

She felt as if he'd slapped her. "I have no intention of disappointing Erik."

His jaw cocked a little in the first indication that he wasn't as removed as he appeared. "Good." His gaze shifted past her. "Looks like Romano's gearing up to write some parking tickets. You should move your SUV before he gets to you." Then he turned and went back inside.

Faith shivered.

The walls inside The Hitching Post were bulging with townspeople. Friends. Co-workers.

Never in her life had she felt more alone.

Chapter Thirteen

One of the hardest things Cam ever did was to leave Faith standing on the sidewalk outside the grill.

But he couldn't stay there with her. He couldn't bear to see her hazel eyes glaze with panic if he so much as mentioned a future.

And now that *that* particular door had been opened inside him, he couldn't be around her and *not* think about the future.

So he walked into the restaurant where it felt stuffy and close because of all the bodies packed inside. He immediately spotted Erik. He'd moved on from Gilmore to Romance—who *had* gotten to play briefly that night and was, not surprisingly, trying to hog credit for a win that was rightfully owned by the entire team.

Cam left Erik be and headed to the bar. On his way, though, someone slapped a long-neck into his hand.

Good enough for him. The beer was cold and maybe, if he drank enough of them, he'd forget the stinging sensation inside his chest. Mayor Brookhurst appeared, looking as self-satisfied as he ever did. "Come on over here, Cam. Want to introduce you around. Have you met Caleb Douglas?" He gestured to a silver-haired man wearing a Stetson on his head and turquoise on his belt buckle.

Cam stuck out his hand. "Mr. Douglas. It's a pleasure to meet you. A person can't live in Thunder Canyon without having heard the Douglas name a time or two." Or twenty, since the man seemed to own half the town, and a lot of the land surrounding it. And for Cam, the greeting was automatic. A throwback to the days of schmoozing clients. But just because he'd retained the ability didn't mean he cared about the life he'd left behind.

Which was a revelation he owed to Faith.

Who couldn't face the notion of a future that included him.

"Fine game tonight," the man drawled, fortunately unaware of Cam's preoccupied thoughts. "Looks like your boy over there's recovered from his incident with my mine. Would've come by to see how he was doing myself, but I've been tied up with business. Understand my wife, Adele, went by the hospital, though. She assured me he was well on the mend."

"He was. And—" Cam looked over when he heard a crash of glasses. He wasn't even surprised when his son stood in the middle of the fracas, looking innocent. "As you can see, he's still keeping things lively."

Caleb's pale green eyes looked amused. "Nothing like a son." He settled his hat again. "Brookhurst here's been singing your praises, but I prefer to draw my own conclusions. Be looking forward to seeing your name on the ballot for council member. It's sometimes good to have new blood from people committed to this old town." He lifted his hand, acknowledging someone's hail. "I'm sure we'll be talking again," he said as he moved off.

Cam immediately headed for Erik, where one of the waitresses had already begun sweeping up the mess. He hooked his arm around his boy and lifted him clear.

"I wanna talk to Faith." Erik's overtired gaze was roving over the people.

"Not tonight. She's gone home."

"Da-ad!"

"You can call her tomorrow." And damned if he didn't envy his kid for that fact. "You might not need any sleep, but your old man does." Cam would first have to eradicate Faith from his thoughts in order to get some sleep, but he had no intention of sharing that particular nugget.

"I gotta get my basketball from Todd. He was gonna get all the guys to sign it for me." Erik squirmed out of Cam's grasp and headed for the knot of players that had commandeered several tables.

Cam watched him go.

"Congratulations on the win." Chris Taylor stopped next to Cam. "Next thing you know, the town'll be expecting you to do this during football season, too."

"Gotta get through baseball first." He didn't for a second believe Faith's brother just *happened* to be hanging around The Hitching Post for the post-game celebration. As far as Cam had been able to tell, Dr. Chris Taylor rarely did anything without purpose.

"Faith was pretty happy to hear you've got Erik starting up with the climbing. And that he's going to do Little League." The doctor made no effort at being subtle.

"She likes my son," he said neutrally.

"She loves *you*," Chris said flatly.

The sting in his chest was more like a wrecking ball plowing through him. "She has a funny way of showing it," he muttered. He didn't for a minute believe that Faith would've told her brother about the episode at his house, either. And just because he hadn't done anything about it just yet, didn't mean he didn't plan to.

Even above the raucous music and voices inside the grill, he could hear the doctor's sigh. "I'm gonna cut to the chase, here," the man said after a moment. "One, because I think you're a decent guy who—judging by the glare you're giving me—has fallen for my thick-headed sister. Two, because my damn pager is liable to go off any second again, and I'm gonna have to book."

"You don't have to cut to anything," Cam assured him, his voice tight. "When it comes to your sister, there's nothing I need to discuss." And "fallen" didn't begin to cover what he felt where Faith was concerned.

"Do you love her, or not?"

Cam's molars ached from his jaw clenching so

tight. "What does it matter? She's made her feelings clear."

"She ran scared, I suppose." Chris didn't look surprised. "And didn't bother to tell you why."

Cam's patience was nil. "Her reasons are her own." Erik had begun bouncing the basketball on the wooden bar. But before he could get over there, one of the waitresses whisked it away with a grin and replaced it smoothly with a bowl of ice cream.

A successful sidetrack maneuver.

"Ordinarily, I'd agree with you," Chris said. "But you know what? I'd like to see my sister be happy again. I thought she was on that track lately. Ever since Erik went down the shaft, anyway."

"Right. She adores my kid. I know."

"Man, you two are suited," the doctor muttered. "Yeah. Faith likes kids. Adores 'em. Which has made it pretty damn hard for her to adjust to the fact that she can't have any."

Cam jerked. "What?"

Chris shook his head. "What the hell do you two talk about when you're together? Or is it just a sex thing?"

Cam's fist curled. "Don't go there."

"Then try this one on for size, and I hope to hell it fits, 'cause when she finds out I'm talking about her business, I'm going to be in the doghouse with her, big time. Dammit." He pulled his pager out suddenly and peered at the display. "The bastard she'd been married to walked out on her about two days after she learned there were no medical miracles that would help her conceive. But Jess wanted kids as bad as she did. Only instead of dealing with the blow the way you'd expect after being married to someone for six years, he told her he couldn't waste any more time waiting for the impossible to happen, so he went out and got himself a woman who could provide them. *I* don't consider it a great loss. The guy never went out of his way to make Faith feel particularly special. Hell, she told me once the guy proposed in the drive-thru at a fast-food restaurant. Just handed over the bag of tacos with a 'wanna get married?' and that was it. No ring. No nothing. But…well, there you go. She still loved him."

"I'm *not* her ex-husband," Cam gritted. "And if she can't see that—"

"Maybe she just needs some help opening her eyes," the other man suggested. "So she can stop looking at the past and start looking at the future. Figure maybe you might know something about having to do that." He slid his pager back on his belt and headed for the door.

Cam frowned, watching the man depart. Then he exhaled and went over to collect his son. But Erik was still eating the ice cream, so Cam stood behind him at the crowded bar, waiting, while Taylor's words drummed inside his head. He stared at the painting of the Shady Lady. But he didn't see the curving limbs discreetly covered by some flimsy fabric.

He saw Laura. As clear as if she were standing in front of him. And she was smiling the same smile she'd worn the day of their checkerboard picnic—as if he'd done something particularly pleasing to her.

Then she turned, her black hair drifting.

And she was gone.

Okay, Laura. I heard you.

Cam's hand closed over Erik's shoulder. "Come on, son. Let's go home."

"I'm not finished with my ice cream." Cam hefted the boy up on his shoulder, and handed him the bowl. "We'll bring the bowl back later."

Then he carried his boy outside and they walked all the way back to the high school to collect his car.

They planned the entire while.

"Um, Blondie?"

It was Saturday morning and Faith was at the station putting the finishing touches on the budget for Jim. "Just a sec, Derek." After she got the paperwork out of the way, she was going to go see Cameron. She'd already told Jim that morning that she needed a few days off, and he'd agreed to cover her territory.

Maybe Faith had ruined things too badly for repair where her relationship with Cam was concerned.

But she couldn't get through another night without doing something. So if that meant taking the chance of him turning her away, or worse, that she'd gain his pity, then too bad.

Either way, she wasn't going to be any worse off than she already was.

And if she had to, she could use the few days off to fall apart.

God, she hoped she didn't have to.

She hoped she could make Cameron understand. That he wouldn't hate her for being so afraid, so—

"Yo. Faith." Derek's voice was a little more insistent. "Seriously. You might want to check this out."

She set down her pen and turned her chair to face him. "Check *what* out?"

Derek was standing at the windows that overlooked Main. He pointed. "Looks like the high school marching band out there."

Faith joined him. Sure enough. There was the band in the same style uniforms they'd worn when she'd attended school there, marching right down the center of the street heading in their direction. "Maybe it's because of last night's game. Winning the state championship."

"Didn't hear about any parade being planned," Derek countered. "They'd have had to have a permit. Fire would've been required to be on hand."

A few other men, still in their turn-outs from the call they'd just been out on, joined them at the window. One of them pointed. "Isn't that the coach?"

Faith nodded. Cameron walked alongside the band, but she couldn't see much more than his head from this angle. "Definitely because of last night's game." She wanted to press her nose against the windowpane, but made herself go back to her desk and the budget.

Telling herself she would go to Cam was one thing. Seeing the man before she'd expected to—though it didn't change her mind now that it was made up—made her feel positively weak in the knees.

And the last thing she needed was for Derek and his band of merry men to see just how female she could be. She'd never live down their ribbing.

It wasn't long, however, before she could hear the beat of the big bass drums and the pipe of the band in-struments.

And she found herself looking toward the window despite her intentions otherwise. Looking, then getting back up, and moving over.

On the sidewalk outside the building, she could see a crowd was forming. People out enjoying the crisp, clear Saturday morning. A few police officers in uni-forms. Cheryl Lansky, even, with her headset still in place and her phone cord dangling back toward the doorway of the police station.

The band had stopped moving down the street and was now marching in place.

"What's that they're playing?" someone asked.

"You are my sunshine, my only sunshine," Derek singsonged.

"Go back to baking," someone else told him and they laughed.

Faith's palms pressed flat against the glass. She could see Cameron far more clearly now, as he rounded the front of the band. He wore blue jeans and a charcoal gray shirt with a down vest over it, and his hair rippled a little in the faint breeze as he stopped to speak to the drum major.

Then Erik darted into view, his young legs pump-ing as he kept ahead of several members of the bas-ketball team who jogged behind him. He held a flat box over his head and as she watched, Cam hastily reached over to rescue it before the boy dropped it.

The band kept playing.

And Cam turned to face the building.

Faith stood, rooted in place.

"What in the hell is that man doing?"

Faith barely heard. Her gaze was glued to Cam's face. He'd seen her through the window. No question. And her heart couldn't make up its mind whether to stall completely or beat as frantically as a humming-bird. Particularly when Cam and Erik walked toward the building, bypassing the gathering crowd.

"He's coming in here."

Faith followed Cam's progress through the window. He disappeared around the side of the building, and a moment later, came through the door.

The firefighters scattered like startled mice. Any other time and she'd have laughed herself silly at the sight of six large men trying to look casual and failing miserably.

Any other time.

Right now, she couldn't do more than stand there in front of the window, without a coherent thought in her head.

Cam pointed at a desk chair and Erik obediently sat and took the box back from his dad. He was grinning as if he'd just discovered a forgotten gold nugget in his pants from the mine shaft.

Then Cam walked right up to her.

She tucked her hands behind her back to hide the fact that they were shaking.

His brown gaze roved over her face, his expression assuring her he knew just what she was doing. "Maybe you better sit down," he said after a long moment. "In case you pass out or something."

She swallowed, pride stiffening her spine. For the rest of her life she'd probably never live that one down. The first and only time she'd ever hyperventilated. "Why would I pass out?"

"Because I'm gonna talk about the F word."

Her eyebrows shot up. "I *beg* your pardon?"

"The *future*."

Her lips parted. Emotion squiggled inside her. Hope. Fear. "What about it?"

He didn't even glance around at their audience. His gaze was focused only on her. "I want one. With you. I know this is fast. We haven't…dated. I haven't romanced you. And I won't push for more than you're ready for." His lips twisted a little. "I'll try not to push," he amended, gruffly. "But I know what you make me feel. And I'm done pretending that it's not happening. And I'm done pretending I don't like it. I love you. And I want you in my life. As my wife. My lover. My partner. My friend."

Her eyes flooded. "Cam, you don't know what you're taking on."

"A golden woman who can stand beside me until we're hunched over in rocking chairs, watching our great-grandchildren sled on the hill behind our house?"

The tears flooded over. Grief sucked hard at her, pulling her under. "That's just it," she whispered. And it didn't matter that she'd planned to talk to him later. The time was now. Avid audience or not. "I can't *give* you children."

His eyes were fiercely soft.

And unsurprised.

He stepped closer. Tilted his head lower toward hers and cupped her cheeks to catch her tears on his thumbs. "We already have Erik. And any more we might be blessed with may not come from *our* cells, but they'll come from our *hearts*. Come on, Faith. There's a world of children out there needing good parents, if and when we decide to add to our family. But the bottom line is that *you* are the one I need."

Oh, how badly she wanted to believe him. "That's easy for you to say now. But you haven't had any time to think about it."

"Your brother told me last night about the reason your marriage ended. And I didn't need any time then. But I wasn't going to show up at your door at one in the morning and casually suggest we get married. You think I'm gonna behave like your ex-husband did, but you're wrong from start to finish. You think you're not the kind of woman to inspire romantic gestures. And you're wrong there, too."

He closed his hands over her shoulder and turned her to face the window again.

The entire basketball team stood there, grinning like darned idiots. And every one of them held out a bouquet of roses. Red ones. White ones. Yellow. It was a veritable garden of them, right there in the middle of winter.

And behind them, the band was still playing that ridiculous song. "You are my sunshine," she whispered thickly and turned back to Cam.

"I'll spend the rest of my life romancing you, Faith

Taylor. Because you are *sunshine* in my life." His voice dropped. Turned fierce. "Do you understand me? You light up the corners. You're the one who's helped me see that what I have here in this town isn't only honoring someone's memory. It's a *life*. And it's good. And with you, it'll be all I've ever wanted. I'm not saying there won't be hurdles. Because there always are. But I'm saying we can take them together. You and me. And that terror over there who's even now spinning around on the office chair—" his voice rose so Erik could hear "—needs you, too."

"Is it my turn yet, Dad?"

"In a minute." Cam didn't look away from Faith's face. "Just give us a chance, Faith. I'm hoping the fact that I *could* make you nearly pass out last week means that this is really important to you, too."

She settled her hands tentatively on his chest. Even through the puffy down vest she felt the charge of his heart. "My *brother* told you last night?"

He nodded once. "I'd have come for you sooner or later, though. I couldn't have stayed away much longer. I thought there was only one thing I needed in this life, Faith. The knowledge that my kid was safe and happy. But there's something else I need now, too. And that's you."

"I was…going to come to you, too," she whispered. "I just…when Jess left it wasn't so much losing *him* that hurt. It was losing the dream of this marriage that was supposed to be as long and enduring as my parents'. But I knew if I were to ever lose you…I don't think I could survive it, Cam."

His breath hissed through his teeth. He leaned down. Kissed her hard. Briefly. "I'm not going anywhere, Faith. My future is here. With you."

Her fingers curled into his vest. She reached up and pressed her mouth to his. Softly. Lingeringly. Then she drew away and sucked in a shaking breath. "What's in the box?"

"What box?" His eyes were gratifyingly glazed.

She smiled a little, loving him so much her heart was cracking wide open with it. "The box that Erik's clutching."

"Right." He slid his palm around her neck, as if he needed to make sure she was going to stay put. He gestured at Erik and the boy gleefully hopped off the chair, only to nearly fall on his nose from all the spinning. But Derek caught him up and set him on the straight course toward them.

When he reached them, Cam flipped back the lid.

Inside was an enormous pink cookie.

"First homemade cookie we ever made," Erik said proudly. "I kinda blew up the mixer, though. Dad was pretty…um…anyhow, it's 'cause of Valentine's Day last week. I never got to tell you happy Valentine's Day."

Faith knelt down beside him, as much because her legs were going to give out as anything. She looked at the cookie.

We love Faith had been spelled out in uneven strokes of white frosting.

She ran her hand over Erik's head. "Nobody but my mom has ever baked a cookie for me before," she admitted.

He looked at her. "I could bake you a cookie every Valentine's Day, maybe."

And that was it. Her heart broke open the rest of the way. And she knew she'd never want to close it again.

Not as long as she had the Stevenson men to love.

"Maybe we'll bake them together," she suggested, laughing a little through the tears that clogged her throat. "See if we can *not* blow up any more mixers."

He suddenly threw his arms around her neck. Cam barely rescued the boxed cookie in time to save it from flying.

"Thanks for rescuing us," Erik whispered in her ear.

She hugged him back. "Thanks for rescuing *me,*" she whispered.

Then she looked up at Cam. He drew her to her feet. "Is this a big enough display for you?" he asked gently.

Outside the window, the players were still standing with the roses. The band still played. Erik had sat down at her desk where Cam stuck the cookie and was busy tearing off a great huge corner of it as his avid eyes roved over the interesting aspects a fire station might hold.

Faith looked from all of it, back to Cameron's face. "I never needed a display." She slid her arms around his neck. "I just needed to believe."

"And do you?"

His eyes were dark. And just as vulnerable as Erik's.

"Yes," she said softly. Joyfully. Peacefully. "I believe. My future is with you, Cameron."

His lashes lowered for a moment. "Thank you." Then his palms slid behind her and he hauled her close.

His mouth covered hers.

And it was *right*.

* * * * *